PURE
ABANDON

JEANNINE COLETTE

Pure Abandon
Copyright © 2015 by Jeannine Colette

All rights reserved.

This is a work of fiction. The names, characters, places, and incidents are products of the author's imagination or have been used fictitiously. Any resemblance to actual persons, living or dead, and events is entirely coincidental.

Cover Design by Sarah Hansen, Okay Creations, www.okaycreations.com
Edit and Interior Design by Jovana Shirley, Unforeseen Editing, www.unforeseenediting.com

Printed in the United States of America
First Printing, 2015
ISBN-13: 978-0-692-44349-1
ISBN-10: 0692443495

www.JeannineColette.com

For Nicole.

PROLOGUE

I'm standing on a corner in the rain. How did I get here?
How did I come to this point in the road?

The corner is wet, and my clothes are soaked, but I can't move. I'm here to see him.

Him.

There he is. Walking out the front door of the hotel. Right where he's supposed to be.

Through the parting umbrellas, I can see his face. Those golden eyes and chiseled chin are striking alongside his broad shoulders and strong thighs.

He's carrying an umbrella, shielding him from the rain.

So in control. So dry.

He's wearing gray. That's the color. The color that defines my life.

Nothing is black and white.

Just gray.

I want to run, dash across the street, and grab him. Hold him in my arms, feel his tongue in my mouth.

I want to caress him, feel his hand under my skirt.

But my legs are lead. I can't move.

He's waiting for me. This is my moment.

But do I turn to him or run away?

Far away.

chapter ONE

There are a few things in life I know to be certain.

The best coffee beans are grown in Guatemala, Humphrey Bogart was the greatest actor of all time, the Mets are the most underrated team in baseball, and I am unequivocally, madly in love with my husband and son.

"It's your turn."

Though, sometimes, I question the husband part when it's three in the morning and the baby is crying.

I pad down the hall, into the nursery, and sooth our baby by cradling him in my arms and singing a lullaby. With a soft kiss on Jackson's temple, I wish him sweet dreams and head back to my room.

"Is he in bed?" Gabriel asks, sounding like he's been up for the last hour. Wearing only a pair of black boxer briefs, his lean six-foot-two frame takes up most of the bed, leaving me a tiny space in the corner.

"He is. If you were up, you could have gotten him."

"It was your turn." His voice becomes slightly muffled as he rolls over and hugs his pillow.

If someone had told me that drunken night at McCloon's that this was the life we would lead, I wouldn't have believed them.

But here we are…taking turns.

I take a deep breath as I slide into bed. Today is a *big* day for me. After walking away from a career I loved, I'm finally going back.

Two years ago, I gave it up. I'd just found out I was pregnant, and due to complications, the doctor ordered me on bed rest. I had been working eighty-hour weeks, scouting locations all over the country and field-producing for a production company. Once the doctor said I had to stop for the sake of my baby, I didn't think twice.

One day, with my feet propped up on the arm of the sofa while lying on my back, Gabriel sat down beside me, and we had a major discussion. We decided that if my job was too high stress to grow a baby, then it certainly wasn't the type to raise a baby with. I lay in bed for seven months and spent the last thirteen at home with my son. While I enjoy my time with Jackson, I've always known I'd go back.

I've barely closed my eyes before the alarm goes off at six a.m. Pushing the comforter from my body, I roll my legs off the bed and pull out into a long stretch. *If I could just rest my eyes for two more minutes…*

"Oh no, you don't!" I say to myself and shake off the need to go back to sleep.

I head into the bathroom to shower and, as my mother would say, *put your face on.* Opening the makeup bag, I unload my arsenal. If I learned one thing from my mother, it was, a girl needs her war paint before she goes into everyday combat. Due to last night's lack of sleep, I have dark circles under my eyes. I slather on concealer, add a pinch of bronzer for color, and line my eyes with a soft black before adding some mascara.

"You look really nice, Kathryn." Gabriel sounds surprised.

I stare back at my reflection. It *is* a vast improvement from the yoga pants, tank tops, and messy bun I've been sporting.

My husband, as always, looks handsome in his navy suit, crisp white shirt, and sapphire tie. It's the one I gave him last Christmas along with new dress socks. A practical gift. I remember when I once bought him a bong and a thong. The thong was for me to wear, and for him to rip off of me with his teeth.

"What do you want to do for dinner?" he asks, combing his hair while leaning over the double vanity. I love his hair. It's dark and wavy, a beautiful contrast to his blue eyes.

"I was thinking we could order in. I want to make sure I spend time with Jackson tonight since I'll be gone all day."

Today will be our son's first day at home without me. I know they say women can't have it all—a career and a family—but I'm certainly going to try. If I have to forgo a home-cooked meal every once in a while, to spend extra time with my son, that's what I'm going to do.

His disapproving eyes meet mine in the mirror. "I let the nanny in while you were sleeping."

I hold up my hand, pointing a finger in warning. "Don't."

His mouth pulls in as he pinches the bridge of his nose. "How can you possibly expect me to be comfortable with having a stranger in our home with Jack all day?" He looks back at me for a reaction. "Financially, it doesn't even make sense. Between the cost of the nanny and the price for commuting, it's just not worth it."

Turning my back to the mirror, I lean against the vanity and face him. "We still have your college loans to pay off, a mortgage and a car payment. I can't stay home forever."

He puts his hands on his hips and lets out a hard breath. "I know; I know."

Gabriel has been against me returning to work. He loves me staying home with the baby. I understand his concern, but I can't take him pressing the issue again.

The last six weeks have been a continuous back-and-forth. Doors were slammed, and the couch was slept on—not by me. It would have ended sooner, but Gabriel was called away on business half the time. He might be a successful attorney, but this is one jury he's been unable to sway. I've made too many consolations in this marriage. I am ready to take back my life.

His eyes soften and he places his arms around my waist and pulls me into him. "I just always pictured you at home, taking care of Jack. Maybe having another…" he says with a twinkle in his eye.

"Hold on there, cowboy. First, one baby at a time. Second, Carmen is an amazing nanny. She came highly recommended, and her credentials are impeccable."

"She'd better be. She costs an arm and a leg." He frowns, and I know he doesn't get it. I'm just glad he's going along with it.

I put my hand on his face and lower his chin, so our eyes are level. My voice is soft yet steady. "She is. I promise. Besides, you hate your job. You don't come home until ten o'clock most nights, and travel more than you want to. Maybe, someday, I'll be able to support you, and then *you* can be the one to stay home."

"Since I work so much, don't you think one of us should be home with Jack?" His navy eyes light up. "How about we make a deal?"

I quizzically eye him but let him continue.

"One year from today, we reopen the discussion. If our family is suffering or if this career of yours is going nowhere, you come back home." He holds up his pinkie finger in front of his face, looking for me to seal the promise. "Deal?"

I wrap my finger around his and kiss our intertwined fingers.

"Deal," I promise. "As long as you promise me one thing."

He raises a brow.

I widen my eyes, so he knows I mean business. "No more talk. We can't keep having the same discussion. No more arguing. You are giving me one year. Good?"

He kisses our pinkies and releases my hand. "Good. Because, in a year, I'll be partner, and you won't need to work," he says confidently.

I cringe at the idea.

"Chinese food for dinner?" I ask, heading out of the bathroom and through our bedroom.

"Don't have to ask me twice." He's fastening his watch as he follows me down the hallway.

We make our way downstairs to the kitchen, where Carmen is feeding Jackson.

"Don't forget, you have to pick up milk on your way home." I grab my purse from the counter.

"Okay. Good luck. Have fun. I love you," Gabriel says, lifting his suitcase from the floor by the front door.

"You, too." I give him a swift kiss and then turn on my heel to Jackson, who is sitting in his highchair with a face full of oatmeal. "And you, too, angel boy," I say to my little man with a big kiss.

And then I head out the door with a stomach full of nerves.

chapter TWO

Asher-Marks Communications is located in a tall, glass skyscraper in Midtown Manhattan. The two-story lobby is intimidating with glass panel windows, and steel bars that run across the vast space.

The name *ASHER* is emblazoned on top of an omega symbol on the black granite wall behind the security desk. Omega is the emblem of greatness, also meaning the end. Ironic since this is the place where I'm hoping to find a new beginning.

The Asher name is well-known in the city. Not as recognized as, say, Trump or Lauren. There is no reality show or clothing line. No high-profile divorces or runs for public office. Over the past fifty years, Edward Asher has become one of the most powerful people in New York City. He is a prominent real estate investor and a major stockholder in various companies, many of which have been relocated to this building. His name can be seen in hospital wings, college buildings, and Minor League stadiums, all because he donates insane amounts of money.

Asher-Marks Communications is one of the Asher businesses, but I doubt I'll ever see him step foot in the office.

"Kathryn Grayson for Malory Dean."

The security for the building is tight with a guard posted at every entrance and two more behind the desk. Not to mention, one at the elevator bank, checking IDs and visitor passes.

I hand over my driver's license. The guard behind the desk eyes me, probably making sure I'm not a terrorist, before taking my picture with a small camera stationed on the counter.

"Twenty-fourth floor." The guard gives a direct stare.

I grab the red visitor pass and make my way to the elevator bank. Once inside, I try to tame the butterflies dancing in my belly.

Breathe, Kat, just breathe.

It was difficult to find a new job in my field that met Gabriel's demands—no travel, easy commute, time with the family—so once Malory called to tell me there was an opening at Asher-Marks Communications, I jumped on board. For one, it's an incredible job. More than that, I get to work with my friend again.

Malory and I met at a small production company six years ago. I was fresh out of college and ready to take on the world. Five years my senior, Malory was my mentor. My very *cool* mentor with whom I gossiped over pink margaritas at Rosa Mexicana. While my life went the marriage and baby route, her career blossomed, taking her to Vice President of Asher-Marks Communications, producing concerts, award shows, and even the Super Bowl halftime show. I was so consumed with my at-home life that I chose nights at home with Gabriel over soirees at Cipriani. My social media has honeymoon photos and baby pictures. Hers has pictures of cocktail parties and posts from celebrities. A lot can happen in two years.

As the elevator doors open, I'm greeted by an impressive reception area of glass and mahogany. A striking young woman with bright red hair is busily shuffling through papers behind her desk. Her eyes light up when she sees me exiting the elevator.

"Ms. Grayson," she says, extending her thin arm out in greeting. "I'm Trish. Ms. Dean will be right with you. Oh, and you can ditch the visitor pass. I'll get you a company badge."

Peeling the red sticker off my jacket, I take a seat on one of the metal-and-leather chairs and wait. A large plasma screen plays a loop of promotional footage—clips of the Academy Awards and the Winter Olympics, followed by a charity concert at The Met. All produced by this company.

"Kat!" Malory walks toward me with open arms.

She has on a black leopard pencil skirt and a blood-red satin top, unfastened one button too many. No one, except Malory with her jet-black hair and piercing dark eyes, can pull off this outfit and make it look professional. She looks so phenomenal; I can't help but feel self-conscious of my post-baby body.

"How are you? How is Gabriel?" Malory asks as she pulls me in for a hello. She even smells exotic with hints of amber and cocoa pouring off her skin. "Don't tell me you're missing him already because, now that I have you here, I'm never letting you leave." She lets out a breathy, deep laugh, making her sound like Lauren Bacall.

I return her embrace, hugging her perfectly toned frame. "I've been so excited to come back to work and to work *here*. I can't thank you enough."

She releases me from our hold. "Honey, I didn't pull any special favors. Everyone was thrilled when you interviewed. That's why you got the job. Erik was begging me to have you start immediately."

"I would have, but we had to get a nanny, and I really didn't feel right until I had Gabe's approval."

Malory grabs my arm, and we start walking down the polished concrete hallway.

"You're lucky." She glides as if she were walking on air. "Most men these days *force* their wives to go back to work. Yours wants you home. It's a good sign. I told him the other day that you need to work. You're not a *stay-at-home*." She says the term as if it's a foul thought. "You thrive on this type of energy. This will be so good for you.

11

Besides, you had to have been bored, sitting at home, feeding Junior all day long."

I stop in my tracks. "When did you talk to Gabe?"

"Last Thursday," she says nonchalantly, pulling me again. "I called, and you weren't home."

That's shocking since I feel like I'm always home. "I was probably at the supermarket. It's a very glamorous life in the suburbs."

"Oh, how I hate that you left the city. Just promise me you don't own a Snuggle and jeggings, and I'll forgive you for leaving me."

"It's called a Snuggie, and I would never be caught dead in one of those things." I bite my lip, thinking how this is actually a lie. Gabriel bought me a leopard Snuggie last year, and I've worn it on more than one occasion. I don't want Malory to know just how domesticated I've actually become. Part of the excitement about coming to work is getting dressed again. "Like my new suit?"

"Girl, it hugs you in all the right places. Especially where those new mom boobs come into play. You seriously don't even look like you had a baby—except for the girls, that is!" Malory laughs and nudges my left breast for fun. She's always been very brash. It's something I'll have to get used to again.

"I have curves I didn't have before. I think I'm carrying some booty, too." I tilt my head back, motioning toward my backside.

Malory smacks my ass. "You needed it. Come, let me reintroduce you to the team. Conference meeting starts in five."

We turn down a corridor and walk along a wide hallway with a wall of glass to our left and a series of doors leading to offices on our right. Behind the glass wall is a conference room with a birch wood table, which looks like it can easily fit twenty people.

Erik, Gretchen, and Heather are in the conference room when Malory and I stroll in.

"Morning, team. You remember Kathryn from the interview process." Malory offers me up as she pulls out one of the orange conference chairs and takes a seat.

"So glad to have you on board." Erik stands and gives me a congratulatory handshake.

"Welcome to the team, Kathryn." Gretchen is equally enthused.

"Kat. Please call me Kat." I return their handshakes, making sure to keep them firm.

"Welcome, Kat," Heather says as if she were sucking on sour candy.

Heather's welcome is the least...welcoming. Even when I interviewed a few weeks ago, she was the least receptive to me. I have to remember to ask Malory what that's about.

Erik Marks is the president and my new boss. He has long black hair and a black goatee. His wardrobe is equally devoid of color—from his T-shirt to his jeans and boots. The look is more biker chic than art-house sophisticate. As casual as he looks, I can only assume he's in head-to-toe Armani.

Gretchen, as I recall from my interview, is a bit, shall we say, high-strung. With her professional attire and a tight updo, I can tell she's never missed a day of work in her life and crosses every *t* and dots every *i*. Heather is about ten years younger than Gretchen, about my age. She's wearing far less clothing—a lot less actually. I suspect her purple chiffon dress is really a shirt.

As the five of us exchange pleasantries, the rest of the staff files in. The entire office consists of thirty-seven people. Less than I thought. I don't know their names or titles but vow to remember them all by the end of the week.

Erik starts the meeting by welcoming me to the team. I gracefully rise from my chair with embarrassment. I feel my ears starting to turn red.

"We are particularly thrilled to have Kat on board because of her expertise in site surveys and logistics, which will come in handy for our next project. We will be covering a charity event right here in New York City, which will be broadcast on network TV on Labor Day weekend. The airtime has already been bought. Now, we just have to fill it. It's a quick turnaround, but I know this team can do it."

There is a buzz of excitement in the room before Erik continues, "It's an integrated project with the Asher family. Seven headliners will be performing at David Geffen Hall in Lincoln Center, and all proceeds will go to fund music programs around the country. This is a New York event, but we're representing the entire country here."

As Erik runs down the list of events, I learn what everyone around the table does.

"Kat, you will be working alongside Heather on full-scale production, making sure the tech team, set designers, and talent are on schedule and on budget, as well as creating the rundowns."

Heather's grimace is obvious from across the room. For a pretty girl, she looks unattractive when she frowns—something I can tell she does a lot.

I turn to Malory. "Is this going to be a problem?"

"Of course. When isn't there a little office drama?" Malory whispers into my ear with a laugh.

$$\Omega$$

An hour later, the meeting is over. Malory and I make our way back down the hallway, turning into a room diagonal from the conference room.

"And this is your office."

My office? I'm shocked, as I didn't expect to have a space of my own. A sleek, rectangular glass desk with an iMac, and a black Herman Miller chair sits against crisp white walls. In front of the desk is a charcoal-colored club chair while mahogany filing cabinets line the wall behind. The space is modern and chic, bare but beautiful.

I leap to the wall of glass at the far end of the room. "I can see the Empire State Building from here!"

"Hey, can I come in?" I hear Erik's voice coming from the doorway. "Again, I really want to welcome you to the team. It's a pleasure to have you here."

It takes everything I have to turn my gaze away from the stunning Manhattan view. "Thank you, Erik. I can't wait to get started. Everyone here seems great."

"Keep that thought in your head because you have a meeting with Alexander Asher first thing on Friday morning. I tried to get you on his calendar earlier, but the end of the week is all he had available. He'll be on the floor for the morning meeting."

I've heard of Edward Asher. Who hasn't? But I've never heard of this Alexander Asher character, and I'm not about to let Erik hear me say that. If I have to meet with him and he's an Asher, then he's clearly a big deal.

"Does he come to all the meetings?"

"Not usually. Since he bought the company, he lets me run things. That said, this project is very important to him, so he'll be quite involved," he explains.

"It should be interesting," Malory says in a low-pitched, singsong voice. Looking down at her feet, she flicks the foot of the chair in front of her with her heel.

Erik clears his throat. "Well, ladies, I'll leave you to it."

I thank him again as he leaves, then take a seat in my new, fancy office chair and recline back. I spin my seat in a circle and come back to Malory.

"So, this is the life you've been living without me?"

She takes a seat in front of me and crosses her legs. "Yes, but you were too busy picking out paint colors for the living room to notice."

I prop my feet on the desk. At my previous companies, I had a cubicle where the person sitting next to me could hear every move and conversation. But in here, I'm free to do and say whatever I'd like.

"So, what's the deal with Heather?"

Malory's cell phone vibrates. She looks down and starts typing a response to a text or email. Without taking her eyes off the screen, she answers my question, "Oh, she's had a stick up her ass since the day she started. She thinks you're here to steal her job. She doesn't like other women, especially attractive women, so you're up shit creek."

If she doesn't like attractive, then she must really hate Malory. She is one of the most glamorous creatures I've ever met.

"This new mom is no sex kitten. Maybe three years ago but not now."

Malory looks up from her phone, her eyes squinting at me, as if trying to decide if I'm telling the truth. "Kat, are you out of your fucking mind? You know you're freaking gorgeous. But don't worry. Once Heather understands you're happily married, she'll realize you aren't the competition."

Heather must be dabbling in the office dating pool. I can understand it. She's young and pretty, if not for the sourpuss face.

"Speaking of happily married..." Malory continues. "This new project is a quick turnaround, which means late nights." Her tone turns curious. "Do you think Gabriel is going to give you a hard time?"

I lean my head against the back of the chair and stare up at the ceiling. "I think he only wanted me to stay home instead of returning to work, so he would feel less guilty about all the hours he spends away from home." As soon as the words pour out of my mouth, I instantly regret them.

The last thing Malory wants to hear are my tales as a suburban housewife. She must think I'm pathetic. *Mental note: keep your mouth shut.*

"Do you still have sex?"

"That's a little personal."

"Well?" She raises a brow, enticing me to indulge.

Just like old times, I take the bait even though it makes me entirely uncomfortable. "Yes, and no. We do, but it's not the same. I can't explain it."

"What did you expect? You're married, and you have a kid already. You're the oldest twenty-eight-year-old I know. That's why we get along so well."

I agree. Malory, on the other hand, is the youngest thirty-three-year-old I know.

She takes my cell phone off my desk and looks at my home screen. It's a picture of Gabriel and Jackson, looking into the camera with their matching features.

"One thing's for sure. You're married to a hot guy. Seriously, the man just gets better-looking with age. I'd be hitting that every night."

Malory always makes comments like that about Gabriel. I forgot how much it irritated me.

"So, who is this Alexander guy I have to meet with?" I say, abruptly changing the topic.

"Asher is, number one, your boss. Don't ever call him Alexander. Mr. Asher will do," she says condescendingly. "He is Edward Asher's grandson and is gearing up to take over the family dynasty."

I roll my eyes at the thought of having to meet with a spoiled brat who's taking over his granddaddy's business. I can't stand entitled people. New York is filled with enough socialites and wannabes already. I don't need to work with one.

Malory points her finger at me as I turn on my new computer and wait for it to load. "Don't roll your eyes. Alexander Asher is on track to become one of the most successful men in the country. He's smart, too. He bought Erik's company and knew enough to keep Erik as an asset. He's also becoming quite the philanthropist."

I'll give him credit for the charity. The rest I'm a bit wary of. "So, I'm meeting with a ten-year-old who made a few bucks from playing Monopoly with the family trust fund?"

Malory returns my eye roll. Apparently, I'm amusing.

chapter THREE

"I can't believe they gave you your own office," Gabriel says, exiting our master bathroom, wearing baby-blue pajama bottoms and a white undershirt.

I take a moment to look him over. Malory's right. He is getting better-looking with age. A Clooney, if you will.

When Gabriel and I met, he was an athletic twenty-one-year-old with boyish charm and a matching exterior. He used to wear jeans, funny T-shirts, and baseball caps. His hair was longer and fell slightly into his eyes. He'd brush it off his forehead when it got in the way or he was frustrated.

Ten years later, he's filled out quite well, thanks to running and push-ups in the park. Gabriel doesn't believe in spending money on a gym when Mother Nature has everything you need. The T-shirts and jeans come out sporadically, but his usual attire is a suit for work and pants and a polo shirt on the weekends. His hair is cut much shorter, and it flatters him.

"So, what are you working on?" He pulls back the duvet and climbs into bed.

"A benefit concert at Lincoln Center." I grab the TV remote and turn on Netflix.

"Who is the concert for?" He lifts his iPad from the nightstand.

"The company was assigned to put together this major televised concert event that will raise money for music programs." I search the selection of classics and select an old Cary Grant film.

"Like a telethon?" he asks, hitting the icon for the CNN app.

I snort. "Yeah, kinda…but a thousand times more posh and without Jerry Lewis. Do you understand how much money this could bring in for music programs?"

"And the revenue your company can draw," he says with his eyes focused on the tablet.

"No, this is all for charity. We're not making any money."

"Who do you think pays your salary?" He puts the iPad on his lap and looks over at me. "I bet, ten cents to every dollar will go to charity, and your company will pocket the rest. No one does anything for free," he says matter-of-factly.

"Gabriel." My voice is stern. He knows I don't want to hear anything negative about my job.

"Kat…" He's patronizing me. "I'm a lawyer. Trust me. Your company is making bank on this."

I know he's right, but it bothers me that he's such a realist. Gabriel is a tax fraud defense attorney. I'm not talking about people who forgot to pay their taxes last year and are being hit up by the IRS. Gabriel represents high-profile clients who hide more money from the United States government than everyone on my block would probably make in a lifetime…combined.

He continues, "What else did you expect, working for a company run by Alexander Asher?"

"You know who my new boss is?"

"Uh, yeah. Did you expect me not to?"

"Well, kind of." I'm too embarrassed to say *I* didn't know who he was.

"The Asher family is synonymous with grandiosity, consumption, and gluttony. I wouldn't be surprised if I had to do some tax litigation for them down the road."

Just what I need—to be out of a job as soon as I found a new one. "Doesn't matter. I have a meeting with the man on Friday, but other than that, he doesn't bother with the company." I turn my attention back to the TV. *Why can't all men be as debonair as Cary Grant?*

"It sounds very exciting." Gabriel rubs his hands over his eyes. "More so than what I have going on. I have miles of paperwork to go over. Tax fraud. Why anyone would commit it, I'll never understand." When his eyes are thoroughly rubbed, he lifts the iPad off his lap and goes back to reading.

The frustration in his voice, mixed with despair, causes me to look over at him. The poor guy works too hard.

"You don't sound too sure about this one."

"This guy is paying a lot of money to stay out of prison. I'll get a good deal, but it's going to take a lot of work." He looks up at me with his cobalt eyes. "Kat, you have to see what my client wrote off. He owes the government three million dollars in back taxes."

I nearly choke on my words. "Three million?"

"This case is going to be the death of me. He recently bought into some lucrative businesses, so if he goes down, a lot of people will lose their jobs." He runs his fingers through his thick hair. "I'll be working some late hours in the weeks ahead. I hope Jack won't suffer because if it." He looks concerned, his eyes tired.

"Are you okay?" Placing my hand over his, I rub my thumb over his palm.

Lifting my hand to his lips, he brushes a kiss over my knuckles. "Yes. Thank you." Gabriel puts the iPad back on the nightstand. He lets out a quiet laugh and lightly shakes his head. "Do you remember when all we wanted was to move to the Caribbean and sail for the rest of our lives?"

"It seemed like a brilliant idea."

The sight of Gabriel with a dark tan, no shirt, and a carefree smile made me weak in the knees when we first met. He still looks great underneath his business suits, but that life we dreamed of wasn't practical.

He opens his mouth to say something but retracts and nods his head in agreement. "We might have been young and dumb, but we certainly had it all figured out," he says, turning off the lamp on his side of the bed and rolling away from me. "Good night."

"Good night." I sigh as I relax into our comfortable bed. Tonight, it's just me and *An Affair to Remember*.

$$\Omega$$

I spend my first few days getting settled into my new position and working with Heather to plan the event at David Geffen Hall.

Every year as a kid, I would go to Lincoln Center with my mom. It was our only common interest. I love the arts, and so does she. She would get us both dressed to the nines, and we'd see the ballet or a concert. I know the venue fairly well. Back then, it was called Avery Fisher Hall. After a sizable donation from the famed entertainment mogul, David Geffen, the building was renamed.

I like to think of it as injecting Hollywood glamour into the New York classical scene. That is my inspiration for the event. Once Erik said we were having a concert there, I knew exactly what I wanted to do.

I walk my files into Heather's office. Since we're both producers on the project, we have to collaborate on everything. While my office is stark white, void of personality, Heather's is decorated in plum and aqua accents.

Aside from telling me to enter, Heather doesn't acknowledge my presence when I take a seat, lay my files on my lap, and open them, ready to start our meeting.

She's wearing a pale pink tube dress with a navy bolero. Her hair is in a high ponytail, showcasing giant gold hoop earrings. She takes her time typing out an email as I sit patiently and wait.

"Okay, let's hear it," she spits out, her eyes still on the computer screen as she types.

I blink a few times. "Hear what?"

"Your ideas. Go."

I take a deep breath and remind myself what Malory told me. Heather thinks I'm here to take her job. I'll just be friendly and let her know I'm not a threat.

Opening my file, I look down at my notes and start. My voice is slightly unsteady, as it's difficult to talk to someone who is looking in another direction. "I thought we could get started on the aesthetics of the event. The red carpet will be filmed for web distribution. We'll have reporters there to photograph the arrivals, so we should set the tone right there."

I look up and see Heather is still focused on her computer screen. She is no longer writing an email but is now looking at shoes on the Nordstrom website.

I continue, "I want to go glam. This is a charity event, but it's a premier charity event. Let's have a black carpet. A red carpet is very Hollywood movie premiere. A black carpet will—"

"Look disgusting," Heather quips, finally turning to face me. "It's a children's charity telethon, not a goth horror show." She turns her attention back to her computer. "Next."

I look back at my notes. "I was thinking of lining the walkways with dahlias for—"

"Next." The word stretches out in mock annoyance.

Apparently, I am not going to win on anything that has to do with the arrival area. I skim through my notes and come to a particularly great idea. "The event is to benefit children's music programs. Why don't we invite a musical prodigy to perform with each musical act? We'll pick the kids based on the genre of music. Like an awesome pianist playing with Coldplay or a trumpet aficionado alongside Chris Bode."

Heather's eyebrows ride up. She doesn't give me any clue as to her thoughts on the idea, but she hasn't easily dismissed it either. She plays with one gold hoop before she finally spits out, "I'll consider it."

I was beginning to think we weren't going to agree on anything.

"It's a half-assed idea though." She turns to me and tilts her head to the side like she's talking to a baby. "Do you really think A-list performers are going to want to be upstaged by some child prodigy?"

My mouth drops as I breathe in the many expletives I'd like to say to her.

Heather takes out her Gucci handbag from beneath the desk and places her date planner in it. "You can leave now." She waves at me in a shooing motion. "I have somewhere else I have to be."

I blink back at her a few times, trying to decide if I should say something or just leave.

When I was in grammar school, I had to constantly hear people talk trash about my dad, Frank "Catch" Grayson, who was a pitcher for a Major League Baseball team. When your parent has a famous profession, people think they can tell you their personal feelings about them. I get it; I do. If my dad pitched a crappy game, they would call him a bum, followed by a few obscenities. What they didn't recognize was, my dad was a part of a team, and the entire team had to work together to win. They also failed to realize it was exactly that—a game. Someone had to win, and someone had to lose. It was the risk you took.

But what irked me the most was how people would take their aggression out on me just because I was his daughter. I mean, my hairdresser's kid went to my school, and I didn't talk trash to him because his mom had given me a bad haircut.

I spoke to my dad about it. He was an amazing sounding board. I felt bad, telling him things the kids at school had said about him. Instead of getting mad, he laughed. He laughed so hard that he almost fell off my bed. I couldn't believe how little he cared.

In that moment, he gave me the best advice. He told me to do what he did when he was on the mound.

"Breathe, Kat. Just breathe."

So, that's what I do.

I take a breath and wait for tomorrow.

chapter FOUR

I planned on getting to the office early to prepare for my meeting with Alexander Asher, but my train is delayed. Not a surprise for the Long Island Rail Road. It can turn a standard forty-minute commute into a two-hour expedition. If Gabriel and I had more than one car, I'd have taken it. Instead, he drove to Connecticut for a meeting, and I'm running late.

To round it all out, after days of blue skies and sunshine, dark nimbus clouds roll in, and as soon as I step foot on the train, the heavens decide to open. This isn't just rain; it's a torrential downpour. Raindrops pound on the roof of the train car so hard, I can hear it through my AirPods regardless of the music streaming in my ears. Hopefully, it will let up by the time I get off because I forgot my umbrella.

When the train reaches Penn Station, I exit and walk up the concrete steps that lead to the central arena, where thousands of people exit and enter every day, traveling in and out of the city.

Working my way past people walking in various directions, I finally navigate over to the underground maze that is the New York City Subway. I transfer to the crosstown E train, hoping to avoid having to walk outside as much as possible.

The subway's doors are about to close as I approach, so I rush and squeeze my body into the sardine-packed car. There is a man singing gospel music on the other end of the car, panhandling for a cup of coffee. If I were closer, I'd give him a few dollars.

Almost the entire car gets off at my stop, and I struggle not to get trampled as I make my way out and up the stairs to street level holding my hands up to shield myself from the rain, which is useless. Just my luck, there is no umbrella vendor insight.

I'm standing at the corner of Lexington Avenue, waiting for the light to change. The rain is coming down harder, and despite the warm air, my toes are getting cold from being wet.

I count the seconds until the little hand of the *Do Not Walk* sign tells me to cross. The sky opens even more, and the rain falls so loud that I can't even hear myself think. People take cover, and I prepare to run across the street.

That's when it hits me.

A car slams into a pothole filled with water, creating my own private waterfall. Like a tidal wave filled with soot, the water saturates me from head to toe.

My arms fly up as I scream in surprise, "Ahh!"

I breathe in erratic pants as I look down at my clothes that are sticking to my skin under my raincoat that is now filthy and destroyed. My feet are standing in a small stream, and I can feel the mascara running down my cheeks. Pedestrians on the corner look at me in shock, thankful it wasn't them.

The car quickly pulls over and comes to a stop. A man jumps out of the backseat; another man follows him, carrying an umbrella. The first man takes the umbrella and signals for the other to wait in the car.

"Are you okay?"

"Do I look okay?" I want to say, but I'm stunned into silence.

"My driver didn't mean to get you. I couldn't believe it. It was like it was happening in slow motion."

My body curves in at the feel of water soaking through my coat. "*You* couldn't believe it was happening? I can't even…" I try to compose myself as the urge to cry takes over me. "I have a really important meeting this morning and…" I don't even know what to say.

The rain is relentless. My hair is soaked, I'm covered in backstreet muck, and this stranger is kindly trying to cover me with his umbrella.

"Let me take you to where you have to go," he shouts over the rain. "You can dry off on the way."

I look at him, weary. *Get in the car with him? Is he kidding?*

He can sense my resistance.

"I'm not a psycho. I promise." He holds out his hand, the umbrella temporarily covering neither of us. He pulls it back in place and gestures to himself with his free hand. "Look, I have a nice suit, a personal driver. I'll even give you my cell phone to hold in case you feel the urge to call the cops." His lip curls up to the side, like he's sneering at me, mocking me. "I'm not usually this nice of a guy, so either get in now or stand here in the rain."

I weigh my options. I can try to run the few blocks or get in the car. He looks harmless, and there is a driver to act as a buffer. A digital clock in the window of a nearby bank alerts me to the fact I am officially late for my meeting.

The rain continues to pour down, and I can't even see the other side of the street. I must be out of my mind. I shuffle my feet and head into the black SUV and out of the rain.

Mystery Man climbs in beside me and I'm immediately overcome with the most delicious smell of tobacco and vanilla. It's intoxicating and divine. I must be hallucinating because this is not the time to be enjoying scents.

"Where are we going?" he asks.

For the first time, I get a good look at him. He's…gorgeous. Beyond gorgeous. At least he doesn't *look* like an ax murderer.

"Forty-Eighth and Third. The Asher Building," I reply, shivering with how cold and wet I am.

He looks at me, puzzled, and motions toward the driver. His eyes never leave mine. "Devon, I believe we can honor this woman's request."

My body jerks as the car pulls away from the curb, and I am suddenly nervous. "This is silly. It's going to take longer, navigating around the street, than it would take for me to walk five blocks."

He smiles, and it's a mischievous smile, almost like a Cheshire cat. "Nonsense. We were headed that way anyway. Besides, I'm sure you'll find this to be a most convenient excursion."

He pulls a handkerchief from his pocket and offers it to me. Tentatively, I take it and wipe down my neck and chest with it. I catch Mystery Man's eyes following the handkerchief. I reprimand him with my stare, and he laughs at the little exchange.

"I'm sorry. I didn't get your name."

"Kathryn," I say automatically and then pause, almost hesitant to give out my full name. "Kathryn Grayson."

"Like the actress," he states. Then, he cocks his head and frowns just a little, like he's thinking.

"Yes."

That point is lost on most people. My mother, the old movie buff, was a fan. She was lucky when she married a man named Grayson. I'm surprised she didn't try to change my name to Marilyn after I married Gabriel Monroe.

"I'm a Lawford man myself," he says with a naughty expression across his faultless face.

Peter Lawford was equal parts witty and sexy, but rumor has it, beneath the charm was a troubled soul. Not many people my age know who he is. From the looks of the man sitting next to me, he's not that much older than I am.

With my hands folded over my bag, I try to look ahead, making sure the driver knows where he's going. My attention can't stay focused long as I risk a glance or two at the man sitting next to me.

His dark blond hair is wet from the rain. It is just long enough to run your fingers through. I can tell from the way his legs stretch across the backseat that he is tall, over six feet. From the way he's sitting, his thighs, lean and strong, are defined through his black suit pants. He has a dominating quality about him.

With his bronzed skin, he looks like he could be Greek or Italian. I can't tell. When he looks up at me, I see golden eyes. I've never seen golden eyes before. I really have never seen anyone who looks like him before. Maybe in a magazine but not in real life. He is quite…breathtaking.

There's a pamphlet on the seat beside me, wedged between us. Upon further inspection I see it's a program for a museum exhibit. On the cover is a black and white photo of a man with a toothbrush mustache and a bowler hat.

"Charlie Chaplin fan?" I ask.

His eyes crinkle. "I go to the Museum of Modern Art often. This showcase was on the directorial advancements of Chaplin. It was one of my favorites."

"What did you like about the exhibit?" My curiosity is piqued.

His elbow rests on the door as his thumb rises to his mouth, brushing the pad of his finger along his lips as he appraises me.

"It's the auteurism approach to film that intrigues me," he says, his eyes steady. "Many people believe the writer is the author. They create the characters, give them names and words to say. Others feel it's the actors who portray the lives on-screen, that they breathe life into the words, and are therefore the most important."

He's just a foot away from me in this car yet, when he speaks, he feels much closer. Almost inches.

"The director," he continues, "is the real God of film. He has the power. The puppet master who controls the strings."

The heat from his body and that wicked scent envelope me. My mouth is dry, and I can do nothing but breathe out in small, shallow breaths.

"I like control. More than that, I like people thinking they hold the power when I am the one who has been holding the strings all along." He isn't angry or crass. The words are merely a declaration.

I study his eyes; this proximity allows me to see the flecks of brown in them that you might easily miss if you weren't really looking. There is nothing sinister in them. Just pure, unadulterated determination.

"I can see how that would be intriguing.'" I breathe.

"You're a voyeur," he states, sitting up straighter, closing the distance between us.

"Why is that?"

"Because you like to stare." His pupils dilate.

My fingers tremble, possibly from the chill of wearing wet clothes. I refold them over one another in an attempt to do something with my nervous energy.

"I'm sorry. What is your name?"

"Alex." He has a devilish grin. "Just call me Alex."

"If you don't mind, I just have to pull myself together." I flip open the overhead mirror and take a look at my appearance—at least, what I can see in the small reflective glass above me. Mascara and eyeliner are smudged around my eyes, and I do my best to smooth it without poking my eye out. "I have a big meeting in about..." I glance at the clock on the front dashboard. "I'm embarrassingly late."

Alex leans toward me and flashes that perfect smile. "I'm sure whoever it is with will understand the circumstances, as strange as they might be." His golden hues hold my gaze. "Pardon me for being up-front, Ms. Grayson, but you have the most beautiful eyes I have ever seen."

I blush at his compliment, yet I feel uncomfortable in his presence. I close the mirror above me and throw my makeup in my bag. Looking out the window, I see the glass skyscraper approaching. "Alex, thank you for the ride. I'll just get out here," I demand.

But the car doesn't stop. It continues past the building and pulls into a parking garage. My heart leaps in my throat.

Where are we going? Where is this man taking me? Oh my God, I'm being abducted.

"It's okay." He puts his hand on my leg. "Relax. You're safe with me. I work in the building, too. This couldn't have been more convenient."

I let out a sigh of relief.

After a quick evaluation, I gain my bearings. The garage is on the other side of the building than the main entrance. The car drives down a ramp and turns a corner before pulling up beside an elevator bank inside the underground garage. The driver—Devon, I believe his name is—gets out and circles around the car to open Alex's door.

I pull my door handle, but before I can get out, Alex has swung around the car and offers a hand.

"Please, Ms. Grayson. It's the least I can do."

I take his offered hand and stand outside the car. Having never been here before, I don't know how to get to my office.

As if reading my mind, Alex motions toward the elevator bank and hits the call button. The doors immediately swing open, and we enter. Just Mystery Man and me. I feel out of place, soaked with rainwater and a dirty dress. This man standing next to me is dry and pristine in a black suit with a crisp white shirt and black tie. The moisture in his hair has dried, and the few raindrops he had on his jacket have evaporated. He stands tall and confident. I feel small in comparison.

My body shivers from the chill of my wet clothes. I cross my arms to regain my warmth.

I hit the button for my floor, but the car doesn't move. Alex leans over and puts his hand on the small of my back. It must be the warmth of his skin that causes me to shiver again. His hand takes up most of my back, and I find myself wondering what it would be like for it to travel around my belly. I shake my head and blink back the odd thought as his other hand reaches around my body. He places a card in the panel and hits a code before the car starts to move.

"You're shivering," he states.

"I'm soaked."

"Silly me. I thought I made you nervous."

My senses are heightened. My eyes focus on his square chin and strong jawline. My nose takes in the sensual smell of his cologne. My ears pound with the sound of my breath speeding up, and my touch tries to not cause my knees to fold at the mere feeling of his hand on my back.

He leans down and softly murmurs into my ear, "Ms. Grayson, how do you like your coffee?" He sounds sensual, as if he were asking me to go to bed with him.

"Um, strong and black." I quiver, swallowing hard.

"Good answer," he says, releasing me in the process.

I didn't realize he had pulled me further into him until I miss the heat of his body.

The elevator doors open.

Trish, the redhead at reception, greets us with an awesome smile. "Good morning, Mr. Asher!"

Asher?

"Morning, Triciana," Alex says and heads down the hallway. "We'll need two coffees…black. Ms. Grayson and I have a meeting. We'll take them in her office."

I stop in my tracks.

Stunned.

Holy shit.

That is Alexander Asher.

Asher!

PURE ABANDON

I am so embarrassed.
No, I am *furious*!

chapter FIVE

"Who do you think you are?" I stamp into my office with my wet head, stopping just past the doorway.

Alexander Asher is standing in front of me, looking as innocent as a lamb. "Excuse me?"

"Did you know you had a meeting with me? When I said my name and the building…you knew exactly who I was!" I can't control myself. My hand has made its way in front of my face, and my pointer finger is waving dramatically in the air. "And that move in the elevator. Do you realize you are my *boss*? That is so wrong on so many levels!"

He walks toward me with a determined look, his eyes intense on mine. He inches closer. The weight of his body leans into me as he swings his hand around my body and slams the door closed.

"I don't think this is an appropriate conversation for the entire office to hear. Do you, Ms. Grayson?" His hand is resting on the door with his arm enclosing my head.

This is not the ten-year-old brat I imagined. This is a *man*. A very arrogant man.

"Will you explain to me just how I ended up in your car?"

"Pure coincidence." He withdraws and walks toward my desk. His presence dominates the space making my tiny office feel smaller. "I am many things, but a liar I am not." He takes a seat behind my desk as if to show his authority over me. "Or you can believe I have a very skilled driver who purposefully plows into potholes on rainy days just so I can pick up beautiful women."

I'm soggy and damp. My hair is a mess of curls and matted ends, but he is staring at me like I'm crème brûlée, waiting to be devoured. I feel my ears turning red at the words this mysterious man is saying.

Well, he's not a mystery anymore. He's Alexander Asher, billionaire, mega-mogul, and my boss.

"Do you really expect me to believe you didn't know who I was?" he asks, incredulously.

"Of course not! I would have said something in the car unlike you."

His eyes shift to the side. "You didn't Google me?"

"Did you Google me?"

"Didn't have to. I have your résumé."

"Well, I…" I have no comeback, especially not when he's sitting here looking all powerful, and sounding so condescending. "You can't flirt with employees."

His teeth skim over his bottom lip as he tilts his head, playfully. "I wasn't the one with a staring problem."

The jest in his tone is unnerving. He's unapologetic in the worst way. I don't know what bothers me more—the fact he's so damn at ease with his actions, or the fact I am mortified by mine. Not that I did anything wrong. I merely noted an attractive man. That's harmless.

I must be getting hot. I take off my trench coat and hang it on the door.

He leans his weight back, causing the chair to recline. He draws his hands up in front of his body and rubs the pads of his fingers against each other. He's wearing an impish grin, and he looks beyond comfortable, sitting in my seat.

"I am very sorry if you were misled, Ms. Grayson, but this is all simply a misunderstanding. I like to think of myself as your knight in shining armor, who rescued you from the perils of the rain. Looks like I was wrong when I said you were a voyeur. You seem to be quite the exhibitionist."

Confused, I follow his eyes, which are no longer holding mine, but are staring down at my chest.

My trench coat must have soaked through to my white blouse, which is now completely see-through. My breasts are exposed through my thin bra, my nipples rock hard from the cold air. I grab my trench and hold it against my chest.

Outraged, I pull the door handle and swing the door open, ignoring Trish, who is standing on the other side, holding two black coffees.

"It's *Mrs. Monroe* to you!" I raise my hand and flash my wedding ring at him, which until this moment I hadn't realized I wasn't wearing. I lower my hand in aggravation and motion toward the open door. "Now, if you don't mind, I need to compose myself and put myself back together."

"Mrs. Monroe?" His brows curve in confusion as his eyes wander around the room.

"Grayson is my maiden name."

Rising from the chair, he adjusts his cuff links and speaks in a professional manner, "Well, we seem to have gotten off on the wrong foot."

"Seems so, Asher." I make a point to leave out the formality of *Mr.*

Poor Trish stands frozen in the doorway, not knowing if she should be coming or going. Behind her, people scurry through the hall.

He passes by me, careful not to brush shoulders, and heads out the door, taking my nerves with him. Mortified, I close the door, trying to block the eavesdroppers' view of my disheveled appearance.

Ω

"What happened to you?" Malory looks at my soot-covered ensemble in horror. She is seated at the conference table, closest to the door.

All heads in the conference room turn as I enter the room, late for the meeting. My clothes are now dry, thanks to the hand dryer in the ladies' restroom, but markings of Midtown muck still give evidence of my interesting morning. I pulled my wet hair into a slick bun. The most polished look I could achieve, given what I had to work with.

"You look like you were run over by a truck," she hisses.

"An SUV actually." I send a death glare down to the head of the conference table, where Alexander Asher is seated.

He looks at me with those penetrating eyes, making my ears turn red again. He stands, keeping his focus on me, and motions for Harvey, a heavyset man, who is sitting on his right, to stand. "Mrs. Monroe, please have a seat. We were just about to discuss the venue for the event."

"No, please, Harvey, stay seated," I say, preparing to sit against the wall. Harvey is already walking toward the other side of the room.

Asher motions toward the chair next to him—"sit."

He is so dominating; it's sickening.

"It's *Mrs. Grayson*, please." I stress the *Mrs.* right back at him.

He looks at me with intrigue as I take the proffered chair

"If we're done here, I'd like to continue with the logistics conversation." Heather breaks the tension. It's the most welcoming thing she's done since I arrived.

"Yes, logistics." Asher settles in and continues the meeting.

Heather polishes her hair and swivels her chair in Asher's direction, gazing at him. "We need to cancel some of the musical acts, or we'll need a bigger venue." She looks at him as if *he* is the bigger venue she needs making a lightbulb goes on in my head. This must be why she doesn't like other women.

"I don't understand. What is wrong with David Geffen Hall?" Asher asks. He is purely business. Not the same carefree yet seductive man I met an hour ago.

"Mr. Asher," Gretchen chimes in, "every single act we've asked is available. This event is going to draw way too many people, and we don't have the air time. This is a huge problem for us. If we don't find a new venue, we're going to have to turn down performers, and I'd hate to risk burning a few bridges."

"The folks at Lincoln Center have donated a lot of their time and more to this event. It would be in bad taste to break that relationship," Harvey adds.

"It would be in worse taste to limit our event." Asher puts his fingers to his mouth, brooding. "What about the Metropolitan Opera House?"

"Unavailable. We inquired when we started the booking process," Heather says. "We'll have to go through the list and limit which performers we have."

It seems like a silly problem. David Geffen Hall holds almost three thousand people. That's a huge audience for a charitable concert, but I suppose it would be nice to have an even bigger venue. Maybe, next time, they should consider a sports arena. Although that would be rather extravagant.

I don't know where the idea comes from or why in the world I say it, but the words just slip out of my mouth. "What about Central Park?"

Heather props her curvy body up to attention. "Out of the question. We're talking security and a bigger production, not to mention getting the mayor's permission."

"Yes, it's just too much to do in the allotted time," Gretchen agrees, while Heather shoots daggers at me for suggesting it.

It was a stupid idea, but I've seen concerts done there before. *Good Morning America* does it every week. But I have no idea what goes into securing a space like that.

I rest my right elbow on the arm of my chair and place my palm against my forehead. It's not even ten in the morning, and this is officially the worst day of my life.

"No, no, wait. I'm the one footing the bill here." Asher places his hands on the table, a pensive look on his face. "That could work. It's been done before. It would be big, much bigger than anticipated. We might be able to get all the networks and streaming services to bid in on this."

My head perks up, as I'm stunned he is actually considering the idea.

"But that doesn't solve the Lincoln Center dilemma. We don't want to insult them." Heather directs her new-found concern at me.

"Keep it," I shoot back and then bite my tongue.

Asher leans toward my chair. "What do you mean, keep it?"

I feel my pulse quickening, the way it has been since I got into his car. I hate being on the spot. And by him. It's all so unsettling. But the adrenaline rush provides me with a moment of complete clarity.

"Do a concert there, too. Keep a top artist and hold a private concert for your biggest donors. Give away some seats to the kids this is benefiting. Turn it into a gala. The event could be a special that you air at a later date."

"You can't really be serious?" Heather is irate. Her body is bobbing back and forth toward the table, looking around the room to see if anyone else agrees with her. "Again, you need the city's approval to use the park."

Asher's eyes look up toward the ceiling, as if he's taking my idea and dancing around with it in his head. He begins to nod as the thoughts work their way through. "The park doesn't concern me. The mayor owes me a favor. A pretty big favor, too, and I've been waiting to cash in on it."

He leans back in his chair and draws his hands together in a triangle in front of his face.

He looks across the table and directs his attention toward Erik. "You know more than I do on this matter. Can you put together two productions, one in Central Park and another at Lincoln Center?"

It looks like Erik wants to say no, yet knows he can't. Instead, he says, "It will be tight, but you know we can."

Heather shoots more hateful glares in my direction, and Gretchen's mouth purses. I don't think she's mad, just overwhelmed by the turn of events.

Asher scribbles a few notes on a yellow pad in front of him. "Good. Two events it is, going on simultaneously. Erik, I will need someone to work closely with my office to make sure the Central Park event has what it needs from the mayor's office."

Heather lurches toward Asher, exuding over eagerness. "I will be in charge. With all due respect, Kat, you are just too new to take on such a large responsibility."

Asher pays no mind to her smug comment. "Heather, I will connect you with my office upstairs to get all the details. Mrs. Monroe, you will be working with me on the private event. Since it has now become a gala, I want to be involved in every aspect." He looks up at me. "And I like the idea about the kids. I'll have my office take care of that."

Heather nearly falls out of her seat. I want to do the same. First of all, I was hired to work alongside Heather, not lead my own project. Secondly, I can't work with this man.

I try to come up with my best plea to excuse myself from the position. "I've only been here a week, and I was hired to work with Heather. Central Park is going to be a large production. She'll need assistance. You should hire someone else to produce the gala." The irony that I'd rather work with Heather is not lost on me.

Heather's mouth falls open as she lets out a loud harrumph. Yeah, maybe my comment didn't quite come out the way I'd meant it to. I was trying to save myself, not make her look bad.

Asher takes a look around the room and appraises the staff. His eyes fall on Trish for a second before he pulls himself back to address the table, "Heather is a fine producer. But you're right. With one producer on the project, Heather will need assistance. Triciana will temporarily be promoted to Heather's production assistant for the next three months. She can handle it, right, Erik?"

Erik shows a hint of apprehension, followed by a curt nod. "Trish is more than capable of assisting. We've done a concert event in the park before. Not as big, but we know what we're looking at. Heather will be fine."

Heather dramatically rises from her seat. "But she's a *receptionist*!" Her voice almost shrieks with the word.

Asher's jaw clenches in agitation over Heather's outburst. While his face is stern, his voice is steady and direct. "No, she is an assistant. Let her assist you. As I recall, you wanted to perform this role on your own. Now is your chance to prove you're as good as your threats."

He just called Heather on her shit in front of everyone. I'd smile if I wasn't an emotional wreck. As thrilled as I am that I'm now separated from Heather, I'm frightened. I'm now running my own event, in way over my head.

To be completely honest, I thought only two producers on the concert was ridiculous when it was just Heather and me. Now, it's just me. This is insane.

My mind is scrambling. I want to cry or back into a corner—or both. This is a colossal responsibility. I look over at Heather, who has an unreadable expression on her face. I can't tell if she's excited to be rid of me or just as scared as I am.

My mouth opens to protest when Malory leans forward and mouths to me from across the room, "You are a fucking rock star."

I close my mouth and hold my breath. If I want to be like Malory and if I want to prove to Gabriel that my career is worth the sacrifices, then I'm going to do this full throttle.

Once my hands stop shaking, that is.

Asher leans forward in his chair, securing the buttons on his well-tailored suit jacket, and continues the meeting. I sit back and take notes as technical terms are discussed and sponsorship requests are detailed. The entire time, I find myself glaring at Asher, wondering how I was such a fool this morning.

At the end of the meeting, Asher turns to Malory. "I expect a full report on ad sales and sponsorships to be in place by next Friday."

Malory nods as she takes notes on her iPhone.

"That's all." Asher rises, and the meeting is over. Just like that.

I hightail it out of there and hide in the safe space that is my office. I am still coming down from my morning aggravation. From the rain to the car ride, the elevator and in this office...

I am relieved to finally be able to take off my shoes, which are still cold and damp. I turn to the computer and pull up a Google search, typing in *Alexander Asher*.

Thirty years old, he is a trust-fund baby, part of the Asher empire, but made his personal fortune investing in several small internet companies and reselling them for millions to the likes of Google, Yahoo, and Time Warner. A graduate of Columbia University, he owns a stake in a small record label he sold to Sony as well as a production house—us—and three restaurants, one each in Vegas, LA, and Miami.

He acquired Erik's company, Marks Entertainment, three years ago, creating Asher-Marks Communications, in which Erik obtained a considerable sum for as long as he was able to stay on board to run the team. I read about the company before but didn't put much research into the acquisition.

What really speaks out is his philanthropy. He annually gives away a vast amount of his fortune to children's charities.

Never married. No children. Asher has been seen with a different actress, model, or super beauty at every premiere, gala, and opening around the city.

As upset as I was earlier, there is no denying that I was affected by his presence. When he touched the small of my back, I could feel his body heat against me. A chill runs down my spine.

I order lunch in an attempt to stay hidden from my coworkers. If my appearance wasn't enough to make me a hermit, anyone who heard my outburst with Asher this morning is definitely talking about it.

I spend the afternoon making calls to Lincoln Center, vendors, and various press departments, letting them know I am the primary contact on the event now. As it's a Friday in the summer, I decide to call it an early day knowing the upcoming weeks are going to be long. I turn off my computer and pack my stuff to head home.

Grabbing my belongings, I am startled by a knock at the door. I let the person on the other side know they can enter, and Trish walks in, carrying a long white box.

"Special delivery!" she exclaims like a singing telegram. "Looks like it could be flowers." She awkwardly carries the box, nearly dropping it, and places it on my desk. "It's really heavy. From your husband?"

I swing the box around, so the front is facing me, and I open the small white notecard on the top.

SO YOU DON'T GET CAUGHT IN THE RAIN AGAIN...

—AA

My heart stops.

I hold the card to my chest, concealing it from Trish, who is staring at me like a puppy waiting for a treat. "Um…yes, these are from my husband. Thank you, Trish. That's all."

Disappointed she can't see what's inside, she slumps her shoulders as she exits my office and closes the door behind her.

I put my hands on the top of the box and open the lid. Inside is a bed of the purest white roses I've ever seen. I pick up some of the stems and breathe them in. They subdue my senses.

I look down and count about three-dozen roses. They are devoid of thorns and cut to a perfect height. I lift a bunch and see something at the bottom of the box. I move more stems to the side, and lying on a bed of white petals is a black umbrella with an intricate antique-white pearl handle. It's beautiful.

I laugh to myself, thinking of the day's events. It's an exhausting day and I can't wait to get home and see Jackson.

Home.

There is no way I am bringing white roses home. That is a conversation I am not willing to have with Gabriel.

I grab the box and my bag and walk out of my office, stopping at the reception desk. "Trish, you should take these." I place the box on the upper counter of her desk. "I don't have a vase or anywhere to put them, and I have such a long commute. Take them home."

Flattered, she takes the box and opens it. "Kathryn, these are gorgeous, and expensive. *Really* expensive. I can't take these." She closes the box. "The graphics team will be in this weekend. Maybe I'll keep them here in the front. Help take the sting out of having to work on a Saturday."

"That's the best idea I've heard all day."

"There's an umbrella in here. You want to keep that. I'll place the roses in a vase and leave the umbrella in a box under your desk. From the way you walked in here this morning, it looks like you could use an umbrella."

I can tell this girl is a good egg. I hope Heather is easy on her. Lord knows we could all use a little saving grace.

chapter SIX

"Your mother's here," Gabriel calls out from the kitchen. He's peering through the blinds while drying his hands on a dish towel. Tossing the towel over his shoulder, he walks to the island and pours gin into two glasses—a martini glass for her, a lowball for him.

My mother, Gwendolyn Grayson, lives for a good time. If there's a party, she's there. When I was a kid, she would rent out halls to host soirees, and wear the most elegant dresses. She frequented nightclubs, went to every fundraiser, and she showed up with bells on. Literally. One year, she went to a holiday party, wearing a red silk taffeta gown with a marabou fur cape lined with reindeer bells.

She can't balance a checkbook, but she can figure out a way to get the senator to come to the ribbon-cutting at the local nail salon. She has the face of Elizabeth Taylor, the body of Sophia Loren, and the flair and style of Zsa Zsa Gábor.

As she gets out of the car, I grab Jackson and head to the foyer to greet her. Gabriel is right behind us.

"Happy birthday!" I shout as I open the front door.

"Let me see my beautiful family!" Gwen throws one arm up and over Gabriel's shoulder as the other swings around, enveloping Jackson and me. She is wearing a flowing pink pantsuit with a floral overlay that sashays as she walks. She makes a dramatic gesture with her arms, so the fabric dances in the air as she talks, "I missed you so much. You make it worth the three hours on the thruway."

"You look like a movie star." Gabriel leans in and kisses her cheek, always the charmer.

"When do I not?" Gwen winks at him and nudges her elbow into his stomach. They both share a laugh as she leans over and gives Jackson a loud kiss on the cheek. "There's my grandson! You've gotten so big."

Jackson buries his face in my chest. He looks up through the long lashes he inherited from his father and gives his grandmother a flirtatious smirk.

"You are going to be a heartbreaker, Jackson Monroe. Stay close to Grandma, and I'll teach you how to win over every man and woman in town." She walks straight toward the kitchen to where Gabriel has the martinis lined up.

"Drink for the birthday girl?" Gabriel adds a few olives to make hers extra dirty.

"You know it, kid." She takes the drink and clinks her glass against his. "Look at my son-in-law, the lawyer. All the girls at the club are just jealous that I have a lawyer in the family."

Ah, the ultimate bragging rights for any parent. If your child couldn't be a doctor or a lawyer, then you must at least make sure everyone knows they were smart enough to marry one. That, or a major celebrity. Gwen would have taken either.

"Don't you roll those eyes at me, young lady. I brag about you, too. You and your big TV career."

"Kat is currently working on a concert program," Gabriel says to Gwen before turning his attention to me. "You should tell your mom when it's airing, so she can watch."

A huge smile crosses my face. It's the first encouraging thing Gabriel has said about me returning to work. Maybe he's settled into the idea since the first week was a success.

Gwen puts her drink on the island and claps her hands together, pulling them toward her chin. "I'll have a viewing party. How exciting!" I can see the wheels spinning in Gwendolyn's head as she plans her next big event. "So, tell me, what has been going on around here? What's the gossip? Kat, are you making any new friends?"

Gabriel sees this as his cue to leave, taking Jackson along with him. He knows I hate my mother's meddling.

"Mom, you know I don't have any friends here," I say, walking to the refrigerator and taking out the dinner salad.

Every time she comes over, she embarrasses me with this topic.

"You moved from the city to the suburbs to raise a family. Now, you're here. You should join a mothers club. You need a network, darling."

I sigh as she leans into me, halting me from moving from my spot by the refrigerator. "Kathryn, you are a wonderful girl with a lot to offer. I don't understand why you don't give any of the women out here a chance."

My shoulders rise as I try to give an explanation. "I don't know. I just don't click." I move around her and walk over to the island. "Besides, I have Malory. She has been a great friend to me. Between getting me the new job and showing me the ropes…" I say, giving the salad a vigorous toss. I look over at my mother, who is giving me the Gwendolyn Grayson stare down. "What is that face for?"

"I don't like that girl. She rubs me the wrong way." Her hand is on her hip, her lips puckered together.

"Please, Mother. You only met her once. You can't stand here and say I need friends and then bad-mouth the first one I talk to you about. I do have friends. They just happen to live all over the country."

"You know I worry about you. Look at you. You have circles under your eyes. You really should wear more night cream."

As she tries to put her hand on my face, I back away, and she flinches.

My mother makes a trip down here once a month to see us, and we always waste so much time with these ridiculous conversations. They consist of her telling me what she thinks I should do and me resisting.

"I know you worry about me, but I'm a grown woman. I can take care of myself." My voice is controlled as I turn my back to her and look at the picture of my father that sits on the counter beside the cookie jar.

I really miss my dad. He was on the road a lot, but when he was home, he was the best husband and dad in the world. He went to every recital of mine when he wasn't traveling. He escorted Gwen to her soirees, and not because he enjoyed them. He went because they were important to her. His life revolved around Gwen. That's probably why, when cancer took him from us, she locked herself in her room for days.

I was thirteen at the time and spent my formative years taking care of my mother. She was too flighty and irresponsible to be left alone. She stopped going to as many functions and moved us to Upstate New York, where her family was from. The fresh air in the mountains was nice, but as soon as I could, I moved back to Manhattan and felt like I could breathe for the first time in years.

I grab the salad bowl and walk it outside to the patio table, where Gabriel and I set up Gwen's birthday dinner.

Our backyard is small but well planned out with a patio made of limestone and a teak table in the center. Gabriel's barbeque is set off to the side. Between the two is a chaise lounge Gwen frequents when she visits.

Gwen takes a seat at the table, repositioning her martini in front of her. Gabriel has already set the main meal on a platter—steaks and roasted vegetables he prepared on the grill. I put a bib on Jackson and we start to eat.

"Did you hear about your cousin Mark?" Gwen asks.

I glance up. "No. How are Mark and Nadine?"

"Probably getting a divorce," she replies indifferently, her bangles clanging as she cuts her steak.

Gabriel and I display equal expressions of confusion. Mark and Nadine are the perfect couple. Two kids, a lucrative business, and a love affair that stemmed from high school.

"What do you mean, they're *probably* getting divorced?" I'm leaning over the table, hovering in her direction.

"She was caught in bed with her trainer. The two were spotted at a motel. Can you believe it? It's so cliché!"

I place my hand over my chest, feeling terrible for my cousin. "Poor Mark. What did he say when he found out?"

"He doesn't know yet. No one has the heart to tell him. Truth is, I think Nadine might leave him first."

Gabriel shrugs his shoulders and takes a bite. "Maybe he doesn't want to know," he says with a mouthful.

"Why wouldn't he want to know?" I nearly shout in astonishment. Clearly, I'm the only one who has lost her appetite.

He swallows and looks at me like I'm overreacting. "Listen, Kat, some people don't want to know. It's easier for them to believe a lie than to face the truth. I've seen it before."

I shoot my husband a threatening look. "Do you know a lot of philanderers?"

"A few men at my office have had affairs," Gabriel says casually. "And do you know what happens when someone tells the wife? That person gets excommunicated from their lives. The couple stays together, and the philandering spouse continues his lifestyle. And the guy who opened his big mouth?" He makes a slicing motion across his neck. "Excommunicated."

I cross my arms in disgust. "That is a crock of shit."

"He's right, darling." Gwen dabs her chin with a napkin. "This happened many times with your father on the road. Trust me, as a baseball wife, I often wondered what went on when he was out of town. But I'll tell you this," she says, leaning over the table, waving her napkin at us. "If someone else had told me your father was having an affair, I would not have believed it. I would have needed to see it with my own eyes."

"Mom, Dad would never have cheated on you." My tone comes off very self-righteous.

"Oh, Kathryn, he had women from all over the country flirting with him, and I know he flirted back. It was in his nature."

"Flirting is one thing. Attraction is fine as well. It's natural." *Isn't that what I've been telling myself?* "But cheating is another thing."

"You're right. As far as I know, your father was faithful till the day he died. Even still, my point remains the same. A person needs to discover these things on their own. It's a process."

The revelation of Nadine's affair is beyond my comprehension, while Gabriel seems so cavalier with the whole conversation.

We finish the meal, and then Gabriel presents Gwen with her birthday gift—a vintage jewelry box made of mirrored glass, which can sit on her bedroom dresser. It will only hold about an eighth of her jewelry, but it's glamorous, and I knew she'd love it.

After cake, I load the dishwasher. I look over at my husband, wearing khakis and a polo, still seated outside with Gwen on the patio. His smile is wide, and his eyes twinkle. I can see how many women would fall for my husband. I remember how easily I did.

Ω

In a rush to make it to class on time, I ran across the lawn at Towson University.

I was walking up the stairs outside Stephens Hall when, of all things, my tote broke, sending textbooks, notepads, pens, wallet, keys...everything cascading down the stairs. I crouched to start picking up the contents as a volley of students ran up and down the stairs, but no one cared to stop and help, except for him.

"Here, let me get that for you." A soft, warm hand reached over and grabbed a book from a step above me.

Mortified, I tried to brush off the kind pedestrian. "Thank you, but it's okay. I can get it," I said, taking the book out of his hand while noting his muscular forearm. I allowed my eyes to travel up and get a good look at the stranger.

He was tall with black hair and oh-my-God blue eyes. With a perfect nose and broad shoulders, he looked like a Kennedy in that all-American kind of way. I had never seen a flawless face before. He was, for lack of a better word, beautiful.

I took a second to wipe the drool from my lower lip.

"Art major?" he asked, looking down at the text he'd picked up. He flashed this jaw-dropping Robert Redford grin.

"Art history minor," I clarified, eyeing the textbook on Venetian art in the sixteenth century. "Marketing major."

As if he really cared what my major was. He was just being nice to a girl who had completely embarrassed herself in front of her peers.

I glanced down at my watch, realizing I was late for my class. "Thank you," I ran up the stairs and spent the next hour thinking about the hot guy and his award-winning smile.

When class was dismissed, I carefully placed my belongings inside my bag. I wrapped two arms around the tote and held it like a package. It was the only way I'd get it back to the dorm.

Outside, I saw him standing by the exit, where I'd left him. I braced myself and my broken bag, and I started across the quad. By bracing myself, I mean, I put my head down and tried to make it across, unnoticed. Unsuccessfully.

"Hey!" he called out. "Let me help you with that."

I stopped in my tracks. Is he talking to me? Oh God, he is.

"No, it's okay. I got this." I held my bag tighter and tried not to look back.

I was halfway across the quad when his long legs strode fast behind me.

"Wait," he called out. "Can I least know your name?"

The beautiful, blue-eyed boy wanted to know my name. This guy had heartbreak written all over his face.

"No." The word rushed out of my mouth, and my feet dashed faster.

My lips, however, couldn't stop smiling.

Ω

By the time the dishes are loaded and the counters are clean, my mind has wandered far away with thoughts of extramarital affairs.

"You are uncharacteristically quiet tonight."

Gabriel comes up behind me and places his arms around my waist. I lean back into the comfort of his body.

"Just thinking." I turn to the Amazon Echo on the counter and lower the volume.

"You only play Sia when you're melancholy." His voice is smooth with concern.

I rest my head in the crook of his neck and let out a breath that makes my lips vibrate. "Why do you think people cheat?"

He smiles into my hair and shakes his head. "I'm not answering that."

"Guilty?"

"Absolutely not," he says, placing a soft kiss on the back of my head. "I don't want you getting any ideas."

"I promise I won't accuse you of cheating on me, if that's what you're worried about."

With an exhale, he releases me. I spin around and prop my back against the sink.

"Why do people cheat?" He crosses his arms and runs his index finger across his lips, pondering the question. "Why do people cheat?" he repeats. "Well, I can't speak for myself because I've never cheated…"

I toss a dishrag at him, which he dodges, and let out a small laugh. "Yes, we've established that, smart-ass."

He makes his way around the center island toward the refrigerator. "Well, there's this one guy in my office—"

"Who?"

"I'm not telling you."

"Why not?"

Opening the refrigerator door, he grabs a beer and twists off the top. "Because you'll start eyeing up everyone I work with because you know their personal lives. Most of the people I work with are good people. I don't need you hating them because of a story I told you." He looks at me with that *you know I'm right* look.

"Fine."

"Okay, as I was saying…" Gabriel waits for me to interrupt, but I don't. "This guy at my office, he's had a long-standing relationship with another woman who works in our building because, as he says, his wife hasn't had sex with him since his kids were born."

"How old are his kids?"

He pauses to think. "The youngest is…seven?" He's clearly guessing.

"That still doesn't give him cause to cheat."

Putting a hand in his pocket, Gabriel leans against the refrigerator and takes a swig of his beer. "I can see how a lack of intimacy could cause someone to stray. How would you feel if I stopped having sex with you?"

"I doubt that would ever happen."

He flashes his Redford grin. "Well, I could just close up shop one day. You never know."

I hate that he's being so offhanded. Doesn't he know I'm very sensitive on the topic? Perhaps he doesn't since we've never discussed it before. We're just coming out of the honeymoon years of our marriage. Before this, everything was fun and exciting. Now, as my mother says, marriage takes work.

He sees my reaction and raises his eyebrow. "Then there's the case of a woman I work with who—"

"A woman!" I can't contain my surprise.

"Yes, Kat, even women cheat."

I scrunch my face at him. "I know. I just didn't expect you to know a woman who cheats on her husband." I prop my elbows on the kitchen island and gaze at my wedding ring. "What is her reasoning?"

"Apparently, her husband let himself go. He won't go dancing anymore or even to dinner. She refuses to divorce because of the kids. I only know this because she has slept with a good friend of mine at the office on more than one occasion, and he told me her reasons."

"What are his reasons for sleeping with her? Is he married, too?"

Either Gabriel works with a bunch of heathens or the law profession is full of more sinners than saints.

"No, he's single. Not everyone is having an affair." When I look up, he's leaning toward me from the other side of the island. He grabs my hand and gives my palm a warm kiss. "You know you have nothing to worry about with me, right?"

"I know." I do. In the years we've been together, I've never taken Gabriel to be a philanderer. It's just not his style.

"You know what we need?" His eyes twinkle with his question. "A date night. Let's put this new babysitter to

58

good use and get some alone time to ourselves for a change."

His invitation works at relaxing my stress, both from the crazy week, and this harrowing topic of infidelity. Just for validation, after Gwen has retired for the night and Jackson is sound asleep, I plan to take my husband to bed and make sure he doesn't ever feel the need to stray.

But after I change Jackson and rock him to sleep, I enter the room to see Gabriel passed out on our bed with the remote on his chest and the TV still on.

Maybe tomorrow.

Ω

The room is dark, except for dim light coming from the credenza and the lights of the skyline beaming in the small space. I stand in my office, facing the windowed wall, looking out to the Empire State Building.

A body approaches from behind; tall and strong, the presence overwhelming. His hands start on my shoulders and glide down my arms, to my fingertips. He takes my hands in his as he uses his mouth to tilt my head and brushes the sensitive skin on my neck with his lips, slowly caressing it with his tongue.

His left hand travels over my shoulder, taking the spaghetti strap of my dress along for the ride. His right arm follows suit with the other strap. My dress falls to the floor and I'm wearing nothing underneath. He is naked behind me, and I can feel his form against my skin. The ridges of his chest, the strength of his thighs, and his rock-hard erection. His solid body pushes against mine as his mouth continues to devour my neck.

I moan in pleasure. I want more.

His hands circle around my waist and drift south to my thighs, stroking the inside up and down, making me wet from just the proximity. His fingertips get dangerously close without touching yet make a promise to be back.

His mouth caresses my shoulder as his hands graze slightly over my nipples, tempting, teasing, causing me to shiver with pleasure. I press my back into his groin and beg with my body to be taken. My core throbs with anticipation.

I want it.

I need it.

His hand wraps around my neck, holding me still, as the other travels back down to my sex. I whimper at the feel of his hand hovering just outside my entrance.

I yearn for it...crave it. I feel a burning inside my belly, and it builds bigger and bigger, higher and higher. I can feel it...almost taste it...

I suddenly pop up. Sweat coats the back of my neck, and my body is still simmering with the heady feeling of lust. It was so real, so vivid, so lifelike, and so...delicious.

I've never had a dream like that before. I want to go back to sleep and continue. I felt every yearning and pleasurable movement, nearly exploding in my sheets.

I had the most mind-blowing sexual experience in my sleep and instead of feeling excited, I'm left confused because man who left me wanton and begging for more was Alexander Asher.

chapter SEVEN

I told Malory I'd meet her for lunch, so we take a seat in a corner booth at Trattoria Dell'Arte. I know she wants to dish on some office gossip. My concern is, I'm the main course.

"You seem to be fitting right in." Malory takes a bite of her salad, looking exquisite in a sheer black button-down with a matching camisole underneath.

"I can't say last week was easy. Sparring with Heather is not fun," I murmur.

Just thinking about how I won't have to face her every day calms my nerves, but having to deal with Asher is another story. I don't know what is worse.

"I heard Heather isn't the only one you're sparring with." Her teeth bit down on a ripe cherry tomato.

"Wow…" I pretend to look at my nonexistent watch. "That took you all of fifteen minutes!"

She sips her wine and gives me a quizzical look through the glass. "The man is unnerving. I should know. I've worked with him for the last three years, ever since he bought Erik's company. It doesn't hurt that he's irresistibly handsome."

I take a sip from my water glass and turn my head to the side, sneaking a look around the restaurant. I know she's reading my expression, so I'm trying to act as cool as the cucumber in my salad.

"Come on, you prude. He's delicious, and you know it. I thought you knew who he was when you took the job, but when I found out you'd never seen him before, I was dying to know what your reaction would be."

"And what was my reaction?"

She lowers her eyes, her brow perked up, almost intrigued by what she's about to say. "You absolutely fell apart," she says slowly.

I shake my head. "Seriously, Malory, I had a fight with the big boss, but now, everything is resolved."

I want to tell Malory about what really went down on Friday. From the car ride to the argument and the roses that were sent to my office, it was the craziest day I'd ever had at any job, and she is the person I want to talk to most.

Malory and I used to have a great rapport, where we would talk about everything and anything that happened at work. Back then, we were colleagues, and while she always held a position above me, she was never this high on the company food chain. Nattering with the vice president about my own personal indiscretions is a huge no-no.

I'm also dying to probe Malory for information, but I don't want her to know I'm interested in anything having to do with Alexander Asher.

Instead, I change the course of the conversation. "How is it going with soliciting advertisers?"

She kicks her head back, shrugging her shoulder. "Easy as can be. Once they hear the Asher name, they start opening up their wallets. We have big companies for the concert in the park. I'm trying to work a deal with some silent donors for the gala you're putting together, but that's going a little slower than planned."

"I can help you with that," I offer while the waiter comes over to refill our water glasses. I thank him and listen to Malory.

"You have enough to do, you little go-getter. Did you see Heather's face when you came up with the idea for two events? I was slightly rooting for Asher to give you the concert in the park just to piss her off."

"Thank God he didn't. She is one scary woman." I see my in for information. "Did something happen between her and Mr. Asher?"

She purses her lips and nods, eyeing me up. "You are a smart girl. I was waiting to see how long until you had everyone pegged. No, as far as I know, she hasn't gone to bed with him...yet. That doesn't mean she can't try. The girl has got it bad!" She lets out an exaggerated groan.

"Has anyone in the office slept together?"

Malory takes another sip of wine, holding the glass in her right hand, speaking matter-of-factly, "Kevin in production and Trish have been dating for a while. Gretchen and Harvey had a thing going, but that's over."

I nearly spit out my drink at the thought of tied-up Gretchen getting it on with... "Heavy Harvey?"

"Oh my God, you have a nickname for him!"

I flush with embarrassment. How rude and juvenile of me. I can't believe I said that out loud.

Malory doesn't seem insulted. "I must say, that's a perfect name for him. And the answer is, yes, Gretchen and 'Heavy Harvey,' as you call him, got down and dirty at a Christmas party two years ago. She was mortified when everyone found out, but it turned out, she kinda liked him."

"I shouldn't have called him that. I feel bad," I murmur into my salad.

"Don't. He's a fat ass. He's been grossing me out for years."

I cringe at her words. I said he was heavy, not gross. The man is actually really sweet.

She continues, "Never underestimate people in this business. Everyone sleeps with everyone. That's how they get ahead."

I wonder what Malory means by that. Correction: I know what Malory means by that but wonder if she has some personal experience. She has come a long way in the years I was out of work. Then again, she lives and breathes this business. This is New York. It's no surprise a woman would hold a high title in her thirties. We're breaking the metaphoric glass ceiling.

I'm not naive. I guess I just have higher expectations for those around me, and I choose to believe Malory is where she is because of hard work.

Malory pays the bill on the company card, and we head back to the office.

Exiting the elevator, I see the display of white roses taunting me, reminding me of Alexander Asher. They are still thick and blossoming, plush and rich.

Walking over to them, I put my nose to their soft white petals. They smell delicious. My eyes widen at the scent…tobacco and vanilla.

The hair on the back of my neck stands on edge.

He's here.

My spine stiffens at the thought of seeing him again, but when I turn around to confront the man who has me on pins and needles, I see no one seated in the waiting area.

Trish isn't at her desk, probably in Heather's office, and Malory went straight down the hallway, headed to a meeting, so it's just me, alone, in the lobby, and Asher is nowhere in sight.

Continuing to look around the room, I follow the scent back to its original location. The flowers. The scent is on the flowers. They smell like him in the most bizarre way.

It is quite possible I am going insane.

"Coffee break?"

I'm holding the phone to my ear, talking to Carmen to check on Jackson when I peer up to see Trish. She's holding two coffee cups in her hands.

Using the universal sign for *just one minute*, I finish my call with the babysitter and make sure plans are set for tonight.

Gabriel and I are supposed to go to dinner. We made plans to go out mid-week since he'll be working this weekend and traveling the next. We hope he'll be able to sneak out of the office at a reasonable hour.

I'm pretty excited about this because we haven't had a date night in months, and I need to spend alone time with him. Any free moment he has is always spent with Jackson. I get it. Gabriel's top priority is his little boy. I love that about him.

I hang up with Carmen, then tell Trish to come in. She places one of the coffee cups directly in front of me on my desk. It's black. She remembered. Then I remember she was front and center last week for my Asher incident.

Tucking one leg underneath her butt, Trish takes a seat, making sure her skirt doesn't ride up.

"You spoil me," I say, taking a sip and hum in approval. When you drink it black, like I do, the quality of the bean really counts, and she has gotten the blend just right.

"Anytime!" Trish has an energy about her that you can't help but want to match. "There's a commercial-grade machine down the hall. It takes seconds. Anytime you want a jolt, just holler." She's swinging her free leg back and forth, as her free hand plays with the tail of her braid.

"How much coffee have you had this morning?"

She relaxes her shoulders, trying to appear more composed. "Sorry. I'm a naturally fidgety person." She raises her cup toward me. "This is my first one."

My shoulders rise as I let out a chuckle. The kid is funny. I guess I could call her a kid. She's only a few years younger than me, but I feel as if I'm much older. The adult in the room.

Looking over the files on my desk, I have a lot to do. Where last week, I was at a standstill, waiting for Heather's cooperation, this week, I can get started on my event. I need Erik's approval, of course, but now, I can get to production. No more being idle. There are so many aspects of the event I can work on now.

Luckily, I feel more in control of the situation. I have my head wrapped around the task at hand. I can do this. At least, that's what I keep telling myself.

"So," I ask Trish, "how's it been working with Heather?" I want to refer to Heather as the ice queen, but I think better of it.

"It's good." Her voice squeaks a little. "Friday, after you left, Heather called me in." She looks down and puckers her brow, as if recalling the memory. "Just as I was about to leave in fact. My boyfriend and I were going to go to a concert, but I had to cancel on him last minute." Her mouth turns into the slightest of frowns before she quickly lifts her head and waves off the notion. "But that was fine. I mean, this is my big break, you know."

"Sounds like you have a great work ethic." I raise my coffee in the air in a cheers motion.

"I hope she recognizes that. I was here all weekend, working, compiling lists of music schools around the country, and calling up the families of musical savants. I also went through hundreds of YouTube videos of kids playing instruments and made a file for Heather to review. Took me days to compile the information. That's what she's doing right now. Watching my videos."

I respect Trish's go-getter attitude. It's inspirational.

I cross my legs and swivel my chair to grab my notepad from my desk drawer. She just reminded me about my idea from last week. I should present it to Erik this afternoon. No, Asher said he wants to oversee this project.

Shaking my head, I push the idea away. I'll go to Erik. Asher doesn't want to be bombarded with every silly idea I have. More importantly, I have no desire to work with the man directly.

"I'm so happy you said that because you just reminded me of something." I flip the notepad over to a clean page and grab a pen to jot down some ideas.

"Awesome. Glad I'm here to help!" She's holding on to her coffee mug with both hands, as if trying to keep warm. While I write, Trish continues with her story, rambling a little, "It's a pretty awesome project Heather has me working on. She is going to have children—like, really young kids who are these incredible piano players and guitar players and drummers—play onstage with each musical guest."

I must have pushed down hard on the pen because it runs away from me on the page, making a deep blue gash across the paper.

That bitch.

Not Trish. She's lovely. She's just doing what she was told to do.

Heather.

She stole my idea, and she's going to take all the credit! Last week, she pretty much told me my idea was crap. No sooner does she separate from me as co-producer than she goes ahead and decides the idea is awesome…which it is…and moves ahead on it. She didn't even wait a minute before setting the wheels in motion.

I have to talk to Erik about this.

Listen to me. I sound like a child. What am I going to do, stomp into his office and throw a temper tantrum? Erik is the last person who would want to hear that kind of nonsense. He's a *we're all a team* kinda guy.

Taking a moment, I think for a second.

It was a good idea. A freaking awesome idea, and I'm happy it's getting done. Let's face it; it's more appropriate for the Central Park event anyway. The talent will be bigger, and there will be more opportunities to showcase the kids. The exposure at that event will be greater as well. We can't do the same thing at both events, so as much as I'd love to do it at the gala, the park is going to be a concert of epic proportions. I'll just have to come up with something new.

Who knows? Maybe Heather is going to give me credit for the idea. I laugh to myself at the unlikeliness of that happening.

I discuss the idea with Trish, not acting bitter in any way, and even give her some pointers. If someone is going to get credit, then I'd prefer it's Trish. Like she said, this is her big break. Malory would have done the same thing for me a few years ago, if the opportunity arose.

At the end of our coffee break, I bid Trish good-bye without giving her the slightest inclination I'm upset. She needs to be level-headed to work with Heather, and I need to keep my head focused on my tasks.

My computer chimes with an alert that I have a meeting in five minutes, so I gather my files and head over to the conference room.

Erik is seated at the head of the table, going over the vendor list I have for the event. We're hiring a design production company to decorate the red carpet area, but we have to tell them exactly what we want and agree on costs. Malory has already approved the proposal, but since it's over budget, Erik wants to weigh in. At the last meeting, Asher said he would be working closely on the project, but I haven't seen nor heard from him or anyone in his office on the matter.

I'm grateful for that.

"You're gonna have to cut this down. There is no way we're spending this kind of money on flowers." Erik looks over the itemized list. "The step-and-repeat needs to be half the size. All the celebrities will be at Central Park. This is just to make the donors feel like big shots."

"You're absolutely right." I nod and then add a note to my long list of things I need to get done. "That amount is there from when we were having the larger event at Lincoln Center. I will fix that." There is no worse feeling than making a stupid mistake. I should have seen that myself.

Malory has a copy of the same document in her hands. She must have missed that item as well. She nods in agreement with Erik and turns to me. "Where are we with transportation costs?"

I furrow my brow. If I knew I was handling that as well, I would have taken care of it. I wish she'd said something about this before our meeting with Erik.

I don't even know who our preferred transportation vendor is. I come up with the best excuse I can on the fly. "Once I know who the guests are and where they're coming from, I'll have a proposal for you."

Malory seems to respect that answer. Erik is still looking over the design specs.

"Slash the floral costs in half and fix the red carpet costs before showing this to Asher." He hands me the paperwork and steps out with Malory to take another meeting.

I get back to my desk and make the necessary changes.

The budget with the floral design company is easy to fix. I'll still get my dahlias. They'll be a mixture of black, purple, and hot pink, but they'll mix in black daisies to fill in the gaps. I want everything to look lush and full. They also opted to sprinkle them with a faint amount of glitter to get them to sparkle under the camera lights.

I make another call to the production design team who is decorating the stage. They are also providing the black carpet for outside. I have them amend that change and ask for new copies of everything.

When the new proposal comes in through my email, I print it and drop it in an interoffice envelope along with the other documents Erik already approved. Taking the envelope, I walk it over to Trish's desk to be sent up to the top floor. If I can avoid having to see Asher, then I will at all costs.

Letting my hair down from my low ponytail, I brush it out to let loose a little. I'm supposed to meet Gabriel in a half hour. I change from my heels to a pair of ballet flats I keep in my bag and marvel at the relief they provide. Gabriel doesn't care if I wear heels or flats, and tonight I'm going for comfort.

I'm just about to head out the door with my bag in hand when my cell rings.

"Hey." I answer after seeing Gabriel's picture light up the caller ID. It's a picture of him in his tux at our wedding. He looked so unbelievably handsome that day.

"Don't hate me." Yup, those are the first words out of his mouth.

I slump my shoulders and drop my bag on my desk. "You're bailing on me." It was a statement. Not a question.

"I am so sorry. I swear if I could leave, I would, but I just got this file on my desk with affidavits and I have to file an appeal immediately." I can picture him running his hands along his forehead and down through his hair.

"You know, for someone who gave me a hard time about working because I won't be there for our family, you are doing a damn good job at it yourself." I feel bad throwing it in his face, but it had to be said.

"I'm not going to argue with you." His voice is deep and understanding. "This job is our future, Kat. This client is very important. If I can at least settle this case, then I'll be made partner."

If he makes partner, he'll work just as hard and long to prove himself. It's in his nature. I know this is all a sacrifice for our family. Gabriel has it in his head this is what I want and we need. It's a grand departure from the things he used to do in life. All he ever enjoyed was sailing, and he doesn't even do that anymore.

"Don't worry about it. I'm tired anyway." I pick up my bag and start heading for the door, listening as he apologizes again but has to rush off the phone.

My sigh is deep as I trudge on home.

I've only been working again for a minute, but I'm exhausted. I race home from work in order to do something with Jackson before he has to go to bed. The sun is out longer this time of year, but the last few days I've been home in time to take our walk. To be honest, I've been keeping him up much later just so we can have extra snuggle time. By the time I get him in bed, I have just enough time to watch my shows and take care of any household chores. No matter how busy you are, clothes need to be washed and floors need to be mopped.

When I can, after Carmen leaves, I take Jackson for a walk in the park. The early summer weather makes for warm evening strolls. As we wander, I point out everything I see... trees, cars, kids, people. Jackson sits up in his stroller, facing me, taking it all in.

Each night, it's the same routine: bath, bottle, and bed. While I can sit and talk to this little man for hours, it melts my heart to watch him sleep. He is so peaceful and full of hope, my hope for a beautiful future for this little boy.

As I lie in bed, about to close my eyes, the downstairs door opens. Gabriel is home. I hear him walk up and, like every night, he heads straight for Jackson's room. I roll over and look at the baby monitor. I see Gabriel lean over the crib and caress Jackson's face with his hand, gentle and soothing, not to wake him. He heads over the rail and gives Jackson a soft kiss on the forehead before exiting the room, silently closing the door.

Gabriel opens our bedroom door and heads straight into the walk-in closet. I hear him changing, kicking off his shoes and hanging his suit up. He finishes, closing the closet door, wearing only basketball shorts and sneakers.

Glancing at the clock, I see it's after ten. Gabriel grabs his Apple Watch off the dresser and places wireless headphones in his ears before walking out the bedroom door. I lay my head back down on the pillow and wait in the darkness.

chapter EIGHT

Waking this morning, I noticed Gabriel was already gone. His side of the bed pulled down as if he slept in it. He must have gotten up with Jackson last night. I don't even remember whose turn it was.

I got to the office on time and had a pretty good day. Sure, I spent a good portion of it being annoyed at Gabriel for bailing on me last night, but two things happened today to make me happy. First, I had a kick-ass meeting with Erik and Richard, the stage manager, as we discussed what was needed from the production design firm we hired to decorate the set. Second, there was no sign of Asher.

All in all, it was a very productive day.

Now, I am home, sitting in my favorite room in the house: The family room.

Gabriel surprises me by coming home at a reasonable time tonight. After putting his briefcase down by the front door, he comes over to where Jackson and I are playing and gives each of us a kiss hello before marching straight upstairs. A few minutes later, he returns wearing basketball shorts and a T-shirt.

Jackson and I watch as he jogs out the front door. Gabriel will run any time of day. I lift Jackson into my arms and head into the kitchen to make dinner. I have become the queen of the quick and easy meal. Tonight, we're having baked salmon with roasted vegetables since it only takes twenty minutes.

I place Jackson in his highchair and take out plates and forks to set the table. Carmen fed the baby dinner before I came home, so I place Cheerios on his tray to occupy him while I finish setting the table.

The timer on the oven goes off and I remove the dinner and set it on top of the oven and wait for Gabriel to return so we can eat.

Twenty minutes later, Gabriel returns. His shirt sticks to his chest from the sweat he accumulated on his run and his hair is sticking up a little on the sides.

"I'll be right back," he shouts over the music only he can hear from his headphones. "Shower," he states while running up the stairs.

Am I annoyed at him still for last night? Yes. Am I perturbed as all hell he's been home for forty minutes and has yet to truly acknowledge us? Yes. Am I going to let it ruin my night? No.

I stare back at Jackson, who I swear gives me a little shrug as if to say, "What are you gonna do?"

I shake my head and shrug right back at him. He returns my shrug with a rub of the eyes. Poor kid has to be in bed soon. Looks like we're forgoing the bath.

Another fifteen minutes goes by before Gabriel reappears. He lifts Jackson out of his highchair and places him on his lap while I get up to serve the now cold fish. I would heat it up, but part of me wants to leave it the way it is just to make a point.

My point is lost because Gabriel eats it up and doesn't say a word. Instead, he talks to me about how the front porch light is out and he has to change it.

I nod and tell him my mother left a voicemail that she wants to come back for a visit in a few weeks.

He nods back and turns his attention to Jackson, telling him about the different types of fish you can find in the Atlantic Ocean.

After dinner, Gabriel takes Jackson upstairs to bed while I clean up the kitchen. When he comes back down, he finds me in the living room, seated on the loveseat with two glasses of wine poured and placed on the coffee table.

He looks down at the wine on the table. "For me?" he asks while grabbing one of the glasses and taking a large gulp.

Gabriel lifts the remote control and turns on the TV. I watch as he changes the channel to the Marlins game, already in the third inning. Sitting on the couch, he takes another sip of wine and settles in for six innings of baseball.

I lean forward and stare at him for a few minutes, his eyes mesmerized by the screen in front of him. It's quite comical how distracted men become when there is a sporting event on.

He catches me staring and motions toward the TV. "The Marlins are playing the Mets. I thought you'd be excited."

It's my favorite team verses his favorite team. I love watching this series with him, but I wasn't expecting him to be home to watch it with me today.

"Slow day at the office?" I ask.

Not taking his eyes off the screen, he answers, "I left early so we could watch the game."

It's a charming gesture, but I'm surprised. "How come you could leave early today to watch a baseball game, but you couldn't leave early to take me out?"

Gabriel catches the tone in my voice and looks over at me. His eyebrows curve in. "That was completely different."

I let out an exaggerated sigh and put my glass down on the table. "It's very convenient that you're available to watch a game with me that you happen to love too, but you can't get out of work to take me to dinner."

Gabriel shifts his weight and places his wine glass on the table next to him. His eyes turn serious as he appraises the situation. "Why are you picking a fight?"

I hate when he does this. I voice my opinion about something and because he doesn't want to hear about it, I'm the irrational one for bringing it up.

"I'm not picking a fight. I'm having a conversation."

"You're trying to argue about something when we should be spending time together."

He's right. I should be sitting back and playfully bantering with him about our favorite teams playing each other, but my feelings are hurt.

"Gabe, I've barely seen you in the last few weeks. I'm sorry if I don't want to spend what little time we have together watching TV."

"Well, I don't know what to tell you. I work way too long and way too hard to do this with you right now. You want me home? I'm home. Tonight, I'm sitting right here and watching the game." His voice is harsh and unapologetic. He turns away from me, giving all his attention to the TV, completely removing me from his line of vision.

Like an insolent child, I stomp my feet and march out of the room. I slam the door to our bedroom and wait for him to follow me to argue. I tear off my clothes and put on pajamas. Climbing into to bed, I pull back the covers and sit up against the headboard with my arms crossed, and stare at the door, waiting for him to come in.

But he doesn't. I don't even hear footsteps. Just the faint sound of the ballgame downstairs in the living room.

Looks like I've "cut off my nose to spite my face," as my mother would say. I never understood that expression, but I know it's what I just did. With too much pride to go downstairs, I turn on our TV in the bedroom and watch the game from the comfort of my pillow. *Stupid husband.*

I watch the game well into the seventh inning, when my eyes grow very heavy and I slowly start to drift until…my body jerks awake.

The room is dark. The TV is turned off, and Gabriel is next to me, sound asleep. I glance over at the clock. It's just after four in the morning. Jackson didn't wake up tonight. That's good.

I lower my head back to the pillow to settle back to sleep when I remember what it was that startled me awake.

I had a dream.

I dreamed of *him* again.

Ω

It's been two weeks since my first encounter with Asher. Every morning, I wonder if today is the day I will run into him again. More importantly, every day, I wonder if today is the day he will return one of my messages.

I've sent every invoice and production idea up to Asher's office, and I have yet to hear from him. I've been moving forward with the preliminary work, but without his final approval, I can't confirm anything. I asked Malory about it this morning, and she told me to wait on Asher.

I feel like I'm in limbo. This event is only two months away. If he doesn't answer me by the end of the week, I'm going to move forward with my plans.

Malory also informed me this morning that I need to buy a dress for the gala. I'd assumed I'd be wearing something professional like a suit since I'd be working. She said I need to dress in formal attire and looked at me like I had three heads due to the fact that I hadn't known this. So, now, I also have to add *find an evening gown* to the list.

Malory and I step off the elevator, and I see those goddamn white roses again.

Yes, they're still alive.

And they're not just alive; they're flourishing.

Every time I see them, I swear they've gotten bigger. I think my mind is playing tricks on me. It's quite possible it is.

As annoyed as I am to see the roses, I can't stop myself from smelling them. That heavenly scent of rose mixed with the manly aroma has become part of my morning ritual.

Looking beyond the flowers, I notice a mound of red hair piled on the desk, buried under porcelain hands.

"Is everything okay?" I say, swinging around the partition to see the usually bubbly and exuberant Trish looking upset.

Trish pops up from her state of distress. Wiping her face with her palms, she tries to gain composure. "It's nothing. Just a bad day at the office."

Trish's eyes drift up to Malory. She must be embarrassed to say what's bothering her in front of someone else.

I turn around and face Malory. "I'll catch up with you later."

Malory looks back and forth from me to Trish. If she didn't wear a constant veil of confidence, I'd think she was offended by being dismissed. With a nod, she turns on her heel and heads down the concrete corridor.

Resting my hand on Trish's bony shoulder, I ask, "Do you want to talk about it?"

Letting out a sigh, Trish resigns and opens up. "It was stupid. I shouldn't have asked."

"Asked what?" I kneel down, bringing myself eye-level with her.

Trish swoops her long braid around her shoulder and plays with it between her fingers. "Well, with all the extra work I'm doing with Heather and having to maintain my post here, I thought now would be a perfect time to ask for a raise."

Asking for a raise doesn't seem out of the norm. I've watched Trish bow to Heather's every whim. The two have been like Wile E. Coyote and the Road Runner with Trish zipping around the office, bouncing from the printer to the lobby, delivering proposals, getting coffee, making phone calls, and from the looks of it… "You didn't get it?"

"No," Trish says, looking at me with big brown eyes. "It's okay. I mean, it's not a real promotion. It's only until the concerts are over, but…" Trish sways her head to the side.

"But what?"

"It's that damn Heather. I'm only an assistant, and she's had me working on things an associate producer would do. I don't mind the work. It's what I want to do. I want to learn more, you know?"

I rub her shoulder with the palm of my hand. "Honey, don't take Heather's attitude personally. She hates everyone. I've been here for five minutes, and I already know that."

"Yes, but Erik was going to give me the raise. He heard my proposal and thought it was valid. I was so excited." She lowers her voice to almost a whisper. "Then, I intercepted an email between Erik and Mr. Asher, where Mr. Asher denied my raise."

"What?" I say too loudly.

"Mr. Asher said due to Heather's review of me and her input on the matter, I was denied a raise, and Erik should evaluate whether I'm suitable to assist Heather during this very critical venture for the company."

My teeth clench, and I can feel the blood simmer in my veins. This has to be the cruelest thing I've been privy to in business. I don't know Trish well, and I have worked with her for only a brief time, but it is painfully obvious how devoted she is to the company and that she's a hard worker.

She's also quite the little spy.

"Trish, do you have access to everyone's email?"

Her face turns green as her eyes grow wide with mild panic. "No, just Erik's. He gave me access last year when he went to Australia and would be out of pocket at times. When he returned, he neglected to revoke my administrative rights to read his email." Trish catches herself. "I swear I never read them! This was a one-time scenario. I just knew something was wrong."

I lean closer and give her frail frame a half-hug. "It's okay. I know you didn't mean any harm."

Maybe it's the mother in me. I feel very protective of this girl. It's nice to know I can be to her what Malory was to me.

Our moment is disrupted when the elevator bell chimes, and the doors slowly open. Trish's eyes light up at the sight of a guy wearing acid-wash jeans and a T-shirt labeling an indie band. His hair is disheveled, and his sneakers are untied. He looks more like a boy than a man, straight out of college. This must be the Kevin I've heard about during our little coffee breaks.

My suspicions are confirmed when he rounds the desk and pulls his distraught girlfriend up from her chair.

"Are you okay? You didn't sound like yourself in your voice mail." Kevin kisses Trish's hair as he wraps one hand around her head and the other around her waist.

It's a beautiful sight.

Memories of Gabriel and me at that age flash through my head. It wasn't that long ago, yet it seems like a hundred years have passed.

$$\Omega$$

After a long afternoon of calls, emails, and a ton of paperwork, I'm spent. Erik wants a finalized itinerary by Friday, but I don't know how I'm going to make this happen. At my old job, we worked on projects like these for months, not weeks. *What if I forget a crucial component of the event, overlook something, or drop the ball?*

I don't know when I became so insecure.

After a meeting with Harvey to go over the first-draft speeches he prepared for the event, I time them out to fit the rundown and make my way to the common area for a coffee.

God bless the Keurig. Seriously, there is no better invention than a machine that makes a gourmet-blend coffee with the push of a button. I pop in a Guatemalan roast and wait for it to produce my afternoon jolt.

I'm standing at the counter, my arms crisscrossed in front of me, as I stare at the piece of paper taped to the cabinet, informing everyone about a blood drive in the sixth-floor infirmary.

The sound of heels clicking down the concrete hallway signals someone is walking toward the break room. I turn around as Heather enters the room. She stops for a second when she sees me.

"Oh, hi." Her disdain for me resonates through her big brown eyes.

Due to her tight pants and form-fitted button-down, I'd like to think her disdain is merely from discomfort. Nope. This chick just doesn't like me.

Heather stands at the other side of the room as I wait for my coffee to stream down. Her tiny frame in sky-high heels and oversize chest fills the room with negative energy. I want to say something to her about Trish, but I can't break the confidence I've earned from my new friend. If Heather knew Trish was reading Erik's emails, she would have her job.

The tension between us could crack a window. It's an odd feeling when you can't stand someone so much that you can't even find it in your heart to make small talk. I wish someone else would just walk in and cut it with a knife.

The last bit of hot water empties into my cup, so I grab it and exit the room. I wonder if my dad made me too passive. Sometimes, I don't want to "just breathe." I want to speak up even if it would lead to unwarranted confrontation.

Why can't I just say something to Heather? Ask her, Why are you so mean?

Just the thought of it sounds so childish. Malory would never let Heather intimidate her like this.

I make my way back down the hall toward my office. When I take a sip, the coffee tastes beyond drab. I must have put the wrong pod in the machine. This coffee is weak and watered down.

Refusing to go back into the kitchen, I stop at my office, grab my bag, and head downstairs to go to Starbucks.

I press the elevator call button. The room is permeated with the smell of roses and vanilla. It makes my blood boil. The elevator pings, and the doors open. I place one foot inside the car and find myself face-to-face with golden eyes.

Double crap. I should have just drunk the damn coffee.

chapter NINE

"Mrs. Monroe," Asher greets me with a wicked smile.

"Mr. Asher." My nod is polite yet unassuming.

His golden highlights shine under the pin lighting, and with long, deft fingers, he hits the *L* button on the control panel for the lobby floor.

I feel him survey me from head to toe as the numbers on the elevator change from twenty-four to twenty-three. A million thoughts swim through my head but all become cloudy from this overwhelming energy I sense from just being with him.

There must be something wrong with the elevator car because I start to quiver.

I risk a glance in his direction, and he's smiling at me.

"Something amusing?"

He places a well-manicured finger along his lower lip and draws in a breath. "I was thinking about the last time we were in this elevator."

"It was an unmemorable occurrence."

I stare at my reflection in the elevator door. My green eyes look back at me, saying, *Keep your cool, Kat.*

"You look lovely today, Mrs. Monroe. Although, I must say, I prefer you wet." He laughs while placing his hands in his pockets, and he rests his weight back on his heels.

From Malory's inquisitions to Trish's tears and Heather's complete takeover of my backbone, I'm frustrated and pissed off.

I lean forward and pull the red elevator Stop button. The cab jolts, and we both lean for the walls to brace ourselves. I've never done that before, and it was a little scary.

Asher looks at me with confusion, humor, and if I'm not mistaken, dread.

"What is wrong with you?" It's the only thing I can get out of my mouth.

"What's wrong with me?" Whereas I'm nervous, he looks calm in spite of my very dramatic move. "This is a bit theatrical; don't you think?"

"I didn't know what else to do."

"Then, why did you do it?" His eyes penetrate mine.

I meet him green for gold. "Because..." I'm exasperated. "You can't just say things like that."

"Like what?" His voice is smooth and controlled. Daring me to incite myself.

"The way you talk to me...it's so...so..." Of course, at the very moment, I'm at a complete loss for words, making me sound like a whiny twelve-year-old girl.

"Inappropriate?" He leans against the elevator wall and crosses his arms in a stance that makes him look like he's posing for *GQ* magazine.

"Yes!" I shift from one foot to the other. I don't know what to do with myself.

"Tell me, what did I say that was so inappropriate that you've taken the liberty to trap the CEO of a major corporation in an elevator?"

Triple crap. He's right. My day just keeps getting...ugh! Oh my God, this is ridiculous.

I lean over to release the Stop button on the elevator but am blocked by a strong hand.

"No, please, Mrs. Monroe. I'd like to hear this out since it was worthy enough of halting us mid-ride." His comment oozes with sexual innuendo.

Maybe it's just my imagination.

"You can't say things like that." I feel the heat radiating on my neck.

"Like what?" He is challenging me.

"Like, 'I prefer you wet.' It is completely uncalled for."

He looks back at me with an amused grin. "Well then, my apologies. If it makes you feel better, you look much better dry and tepid."

"Dry and tep—" My mouth stops mid-sentence. I can feel my ears turn red and my brows furrow.

Does this man really just say whatever comes to his head? And what does that mean...dry and tepid? Was that a dig at my personality? He'd claim it wasn't.

"Relax."

"Relax?" My question is more of a rant than a concern. "You are the most diabolical man I have ever come across. You say whatever comes to your mind, not caring if it's mean, crass, inappropriate..."

I begin a mini pace back and forth in the elevator. Asher enjoys the floor show.

"You hit on me in an elevator, knowing full well that I am your employee, then ogle my breasts through my wet shirt, and take the next opportunity you have to discuss my being wet in an elevator." I run my hand over the back of my neck. "You have yet to approve any of my proposals. I mean, at this point, I'd prefer to hear you tell me they're complete shit than have you utterly ignore me. It's belittling and degrading."

I'm on a roll. For someone who bites her tongue, I have finally found my voice.

My pace quickens, and my hands move freely in front of me like an old-school Italian accenting every word with a dramatic gesture. "You want to play puppet master. You want to hold the strings and have all the control. Meanwhile, there are people upstairs who work hard and diligently and who deserve your attention, but you disregard them because of someone else's report."

"What are you talking about? Who am I *disregarding*?"

Of course that got his attention.

He's staring at me with a look of confusion and concern.

"Kathryn." His voice is stern and determined.

Leaning forward, Asher puts his hand on my arm, halting my movements. I look up into his perfectly sculpted face as he arches his eyebrows.

"Tell me."

What's the use? I already dug my own grave. I might as well lie in it.

"Why did you deny Trish a raise?"

His hand still on my arm, Asher quizzically looks at me, as if he just can't seem to understand what I'm saying. At this moment, I realize how close he's standing to me. I can feel his breath on my skin and the heat radiating from his arm on mine.

His mouth opens to say something when a buzzing noise sounds from the speaker on the elevator panel.

"This is Asher Security. We registered that the Stop button has been activated in your car. Is everything okay?"

He releases my gaze but keeps his hand on my arm.

"This is Alexander Asher. Yes, everything is okay. There seems to be a computer glitch with the cab. Please override the system and return us to the lobby. I'd like this car retired for the rest of the day, and have someone take a look at the control panel."

"Yes, Mr. Asher. We'll have you moving momentarily."

The speaker is silent once again.

Thank God this enigmatic man is so quick on his feet. Bad enough I'll have to endure the embarrassment and office gossip that will follow after being stuck in an elevator with the big boss...a week after a recent outburst, no less. At least I have a valid story to go with why we're stuck in here. No one has to know I pulled the trigger.

Asher's eyes look back at me. He's still holding on to me when the elevator starts to move again. When he finally lets go of me, I take a moment to check my appearance. From the reflection in the door, I catch Asher staring at me, his hand rubbing the back of his neck. He looks out of sorts. I want to thank him for what he said to security, and I also want to find out why he denied Trish her due.

But I don't say a word.

I don't know what I expected when we arrive at the lobby. Hordes of people waiting for the elevator, police, firemen, the media! Instead—and thankfully—the elevator doors open to a seemingly empty space.

Chin up and hands at my sides, I make my way out of the building and down the block before I even remember where it was I was going in the first place.

Ω

As soon as I walk through the door, I slam my keys on the side entry table.

"Are you okay, Ms. Kathryn?" Carmen comes running to the entryway, Jackson in arm.

I reach over to grab the angelic little bundle. "Yes, sorry."

Carmen grabs my purse from my shoulder and delicately sets it on the table next to my keys. Grabbing my hand, she says, "You work too hard." Ushering me into the kitchen, she pulls out a chair. "Rest your feet and let Carmen take care of everything."

I do as Carmen suggested and seat myself, propping Jackson on the table. He babbles and laughs at my funny faces as piles of drool fall onto his bib.

"Do you like sardines, Ms. Kathryn?" she calls from inside the refrigerator door as she produces a large bowl. "I made chicharron with pepesca."

She leans down to show me the bowl in her hands. The little fish with their heads still attached look up at me.

"Uh, no, thank you, Carmen. I'm full." I smile up at her.

Besides, I was thinking Gabriel might want Chinese tonight.

I lean over and give Jackson a raspberry on the side of his neck.

"Mr. Gabriel called. He has a dinner tonight in the city. He asked me to prepare something for you." She places the bowl back in the refrigerator and turns around.

I put Jackson down and walk toward the entryway. Picking up my purse off the table, I search for my phone. Flipping it open, I look to see if I have any missed calls. None. The last call I received was from Harvey earlier, telling me he'd be a few minutes late for our meeting.

"Carmen," I call, "what time did Gabriel call?"

She replies from the kitchen, "Around two o'clock."

I was in the office at that time. He should have called my desk. He has my number. I place my bag back on the table and make my way toward the kitchen.

"You should go home. You worked hard today. I think I'll take Jackson to the park, and then we'll have some of that delicious meal you made for us."

Carmen eyes me for a moment and then makes her decision. "Okay, Ms. Kathryn. I'll see you Monday." She grabs her tote from the closet and slings it around her shoulder.

I watch her walk down the street until she gets to the corner and then gather my and Jackson's things to go for a walk ourselves.

Jackson and I take a stroll around the park and stop near a grassy knoll. Grabbing a blanket from under the stroller, I open it and spread it out on the ground. The sun is just about to set, so I take Jackson out of his stroller to let him play on the blanket. I know it's getting late, but it's the only time I have my little angel these days. Our nights are our special time.

I stretch out my legs and try to pull the grass off my heels. I should have changed into sneakers before venturing onto the dirt terrain. As I'm scratching dirt off the bottom of my shoe, I hear a woman's voice.

"Is that Jack?"

I look up to see a blonde woman jogging up the hill. Very blonde and very fit. She looks younger than me but not by much. Her hair is swung up in a ponytail, and her very yellow Nike tank is clinging to her like a second skin. Her shorts are also very short.

Everything about her is *very*.

Jackson looks up and squeals with recognition.

"I thought I recognized this little guy!" she says, panting and pulling earbuds out of her ears.

I reach over for Jackson and swing him onto my lap. This mama bear is protecting her cub from the platinum lioness. "I'm sorry. Do I know you?"

She laughs and places her hands on her knees, still catching her breath. "I'm friends with Jack and his daddy."

I glare up at her. "You know Gabe?"

"Oh!" She looks surprised, her gaze settling on my left hand. "You're his wife?"

I slowly nod my head.

"I'm sorry," she continues. "I didn't know he was married. You're so young. I thought you were the babysitter."

Babysitter would be flattering if I wasn't still wearing my work clothes. In this case, it's just laughable—and not in a funny way.

Staring blankly at this woman, I appraise her. Blonde, tan, young, and fit. I don't know her, but clearly, my husband and child know her. I look down to see Jackson smiling up at her. I wish I could telepathically tell him to scowl at her. My little cub is falling prey to the predator.

My mouth finds a way to catch up to my thoughts. "Who are you?"

In the utmost cheerful way she could possibly reply, she says, "I'm Becca!"

Of course she is. Not to judge, but she really doesn't look like a Maude or an Arlene. She looks like she should have two pom-poms in her hands and be doing the splits. Again, I'm not judging. Just observing.

"You know my baby?" I stand and gather my blanket and baby.

"Yes, Jack and I see each other every Saturday. Isn't that right, buddy?" She shines a luminous smile that shows either her skin is too tan or she uses way too many whitening strips.

If Gwen were here, she would tell me to stop judging and make a friend with this woman. I guess I could. She looks friendly enough. A little too friendly, but if Gabriel knows her, then she can't be that bad.

"Jackson and I are here all the time. Surprised we haven't run into you before."

She looks up at the setting sun and then back at me, bouncing on her toes to keep moving. "This is an early run for me. I'm usually out here later than this. I like to run with the wolves, you know."

We live in a nice neighborhood, but a pretty girl like her running at night is not a good idea.

"That doesn't seem safe."

Becca gives me a half-smile. "That's what Gabriel said. He runs with me sometimes. Keeps the wolves away."

My body halts for a second at the realization of her words. I don't want to make assumptions, but isn't it odd for a married man to be running with a pretty blonde? Then again, I'm not a runner, so I have no idea what runner's etiquette is.

I lower Jackson into the stroller and buckle him in. "Jackson and I need to go. It's getting late."

"Of course. Jack needs his bath, bottle, and bed, right?"

I just stare at her, dumbfounded.

The lioness shuffles from one foot to the other, trying to bring her heart rate back up. "Peace out! It was great meeting you. Later, Jack!"

Off she goes into the wild.

Who was that woman?

Maybe I shouldn't be so skeptical. She's probably very nice.

Who am I kidding? I hate her.

I hate her blonde hair, her tanned skin, her toned abs, and the fact that she calls my kid Jack just like my husband does.

chapter TEN

They are driving me crazy. Last week, I could swear the flowers were even fuller, and doubled in size. Today, I can barely see the fiery little redhead beyond the lavish display.

"You must have one green thumb."

Trish giggles. "Maybe a black thumb! I am the worst with flowers. In fact, I've killed every plant I've ever owned."

"Then, how are these still so perfect? They look like they were just delivered."

Trish gives me a curious expression. "That's because they *were* just delivered. There has been a fresh shipment of roses every day. Mr. Asher loved the ones your husband sent you, so he has a fresh bouquet delivered every morning. Although they seem to be getting bigger by the day!"

While it's good to know I'm not crazy, I can't imagine what kind of trick the man is playing. Not to mention, this is a colossal waste of money.

Once in my office, I place my bag on my desk and turn on my computer.

Gabriel and I have been fine since our argument over the baseball game. By fine, I mean, we're existing.

I asked him about the girl in the park over the weekend. He looked at me like I was crazy before realization crossed his face, and he laughed and said she was just some girl he runs with sometimes to keep pace. He actually referred to her as the "bouncy blonde." He didn't know her name, which I found odd since she knew so much about him. He just shrugged it off and said she got extra chatty a few weeks ago when he was out with Jackson. He seemed surprised she'd remembered so much about their conversation since he hadn't even remembered it until I brought it up.

While Gabriel parked himself at the kitchen table this weekend, filing an amendment, I took the time to hang out with Jackson, my sweet boy.

This week, the little angel has decided to play favorites with his toys. If he's playing with his set of blocks, he always goes for the round blue one. If he is playing with an animal puzzle, he always wants the cow. His cruising is getting good. Pretty soon, I'll have a little walker on my hands, and then I'll be truly exhausted.

Gabriel, too.

He's been so caught up lately with his big case. Our life has certainly changed from that first night ten years ago. I don't know what my life would be like if I hadn't walked into that bar.

Ω

As soon as I entered McCloon's, the sounds of the Spin Doctors sang in my ears. No matter what year, "Two Princes" never got old.

And just like a mirage, he was standing there—the boy with wavy, dark hair and navy-blue eyes, who had helped me with my books outside of class. Blue jeans and a pair of Lacoste sneakers, he was the epitome of a relaxed college guy.

I should have been used to seeing his face.

Three times a week, for the last month, he'd stood outside my building and asked me my name. It became a bit of a game for the two of us. He'd ask, I wouldn't answer, and then he'd walk me to my Art Theory class on the other side of campus. Every day, he would tell me a different story about himself or something he'd learned in class. I'd become used to our walks, so much so that my Behavioral

Science lecture in the building became my favorite because it meant I'd get to see him after class.

He always made a point to tell me where he'd be later that day. I'd want to go, but I'd find an excuse not to.

After a month, I had no more excuses.

"It's you," he said, his eyes wide with amazement.

"It's you," I reciprocated.

He was much taller than me by a whole head. I had to look up at him when he spoke, "So, are you going to tell me your name yet?"

I stood there, unable to contain my blush. He made me feel the need to play coy. Before coming out tonight, I'd decided that if I saw him, I was going to tell him my name. Yet, for some reason, I just couldn't form the words. All kinds of awkward and embarrassed, I walked over to the beer pong table, trying to think of something clever to say.

He was quickly behind me. "Let's make a deal. We'll play for it. If I win, you tell me your name. If you win, I'll leave you alone for the rest of the night."

I was going to tell him my name anyway, but I enjoyed a good game. I also happened to be really good at beer pong. Shame since I really didn't want him to leave me alone.

"I'll take that bet." I finally found my voice, realizing I might have to throw the game.

He grabbed plastic cups and started arranging them in a triangle, filling each of my cups with beer well above the normal amount.

"I think that's enough!" I said, putting my hand over his, halting him from pouring any more.

"I'm just hedging my bets," he said, releasing that Robert Redford grin. "Ladies first." He motioned for me to take the first shot.

Leaning over, I sank the first two balls. As the rules went, that meant I got to go again. I sank the third but missed the fourth. Each time I got a ball in the cup, he had to drink. My eyes watched him bring the cup to his mouth, his Adam's apple enlarging each time he quenched his thirst. I had kissed three boys before that day, and at that moment, I really wanted to bring that number up to four.

Putting the cup down, he licked his lips before going all Sundance Kid on me again. "If I didn't know any better, I'd think you were trying to get me drunk. I must warn you, I'm an easy lay when I've had a few drinks."

My eyes widened at the word lay, *but I kept my wits about me. Watching him lean across the table, I felt a twinge deep inside me. A burning I'd had before but become accustomed to ignore.*

"Since I don't know your name, can I at least know your birthday?"

"Why?" I asked.

"So I have time to pick out the perfect gift," he said, leaning forward, ready to make his shot.

Inching on his toes, he raised his arm in the air and out in front of him, causing his shirt to rise. His white T-shirt inched up, revealing his boxers peeking out over his belt buckle. My eyes traveled further north to see what else was under that shirt. I could see these sculpted abdominal muscles that came to a V above his groin. My roommate called this "the pathway to paradise." Long and lean but pure muscle, and I'd never seen anything like it.

I swallowed hard and tried to refocus on what we had been talking about. "September 27."

When it was my turn, my nerves were so at odds with my brain that I completely missed the two cups.

Seeing I'd lost my focus, he put his cup down on the table and made his way over to me. His eyes were unsteady but not from drinking. He looked like he was trying to decide something.

"Just so you know, once I know your name, I plan on asking you out, and you will say yes."

Butterflies took over my stomach. "I will?"

Running his tongue over his lower lip, he stared at me, taking me in, and gently placed his hands on my waist. "You will. I need to tell you something."

So aware of his fingers on my body, I was afraid to move or else he'd take his hands away. "What's that?"

"Gabe," he said.

I looked at him in confusion.

"My name is Gabe. I needed you to know the name of the guy who is about to kiss you."

My mouth opened on the inhale, and it wasn't enough time for me to catch my breath before his lips were on mine. Let me tell you, number four was a really good kisser. Our mouths moved so familiarly that you wouldn't have believed it was our first kiss.

I had never gone at it with a guy in a bar before, but I was so attracted to him that I couldn't pull myself away. I could feel his heart racing as he grabbed the back of my head with his right hand, running his fingers through my hair. My body melted right into him as I wrapped my arms around his neck. His left hand traveled down to my lower back and held me.

We heard catcalls and hollers from our fellow collegiate drunkards, some shouting things like, "Get a room!"

After he kissed me a few more times, my lips felt naked.

Slightly out of breath, he leaned against my ear and whispered, "Let's get out of here."

$$\Omega$$

My office phone rings, pulling me out of my daydream. It's easy to get lost in the memory of when Gabriel and I were falling in love. I answer the call and tend to the person on the other end. It is someone from Lincoln Center, confirming an appointment I made. When the call is done, I hang up and look over at my cell phone sitting on my desk.

I light up the home screen and see a photo of Gabriel and Jackson looking as beautiful as ever. Jackson with dark hair like his dad and cobalt eyes to match. They are definitely twins. I hope Jackson grows up to have Gabriel's perfect nose, too. Gwen always comments on the slight crook of my own. She wanted to get it fixed, but I refused. Gabriel always tells me I am perfect.

I forget sometimes how kind Gabriel really is. Perhaps it's because our personal interactions are few and far between. Maybe a vacation will do us good. That's what we need. A romantic Caribbean vacation, just like our honeymoon when we sailed from the Keys to the Grand Caymans and beyond. Of Gabriel's many talents, sailing is one of them. I guess that's what you get with a kid who grew up in sunny Florida.

I close my eyes and remember seeing him at the helm of the boat with his blue polo and aviator sunglasses, the wind blowing in his hair. He looked to be the epitome of peace and happiness, and I could picture him sailing forever. We danced throughout the islands, ate more shellfish than should be legal, devoured conch, and drank tequila. We made love on that boat every day and watched the sunset with our toes in the water. It was pure bliss.

We made a promise to travel the world together on that boat, but deep down, we knew that was impossible. He had a law career to nourish, and I was busy working on my own career.

That was when we received the greatest news a couple could expect—a baby was on the way.

We bought a house and a car, and we moved to the suburbs. We have been winging it ever since.

And here Jackson is with his perfect face and perfect toes, perfect dimples and perfect devilish glare in his eyes when he sees something he wants. It's the same look Gabriel had that night he saw me walking into that bar.

While I can daydream all day, I have to get back to work.

Looking back to the newspaper on my desk. I jump to the Entertainment section and read up on the celebrity gossip and the face on the page nearly jumps off the paper at me.

There he is in a black tuxedo with the top buttons of his shirt undone and a beautiful brunette on his arm. The title reads, *Alexander Asher and top model cozy up at the Metropolitan Opera House Benefit gala.*

A knock at the door jolts me from the editorial.

"Come in," I say, closing the paper and straightening myself for the unexpected visitor.

"Am I disturbing you?" Trish enters, wearing an adorable checkered skirt and white blouse.

"No. Please sit," I say, especially since she comes bearing a gift in the form of coffee. It's particularly sweet because she brought me a cup and not one for herself.

I feel like I was just talking to her about the flowers five minutes ago. A look at the clock startles me as I realize I've wasted an hour in my office, caught up in my own head.

Trish takes a seat. She has a stack of papers in her hand and a beaming smile on her face. "I came to tell you I got that raise."

"Congratulations! I see Erik took care of the misunderstanding then."

I might not have seen Asher in days, but I can't erase my embarrassing outburst in the elevator.

"Actually, Mr. Asher called me up to his office personally. It was very intimidating."

"I can imagine," I say from experience. "What did he say?"

"Well, he sat me down in his office and asked me everything from my duties here at the office to the new ones I have acquired, working with Heather."

"Were you nervous?" I ask because her body is radiating with unused energy she's clearly been storing up.

"It didn't help that at the end of the conversation, he just dismissed me. Just like he was done with me or something."

I am not surprised. "When did you have this conversation?"

"Last night, after you left. I was going crazy all night. I didn't know what it meant. Kevin told me not to worry and that I should quit if Asher refused my raise."

"But you got the raise, right?"

"Yes. Well, not officially." Trish turns beet red and bows her head in embarrassment.

"Have you been reading Erik's emails again?"

She peeks up at me with a look of shame. "Guilty."

"Trish, you have to stop that. If I find out you're doing it again, I'll have no choice but to tell Erik. Please don't put me in this position."

"I know; I know. It's just…I've been so consumed with these feelings of anger over the matter, and I'm not an angry person. I didn't know what to do with myself."

With just one look at her remorse, I know she's telling the truth. This girl doesn't have a vindictive bone in her body. Of course she wouldn't know how to handle her feelings in this matter.

"Well, I guess the damage is done. What did the email say?"

"Mr. Asher told Erik that after reviewing the matter and having a personal conversation with me, he found me to be a bright and capable young woman who is invaluable to the project." Trish's beaming smile is back.

"He's right about that." I can't help but match her grin. It's infectious.

"And he said Heather's review of me is without merit and that Erik should give me a raise as he sees fit and consider me for a promotion when the project is over, as I am—and I quote—*overqualified for her current helm*." Her posture straightens, and her chin lifts to the north in a sense of pride.

"Right again. I'd say, you really impressed him. I hope Erik gives you a decent increase."

"I know he will. At least what is fair, of course. Erik is just that way. You know, all for one and that kind of thing." She bobbles in her chair like there's a spring underneath her.

"I do." It's the one thing that keeps me sane around here. "Again, I'm very happy you have some closure on the matter."

Trish lets out a laugh. "I feel much better." She holds the papers straight out, putting them in front of my face. "Mr. Asher told me to give these to you."

I take the papers from her hand and look over them. They're all the proposals I've been sending up to his office for review. I flip through each contract in my hand, and Asher's signature is on all of them, approved everything.

I look up at Trish, who is playing with the hem of her skirt. "Did he say anything when he gave these to you?" I ask, hoping for some inclination of his feeling toward me after my ridiculous outburst in the elevator.

"No. He just told me to take them to Mrs. Monroe. I almost didn't know who he was talking about."

I hate how he uses my married name. It's like he's using it as an insult.

It doesn't matter anyway. Now that he's approved these contracts, I can get to work and hopefully get to the end of this project without having to see him. If I can do everything over interoffice mail and email, then I'll be very happy to never see Asher again.

Trish looks at me as if she could read my mind. She leans forward a touch to tell me, "He'll be at the meeting on Friday." It is a warning in the sweetest tone.

I laugh. Like, really laugh. This girl totally gets me. "Is it just me, or is that man confusing as all hell?"

She nods her head in agreement. "He is really bananas. Sometimes, we don't see him for months. He usually deals directly with Erik, and when he is around, he's so serious. Erik always comments on how cool the guy is, but I've never seen it though."

I saw a tiny glimpse of a relaxed Alexander Asher that first time I met him. Every time since then has been extreme.

"But he's not supposed to be around until Friday, right?"

"Right. You're safe for a few more days," Trish answers as if she knew I had an undercurrent of regret and hostility building up inside of me. Although she'd probably say that to everyone in the office since we all seem to be on edge when he's around.

chapter ELEVEN

"You know what you need? A drink!"

Malory, as vice president of Asher-Marks Communications, requested my presence for an emergency meeting…at the nail salon.

"Malory, I'm not going out for a drink in the middle of the workday. It's bad enough that you have me getting a manicure when I have a desk full of work to do!"

Crossing her legs and swiveling toward me while keeping her hands in place for the nail technician, Malory leans her head to the side with a condescending look in her eye. "Kat, you worry too much. How is this any different from taking a lunch?"

I roll my eyes at her and stare at the simple yet classic color I chose for my nails. "I don't worry. I'm just practical. A mani during my lunch hour seems like…cheating."

Pursing her lips, she gives me her scowl that's equal parts serious and sexy. "You know what they say about nail polish. You are the color you wear."

I look down at the rustic bronze color being painted on my nails. It has a subtle golden shimmer that's restrained yet warm and sensuous.

Malory raises her eyebrows and motions toward the bottle of Essie nail polish. I turn it over to see the clever name—All Tied Up.

"Funny," I chide. "What does yours say?"

"Fear or Desire!" With a wicked laugh, she swivels back to face her technician. "For the record, the drink in question is after work. I thought we could go out, just the two of us. Maybe even get our flirt on."

I shake my head. "As much as I'd love to have my ego boosted by a stranger at a bar, I cannot. I have to be home, so the sitter can leave."

"Well, make sure the sitter stays late next Thursday. Everyone's going out for Heather's birthday. You can't be the only one not going."

"First of all, if Heather had anything but contempt for me, I'd be enticed, but the answer is no. I have to get home to Jackson."

Flipping her black hair behind her shoulder with one fluid motion of her head, Malory shrugs. "I had to ask. Should've known you'd be a party pooper. Are you twenty-eight or fifty-eight? I seem to have forgotten."

"Excuse me for being *all tied up*, pun intended."

Speaking into the air, as if talking to herself, yet knowing I'm in earshot, she says, "I don't want you waking up one day and regretting your youth passed you by while you were focused on raising a baby."

"Going out for a drink for Heather's birthday is not going to fill some void. Thank you for the offer, but I'm otherwise engaged."

If Malory hears the disdain in my voice, she doesn't let on.

Instead, she throws this zinger at me. "Gabriel doesn't seem to have a problem with canceling plans on you."

My mouth falls open, and I have to remind myself to breathe. Malory laughs to herself and asks the cosmetologist for a wax while I stay silent.

As we arrive back at the office, Trish greets us with a concerned look on her face. "Mr. Asher called a three o'clock staff meeting."

I look down at my watch. "That's in five minutes. He wasn't supposed to be here until tomorrow."

"I know." Trish whisks her redheaded body out from behind reception. "His receptionist called around two. Erik is in a panic. I've never seen him so unsteady. I've been running around, trying to gather the crew and get the conference room in order."

Shit. I haven't polished off my spreadsheet. I spent the last four days taking all the materials Asher had signed off on and getting them in production. I was hoping to finalize that tomorrow morning.

I rub my palms together and bite my lip. A few weeks ago, I didn't even know who this man was, and today, I'm falling apart at the thought of seeing him.

I run down to my office, peering into the conference room and other office spaces on my way down. Everyone is frantic, dancing around like little mice scurrying from the presence of a cat. All the excitement is making me jittery.

I print up what I've completed and grab a notepad from my desk.

Glancing in a mirror on the way down the hall, I check my appearance. My brown locks are up in a French twist. My navy skirt still looks crisp. Thankfully, I have freshly painted nails. Hopefully, no one will notice how fresh they are. I tug at my blouse and adjust my necklace. With my paperwork in hand, I confidently stroll into the conference room.

Just like last time, there is a lone seat next to Asher, meant just for me.

He starts by inquiring about ad sales and then moves on to the technical and graphics teams. He listens to everyone's progress reports and makes decisions on what should be executed next. He has a way of being stern and abrupt without being harsh or mean. One by one, he calls on each member of the production team, listens for the issues at hand, and resolves them. The man has a way of seeing the big picture and filling in the blanks. No matter how big or small the problem might be, he has an answer.

I find myself staring at his full lips as they speak with ease. I imagine all the women he's kissed with those lips.

"Mrs. Monroe, how are you doing on the Lincoln Center itinerary?"

Fumbling for my papers, I spew out what I've committed to memory, "The rundown for the televised portion of the evening is still being laid out. I've submitted an itinerary to Erik." I hand Asher a printout. "It can also be found in the company Dropbox."

Asher's eyes skim the document as I continue, "I was only able to make final confirmations with several vendors this week, but as it stands, deliveries will be made, beginning at three in the morning."

I rush through a list of who's arriving and what they're setting up as well as their estimated time of setup from start to finish. "Guests will arrive at six o'clock…and Gretchen and I are working on an opening act for the performance. There seems to be some confusion on who should be appearing at the park event and who should be at the Lincoln Center gala. I'm hoping for someone hot, like the new pop star Ashley Sands."

I swallow hard and wait for a response, unsure if I should continue.

"That's an *interesting* idea." He stresses the word *interesting* with a condescending tone and continues, "But this is a group with a lot of wealth and class. The Philharmonic will open the event. It's their home venue, so they should be the ones to open the event."

Is he insinuating I don't have class or wealth?

I feel like he's putting on a show. As if he were saying, *See, I can be a nice guy, but don't forget, I am in charge here, so if I don't like what I hear, I can change it at any time.*

Nonetheless, my inner sparring warrior takes her stance. "With all due respect, the Philharmonic is impressive, but we should open the show with a bang or else the event will feel uptight and unwelcoming."

Take that, Asher. I just called you uptight!

He looks at me with a smirk. "We don't want to be uptight, Mrs. Monroe." He takes out his cell phone. "I'll call Crystalis. Her album is number one on the pop charts. I'll tell her to perform at the gala after the Philharmonic."

Crystalis is the current princess of pop. Her current single is being deemed the song of the summer, and since last year, no one has been able to listen to the radio for more than twenty minutes without hearing one of her songs. Of course he would have one of the biggest talents in the world in his personal Rolodex.

Heather nearly leaps across the table. "Crystalis is performing in the park!"

Gretchen puts her hand on Heather's forearm and gently guides her to sit back in her chair.

Turning to Asher, Gretchen explains, "Her publicist agreed to the telecast. They would never let her do a benefactor gala with limited exposure."

Asher finishes typing into this phone, which I can only assume is a text to one of the most famous women in America right now. He puts down the phone and sits back in his chair, looking directly at Gretchen and Heather, unaffected by their concerns. "She knows this is for the children. She will perform wherever she's needed. She doesn't need the coverage."

Heather and Gretchen know there's no use in arguing. Instead, Heather's grimace sends negative vibes to my side of the table, and I try to shoo them away. It's not my fault that Asher gave me her performer. I wanted someone else.

Asher turns back to me and points to the document in his hand. "I liked your idea about giving seats to the kids. Give them more. You only allotted two hundred. Double that."

Despite my surprise, I affirm vigorously. There are plenty of seats in the venue, and I know they haven't all been sold.

"You will also need to block time for a special performance. I'm working with a group of children who will be playing for the grand finale." He pulls out the incomplete rundown sheet. "Give them four minutes."

I look for Erik or someone else to interject, but they do not.

"Um, that might be difficult. The event is only two hours. With commercial breaks, that leaves us with eighty minutes of airtime. Between the Philharmonic, Crystalis, the two other acts Gretchen booked, and the speeches that have to be made, you have no time left."

You could hear a pin drop in the room. There are dozens of other people here, yet everyone is completely focused on the man to my left.

Including myself.

He takes a beat, clearly thinking over the matter. My heart skips when he speaks again. Not because he's intimidating me. But because his tone is sincere. "I want the kids to have four minutes. It's important. Take a look at the rundown and see if you can move the timing around."

I let out a breath and look down at my notepad.

I think it's the end of the discussion, but he speaks again and completely catches me off guard, "If anyone can make this happen, it's you."

I would probably ask him what kind of game he's playing, but I can't. Not only because we're in a room full of people, but also because I, for the first time, don't think he's playing a game.

Is it possible the bastard can be sincere about one thing in his life?

When the meeting ends, I grab my belongings and rush to my office. Between Asher and Heather, I need to get far away. There's no doubt in my mind that Heather is stomping her feet in front of Erik right now. I, on the other hand, am ecstatic. I have the number one performer in the country for my event. I'll have to get a list of requirements from Gretchen and work with Harvey on introductions.

I close the door behind me and start working on my notes from the meeting. I have calls to make and an itinerary to change, and the New York Philharmonic to book. Knowing I have the Asher name behind my back, I have no doubt they will make themselves available to perform.

I take a seat in my sleek leather chair and start typing away.

I don't hear the door open or hear him come in. I actually don't know why I look up, but there he is, leaning against my wall with his arms folded, staring at me.

chapter TWELVE

"You don't like my flowers?"

He has removed his tie and jacket since the meeting, leaving him in black slacks and a dress shirt, his sleeves rolled up. He looks relaxed, yet his eyes gleam, determined.

My body pulls a Trish, and my leg starts bouncing under the glass table. Tucking a stray hair behind my ear, I try to appear as professional as possible. I offer a polite smile and fold my hands on the desk in front of me. "While they are exquisite, I'm afraid I cannot accept them."

Keeping his eyes trained on me, he asks, "And why can't you accept them?"

Keep your cool, Kat.

"They are rather inappropriate, Mr. Asher."

"Why ever so formal, Mrs. Monroe? Pray tell, why are they inappropriate?" His lips turn up in an indecent grin.

"Why do you insist on calling me by my married name?"

"Why do you answer a question with a question?"

He has a way of drawing me in with his charm, but I have to stay on my toes. So far, I'm three for three with failed attempts at talking to this man. One of which I can't blame him at all for. I need to maintain proper decorum.

"Mr. Asher…"

Unfolding his arms, Asher takes a step off the wall, closer to my desk. "Alex. Just call me Alex."

Ah, those famous words from the limo. *"Just call me Alex."*

Irritation sends blood pulsing through my veins. I keep my voice even and cross my shaking leg under my steady one. "Mr. Asher, with all due respect, I'm a married woman, and I cannot accept flowers from another man. Especially when he's the one signing my checks."

His face turns serious as his eyes squint, appraising me. "Do you always uphold such high moral ground?"

With his palms placed on my desk, he leans forward, driving that divine scent into my personal space. Our eyes lock. I stare at them like someone mesmerized by a pinwheel. Those flecks of gold and brown are a kaleidoscope for the devil.

He inches his body toward me until he's so close that I can feel his breath on my skin. I want to turn around and push my chair away from the desk. But like always with this man, I freeze.

"Relax." A slow, sexy smile creeps across his face before he pulls away and collapses into the chair in front of my desk.

What the...

Well, it looks like we'll be going four for four with awkward encounters.

Asher sits back...no, lounges back in the seat with his arms spread open. He fills it far more than Trish. In fact, he makes the chair look small.

Oddly enough, his order to relax actually does calm my nerves a bit. It was in the tone. It was...earnest?

I stare at him, dumbfounded.

"You intrigue me." He crosses his right leg over his left knee. "You are the only person in this damn place who tells it like it is. I like you. I want to get to know you intimately."

I must look like a deer in headlights. He leans his head back and laughs. A real laugh. Like a guttural, deep-in-the-belly laugh. It's low and smooth.

"No, no, not like that." He holds up his hand while the other sits on his chest.

If not like that, then what?

He pauses as he tries to assess how to proceed. "Gray. May I call you Gray?"

I shake my head. "No."

We're not doing nicknames.

He mouths the word *no* as a question, his lips forming a perfect O.

He placing his elbows on his knees. His legs spread wide, hitting the sides of the chair. "That's fine. I like your name. Kathryn." My name slides off his tongue like a dare. "It's beautiful. It means pure."

Pure? I'm far from it. Maybe once, a long time ago. Speaking of pure…

"The white roses. They have to go."

"The roses were meant as a peace offering. I should have told you who I was, but I swear I didn't know who you were when you got in my car."

I blink at him, unsure of whether to assume he really did or did not know. "So, you weren't being inappropriate?"

He takes a deep breath. "To be honest, yes, I was coming on to you in the elevator, but I swear that was before I knew you were married. Scout's honor."

"You said I intrigue you. Intrigue how?"

"Fascinate, interest, beguile. Are you really going to make me list every SAT word I have in this head? Because I've got a lot of them. Appeal, bewitch…transfix…" He counts off the various words.

"I know what *intrigue* means. The question is, how?"

Clearly amused by himself, he smiles and then shrugs his shoulders. "You're intense. You're honest, and you don't take shit from anyone, especially me."

Okay, that is so not me.

He continues, "I would have written you off, but there's something about your work. You understand what I want to do with these concerts more than anyone else here."

He *seems* genuine, yet, as with everything with Asher, I tend to stay on my toes, not knowing what he's going to say or do next. This is something I didn't see coming. Not today anyway.

My interest is piqued. "What do you mean, you want to get to know me better?"

The corners of his eyes crinkle just enough to make him look like someone I'd want to get to know on a friendly level. Not the ultra-serious businessman who's had me reeling for the last few weeks.

"You are a breath of fresh air. Women always tell me exactly what I want to hear, and I know it's because they want to get in bed with me to become the future Mrs. Alexander Asher."

His conceit knows no bounds.

"That is the most self-obsessed thing I've ever heard."

His smile broadens, revealing beautiful white teeth. "See, that's what I mean. You don't feel the need to lie to me or jump through hoops. As hard as it might be for you to believe, most women see dollar signs around me and only want me for that single purpose."

Clearly, he doesn't realize how gorgeous he is? I'm sure he'd get plenty of women if he were dirt poor, personality aside.

"And the men around here," he continues, "they all want promotions or event tickets, trips on the private jet—"

"Mr. Asher." I use his name in an attempt to keep this relationship as professional as possible. "I doubt there isn't a single person who can be up-front with you."

"You are a rare breed. That's why I'm here to apologize and ask for a truce. I mean it. I want to be your friend."

This is so awkward. I don't even know where to begin. Let's forget the fact that I've had some very odd dreams about him. One that happened to take place in this very office. Yes, we're going to forget about that.

This whole situation is just…

"Again, it's inappropriate. For starters, I am your employee. Secondly, I'm married." I flash my ring finger at him. Yes, today, I am wearing one.

Asher nearly jumps out of his seat. "That's exactly what I like about you. You're taken. You have no interest in me, and I have absolutely no interest in you. I can relax. Be myself. I know you're not after anything."

"Mr. Ash—"

"Please, call me Alex. You said it in the car. I like it when you say my name." My mouth opens, and he waves me off before I can say anything. "And, no, it's not inappropriate. Consider yourself my consigliere, my right-hand man, my secretary of state."

He's being playful, and it makes me smile, a tiny sliver of a smile I know he's getting a kick out of.

"I'll take the title of work friend. But first, you must earn someone's friendship."

His brow puckers, as if he's never thought of that. Distorting his face, he looks as if he's processing something.

I decide to put him out of his misery and change the topic. "Why are you here?"

With his furrowed brow, he looks back at me. "I thought I just explained—"

"No. Why are you in the office today? You weren't supposed to be here until tomorrow. You have the staff going crazy."

"I have a very important date tomorrow." He's back to being Mr. Casual, leaning back in the seat.

"A date?" The words come out slow, accusatory. "You cause chaos among your staff because you have a date tomorrow?"

"Not the kind of date you're thinking of. I have somewhere very important to be every Friday afternoon until the concerts. And, yes, if I want to surprise my staff with a meeting, then I will. No one has ever become a successful CEO by playing it safe with the staff."

"You really do love yourself, don't you?"

"Confidence, Gray. It's the key to success."

"Smug is more like it. And I said, no nicknames."

"That was before we were friends." He pauses to look around the room. "Where is the umbrella?"

It's still under my desk in the box. "It hasn't rained, so I haven't had a chance to use it."

His eyes light up, and a satisfied smile brightens his face. "You're keeping it. Good. I picked it out just for you. My olive branch."

"Olive branch accepted. But no more gifts. I mean it, Asher!"

"Asher? I like the stern tone in your voice." He's mocking me with his eyes and his mouth.

"I'll keep the umbrella, but the staff enjoys the roses. Remember, no more gifts!"

"Okay, okay. No more gifts. I've never had a woman tell me that twice."

"I'm glad you're counting." I laugh lightly.

I really want to dislike this man, but he's so magnetic. As hard as I try, my eyes never leave his. The current between us is building. I know he can feel it, too. Thank God for the desk, acting as a barrier to our indiscretion.

Breaking the spell, Asher shakes his head and stares at the floor. He takes a breath and puts his hands on his legs, rising from the chair.

"That's all." Just like that, the playful man is gone, and back is the commanding CEO. "I want to see the new rundown with the amended time next week. Call my office and make an appointment."

I feel slightly displaced. "Yes, sir."

He is half out the door, his back to me, when he halts and speaks over his shoulder, "And, Gray? Have a great day."

Asher exits my office, closing the door behind him.

My shoulders drop, and I realize how tense I am. I don't think I've relaxed in the last two hours.

Ugh, and I said, no nicknames.

chapter THIRTEEN

Just because Asher has decided to form a truce between the two of us doesn't mean I'm not on pins and needles with the thought of going to his office. I tried to get out of it. After perfecting the rundown this morning, I emailed it to him, hoping he'd approve it, as he had the last set of documents.

To my surprise, my computer lets out a ping sound, signaling a new email in my inbox.

> JULY 8 AT 10:04 A.M.
>
> TO: GRAYSON, KATHRYN
>
> FROM: ASHER, ALEXANDER
>
> SUBJECT: YOU, ME, MEETING…
>
>
> NOW.
>
> :)

At least he used a smiley face.

The elevator takes me up to the penthouse. It feels a long way away from the twenty-fourth floor.

When the doors open, I'm greeted with a reception area similar to the one Trish sits at but more grandiose and missing a redhead. A woman, who I assume is Asher's assistant, Cecelia, greets me. I had to call her, rather embarrassingly asking if I should go up to the penthouse or if the meeting would be taking place in my office. I really had no idea.

She answered with a serious tone, "Mr. Asher travels for no one."

I wanted to be snotty and tell her he'd been in my office twice since I met him, but the point was moot.

"Mr. Asher will be with you in one moment. Please, have a seat." Cecelia's tone is far more cordial than it was earlier.

Although she does take a minute to assess me from head to toe—peeking down at my navy dress with a boatneck, long sleeves, and a hemline that falls at the knee. I look like a professional. I'm sure Asher's had a few Heathers come through here with their short skirts and low-cut shirts. Cecelia must have a field day with people-watching.

The seating area is like the one downstairs with its white leather sofas and chrome furniture. Instead of plasma screens, a massive fish tank takes up most of the wall. Inside are the most exotic sea creatures I've ever seen. Vibrant-colored exteriors with exquisite forms. Gabriel would get a kick out of this.

Cecelia disappears behind a large mahogany door and reappears seconds later to tell me I can enter.

Asher's seated at his desk, in front of a giant window of floor-to-ceiling glass. His back to me, as he's on the phone. I stand in the center of the room and look over the space.

There is a seating area set up like a mini living room, a small conference area, and a bar. Behind the apropos bar is a large television screen in which, if you look closely, you can see the seam where four individual screens meet up. The screens are currently acting individually, playing CNN, MSNBC, FOX News, and BBC.

Asher swings his chair around and keeps a serious expression on his face, even after he sees me standing here. He continues to talk to the person on the other end of the call while I walk forward and situate myself in one of the desk chairs.

As I spread my files on the table, Cecelia walks in with two cups of coffee. "Two black, as you requested."

I glance over at Asher, surprised he remembers how I like my coffee. Cecelia leaves the room and closes the door behind her.

Asher dismisses his call in the same way he's ended every conversation and meeting I've ever witnessed. Abruptly. Not knowing which version of Asher I'm going to get today, I wait for him to speak first.

"We never did get to have our meeting. The one when we were so rudely interrupted by the rain." Idyllic eyes twinkle as he motions toward the black coffees.

Taking a sip, I force my shoulders to relax. "You're the only other person I know who likes their coffee black."

"Something else we have in common," he says.

It takes me a second to realize what he means. Well, to be honest, I don't entirely know what he means, and I'm not going to ask. I'm pretty sure he's talking about our common interest in the arts and in this project. He's keeping a tally of our interests. Is that weird? Maybe he really doesn't have anyone around here he can be on friendly terms with.

I take out my copies of the rundown and place one in front of each of us. Slipping into business mode, Asher goes through the entire document, minute by minute, second for second. He probably doesn't know what he's looking at. He's a money guy, not a producer.

"A bar in the office. Very young mogul meets old-school businessman. I approve."

My awkward comment is met with his intense silence. I inhale through my nose and play with my fingers.

Asher leans back in his desk as he assesses the document. I've added the time he requested, but I had to considerably cut down on the three celebrity acts to make up the difference. I also took time away from his speech. Let's hope he's a quick talker.

His blond hair looks darker in the dim light of the office. Everything about him seems a little darker. The light pouring through the giant window behind the desk casts a shadow in variations of black and white around his solid frame.

I shift my weight in my seat. "An additional commercial block is built in there. Malory has been doing a kick-ass job at securing ad space."

"She should be. We've contracted out the half the ad sales to another company," he says, flipping the page.

I swallow. My nails are incredibly fascinating to me right now. I don't do well in silent situations. It's like I have this innate desire to fill the empty void with chatter, yet once I say something, I immediately wish I'd kept my mouth shut.

So, I just sit and stare. At least the view is nice.

Asher's lips pucker, and he slides the pen down the document, reading every word and number on the page. His eyes skim over the same portion of the paper a few times, trailing back and forth from left to right. Either he disagrees with something on the page or...

"You don't know how to read a rundown, do you?"

His head pops up, betraying a mixture of surprise and insult that I asked the question.

What the hell is wrong with me? For someone who has spent her life keeping her idiotic thoughts to herself, I certainly have diarrhea of the mouth when I'm around this man.

I lower my lids and let out a sigh, feeling so foolish for accusing my boss of not knowing how to read a simple production document. A second later, when I open my eyes, I'm stunned when I see something besides an affronted mogul.

The left side of his mouth is curled up, and he lets out a light chuckle from deep in his throat. "You got me. I have no idea what I'm looking at."

A gush of air washes out from my lungs. With that air comes all the nervous energy I normally carry when I'm around him. I let out a huge laugh with an unattractive snort and then try to cover it up with my hand.

"Amused?" he asks.

I gather my wits and wipe a tear from my eye. "No. I mean, yes." I cough and then take a deep breath, sitting up straight again to regain my self-control. "I'm sorry. That was rather unprofessional."

Asher drops the document on his desk and folds his hands into each other and placing them on his desk. "It's okay. Maybe you can show me what I'm looking at."

This should be interesting. One would think someone of his stature would know how to do just about anything.

I grab the arms of my chair and scoot myself closer, so I can lean forward and look at the rundown he placed on his desk. Using my pen, I point to the column all the way to the left and tell him the program is portioned out into blocks, categorized with letters of the alphabet. Each block contains a segment of the event, whether it be a speech, a performance, or an interview. Pretty much every element of the show is given its own block, and with each block comes a set amount of time.

If Asher knows any of this already, he doesn't allude to it. He lets me move along, explaining each portion of the document, how to read the time that's been allotted, where the commercial breaks are, and the various elements that will be in place for each block of the show.

He's a quick study, and he starts making changes immediately. They're good but not simple. The tricky thing about creating a rundown is, making one change has a domino effect on the pieces before and after the change.

We take our pens and start marking up the pages. His black ink and my blue shoot over the white pages like a piece of modern art.

"You can't do that," I say.

"Why not? We just took thirty seconds from Crystalis's performance."

"Because you have to hit your commercial break at exactly nine thirty-four or else the network will cut you off. Network commercial breaks go to air whether you're ready for them or not." Looking down at the paper, I don't even know which changes I'll be able to keep. The page looks like a toddler got his hands on a pen and started scratching up the paper. "Let me work on this some more, and I'll get it back to you."

I grab the papers from the desk and stand up. I've been in the office for half an hour. He must have another appointment after me.

"Why don't we keep going?" He stands and grabs his cell phone.

Watching him make his way from behind his desk, I explain, "We could, but you really need to be on the computer to do this, and the software is in my office—"

"So, let's go to your office." Asher's hand is on the door. He opens it and calls out to Cecelia, "Cancel my afternoon appointments."

My feet are still planted on the floor as Asher looks back at me, holding the door open.

I'm baffled he canceled his afternoon appointments to work on a rundown with me from my office. I suppose the lesson here is, I should stop being surprised by anything Asher does.

Shrugging, I move one foot in front of the other and lead Asher down to my office.

The elevator ride isn't nearly as exciting as the last two I've shared with him. I'm surprisingly comfortable this time. Perhaps it's because the elevator stops on a few floors on the way down to accommodate other passengers. The company is very welcome.

We make our way to Asher-Marks Communications, ignoring the stares of colleagues who see Asher on the floor…with me.

We take seats at my desk—me on my side and him in the guest seat. After I log in, I pull up the software and then tilt the computer, so we both can see. We go through the notes we made together and start making the changes. I state why we can't do things, and then he tells me I have to. Somehow, I manage to make it happen.

At noon, he orders food for lunch, and Trish brings it in when it arrives. By one, Asher asks to see the production details I have so far. He isn't impressed by how much work still needs to be done on them, and I explain he has been the major holdup. He laughs, apologizes, and then tells me what I need to have completed by the end of the week.

He's authoritative, but not bossy. He's direct but not mean. He has a way of saying things about my work that I don't find condescending. And while, just last week, I thought he was the rudest person on the planet, this afternoon, I find myself respecting his opinion.

Why? Because he is so passionate about this project, it's hard to fault him on anything else.

By two, my stomach is full, and my desk is stacked with files. Asher stands up and puts his suit jacket back on. He took it off, along with his tie, when the Thai food arrived.

"I have a penchant for ruining ties with my lunch. You'd probably cry if you saw the amount of money I spend on ties every year."

I find his charming yet earnest comment out of character. "I can't imagine you have such casual lunches."

"Never." He grins. "This was surprisingly enjoyable. We should do it again." Fixing the tie around his neck, Asher looks down at me, still seated behind my desk. "You know, doing the concert in the park was a good idea. Doing two events was a great idea. Although, I must admit, if anyone else had mentioned it, I wouldn't have approved it."

I cock my head to the side. "Then, why did you?"

He swings the tie around the knot he just formed and up from the back to secure it in place. "I like to challenge people. I wanted to challenge you."

I bite down on my lip. "Why?"

Looking down at me, his eyes turn serious, like molten lava from a volcano. They find mine, as they do every time he wants me to know he means what he says. "Because I can."

It's the last thing he says before turning around and heading out of the office. Exhaling, I slump in my chair, trying to comprehend how my relationship with Asher has done a one-eighty.

My office, the one that seemed so small moments before, now seems huge. I glide my hands along the glass of my desk, hoping the cool, smooth surface will bring me back to reality. I look for something to fiddle with and end up with a pen. My space is so impersonal. I need to bring in pictures of Gabriel and Jackson. Their smiling faces will help ground me when things become too intense. I upload the photo from my phone and add it to my computer desktop.

I have a security list I have to submit to Marci, the woman in charge of compiling all the lists and making sure only the right people are allowed backstage. I stare at the list I started earlier, looking for a distraction.

An hour later, I have yet to add a single thing to the document, and I've chewed the cap off my pen. I'm far too distracted by my previous company.

I'm only pulled back into reality when my phone rings.

"Hey, baby." Gabriel is unusually chipper for midweek.

I instantly feel calm. "I needed to hear your voice."

"Everything okay? Asher riding you hard today?"

I nearly fall out of my chair. My pen, however, does fall from my hand. Thank God it was the only thing I was holding.

"Not exactly. Just…overwhelmed."

"That is a way to describe you in most scenarios, Kat. But you always manage to come out on top."

"Thank you. Where are you?"

"I was calling to say I'm heading home early. I can't take the office anymore, and I just want to hang out with Jack. Maybe take him to the park or something."

"That sounds great. I'm jealous." I smile back at the desktop photo of Gabriel and Jackson.

"Since you're having a crazy day, why don't you go get a manicure or something on your way home? You need some alone time. Jack and I can do some male bonding."

"You're amazing, Gabe, but I'm good. I'll just come home."

"Are you sure? You should do something for yourself."

I look at the calendar on my computer and see the interoffice event scheduled for tonight.

"Well…my coworkers are going out after work for drinks for Heather's birthday. Do you mind if I do that instead?"

"That sounds like fun. You need to make more friends."

"I find my life is quite full. Why do I need anyone but you and Jackson?"

"That's why we love you. Go out tonight. Have fun. Just promise you'll take a cab home."

"I will. Talk to you later."

"Bye, baby."

Yes, a drink is exactly what I need to unwind.

chapter FOURTEEN

Malory and I step into the Whiskey Blue at the W New York Hotel. With its navy snakeskin-leather club chairs and dim lighting, the place is a modern-day take on an old New York gentlemen's club.

The place is swimming with suits and Louboutin-wearing women hoping to meet seven-figure-earning moguls who will be their future husbands. These women are dressed to the nines.

Before leaving the office, Malory insisted we freshen up. I touched up my makeup and let my hair down while she took the liberty of removing my cardigan. That was before the inquisition about Asher's visit to my office started in the cab ride over here.

I rolled my eyes. "Please tell me I can go to the ladies' room without someone tracking my every move?"

Malory laughed. "It's not your moves they're tracking. It's Asher's. Everyone saw him go to your office."

The cab cruised up Park Avenue. I only had to make it a few blocks before exiting the conversation. As much as Malory had been my closest confidant at our previous job, I just didn't want to give her any reason to think something was amiss with Asher. I valued her respect too much.

Malory's eyes studied me, but I never faltered. Our conversation shifted to shoes, and by the time we arrived at Lexington and 49th, we decided to swap. Her red stilettos gave me the added color she'd said I needed for a night on the town. I traded her my beige patent leathers, which, of course, she made look sexy as hell.

"Damn, girl, your legs are killer in those shoes. You should wear higher heels from now on."

"No, thank you," I say as I almost lose my balance. "Three-inch heels are as high as I need for the workday. How do you last in these things all day?"

"It's what I do in them at night that should be the question." Malory gives me a wink, and I laugh.

Unsure of my footing in these shoes, I take a seat at the bar, thankful there's one available, and order a glass of wine. Almost everyone from the office is here, some with their significant others, occupying booths and barstools, while Trish, Malory, and I are at the bar. Heather is at the opposite end of the bar, chatting up some Fortune 500–looking guy. I can't help but hope he's really the mailroom boy in disguise.

Trish, as it turns out, is pretty funny. Give her a drink, and she opens up into a great storyteller. She even has a few dirty jokes that have Malory and me bending over the bar in laughter. I don't know if it's the drinks or the fact that Trish, this very sweet little redhead, is telling dirty jokes. I decide it doesn't matter and lose myself in the conversation.

The evening also allows me to see how my coworkers interact outside the office. Erik is just as I would have imagined. He's sitting at the booth in heavy conversation about work with Harvey, Kevin, Gretchen, and Richard. They're all hanging on his every word. Especially since, every so often, Erik orders a round of shots for the team. That is exactly how I've interpreted Erik since meeting him—all work but a lot of fun.

Gretchen is still head to toe, in her work attire. Where I let loose a little, she still has her shirt buttoned to her neck and blazer fastened around her waist. I think she only wears jeans to the office just to prove she's not completely uptight. When she does, they're trouser-cut. I also watch her chemistry with Harvey and smile at how relaxed they seem with each other. He's a good man to talk to. Even in the office, whenever I have a question that might seem silly or embarrassing, I always ask Harvey because I know he won't judge. Shame on me for judging him.

Heather is in her full glory, having changed into a sequined cocktail dress shorter than anything I've seen her wear to date. She's in full conversation with Mr. Fortune 500. Even when I went over to wish her a happy birthday, she gave me a quick, "Thanks," and averted her attention to everyone but me.

Two hours later, I'm quite buzzed. My second glass of wine is sitting in front of me at the bar. Couple that with the two rounds of shots Erik ordered for us, and I'm feeling good. Really good. So good that when Trish starts talking about how she and her boyfriend, Kevin, used anal beads the weekend before and describes it as, "Mardi Gras in my pants," I literally fall off my chair from laughing so hard.

On my way off the chair, I try to grab hold of the bar, but someone from behind catches me before I hit the floor. Like a rag doll, I'm lifted up and onto my chair. I really can't have any more to drink.

As I gather myself and wipe the tears of laughter from my eyes, I look up to see Malory and Trish staring over my shoulder, their jaws falling to the floor. I don't have to turn around to know who's behind me. The smell of tobacco and vanilla causes me to sober up.

"I see you guys are having a good time. Please, ladies, don't let me disturb you. Though I'd love to know what's so funny."

I slowly turn around to see Asher standing tall, picture-perfect, as if the day had just begun. He towers over the three of us, as intimidating as ever. I can feel the heat of his hand on the back of my chair as he leans over to get the bartender's attention.

"Auchentoshan, twenty-one," Asher orders his drink and puts his black label Amex on the bar. "And the tab for all this." He makes a motion with his hand toward the members of Asher-Marks who are out celebrating.

Trish takes a sip of her Captain and ginger, trying to wipe the flush from her face. There's nothing more embarrassing than being caught by the big boss, doing shots and talking about sex.

Malory isn't concerned in the least. She is confident and brilliantly beautiful. She has no need to even hide behind her glass.

"Fine choice of scotch." Malory swivels her chair, so she's in direct line with Asher. "Though I always took you as a Macallan kind of man."

The three of us watch as he draws his lowball to his lips and takes a sip of the malt liquor, letting it swim around his teeth before swallowing.

"Macallan 1939 is my vice. But there's a time and a place for largesse," he says with a wicked smile. "Are you a scotch drinker, Ms. Dean?"

"Only with a cigar." Seductiveness leaks into her voice.

I've never seen her interact with Asher before. If she wasn't like this with everyone she meets, I would think she had a thing for our boss.

"May I?" Malory motions toward Asher's drink.

"Be my guest." He leans into her, offering up the golden liquid.

Malory raises it to her lips, repeating the savoring process Asher did a moment before, never taking her eyes off Asher as her tongue rims the glass.

Trish and I exchange a glance. So, I'm not the only one who noticed that.

"Vanilla and honey. A nice blend."

Their eyes remain connected as Asher's lips curl up to one side like the wicked man he is.

I grab my wineglass and take a sip.

Trish breaks the tension. "Speaking of, the flowers on my desk have an incredible aroma of vanilla."

I nearly choke on my pinot. Instead, I spit it across the bar. Malory and Trish step back in surprise. Asher looks unaffected by the scene.

"Went down the wrong pipe." I swallow.

Like a bolt of lightning, Heather is at my side, taking the space between Asher and me. I'm surprised it took her this long to approach him, yet I'm happy for the diversion.

"Mr. Asher! I'm so happy you came out for my birthday. I thought you had plans tonight." Heather's short dress grows shorter as she leans over further to cut the line of sight between me and the devil with golden eyes.

"I'm glad to see everyone, but I'm not here to enjoy the festivities. I'm on a date." Asher raises his glass and nods toward a leggy young blonde on the other side of the bar.

She's wearing a long-sleeved black dress with a micro skirt and dangerously low neckline that reaches her navel. She's standing there, looking bored yet waiting dutifully for her mogul to wrap up with his minions.

"You should ask her to join us," Trish cheerfully offers.

"I don't think that's a good idea. I never mix business with pleasure."

I can't see Asher's expression as he utters these words. I wonder if he's directing them toward someone.

"Asher, we weren't expecting you." Erik walks over from his booth. "Not like you to join us at our little get-togethers."

"I like to make unexpected appearances now and then." His demeanor is calm and authoritative. He's still in workplace mode.

"Don't we know that from this afternoon?" Erik reaches up to set a friendly pat on Asher's shoulder. "If you don't mind me stealing these ladies…Heather, Malory, Harvey, and I have a bet I need you to settle."

"Sounds intriguing." Malory willingly takes my patent leathers over to the booth while Heather sulks away from Asher.

Erik gives Asher two taps on the back and follows the girls over to the booth. I immediately hear an uproar as the girls approach. Apparently, they're reliving some old escapade and trying to decipher whose version of the story is correct.

Trish is still at the bar with Asher and me, feeling out of place. "I'm going to see what all the commotion is about."

No, little redhead, don't go!

Asher takes Malory's seat next to me. We're each sitting at a corner of the bar, so our chairs easily swivel toward each other.

I must leave when I finish this last glass. A cab is definitely in order.

"Are you going to let your date stand there all night?"

He rubs his pointer finger along the rim of his glass. "I have a perfectly good twenty-one-year-old scotch in front of me. Why should I let that go to waste?"

"You can drink your scotch with your twinkie." The liquor is making me feisty.

"For starters, that is not a twinkie. Her name is Monique, and she happens to be a very wealthy socialite."

"That must be comforting. She clearly doesn't want you for your money. I heard that's a major concern of yours."

"She might not need my money, but she definitely wants the power. Monique is like the others. She'll stand there all night if I ask her to." Asher flashes a smile, showing off his perfect teeth and full lips.

"Then, why bring her at all? If you don't even like her…"

"A man has needs. She'll do for tonight."

I down the last of my wine. "You are disgusting."

"I am honest. I told you, we're friends. We're honest with each other."

"It still doesn't mean I can't be repulsed by you." I barely get the words out as I dismount from the stool and grab my purse.

I turn to walk away but am pulled back by Asher's hand on my arm.

"Please, don't let me offend you. We're having a nice night. I haven't had the chance to tell you how lovely you look. I like your hair down. It's very becoming of you."

"Thank you, but really, it's late, and I have to go. Plus, you have a twinkie to tend to."

He rises from his chair, leaving his scotch. "The twinkie can wait. How are you getting home? You've had a lot to drink, and in those shoes..." His voice trails off.

"I'm taking a taxi home. I'll be fine."

"I'll walk you out." He places a hand on my back and ushers me toward the door.

"No, people cannot see me leave with you. They'll get the wrong idea. It's entirely—"

"Inappropriate," Asher finishes my line. "Come on. I'll walk you out and come right back. It's the responsible thing to do. Besides, I want to see how long I can make the twinkie stand there." He beams in a devilish grin that takes up his entire face.

He's so mean, yet his boyish charm makes him disarming, and I can't resist.

Turning on my heel, I follow him out of the hotel and walk to the curb to hail a taxi. My hand is high in the sky, trying to flag a car, when I turn around to see he's standing on the sidewalk, hands in his pockets, staring at me.

"Enjoying the view?"

"You have no idea." He leans back on his heels. "You really should wear fuck-me shoes more often."

"These are not fuck-me shoes, and they're not mine. Asher, I am a marr—"

"Married woman. I know." There he goes, finishing my sentences again. "You know, just because you're married doesn't mean you can't get spicy like this every now and then. It's a good look for you."

The air outside is cool, yet I can feel my skin heat up. Standing under the streetlamps, Asher looks divine. The shadows highlight his square jaw and perfectly formed nose. His hair glistens, and his eyes light on fire. Even in my five-inch heels, I feel small compared to him. He commands attention, and I can't help but give it to him.

"Enjoying the view?" he teases, repeating my line back at me.

I blush in embarrassment.

"It's the lighting. New York City streets at night make people look so…"

"Angelic." His words are precise. "You look divine, standing there in the light. Pure," he says before getting a very serious look on his face. "I meant it when I said you looked beautiful tonight."

"You never said I looked beautiful."

"I was thinking it," he says, and I am vaguely aware that a black SUV has driven up alongside me. "Your husband is a lucky man." He steps around me and opens the back passenger door. "Devon will take you home."

I open my mouth in protest, but he puts his finger over my lips.

"Devon is taking you home, and that's final. I have some company to entertain upstairs, so I won't be leaving for a while. He's all yours."

"Thank you, Alex."

"Alex? What happened to Asher?"

"I only call you that when I'm mad."

"Well then, let's hope I stay on your good side. I like it when you say my name. Knowing our track record, I'll do something to have you calling me Asher by morning."

"Good night, Asher."

"Already?" He laughs.

"Why wait till morning? If it's a given, I might as well just call you as you are." I walk over to the open door, about to get into the car as he holds the door behind me.

"Savory or sweet?" he asks, causing me to turn around.

"Excuse me?"

"Breakfast. Do you like savory or sweet?"

It's an odd question, but he is an odd man.

"Pancakes."

He seems to find this answer acceptable. "Sweet dreams, Gray."

"Enjoy your twinkie."

I climb into the backseat, and he closes the door of the car.

Maybe it's the wine talking, but I have to admit, I'm starting to like nicknames.

chapter FIFTEEN

The sun beats down on the New York City pavement as I exit the subway terminal and walk briskly to Lincoln Center. I haven't been inside David Geffen Hall in over two decades and want to reacquaint myself with the venue before finalizing production details for Asher's report.

A bright young woman named Claudia escorts me through the campus and gives a guided tour of where the gala will take place. The limos will pull up on Broadway, and the guests will walk out on a black carpet. The paparazzi pit will be on the far-right side of the carpet. At the end of which, a station will be set up for interviews by select media outlets. There is a giant fountain outside. I can imagine it lit up and glowing in the evening with spotlights illuminating the space for the event. It will look spectacular. I request rows of lit trees be placed around the perimeter to create an elegant, ethereal feeling. We make a deal for the venue to pick up the added expense.

Inside, I ask to see the concert halls. They are exquisite. David Geffen Hall is nothing short of spectacular, adorned with gold filigree and velvet seating.

Claudia's phone rings, and she excuses herself. I leisurely glide my fingers over the front of the stage, taking in its enormity up close. My thoughts are halted by his husky voice.

"Have you ever performed?"

I freeze and look up onto the dimly lit stage. Walking out from the left wing, he's dressed in dark jeans and a black button-down shirt with the top button undone. He looks polished and perfect.

"Mr. Asher. It's a pleasure to see you again, albeit a surprise," I say, adjusting my bag on my shoulder.

"I could say the same thing." He strolls across the stage and takes his place above me, eyes gazing down at me. "Mr. Asher? Since when did we go back to formality?"

I stare up at him in awe. His golden highlights are combed flawlessly, glistening in the soft light of the stage.

"Did you enjoy your twinkie?" I ask.

"Turns out, I'm not into sweets."

"No?"

Asher tilts his head to the side. "No, I want something a little more savory. Say, Gray's Papaya."

We might be on friendly terms now, but his innuendos still make me uneasy.

I give him my best deadpan stare. "I think you should stick to dessert."

"Come up here," he commands, holding out his hand.

After a beat, I raise my hand and grab his. I walk up to meet him, careful not to trip over my wobbly feet.

I look out at the scene in front of me. The massive theater with over twenty-seven hundred seats is illuminated in golden hues. The lights on the balcony aren't lit, but I know they're spectacular when turned on.

The stage is lined in wood, and for our event, it will be covered in backdrops, plasma screens, and a top-of-the-line lighting system. Erik, Richard, and the technical team have all been working hard, making sure this place will be gorgeous.

My eyes travel around the room and fall on my hand, still enclosed in Asher's. I quickly pull it back.

"Feels incredible, doesn't it?"

He's right. The feeling is extraordinary. Standing here, facing hundreds of seats...I feel larger than life. The corners of my mouth turn up in a smile, but it fades when I realize he's staring at me.

With a puckered brow, he looks at me, as if trying to answer a plaguing question inside his head. He shakes it off and moves toward the back of the stage.

"I used to perform on this stage when I was a boy."

"What do you play?"

"The cello."

My face must register surprise because he laughs, and for the first time, I relax. He has a great laugh.

"This is something I am very passionate about. Music is my life. That is why these concerts are so important. Through music, you can express how you feel. Through music, you can find yourself. There is no greater way to bring people together than with a song." His passion for the subject is genuine. He seems so vulnerable, as if music were a beautiful woman he couldn't get enough of.

The room goes silent. I realize I've been too quiet, probably because I've been busy assessing him, admiring him. Mega-mogul, philanthropist, and musician...the list goes on.

"May I ask you a personal question?" he says, taking a step closer.

I nod and wonder how personal he plans to get.

"Why do you go by your maiden name?"

The deadly question that has plagued my marriage. The answer is because it's my name, my given name, and I've never understood why women have to give up their name for their husbands. Why can't it be the other way around? My son has Gabriel's last name.

I am a Grayson. That's who I am.

"That is a personal question. But to answer it, I would have to say, it's because I don't believe in conformity."

His cheeks rise to meet his eyes. It's as if I said the exact thing he'd wanted to hear.

"Do you hear that?" he asks.

"Hear what?" I strain to find the sound.

"Music. Dance with me."

"But I don't hear any—"

Before I can finish, he pulls me up against him and moves me across the stage.

My hand rests on his shoulder; I can feel the muscles beneath his shirt. My other hand is in his palm, his soft skin holding mine. We glide across the stage to imaginary music, and before long, I can hear it pulsating through my ears. My body against his, I feel safe and secure. It feels like home.

"Will you accompany me somewhere?" he asks, his voice like smooth caramel.

"Today? My boss might be upset that I'm not at work," I tease.

Asher cocks his head to the side and gives me a wink. "I think I can persuade him not to be too upset."

As we exit the building, he leads me to an alleyway on the side. Expecting to hail a cab or hop into a black SUV, I'm intrigued when he stops in front of a motorcycle.

"Here, put this on." He hands me a helmet.

"Do you always carry a spare?" I say, hesitation in my voice.

"I was hoping I might have company today," he says with a glimmer of mischief.

Reluctantly, I take the helmet and place it on my head. He walks toward me to straighten it out and fixes the chinstrap. I feel like a child being protected, and for some reason, I enjoy it. He places his helmet on and climbs onto the bike. With his dark jeans and leather jacket, he looks like a guy I could have a beer with, not the in-control CEO who has been dominating my thoughts for the past month.

He takes my hand and helps me onto the seat of the motorcycle until I'm straddling it.

"Put your arms around me and hold on tight."

I reach around him and place my hands on his stomach. Asher grabs my hands and pulls them tighter and higher. A charge stirs inside me. He kicks the bike into action, and we take off. I'm delighted to hear music, beautiful orchestra music, ringing in my ears. These helmets have speakers! I can hear the sounds of the New York Philharmonic gracefully dancing through my head. I feel like I'm floating.

We drive up Columbus Avenue and head straight toward Harlem. The hot July morning is cooled by the breeze we create. We drive through the cultural center of the city, passing bars, restaurants, and stores, all new to the revitalization of this once-depressed area. We pass through some blocks Gwen would never be caught dead in and pull up to a school made of brick and mortar.

Asher dismounts from the bike and grabs my hand, helping me off. I would tell him I could do it myself, but I've never been on a motorcycle, and my legs are still vibrating from the short ride.

I hand him my helmet, and he rests it on the motorcycle, not caring if someone will try to steal it. Come to think of it, I don't think we're even allowed to park where we are. Asher doesn't seem to have a care about that either.

I shrug my shoulders and follow him inside. He has this way of walking in front of me without looking back to make sure I'm here. It's like he knows I'm just going to go wherever he tells me to.

The building is fairly empty, as school has been let out for the summer. A few students are occupying classrooms. I try to peer into the rooms to see what they're doing, but Asher's long strides are difficult to keep up with. We continue through the halls until we approach a classroom filled with twenty or so children and their parents. The children are talking on one side of the room while the parents are on the other.

Everyone stops their conversations and focuses on the door as soon as he enters. Pleased expressions cross the parents' faces while the children run up to him.

An older woman, who appears to be in charge, ushers the children away from Asher and tells them to take their places by their instruments. They all take a stand by a cello. Their backs are to the audience, and they're facing a wall.

In front of the children, facing us, is the same instrument, double in size. Asher motions for me to take a spot, standing next to one of the parents, while he moves to the front of the room.

Asher takes his place, seated behind the cello, and looks to the kids.

"Mr. Asher! Mr. Asher!" A young girl about seven raises her hand to gather Asher's attention. "I have a special song for you."

His jaw widens. "I'd love to hear it, Jaelyn," he answers the girl with familiarity.

We're at a music class, and I'm trying to figure out if Asher is the regular teacher or a part-time volunteer.

The young girl bows down on her cello and starts to play a beautiful melody far beyond her elementary school age. She makes a few mistakes, but Asher doesn't correct her. When she concludes her musical interlude, she looks up at him with a big grin on her face. She has clearly been anxious to play that for him.

"Thank you, Jaelyn. I can tell you've been practicing." He leans forward and touches the little girl's cheek, causing her to blush.

I want to assure Jaelyn he has that effect on women of all ages.

Asher removes his leather jacket and begins a cello lesson. He's amazing. When he talks to the children, his patience and manner with them are surprising. I didn't see him as being a teacher.

With the twenty children surrounding him, Asher teaches them how to play their instruments, and while the sounds from the children in unison leave much to be desired, you can tell he has made a lot of progress with them and that they're desperate to please him. Equally impressive is the amount of parents surrounding the lesson. I wonder if they're here for their children or to steal glances of the beautiful mogul.

A tall woman leans over to me. "Isn't he amazing?"

"Yes, these parents must spend a lot of money to have Alexander Asher teach their children to play the cello."

"Oh no." She corrects me, "Mr. Asher volunteers his time every week. These are underprivileged children. This is his way of keeping them off the street."

I'm confused. "But the cello is an expensive instrument."

"All donated by Mr. Asher. He teaches a class here but funds the program in seven schools across the city."

So, this is where he is every Friday. He said he had a standing date until the concerts. These must be the kids he's having perform at the gala.

Perhaps he is for real. But why would this man, who lives his days and nights carefree, spend so much time helping children? I've seen his bio. He donates millions to children's charities. I assumed it was a publicity stunt, but seeing him with these kids, knowing he's here with them every week...you can't fake that kind of generosity.

The class ends, and the students each hug or high-five Asher. He pays attention to each child and asks them questions about their school week and if they've been good to their parents.

"I'm impressed."

"I'm glad. Come," he says, placing his hand on my elbow, escorting me back to the bike. "I have one more place I'd like to show you."

This man could ask me to go anywhere right now, and I'd follow.

chapter SIXTEEN

We drive up the West Side Highway as I listen to Snow Patrol sing about love and forgiveness. I don't know where we're going, and for the first time in a long time, I don't care. I don't care about having a plan or list to follow. I feel like I'm a teenager again. Carefree and wild.

The lesson lasted an hour, and he stayed almost as long afterward, talking to the families. He invited everyone to the concert on Labor Day weekend and is even giving them prime seating. With a theater of over two thousand seats, you'd think he'd only leave the house seats for the high rollers, but I guess, to Asher, those kids are the high rollers. They are why he's hosting this event.

It never dawned on me why we were doing this concert. I know Gabriel said the company was making money, but there had to be more to it than that. Erik said this was an Asher family event. What he really meant was, this was an Alexander Asher event.

The afternoon sun gazes down on us, and the wind from the Hudson River cools my skin. As we drive north, I feel removed from the city, but we're very much in it. We've been driving around on the motorcycle for quite some time, yet we haven't gone far at all.

We drove through Central Park and stopped to survey the area where the other concert would be held. Asher wanted to get a feel for where everything would be and look at the layout. I stayed, yet gave him some time as he made a few calls. One was to Erik to let him know of a few concerns. I tried not to eavesdrop. Instead, I just hung back and enjoyed the sun. After the park, we took a drive across town and onto the highway.

Asher exits and drives up to a place I haven't been since I was a kid on a school field trip—Grant's Tomb. Devon, his driver, is waiting for us with a large plastic bag from the gourmet market Citarella. He takes the bag, and we walk side by side down the corridor of trees, which leads to the glorious stone monument. It's amazing how a mausoleum can be so ethereal.

Taking my seat at the top of the grand staircase, American flags hanging over me, I place my hands around my knees, looking out at the harbor. It is beautiful in the afternoon light. The day has been stolen away from us, yet with the promise of a summer sunset, there's still plenty of time left before we have to go back.

Asher places the bag down and takes a seat beside me, leaning back on his elbows. His long legs stretch down the stairs as he looks up into the trees. My eyes trace his frame from his toes to his fingers, which were recently playing the most soothing melodic chant I'd ever heard.

"You play beautifully," I say.

His eyes meet mine as he tilts his head to the side and grins. "Thank you."

"Who taught you?" I ask, running my fingers through the front of my hair and tucking it behind my ear to gather it back in place. There's a slight breeze, and wisps of my hair are lightly blowing in front of my face.

"My mother." He pauses as if drawing back a sweet memory. "She was a concert cellist. Studied at Juilliard."

"Did she play professionally?"

He tilts his head down and lets out a sad smile. Shaking his head slightly, he replies, "No." He raises his head and looks back out to the river. "No. She gave up on her dream, but she never stopped loving to play. She made me practice every day. She instilled the love of music and culture into everything she did."

"Then, I take it, she would approve of your choice of meal locations," I chide.

He lets out a light laugh. "Yes. Yes, she would. My mother was somewhat of a historian. She loved history, the arts, museums, and fine food." He lowers his head away from the sunlight and trees. "Not a bad role model to have, I suppose."

"It sounds like she's a wonderful woman. Does she get to see you play often?"

"No. She passed."

"How old were you when she died?"

Asher looks at me, as if debating to answer. I can see he doesn't talk about this often.

Bending his right leg, he places his elbow on his knee. His hand travels to the back of his neck and plays with his collar. "Ten." He sighs. "My mother died on my tenth birthday."

My eyes widen as I try to bite back the tears building behind my eyes. My mind immediately goes to Jackson. Picturing my sweet, blue-eyed baby all alone. It's hard to imagine a golden child left broken from the loss of his mother. I push the thought into the back of my mind. I cannot get emotional.

"And your father?" I pry.

With his eyes fixed on the scenery below, he nods his head in affirmation that he, too, passed on. I feel like the air has been wiped from my chest.

"Don't look at me like that." He's not looking at me, yet he seems to know exactly what I'm thinking. "I'd hardly call myself an orphan. My grandfather wouldn't stand for it. His motto is, 'Never look back, only forward. Take no prisoners. Run the empire.' And that's what I've done."

When Malory told me about Alexander Asher weeks ago, I pictured a disingenuous, spoiled kid who didn't know what it was like to live in the real world. While Asher might not have wanted for anything material in his life, he has certainly known pain.

"It sounds kind of lonely, being your own empire."

His eyes dart back to me, and I know I've hit a nerve. Both his and my own. His eyes do something to me whenever they look at me. While I know nothing about him, he acts like he can see right through me. My emotions are transparent, and he's breathing them in.

"You are an enigma, Mrs. Monroe. You are the only person who doesn't seem to know a thing about me. How is that?"

"I suppose I've been preoccupied."

"I suppose you have. With your husband?"

I blink at him. "Asher, my husband is not the punch line or your defense for everything I say to you. You have to stop doing that," my voice says in a scolding manner.

He winces. "My apologies. I didn't know it bothered you so much."

"And I see I'm back to Mrs. Monroe." I lean into him. "How many defense mechanisms do you have?"

He looks dumbfounded, and I know I've just hit the bull's-eye. For a man so powerful, he has enough tells to ruin a game of poker.

Asher opens the Citarella bag and starts to unpack a simple lunch. Simple as far as what I would expect from someone of his wealth and position.

From the bag, he produces two prosciutto, eggplant, and mozzarella sandwiches on baguettes, an apple, an orange, and two small bottles of Pellegrino, each with its own cup.

Holding an apple and orange in each hand, Asher gestures for me to pick one. I choose the apple and immediately take a bite out of it. The fruit is crisp, and the juice runs down my chin. I raise the back of my wrist to my face to quickly retrieve the mess. Someone thinks this is amusing.

Seeing the mood is lighter, I try to broach the subject again. "How do you ever get to know someone then? If everyone knows everything about you, then there's no reason to have a conversation."

"When I get to know someone, particularly women, there is no conversation involved." Asher winks as he pours sparkling water into one of the cups.

"Calm down there, Casanova." I take a cup from his hand. "What do you do when you're not entertaining the women of New York?"

Bringing his legs up a step closer, Asher places the bottle on his other side. With his cup still in his hand, he turns his body back toward me and rests his elbow on his knee. "Well, you already saw my true passion—the cello. I also play the piano, but that is for very private audience."

His smile is enigmatic, and I'm pretty sure I just saw a diamond glisten in his teeth. Man, this guy has a great smile.

"I'm sure." Rolling my eyes, I take a sip. "What else do you do? Do you play any sports?"

"Uh, no."

"Why not?"

"Group sports are not my thing."

"So, you won't be playing on the company softball team?"

"That's a definite no."

"Snob."

"Meddler."

"Narcissist."

Asher takes the rest of his wine and finishes it in one gulp. "Do you want me to tell you about myself, or shall you continue to berate me with foolish names all day?"

I can't help but show my grin. "Fine. What do you do in your free time?"

"Well, I work…a lot." He lifts the orange and begins to peel away the skin. "My grandfather, as I'm sure you do know about…" he says with a wink.

I cringe at the notion that I'm the worst investigator in the world.

"My grandfather believes in hard work and only hard work." He pops an orange slice into his mouth. His lips glisten with the juice in the sun. "Yes, *all work, no play* has been the way since I was ten years old. Aside from the office, I work toward funding music programs and helping kids."

"Why?"

He takes another slice and furrows his brow, as if he doesn't understand the question. "Why all the work?"

"Why the music and the kids?" I bite my lip, thinking of how to deliver my next statement. "You don't seem like the caring, giving type." I wince.

He bites back, "That was mean."

I smile sweetly. "That was honest. You said you liked honest."

He peers down at me. He's only inches beside me, yet he feels like he's mountains above me. "I do, but it doesn't mean I like to hear it."

Asher might not like it, but I might not get this opportunity again.

"So, why the music programs, the grand concert in the park to raise money for music education programs? Is it a big tax write-off?"

A frown creases his face. I know I've hurt his feelings.

"I'm sorry," I say quickly.

"Don't be. I know that's how my grandfather sees it, but the motivation behind all of it is completely personal."

"Can I know the reason?"

He thinks about this for a moment. "No."

"Why not?"

"I have spoken entirely too much about myself today. We're done talking about me. Now, about you…"

Slowly unwrapping my sandwich, I look down at my lap and try to think of something interesting to say about myself. I don't play any instruments or have my own charitable foundations. I don't own a company, nor am I well versed in culture, history, or can play an instrument.

"You are fascinating to me. You know this. I want to know you better."

I take a bite of my sandwich and ponder what I could possibly talk about. The truth is...

"I am so boring; I can't think of a thing to say."

Asher places his fingers on my chin and raises it to meet his gaze. "Fascinating." The singular word departs from his lips.

I could answer that comment with a single word myself—*mesmerizing*.

"Okay then." He chides, "If you aren't going to freely give up any information, I will ask the questions."

I open my mouth to begin to protest, but Asher answers my concern in time, "I promise not to ask a single question about your husband."

My shoulders relax, and I nod in approval.

"Since being friends seems to interest you so much, who are your friends?"

"Well, Malory is probably my best friend, although I don't see her that often or talk to her as much as I'd like."

Come to think of it, she's a weak excuse for a best friend. Lately, every time I'm around her, I'm either insulted by or uncomfortable with one of her comments.

"Malory is your best friend?" This time, Asher is shocked.

"Yeah. Well, I guess. I left my childhood friends when I was thirteen and moved to upstate New York. I didn't keep any friends from that part of my life. I went to college in Maryland. All my friends went on to live in Virginia, California, Florida. Not too many came to Manhattan, and the ones who did, well, they led a different lifestyle than the one I wanted."

"Park Avenue princesses?" Asher nods in understanding. "I know a few of those."

"I tried city living, but I guess I just don't fit in. I don't have the clothes or the attitude to keep up. I always felt inferior in some way. I thought I wanted the house on Long Island, kids, vacations…something simple." What am I saying? "Am I rambling?"

"So, what about the women of Long Island? Do you have any friends there?"

"No." I swallow another bite of my sandwich. "I don't fit in there either. I'm not built to be a coupon-cutting, high-waisted-jeans-wearing woman who stays home all day." I take a breath. "Truth is, I've never felt more displaced in my life. It's like I'm riding on the border of two countries, yet I have citizenship in neither. It's a terrible feeling." One that, up until this moment, I didn't realize.

Asher takes in what I just said and digests it. He also seems to understand I'm evaluating these feelings as well.

Thankfully, he changes the topic. "You said you traveled a lot with your dad. What did he do?"

"He was a baseball player," I say matter-of-factly.

"Like, a Major League Baseball player?"

"Yep," I say, taking a final bite of my baguette.

I watch Asher's face out the corner of my eye as he studies me, and I can see the wheels in motion.

"Is your dad Catch Grayson?"

I swallow and nod at him.

"Really? This entire time, I've had Catch Grayson's daughter working for me, and I didn't even know it."

"Since you're not a sports guy, I would have assumed it wouldn't matter if my dad were Mickey Mantle."

"I might not like to play company softball, but I am definitely a baseball fan. I am a red-blooded male, you know," he chides.

As if I haven't noticed his maleness.

"Dad played in Texas and then for the Reds before we settled here in New York, when he played for the Mets. He was...amazing."

"And your mom?"

"Gwendolyn? She's flighty and immature yet quite possibly the most charismatic person I've ever met."

I look up to catch golden eyes staring into mine.

"She sounds like her daughter."

Little does he know, I am nothing like my mother.

I feel really uncomfortable and unbearably shy at this very moment. I rest my face in my hand and look out over the harbor. I respect that he doesn't try to pry more about my story, as I did to him. There is something natural to this relationship. There's a level of understanding that we so easily have for one another.

"Tell me something no one knows about you."

He arches his eyebrows. I believe he's intrigued by my question.

He takes a moment before answering, "I don't like sleeping alone."

I raise a brow.

"Not in that way." His voice is condescending. Asher runs his hands through his golden hair and clarifies, "I don't like to be alone."

I redden, thinking of how I have so clearly misjudged this man. Perhaps I can help him, guide him. He doesn't have a woman in his life, and maybe he needs a motherly figure. He hasn't had one since he was just a boy. My stomach sinks at the thought.

"Don't read too much into it. I am a successful man because of my past. I'm okay with it," he says in an authoritative voice. It's not a recommendation. It's an order.

And because he said it, I can't help but want to read way too much into it. For someone who portrays himself to be confident and controlled, he has a vulnerability that is masked by a dark suit and handsome face.

Alexander Asher has just peeled away a layer of himself, and I want to know what else is beneath the skin.

So, of course I need to know. "Why did you tell me that then?"

Asher's eyes search my face, as if trying to figure out the answer. "I don't share my feelings with anyone. I can't trust anyone. But I trust you. I don't know why, but I trust you, and I like talking to you. This is new for me, so please don't make me regret opening up to you."

"I won't. I like spending time with you." I mean it. "I'm glad we're friends."

"Me, too." He stands and holds out his hand to help me up. "Now, let me get you home before your husband starts to worry."

The ride back down Henry Hudson is slower on the return. Asher seems to be savoring the last moments of our perfect day. Sarah Brightman sings of Eden in our ears. I wonder if his iPod is on shuffle or if he purposefully picked this song of best friends and enemies and never trying to go too far. I decide not to analyze it and enjoy the sweet operatic.

Asher offers to bring me home, but I can't bear the thought of my neighbors seeing me on a motorcycle, not that I know any of them. Getting dropped off at the office is out of the question. Lord knows the gossip I would endure.

We pull up to Penn Station, so I can catch the train home. I climb off his bike and thank him with a nod. Asher pumps the throttle, and with one smooth action, he has the motor running and sets off down Seventh Avenue.

So much for not analyzing everything in my life. I now have a long train ride to think about…everything.

Asher was amazing with the kids. I could tell they loved him with the way their eyes lit up when they saw him. I felt honored to be there with him.

And then there was the personal side. Alexander the man. I can't help but recall how natural the afternoon felt. He shared stories of his childhood. Being an orphan. It all sounded so sad. He admires his grandfather and took the tools he had been born with and skills he'd acquired to amass his fortune. It was just beautiful. Yet something in his words let me know he substitutes his grandfather's approval for love.

I want to know more about Asher, and I'm no longer worried about what that might insinuate.

Alexander Asher can have any woman's heart. He doesn't want or need mine. He dates models and famous actresses. He is seen with the daughters of the wealthy, and I'm sure he has a few prospects lined up. He's probably dating someone right now.

What could he possibly want with me? I'm a wife and a mother. I'm old news. Used. I have nothing to offer him.

No, this is merely a new friendship, which I am more than happy to have. It pays to have friends in high places.

chapter SEVENTEEN

"*This* is your boss?" Gwen looks at the cover of *New York Magazine* and quickly opens it.

Ever the dutiful grandmother, she came over to spend time with Jackson. And by spending time with Jackson, I mean, she's lounging on my outdoor chaise, reading a magazine, and drinking a martini.

"Yes, Mother." I feign indifference.

We're in our backyard on yet another beautiful summer Sunday. So far, we've had gorgeous weekends this year. Makes up for the crappy winter we had. On days like today, when everyone is outside, you can hear the laughter and the noise coming from other people's backyards.

Gabriel is standing at the barbecue on the far end of the stone patio, wearing khaki pants and a pale blue button-down.

"Honey, he is…he's just so…" Gwen is at a loss for words.

"Dreamy?" Gabriel teases while flipping burgers.

I roll my eyes at him. "He is not *dreamy*. That term should be reserved only for fourteen-year-old girls talking about A.C. Slater or anyone in *Teen Beat*."

Walking over to the grill, I hold the plate as Gabriel takes chicken off the metal racks.

"Asher is…" I look for the words. "He's…" Exotic, mesmerizing, Apollo-esque. "He's…okay-looking, I guess."

Gwen doesn't even look up from the magazine. "This man is what fantasies are made of."

I think I see a little drool seeping from her mouth.

I walk the plate of chicken to the table, and as I pass behind Gwen, I catch a glimpse of the two-page spread of Alexander Asher. I stop in my tracks.

He looks good. *Really good.* Who would expect him not to?

On the left is a photo of him in his office. From the window, you can see all of Manhattan with a spectacular view of the city. He's standing in front of the glass, wearing a black pinstripe suit with a crisp shirt and black tie. I've seen this look on him before. It must have been taken the day I trapped him in the elevator.

With one hand in his pocket and the other on his lapel, he looks commanding, pensive, and smoldering. It's the exact Asher I thought I knew at the beginning of the summer. Now, I know so many more sides. The sad Asher who lost his mother, the grandson who lives his life to win over his grandfather's attention, the giver of music, the teacher, the smart-ass, and even the nice Asher. There are so many sides to him that you can't see in this picture.

My favorite is the messy eater. I've had four other meetings with Asher since our first official one in my office. All have been in his office and all have been over takeout. The man wasn't lying; he ruins a lot of ties. I only get an hour or so of his time, and it's a shame that we spend so much of it talking about everything other than the event because I leave without getting any work done.

The good news is, I haven't had a single dream about him in weeks.

"What does he have…yellow eyes?" Gwen asks.

"They're a deep gold. Like the color of honey." The words come out of my mouth before I realize it.

Gwen turns around and gives me an inquisitive look. "I didn't think you would have noticed."

I back away from the magazine. "They're hard not to notice, but they're nothing compared to Gabriel's." I smile over at him. Hopefully, he didn't catch my comment about Asher's eyes.

He's looking over at us indifferently.

"That's right, Gabriel. You have the market cornered on beautiful eyes." Gwen looks up from the magazine and gives me a wink. Nice save. "I'm especially grateful you passed them on to my grandson."

Thank you, Mom.

With the spatula still in his hand, he saunters over to Gwen. He stops to look over her shoulder, appraising the man in the photo. He knows more about the Asher family than I do. Clearly, he knows what Asher looks like.

"He's not too bad." Gabriel walks back to the grill, shrugging his shoulders. "And Photoshop does a lot."

"Are you jealous?" Gwen asks, swinging her body around to gauge Gabriel's expression. She turns to me and says, "That's good. Very good."

Gabriel laughs off Gwen's comment and returns to cooking. He knows he has nothing to worry about. Doesn't he?

"Pay her no mind. My mother loves drama," I tease.

"Say what you will, but it's good for a couple to be a little jealous." She looks up from the magazine. "You know, when your father was touring in the majors, I would hear all these stories of women throwing themselves at him. Was I jealous? You bet your ass I was.

"But instead of getting all worked up," she continues, "I just made sure your father had something to remember me by before he left the house."

"Like what?" As I ask the question, I look over at Gabriel, who has his head tilted to the side with his hands thrown up in the air, as if asking me, *What do you think she gave him?*

Realization dawns on my face.

"Gross! Seriously, Mom, keep these comments to yourself."

Gabriel laughs and places the chicken out for lunch.

Gwen reluctantly puts down the magazine and walks over to the table. "So, what is on the agenda for this afternoon? When Jackson wakes up from his nap, I thought we could go to the mall. I need some new clothes and the one up in the sticks has the most hideous choices." She takes a seat across from me.

I load my plate with chicken and salad. I should pass on the burgers.

"Mom, your Macy's has the same crap our Macy's does."

"Rubbish! You have more department stores here, and there's even valet. Trust me, your mall is nicer." Gwen takes a sip of the apple martini he prepared. "Gabriel, this is delicious."

"That's why you love me, Gwen." He picks up his beer, and the two of them cheers.

"If you get sloshed, then there's no shopping for you," I say condescendingly, pointing my finger in her direction. "I hate the mall as it is. The last thing I need is a lush of a mother falling into the clothing racks."

She waves me off. "Hush! You're so high-strung. When did you stop knowing how to have fun?" She takes another sip.

Me? I'm a ton of fun! Aren't I?

"You two have a great time at the mall. Besides, Kat needs to pick up something for the gala." Gabriel takes a seat next to me, draping his arm around the back of my chair.

Ever since Malory told me I had to wear something formal, I've sort of been blocking it out. I can't just wear any old thing. It might be a big production, but the concert is indeed a gala, and I'll be representing Asher. I have to wear something spectacular.

I nod in agreement. "Let's go to Bloomingdale's."

He whistles through his teeth. "Breaking out the big guns."

Oh.

"No. I'm kidding." He places his arm around my shoulders and kisses my hair. "You two have fun. You deserve it, baby. My working girl."

He can be so sweet sometimes.

"Just don't spend too much."

And there it is.

Does the man realize he's sending me shopping with Gwendolyn Grayson? The woman was born to shop.

Ω

Once at the mall, we valet in high fashion and saunter into Bloomingdale's. Gwen is well ahead of me as I stroll Jackson through the racks of clothing. Gabriel wanted me to leave him home, but since being at work all week, I cherish all the time I can get with my sweet angel on the weekends.

I find Gwen in the women's section, looking at a table display of sweaters. She's holding up a powder-blue crewneck sweater against her chest.

"Aren't these gorgeous?"

"Mom, it's the middle of the summer. It's a little warm for cashmere."

"Honey, it's never too warm for cashmere," she admonishes. "I'm buying three!" she exclaims, picking up a blue and a green for herself and then grabbing another.

"Who's the gray one for?"

"You, dear. You need a little luxury," she says, tossing the gray piece of luxury at me.

I spin Jackson's stroller and meander through the racks.

Gwen stops at every rack, remarking on how gorgeous each outfit is. "Look at the cut on this," and, "Isn't this color just divine?"

When I said the woman was born to shop, I meant it. How she affords it all, I'll never understand. My dad had a lucrative career, but she shops like she's a Rockefeller.

Grabbing one item after the next, Gwen takes her armful of clothes into the dressing room, and I have a seat on a bench, waiting for her to come out.

Gwen tries on a series of ensembles. If she's tried on twenty, she hasn't tried on enough.

After forty minutes, Jackson gets antsy.

"Mom, I'm going to push Jackson around a little. He's tired of sitting still."

"Okay, dear," she calls from inside the dressing room.

Grabbing my purse, I stand and start to move.

"Just real quick," she interrupts my departure. "What do you think of this one?"

She's standing in the doorway, wearing a short-sleeved, cowl-neck black top and leopard-print pants. As wild as they are, the pants are tasteful. The gold belt, on the other hand, is a bit…much.

"It's perfect. Definitely get that one."

I push the stroller out of the women's department and browse through the makeup section before stopping at one of the jewelry counters. I enjoy looking at the gemstones under the twinkling lights. As I admire a beautiful bangle bracelet, a scent permeates my senses.

Tobacco…and vanilla.

I freeze in place.

He's here.

Hastily, I turn around and scan the room for Asher, but he is nowhere in sight. Like a bloodhound on the hunt, I follow the delicious scent to see where he went.

"Would you like to try some? Perhaps for the man in your life?" a salesgirl calls over to me.

The pesky salesgirl is on a scent-selling mission. "Here. We have these great scent cards." She takes the fragrance, sprays it onto a rectangular piece of card stock, and fans it out in front of her.

I try to walk away, but she's shoving the fragrance card in my face. Reluctantly, I take it from her and start to stroll away.

But here it is.

In my hand.

I raise the card to my nose and savor the delicious fragrance.

It's his damn cologne.

Turning around, I head back to the salesgirl and look at the black-and-gold bottle in her hand. The man wears Tom Ford.

"I'll take a bottle of that," I say, pulling my wallet out from my purse. Yes, my own personal Alexander Asher in a bottle.

"There you are!" Gwen pops up beside me. "What are you buying?" she asks, scanning the counter. "Cologne for Gabriel. How sweet. Let me smell."

Gwen picks up the tester bottle and sprays it on her arm. She raises her wrist to her nose and takes in that heavenly scent that's had me going wild all summer.

"This is divine. Smells like an old English gentlemen's club. Very heady. Very male." Gwen has just described the man more than the fragrance.

"That will be two hundred fifteen dollars," the salesgirl chirps.

My jaw falls to the floor. "For two ounces?"

Of course Asher would have the most expensive cologne in the whole goddamn store.

"It's one-point-seven ounces, but you can't put a price on this kind of luxury." Pesky beams.

I hand over my credit card and glance over at my mother.

"Don't look at me. I just spent four hundred dollars on cashmere!" Gwen saunters off.

With my bottle of Alexander Asher and my mother, who now smells like him, we make our way up to the women's evening gown section.

The gowns are stunning. Row after row, there is one more beautiful than the other. I don't know where to start, so Gwen grabs several and makes a room for me. I scan the price tags to make sure she's not going overboard. The prices are fine, but the sizes are all wrong.

"Mom, these are too small." I hold up the tag in my hand.

"No, Kathryn, your clothes are too big." Her eyes look me up and down. "You've lost a lot of weight. Trust me; they'll fit."

I roll my eyes and head into the dressing room. The first is a pale pink A-line that, to my surprise, fits. Maybe I have lost weight. I don't know how. I feel like all I do is eat with Malory.

I open the door to show Gwen the pink dress, and she shakes her head in disapproval.

Next, I try on a strapless plum satin number. It's slimming and sophisticated. I love it! Opening the door, I look out for Gwen.

"What do you think?" I beam.

Gwen tilts her head to the side and twists her mouth. "Not for you."

"I like it!"

"Kat, it does nothing for you. It's too boring. Try on the red one," she directs.

Fine! I slam the dressing room door like I'm a fourteen-year-old.

Gwen lets out a laugh. "You'll never change!"

The red dress has a two-part neckline, where I get my head stuck in twice before finally figuring it out. I'm so aggravated by the time I get it on properly that I automatically hate the dress, no matter how it looks.

I open the door to Gwen standing in front of me, holding an ivory dress.

"Try this on."

"You haven't even looked at the one I have on!" I huff.

"I hate it. Here." She shoves the dress in my hand. "This is the one."

I hold up the ivory dress. "I am not wearing white. It's not my wedding day."

"Put it on." Gwen walks away.

Flashbacks of my prom, formals, and even wedding-dress shopping pop in my head. The woman is maddening to shop with.

And just like with my prom dress, formal, and wedding dress…she is right.

The gown is exquisite, worldly, and makes me look like a goddess. It is a Theia form-fitted number with a low, soft V-neckline and spaghetti straps. The silk fabric clings to my body but hangs delicately as it swoons down my hips into an elegant cascade of petals. The hemline drapes gracefully on the floor. I look like a goddess walking on a bed of floating white rose petals.

Ivory on ivory, it is the epitome of classic. I'm in love.

I open the door to allow Gwen to gloat, but she isn't there.

"Mom?"

Picking up the bottom of the dress, barefoot, I sneak out of the dressing room. *Where did she go?*

As I'm about to turn around back into the dressing room, I hear a familiar voice.

"He wanted to spend time together tonight, but I was already at the mall. I mean, he can't ask me to spend time with him at the last minute. A girl needs to pamper!" She lets out a laugh.

Hiding behind a rack of clothing, I eavesdrop on the conversation.

"You have to see him. He's gorgeous! And his body is to die for. Yeah, yeah. We run together in the park. Yes, totally hot bod. It makes it all worth it."

What is worth it? Who is she running with? And is she talking to herself?

I slide down to the floor and squat low, so she doesn't see me. I have to get a glimpse.

Putting my hands on all fours, I crawl around the rack. Shirtsleeves and price tags hit me in the face as I peer around the side of the rack.

It's *her*.

The lioness!

The girl from the park, who knows my husband and calls my son Jack, is on the phone and looking at a display of undergarments. Very sexy undergarments, I might add.

What's her name? Beth, Brie, Bailey...

"We are seeing each other Tuesday. I know, right?" she continues. "I have to find something killer to wear. We are going to..." She starts to walk away.

I can't hear. I crawl closer.

I'm about to round the corner when I'm interrupted by a pair of feet. I don't know those feet. They are clad in black Aerosoles. Cowering, I hesitantly gaze up. I've been caught by a salesgirl.

"Excuse me, miss. May I ask why you're crawling on the ground in a thousand-dollar dress?"

I slowly creep up to a standing position.

"I, um..." My mouth goes dry.

She crosses her arms and taps her foot. This day just can't get any worse.

"There you are!" Gwen emerges by my side, holding Jackson. "Oh, don't you look beautiful!"

My scowling eyes meet hers. "A thousand dollars?"

"If you don't like it, don't get it," Gwen suggests nonchalantly.

I turn to the salesgirl. Her lips are set in a hard line, and she's raising an eyebrow. There is no use arguing with either of them.

"I'll take the dress," I mumble beneath my breath.

The salesgirl gives me a smug look. "I'll ring you up."

As she walks away, Gwen hands me a shoebox. "Here, these will look perfect with the dress!"

I look at the expensive, high-end label on the box and shake my head. "I think we've done enough damage."

"Try them on, Kathryn. Listen to your mother." Gwen tries to shove the shoebox in my arms.

"No." I shove it back.

"Kat," she admonishes.

"No." I push the box away again.

"Kat—"

"I said, no!" I shout.

Gwen's eyes widen in surprise.

"Is that Jack?" an excited voice calls from beyond the rack.

Are you fucking kidding me?

The lioness pops up her bubbly head and leans over to give Jackson a kiss.

Gwen looks at her and smiles. "A friend! Hello, dear. I'm Kathryn's mother, Gwendolyn. You can call me Gwen." She holds out her hand.

"Hi, Gwen." She shakes my mother's hand. "I'm Becca."

Becca!

The lioness who was just on the phone—talking about, who I presume is, *my* husband—is kissing *my* baby and shaking hands with *my* mother while I'm standing in a thousand-dollar dress I just dragged across the floor.

I grab the shoebox from my mother's hand. "Give me the damn shoes!"

chapter EIGHTEEN

"What do you mean, you think Gabriel is cheating?"

I'm a chickenshit. I can't talk to Gabriel about it. Mostly because there has been zero privacy in my house since Gwen is staying for a few days. Lord knows I can't talk to my mother about this.

Even if I did talk to him, if he's having an affair, he's not goanna say, *since you asked, yes. Yes, I am having an affair with the blonde with big boobs from the park. And, yes, she did buy sexy lingerie to wear for me. Thank you for asking.*

Instead, I held my breath until I saw Malory, my sounding board.

"Part of me thinks he is, and part of me knows better. I mean, this is Gabriel we're talking about. It would be so out of character. He's one of the good guys…right?" I ramble, disgusted that I'm even thinking this. My foot is shaking a mile a minute, and I've chewed through two pen caps this morning alone.

"Yes, Gabriel is definitely one of the good guys." Malory tries to comfort me, her hand leaning across the desk to touch my arm. It's an odd gesture for Malory. It seems forced.

"But you say it all the time. He is good-looking and successful. I mean, why wouldn't women be thrusting themselves at him all day long?" My head falls in my hands. There is a mountain of work on my desk to be done, but I can't concentrate. "There is this girl in the park…"

Malory scowls. "What do you mean, this girl in the park?"

"Blonde, perfect, and well acquainted with my husband and son." The thought makes me shiver. "And to top it off, I heard her talking to someone about this guy she's seeing."

I let out a breath of air. I feel defeated. "There was something she said. She made a reference to the guy making it all worth it. Like there was an obstacle they had to overcome." My fear is that the obstacle is me.

"Tell me more about the girl. What does she look like? Is she young?"

"I'd say early twenties. She was—" The ringing phone interrupts me. I put my finger up to Malory. "Hold that thought."

I pick up the phone. "Hello?"

"This is Cecelia from Mr. Asher's office. He's requested your company. Shall I alert him of your availability?"

Is this the right time to be dealing with Asher?

He's your boss, Kat. Yes.

"Yes. I'll be up in five minutes." I hang up.

Malory's black eyes question my phone call.

"Asher has summoned me," I answer her unspoken question.

"Huh," she replies with a raised eyebrow.

"Huh?"

"Yeah, huh. Shall I say more?" Her lips fix into a smirk.

"You've said enough." I stand, grabbing my files for the gala. I'm sure he wants to go over the permits and timeline.

"If he's having an affair, you want to catch him in the act. Otherwise, he'll just cover his tracks," Malory says, and I nod in agreement. I should be taking notes. "Do you have any proof of this alleged affair?" she questions.

"No." There is comfort in that fact.

"Whatever you do, do not—I repeat, *do not*—talk to Gabriel about this. We need to come up with a strategy first." Malory stands and smooths out her onyx dress. "Did you drive in today?"

"Yes. Why? Do you need to borrow it for some reason?"

She grabs her bag and thinks for a second before changing her mind. "No. I just wanted to know if you had a train to catch. When you get back, I still have questions for you. I want to know who this younger other woman is."

I stall at the door before answering, "If my husband is sleeping with another woman, does it really matter how young she is?"

Malory stares at me blankly as I walk out of the room.

$$\Omega$$

Upstairs in Asher's office, I take a seat and stare at the big-eyed fish. They're so naive, thinking their perfect little aquarium is a paradise just for them when, in reality, they have no idea there is an entire ocean out there. They only know what they've been lied to about.

The large door behind me opens, and a dark-skinned woman with hazel eyes and a tiny frame exits Asher's office. She's buttoning the top button of her blouse as she saunters over to the elevator. She should at least have the decency to put herself together inside the office.

"Ms. Grayson." Cecelia draws my attention away from my staring. "Mr. Asher will see you now."

"Close the door," Asher calls over from the bar area.

I compromise and leave the door slightly ajar, as I do every time I'm in his office.

"Afraid someone might think we're being…oh, what's the word? Inappropriate?" Golden eyes leer at me.

"Did you enjoy your twinkie?" I say, referring to the woman who just left Asher's office. I hope he can hear the disgust in my voice.

"That," he says, pointing toward the door, "was not a twinkie. That was Simone Davenport."

"Do Simone Davenports not have the same cream filling as the rest?" I sneer.

Asher waves me into the room and motions toward one of the barstools. "Simones are part of the business world. Daughters of men with a lot of money and power. So, if you fuck over a Simone, you'd better have your balls in a vise." He makes a mock cringing face, like he was just kicked in the balls. "But we do have an arrangement. We see to each other's needs."

He is so full of himself.

"All men are swine."

"Only the good ones." His chiseled chin rises as he holds up a glass. "Drink?"

There is one thing to say about Alexander Asher. He doesn't hide who he is. Sure, he has secrets. But women know what they're getting from him. They know he's a cad and noncommittal. He doesn't lie, and he certainly doesn't sneak behind anyone's back.

The thought is lightly refreshing. I could use a good dose of honesty right about now.

I let out a deep breath and toss back my shoulders, making my way toward the bar. "I don't drink on school days."

"Only school nights?" he teases.

"That was a special occasion."

"Heather's birthday was a special occasion? Have you two become buddies or something?" Asher lifts the rocks glass to his lips and takes a sip. The alcohol must burn a little because his throat clenches.

"As much as I'd love to banter back and forth with you, I have a gala to produce."

"Right," he says, putting the glass down on the bar. "I have something to show you."

He is giddy with excitement. It's so un-Asher that it makes me smile for the first time today.

Asher walks over to his desk. Propped up against the side is a large poster-sized picture. He lifts it with both hands and turns it around. He is wearing his megawatt smile in anticipation of my reaction.

I can't help but let out a small laugh. In his hands is an original vintage movie poster for the film *It Happened in Brooklyn*, starring Peter Lawford and, my namesake, Kathryn Grayson.

"I thought we could hang it in the conference room," he proposes, looking down at the poster in his hands and then back up at me, waiting to see how I'll react.

I can't argue with him about buying it for me because he didn't. He bought it for the office. That's acceptable. I won't admit it out loud, but I kind of like that he bought it because of me. It's a sweet gesture.

"It will look great in the conference room. I approve. Now, let's talk about the gala."

"Yes." He places the frame back on the ground and suddenly becomes very serious. "The gala. Come, take a seat."

We walk over to the table, and Asher holds out a chair for me. The swell of every emotion dancing earlier in my belly—from anger to excitement and absolute anxiousness—is settling. Maybe it's the scent of vanilla or the way his voice has this melodic sound to it, but I am undeniably relaxed in his company.

Crazy, right? I know.

Right now, I'm a far cry from the anxious twit I was this morning.

Working together, we have a commonality in this job that puts us on the same playing field. When we went to the tomb, we shared stories of family and honesty reserved for intimate friendships. I feel like he's known me forever. We've come so far in a short amount of time.

Maybe Asher can give me some advice. Malory is no use.

"Can I ask you a question?"

"Of course."

I twist the words around in my head for a minute. I don't want to give too much away. "If you believe something in your gut but you have no physical proof it is what your mind thinks it is…do you…"

My eyes feel heavy as tears try to inch out from behind them. I swallow them back to the point that my throat feels like it's going to burn.

My eyes betray me by letting go of a single tear.

"Kathryn." His warm, strong hands grab mine and hold tight. He tries to catch my gaze, but I sit, staring at the empty space around me. "Look at me."

Tentatively, I raise my head and compose myself, the drop falling down my cheek. "I'm sorry. I feel so foolish." My head falls again in embarrassment as I wipe away the solo tear with the back of my hand.

"Never say you're sorry to me." He dips his head until it's within my gaze and holds his eyes to mine, forcing me to raise my head along with his. He's not touching me physically, yet he can control me with just the look of his eyes. "And never lower your beautiful face."

"You never call me Kathryn." I let out a shy smile.

"Only when I'm not mad at you."

"Very funny."

"Listen"—his voice is low—"I don't know why you're distressed, but I can tell you this. This business, everything is numbers and bottom lines. But sometimes, something might look great on paper. Hell, it might look like a fucking cakewalk. But if my gut says it's wrong, then I walk away.

"The same goes for when I know I should be doing something about it," he continues. "If I know it's right, if I feel it's right, then I have to do it or else it's all meaningless." His eyes look to mine for understanding.

I try to comprehend his words. "What do you do if the issue at hand is personal? If it's not business?"

"Then, I follow my heart. I'm impulsive that way."

"I was afraid you'd say that." My breath leaves my body.

"Listen, the world isn't all black and white. Sometimes, it's…gray, Gray."

I smile reticently, my body at ease and my mind at rest. "Are you mocking me?"

His lips cock into a crooked smile. "I believe I am."

My heart knows I'm going entirely overboard. My brain knows what it saw and heard, but what was it I thought I saw or heard?

When did I become so insecure? Perhaps I always have been, yet Gabriel has never given me the opportunity to see just how insecure I am over him. He's always been so attentive. His world has revolved around me. Am I being so self-indulgent that I can't imagine him having another life aside from the one I'm in? He's a hardworking man. I can't be so jealous of the time he puts into his career. Isn't that exactly what I asked him not to do with me? I wanted to have a staple of my own, a place where I was important and productive outside of our marriage.

And that stupid, pesky blonde from the park? Gabriel's a nice guy. He makes friends easily. Always has, always will. It's fine that he runs with her. I have lunch with Asher, and there's nothing indecent going on here.

As for that conversation I heard in the store, I must have misheard. My imagination runs away from me sometimes. Gabriel is a good man. He's my man. I can't believe I almost let Malory help me dig myself into a deeper hole of despair. When, here, Asher is being the voice of reason.

When I pull my thoughts back to the now, Asher is looking at me with a peculiar mix of intensity and contentment.

"Thank you," he breathes.

"For what?"

"Confiding in me. It's new for me. I like it." His voice is low.

"You're a good friend," I whisper.

"I try."

A beautiful piece of artwork hanging on the wall over Asher's shoulder catches my eye. A jeweled gold cross—adorned with emerald, sapphire, and citrine stones—lies against a black backdrop. The alpha and omega symbols hang from the arms of the cross. Asher follows my gaze.

"It's called crux gemmata," he explains, looking at the early medieval art. "Do you see the tree in the center of the cross? It symbolizes the story of Adam and Eve. The first original sin."

"It's stunning." My eyes meet his again.

"Feel better?"

"Surprisingly, yes." A grin crosses my face.

"You have a beautiful smile, Gray."

Breaking the intense eye contact, I rise from the table. "Enough with the compliments. I think we've crossed enough lines this afternoon."

Asher swiftly rises. "Don't start with that again."

I hold my hand up in protest. "No. You misunderstood. I'm not admonishing you. Thank you. I mean it. I feel much better."

"You should." His words are sincere. "You have me."

I do.

When I'm back to reality on floor twenty-four, my redhead is barely seen over the ever-growing display of white roses.

"Do you have any stationery?" I ask.

She hands me an envelope and a notecard emblazoned with the Asher signature and omega logo.

I take it to my office, scribble a note and seal the envelope before placing it in the small Bloomingdale's bag

I have in my purse. I never took it out from this weekend. Frankly, I had no idea what I was going to do with the cologne.

I walk back to Trish's desk and hand her the bag.

"Please deliver this to Mr. Asher's office. You can leave it with Cecelia."

Ever the eager beaver, Trish grabs the bag and heads toward the elevator to make the delivery.

Stopping for a moment, I lean over Trish's desk and smell the delicious white roses laced with tobacco and vanilla. Tranquility swims through my bloodstream.

Turning on my heel, I head back to my office with a foolish grin on my face. My office is still bare. Its stark white walls and spacious furniture might seem cold, but this little space has become my home away from home.

I don't believe I have anything personal in here.

Then I realize I do.

Bending down under my desk, I grab the black umbrella. I hold it by its beautiful white pearl handle. It really is pretty. The sight of it elicits a fond memory. I can't believe, just two months ago, I thought this man was crude and wildly inappropriate. It's odd to think he has become one of my best friends.

Maybe Gabriel was right. I do need more friends.

chapter NINETEEN

My desk has become a paper land mine. For a job that is so creative, there is an awful lot of paperwork that goes into it.

We have a production meeting at eleven, so I came in nice and early to prepare for it. I feel good today. Today is a new day. I'm going to follow my heart. And my heart says, my husband loves me.

I woke this morning draped in two hundred pounds of Gabriel. His hair is getting a touch longer than usual, and it brushed against my face as he woke me up with soft kisses and a little tickle. We didn't have the opportunity for more because Jackson was up and ready for some attention as well. From the bed, I admired Gabriel's backside as he undressed for the shower. It was a beautiful sight to see.

Stepping out of bed, I nearly slipped on a magazine. I lifted it up to see the cover with Asher's picture. It was the same one Gwen had been reading this weekend. Gabriel must have fallen asleep while reading it.

The phone rings.

Shaking off the memory of this morning, I answer it in my most professional producer voice, "Kathryn Grayson."

"There is a delivery here for you. Shall I bring it to your office?" Trish is on the other end.

"No. I'll be right there."

Trish has been working hard under Heather. Between that and answering the main phone, signing for deliveries, and keeping this place in order, she has more important things to do than deliver my package.

The display of white roses is extra obnoxious today. Asher is really getting carried away. Sitting next to them is a package with a large red bow on top.

"Looks like someone sent you a present." Trish beams. "Can I watch you open it?"

As I have nothing to hide, I allow Trish to stand by while I unwrap the silky red ribbon of the large white pastry box.

I open the lid and find packages of, as the slogan goes, the "golden sponge cake with creamy filling."

Asher can be very funny.

"Who would send you a box of Twinkies?" Trish's face is twisted.

I partake in the second lie I've ever told this girl. "Must be from the Hostess Brands people." I feign being confused. "Twinkie?" I offer.

Trish grabs the cream-filled delicacy and smiles.

Walking back toward the office, I open the card that came with the package. I didn't want to open it in front of Trish.

The note is short and sweet.

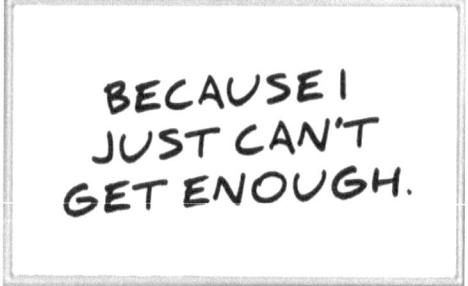

No signature.

I smile inwardly and leave the box on my desk. It's almost eleven, so I gather my notebook and files and head to the conference room.

In the conference room, Erik, Malory, and I take seats next to each other, facing the wall of vintage advertisements, while Harvey, Gretchen, and Heather sit across from us.

As I take my seat, I look up and see the vintage movie poster Asher purchased hanging proudly. Kathryn Grayson looks ethereal under the handsome Lawford.

Everyone seems to have their portion of production underway. Erik has been working with his crew to secure equipment and make sure they can capture every aspect of the Central Park concert for viewers at home. He is also planning on setting up a crew at the Lincoln Center gala. It won't air the same night, but they might be able to sell it as a special down the road. He's giving one of the tech guys the opportunity to direct. It sounds like a great idea.

Malory has sold the rights to the broadcast and is packing the gala with an elite crowd who are paying thousands of dollars to attend.

Pressure's on. This thing had better be perfect.

Heather, as evil as she is, really has her shit together. Her concert is planned out, vendor contracts signed, timeline and logistics clear. Her speeches and dialogue throughout the program are all in review stages. She's hired a well-known name in radio to be the announcer, and she has an even more well-known late-night personality ready to host the entire event. That's really smart.

Asher approved another television personality to host my event as well, but he's not nearly as funny, and his people are a disaster to work with. I look down at my production notes. I have many loose ends. If I had Trish working with me, I'd be as far ahead as Heather is.

Harvey is going over the scripts for the Central Park concert when Gretchen's eyes shift to the glass wall behind me. Heather notices Gretchen's distraction and follows her gaze.

"Who is that?" Heather's doe eyes widen. She nearly foams at the mouth.

Malory and I turn around to see a man with dark, wavy hair, an athletic build, and navy-blue eyes behind the glass, looking for, what I presume is, my office.

Why is Gabriel here?

I turn to Erik. "If you'll excuse me, that's my husband."

Erik nods in permission as Heather chimes, "You've got to be kidding me."

Malory scowls back at Heather. "What bothers you more—the fact that she gets to leave the meeting or that McDreamy over there is here to see her and not you?"

Malory's mad, though I'm not a hundred percent sure it's directed solely toward Heather.

I exit the conference room as fast as possible.

Gabriel sees me through the glass panel and relaxes.

"What are you doing here?" I guide him down the hall to my office.

"I was in the area and thought I'd stop by and see this fancy office of yours. Besides, I know you love surprises."

He looks handsome in his business suit, his blue tie bringing out his eyes. No wonder Heather nearly convulsed.

"Thank God. I thought something terrible had happened." I take his hand and escort him into the office. "Well, this is it." I hold out my hands, gesturing at the stark space of white walls, modern furniture, and paper...everywhere.

"You really do have a view of the Empire State Building."

"Yes, almost all of the offices on this floor have this view."

"This is awesome, baby. You've really made it." He sits on my desk, taking in the room. "If I didn't know better, I'd ask who you slept with to get this kind of view." He's kidding, yet his eyebrows are raised at me questioningly.

"Gabe!" I admonish, crossing my arms and cocking my head to the side.

"I'm joking," Gabriel says with a sarcastic tone.

"You'd better be."

"Where is that big boss of yours anyway?"

"Erik? He's in the meeting I just left because you surprised me at work. Which, as a matter of fact, I love, but really hope I don't get in trouble for it."

"No, the *big* boss…Alexander Asher. Where does he sit?"

"Asher?"

The man is part of an empire. He would never sit on the floor of the communications company he owns. It seems silly Gabriel would even think he would.

I take a step back and assess my husband. "You're jealous!"

I knew Gwen and her ridiculous comments were good for something.

A smile stretches across my face so wide that my mouth opens in surprise. Despite my annoyance, I am utterly flattered that Gabriel would be jealous of Alexander Asher. After the crazy few days I had with my head reeling from thinking Gabriel was cheating to my relief to understanding that he's not, this is a welcome development.

"Yes, Asher. Where is his fancy office?" he asks, looking around the room as if there were a secret door that led to Asher's office.

"It's all the way upstairs in the penthouse. He doesn't come down here, except for a meeting every once in a while. I hardly ever see him." Okay, it's a lie but a white lie.

Gabriel glances down at the white pastry box I have on my desk. "Why do you have a box of Twinkies?"

If I tell him who they're from, he will never believe my white lie about hardly ever seeing Asher.

"The Hostess people sent them. They probably want to sponsor an event or something. I get pitches like this all the time," I ramble.

Where's the card? My eyes skim rapid-fire over the desk. I have to hide it.

Gabriel takes a seat in the chair in front of the desk. "No pictures of me or Jack?" He sounds disappointed.

"I keep on meaning to bring a photo or something, but I always seem to forget. You know it's very hard, being a working mom." It's true. Work all day and then take care of the baby at night. It's a lot.

"But I do have you as the screensaver on my computer." I motion toward the screen as I swivel it around for Gabriel to see a photo of him and Jackson taken just weeks ago at the house. It's one of my favorites.

This seems to appease Gabriel.

Trish knocks on the door and walks straight into the office.

"Sorry, Kat, but I heard your husband was here, and I just wanted to come and introduce myself." Trish steps back and appraises my husband who stands to greet her. "Wow, you're tall."

Gabriel breaks out his Robert Redford grin and shakes her hand. "It's a pleasure to meet you..." He waits for her response.

She catches her breath. "Trish! I'm Trish, the assistant. I must have stepped away when you entered, or I would have escorted you to Kat's office. But I wasn't at my desk. So, I couldn't greet you." She's babbling. Clearly overtaken by the blues.

I roll my eyes at her gushing. I used to be that girl.

I take the moment to look down at my desk. The card from Asher is sticking out from under the box. I pull it out further and swipe it into the trash can beneath the desk.

Gabriel finally releases her hand. "It's a pleasure to meet you, Trish. Kat has told me a lot about you."

He's such a charmer. I haven't told him a thing about my job at all...except for the concerts and my office. But

186

the people? Nothing. That's so rude of me. I love Trish. I have so much to tell Gabriel about her.

Trish absentmindedly grabs her braid and looks toward my desk. "The Twinkies." She laughs. "Isn't it funny that the Hostess people would send you a box full of cake?"

"Very." I grab the box and hold it out to her. "Why don't you leave these at reception, so everyone can enjoy them?"

A light goes off in Trish's head. Crap, I know where this is going.

"Did you see the flowers in reception?" Trish asks.

The flowers! Trish thinks they're from Gabriel. Well, she thinks the first set was and that Asher has been supplementing them.

I look over to Trish. "Will you please make my husband a cappuccino?"

Gabriel turns to me, confused by my abrupt command. The good thing is, he doesn't think twice about Trish's question, nor does he attempt to answer it.

"No, Kat, that's fine. I'm just leaving," he says.

"So soon?"

"Yes. I have a meeting a few blocks from here."

He looks just as disappointed to go as I am to see him leave.

"I'll walk you out." I lead Gabriel out the door and down the concrete hallway with the box of Twinkies still in my hand.

Trish makes her way toward Heather's office.

"Thank you for coming to visit." I truly am happy he's here.

"Absolutely. I'll try and do it more when this trial is over."

Once we're at the elevator, I hit the call button and stand with him, waiting for the car to arrive.

As the elevator doors open, I lean up and give him a good-bye kiss on the lips. The kiss is sweet and appropriate for the office. Still, I hold on to it entirely too long. His tender, velvety lips feel so good against mine.

"Ahem."

We are interrupted by the sound of someone clearing their throat, and it's not Trish.

Inside the elevator is a pair of golden eyes. Gabriel and I unlock our lips, and the three of us make eye contact. Gold to green to blue. We're like the crux gemmata of early Christian art. Jeweled crosses in precious metal that hang above altars with the alpha and omega signs in juxtaposition.

A symbol of the beginning and the end.

You can cut the tension with a knife. At least, I can. I wonder if Gabriel can feel it.

Asher exits the elevator, holding the doors open with his arm. "Going down?" He's being snarky.

"Mr. Asher, this is my husband, Gabriel Monroe. Gabriel, this is my boss, Alexander Asher."

For the first time, I'm able to appraise the men properly. Gabriel is a touch taller than Asher, yet the men are equally as handsome in entirely different ways. Gabriel with his fit frame and all-American good looks. Slick, dark waves of hair, fair skin, and navy-blue eyes. Asher is exotic with bronzed skin and a rock-hard physique, but his blond highlights and citrine eyes make him mesmerizing for all the wrong reasons. Gabriel's nose is a little straighter, Asher's jaw a little squarer and manlier. Gabriel's eyes are bigger and brighter; Asher's lips are fuller, his smile broader. They are the black and white, the yin and yang of my life.

Alpha and omega in the flesh.

But which is which, I don't know.

Asher holds his hand out to Gabriel. "Mr. Monroe. I have heard a lot about you. It's a pleasure to finally meet the *husband*." He puts emphasis around the term.

It doesn't help my story of me hardly ever seeing Asher. Nevertheless, I don't think Gabriel notices.

Gabriel shakes Asher's hand. "Pleasure to meet you." He quickly removes his hand and places his arm around my waist, marking his territory. "I was just paying a surprise visit to my *wife*."

Yep, it's a pissing match.

Asher laughs it off. "Well, I hope you do stop by more often." He eyes the box in my hand, lifts the lid, and takes out a package. "Twinkie?" he offers Gabriel.

"No, thanks." Gabriel turns to me and places another kiss on my lips. "I have to go. I'll be home late tonight. Don't wait up, okay?"

I nod in understanding and watch as my beautiful husband gets into the elevator.

As soon as the doors close, I hit Asher in the arm.

"Ass!" I say before I storm down to my office, thankful there is no one in the front reception area.

I can hear his chuckle over the sound of my heels pounding down the concrete hallway.

$$\Omega$$

I arrive home to a partially empty house. Gwen is at dinner with friends, and Carmen leaves as soon as I get home.

Jackson and I play with his building blocks for a while.

Build them up. Knock them down. Repeat.

We partake in our nighttime ritual of bath, bottle, and bed. Even the lioness knows of this.

No, Kat, don't go there!

No is right. Not my husband. My jealous, beautiful, blue-eyed husband.

Once Jackson is snug in bed, I glance at the clock. It's nine o'clock. It's early, but if I want to get into work early again, I need to get a good night's sleep.

My eyes open to the sound of shuffling feet. Gabriel is home.

Making his way into the walk-in closet, he kicks off his shoes. I sit up in bed and watch as he unknots his tie and hangs it on the tie rack before his long fingers unbutton his shirt from collar to hip. My eyes watch as he slowly peels his shirt back, revealing his exquisite build. There is no sweeter sight than a shirtless man in dress pants with the top button undone. As if he knows I'm watching, he takes off his pants, revealing his incredible physique. Tall and strong yet not bulky. He's toned in all the right areas, and he has incredible definition. His arms and chest are his best features. Looks like he's been keeping up with his push-ups in the park.

When he's shed his suit, wearing nothing but boxer briefs, I'm reminded of our first night together.

Ω

Gabe knelt down next to the bed in front of me and looked deep into my eyes.

"Are you sure you want to do this? You had a lot to drink."

I smiled at his compassion; it was so unexpected. It made me want him even more. "Yes."

Standing up, Gabe removed his baseball cap, revealing his long, dark waves that had been hiding underneath. He threw the cap on his desk and turned on his iPod. "Crash into Me" began playing. Dave Matthews had no idea he had written that song about this very moment.

In slowed perfection, he rolled his shoulders forward and grabbed the hem of his shirt, lifting it over his head. His breath hissed when I leaned forward and touched his chest. It was smooth and creamy, like silk. My hand trembled ever so slightly.

"Relax."

I let out a breath and felt my shoulders lower.

"You are so beautiful. I haven't been able to think of anything but you, right here, for weeks." His voice made me quiver in a way I'd only read about in my young adult books. "But I can't do this." My eyes must have given away my disappointment because he winked joyfully. "Not until I know your name."

I blushed at the thought of being half-naked on a bed with a guy who didn't know my name. "Kathryn."

He repeated my name, and I felt his breath hit my skin. Gabe moved his hands around my back and unhooked my bra. The straps fell to the sides, so I was completely exposed. He leaned forward and trailed soft kisses on my neck, stopping for a second at my clavicle before continuing his delicious journey south.

I let out a moan and grabbed his arms. I didn't know what else to do with my body. I wanted—needed—to feel him, all of him. And I told him so.

After an endless amount of foreplay, my heart raced a mile a minute from the incredible feeling of having him all over my body, from anticipation of what was about to happen. He grabbed a foil packet from his end table. I nearly stopped breathing at the thought of what was about to happen.

Easing his weight onto my body, Gabriel slowly lowered himself down and into me. I took him in, welcoming, widening, and accepting him into my body as one. He pulled himself out before shifting his weight back into me, forcing my body to convulse as I took the pain and pleasure at the same time.

"Do that again!" I begged.

And he did, faster and faster. Our mouths found each other, and we were all lips and tongues, taking breaks only to say each other's names, names we'd just learned, yet we said them over and over like they were a mantra until we were breathing so hard that we couldn't speak.

"You're going to be the end of me," he said as he rolled over to place a loving kiss on my forehead. His hands laced in my hair and swirled the soft tendrils along his fingers.

I nuzzled closer to him, nestling myself in his arm. "I've never felt that before."

He looked down at me, confused. "Felt what?"

"An orgasm. That was...I can't even describe..."

Gabe let out a chuckle. "I'm sure that's what you tell all the guys to make them feel good."

"That would be impossible."

"You weren't"

He looked puzzled, and I suddenly felt so self-conscious.

Should I have told him that? Is that something I possibly should have told him before I got naked in his bed?

"Were you a virgin?"

Half-hiding myself under the sheet, I nodded in mortification.

He looked down at me and smiled, pulling the sheet off my face. He kissed me with the most tender kiss I'd ever felt in my life.

"You are the greatest surprise I've had in a long time. Who are you, and where have you been these last three years?"

I giggled. "Saving myself for the right moment, I guess."

"Stay the night. I don't want you to go."

"I won't."

A look of alarm crossed his face. "You won't stay?"

I laughed again. "I won't leave. I'll stay as long as you want."

And I never left.

Ω

"Shit. You scared me," he says, taking a step back when he sees me.

Not the reaction I was hoping for. I lean over and pull down the duvet on his side of the bed. Gabriel climbs in and adjusts his pillow.

"What are you still doing up?" he asks.

"Waiting for you. What time is it?"

"After midnight." Gabriel rolls over, facing away from me. "I'm beat, baby. Go back to sleep." He adjusts his pillow one more time and settles his body into the mattress.

I move toward him and press my chest against his back, draping my right arm around him. My head is buried between his shoulder blades, so I take the opportunity to place soft kisses along his back.

The action causes Gabriel to roll over toward me, onto his back. As Gabriel's arm snakes around me, I find my new home in the crook, lying with my arm across his stomach.

Raising my hand, I gently run my fingers through the sprinkle of hair on his belly that leads to a very happy place. My fingers draw small circles from his navel and start their descent to the elastic of his boxer shorts.

My fingers cross the barrier, and as I am about to grab hold of my prize, Gabriel's hand lands on top of mine and lifts it up and out of his shorts.

"No, baby. I'm tired. Not tonight," Gabriel says as he rolls back over, away from me.

What kind of man refuses sex with his wife? After his office visit today, I was sure he would want to make love tonight. Instead, it's the same story.

I feel like Jackson's building blocks.

Build them up. Knock them down. Repeat.

chapter TWENTY

I arrive at the office later than expected. I overslept, and of course, Gabriel had already been gone. Gwen was still there, so I left her with Carmen. I couldn't deal with her this morning.

And those goddamn flowers are blocking the redhead!

"Trish, is Malory in yet?" I scowl.

"Yes, she's in her office." Trish rises and rounds the reception area. "Kat, I have to talk to you."

"Not a good time." I walk past reception and head down the concrete hallway.

"Listen, I was reading emails this morning and…" Trish follows me. She has a frantic tone to her voice.

"No!" I say condescendingly, stopping in the hallway to put the little redhead in her place. "Trish, what have I told you about reading other people's emails?"

She looks me square in the eye, remorseful yet determined. "I know, but listen. I was looking for—"

"Say one more word about emails, and I am marching right into Erik's office."

"But I—"

"Enough!" I turn on my heel and head down to Malory's office.

She's sitting at her desk in red from head to toe. She looks exquisite, her jet-black hair smooth, silky, and falling just below her chin. The phone is to her ear, but when she sees me enter, she puts it down.

Her office looks like mine but bigger and professionally decorated. Okay, it looks nothing like mine, except for the view.

I close the door behind me and take a seat on the black-and-white love seat in the corner.

"I need to talk to you."

If anyone knows how to win a man over in bed, it's Malory. Many times over, she's alluded to her sexual prowess in the bedroom. As often as I've thought that she is brash and tried to shy away from the conversation, I've always felt myself keeping little mental notes.

"And I need to talk to you. What's going on with you and Asher?" She swivels her chair to face me.

My mouth falls to the floor. *Asher?* She can't possibly think something is happening between the two of us. It is a purely professional relationship. She knows that. Doesn't she?

"Why do you ask?"

"Kat, I've been watching the two of you since you started. He has paid more attention to you than he has anyone in the three years I've been here. Yesterday, he was in the conference room with the maintenance crew, hanging up that ridiculous poster." She is looking me square in the eye. Her words are direct, yet I can hear the approval in her voice.

Malory has mastered the art of swaying a conversation. I've seen her do it a thousand times, and right now, it feels like she's swinging me toward Asher.

I press my lips together, trying to keep my bottom lip from quivering. "I actually came here to talk to you about Gabriel. Yesterday, when he was here…I thought everything was good, but then last night, I tried…and he…" Words fail me.

"So, what does this mean? Are you leaving him?"

"No."

Malory leans back in her seat and crosses her arms. Her eyes squint in observation, looking at me as if I were a criminal under the heated light of an interrogation office.

"Why wouldn't you?" she asks. "If he's having an affair, why would you stay with him?"

"You think he's having an affair?" My head falls into my hands.

"Don't you?" Her words are curt.

"I haven't even spoken to him about it. I mean…" *Leave my husband?* I haven't ever thought of that.

"I think you have to ask your husband about the woman in the park. If you think something is going on, then it probably is."

"You mean, follow my heart?"

"Your heart, your brain, your gut, your vagina…whatever. You can't play the *poor me and my marriage* card every day. It's getting old."

I raise my head and look at her in utter confusion. "I don't complain about my marriage."

Using a mocking tone, she recites my words, "*He works a lot. We have sex, but it's not the same. He used to take me sailing. He used to play games with me. He used to* this *and he used to* that." Her words cut at me like a knife.

I don't even know how to respond. I stare at her in bewilderment as I watch her get up from her desk.

"Shit or get off the pot, Kat. It should be easy since you have a golden god kissing your goddamn feet." With that, she leaves the office.

I walk back toward my office in disgust. How dare she! My sounding board. My best friend. Of all the…

First, it was, *Don't say anything to Gabriel.* Now, it's confront him.

And that Asher nonsense!

I bet she's jealous of my friendship with Asher. I saw her moves on him at the bar. She thinks I'm after her man when it couldn't be further from the truth. Heather isn't the one I have to watch out for. It's Malory. If she is attracted to Asher, why doesn't she just go for him? She's stunning and totally his type.

I feel like I'm lost in a head trip. *Poor me? Getting old? Leave my husband? What the hell is going on with my life?*

Breathe, Kat. Just breathe.

I power up my computer, grab the phone, and start placing calls I've been neglecting. Three weeks left, and this event has to be perfect.

And it will be…after I call Gabriel. I just need to hear his voice, and I'll know. Know what, I'm not sure.

"Hey." He picks up, sounding his usual self.

My stomach is in knots, torn between my brain and my heart.

"You left early this morning." My voice breaks.

"Is everything okay?" he asks, sounding distracted.

I can imagine him sitting at his desk with his sleeves rolled up, going through a thousand-page deposition in front of him.

"I miss you, Gabriel. I really miss you." Tears threaten to escape my eyes.

"Miss me? Kat, what's going on?" He's worried.

"Yes. I need to talk to you. Tonight?" I plead.

"Of course," he promises. "Are you sure everything's okay?"

Just hearing his voice quiets the irrational voice inside my head that's making me go crazy.

"It's better now." It is. "I love you."

"I love you, too." His voice is sincere.

I hang up, feeling much better.

A knock on the door interrupts my thoughts. I swallow my insecurities and gain my composure. Wiping under my eyes to make sure my makeup is not smudged, I turn my head to the doorway to see Erik standing there, clad in his signature black.

"What can I do for you?"

"I came by to pick up the final production notes." He's holding a black leather satchel and an iPhone in hand.

"I'm still finalizing my packet for the event."

Was I supposed to have it ready? We just had a meeting yesterday. He knows where I am in production.

Erik looks displeased. It's an odd reaction from someone who has been over-the-top welcoming to me.

"Kat, we have to talk about your performance here. You are constantly behind, and with the tight deadline we're on, it makes me question whether you're able to handle the job on your own." His eyes are laced with disappointment.

"I didn't know I was behind," I nervously reply. I've been working really hard, and I am on top of all of my work.

I shuffle through the files on my desk, eager to show Erik the progress I've made—substantial progress. Haven't I?

The vendors have been contacted and contracts written up. I haven't finalized a few things, but that can be done next week.

My rundown is still in flux, but Gretchen has added some sequencing issues as per the talents' time requirements in their contracts. So, I have a lot of work to do there.

Malory has been reviewing the elements in the broadcast and the sponsorship inserts. I don't have those complete either.

There is still back-and-forth going on about the set. The site survey was great. That woman...oh, what was her name? Claudia! Yes, Claudia. We were going over logistics, and she was answering my questions, but then I...left...with Asher.

Harvey and I have gone over the speeches, and I still have to write a few more inserts in the copy.

I am really far behind. I immediately feel deflated. The roller coaster of emotions I've been feeling the past few weeks is really taking a toll on me.

How can I go from high to low so fast? It makes the lows feel even…lower.

"I'm sorry. I didn't know my notes were due already. There's still another three weeks."

I bite my lip and wait for a response. I can't stand the look of disappointment on his face.

Please, don't let him fire me.

"Richard and I are heading over to Lincoln Center to discuss camera placement and lighting. I expect those reports on my desk by end of day Friday." He turns to leave and then stops and sighs. "I have high hopes for you. Friday." It's a command more than a compliment. With two taps on the door, he leaves.

I look around at the papers on my desk, trying to figure out how I let so much get by me. It wasn't that long ago that I was the go-to gal, the one you could rely on, who picked up everyone else's pieces. I came here two months ago with that same attitude and fresh ideas. Then, I got distracted, letting my head get away from me.

And I know exactly where it's been.

Ω

The house is quiet when I get home. Gwen is still here, so she can spend time with Jackson. It's sweet of her, though part of me can't wait until she goes home. She meddles. I want to talk to Gabriel about Becca again but can't with Gwen around. She will either take his side—or worse, take mine. I don't know if I'm ready for that…yet.

"You look beat. You really should wear more rouge." She's thumbing through *New York Magazine* again.

It's been circulating my house all week, yet I've neglected to pick up the damn thing and read it.

"Thank you for the words of encouragement, but I had a very trying day at work." My body falls to the couch in defeat.

"I'll tell you what I'd like to try…this boss of yours. Did you know he's been linked with two Hollywood actresses and three socialites in the past year alone?" Her eyes widen as she scans the photos.

"Yes, he is quite the playboy, Mother. I'll put in a good word for you if you'd like a piece." I cover my face with my arm. I wish I could just block out everything Asher and Asher-Marks Communications for a few moments.

"Did you know he is the sole heir of the Asher fortune? When his grandfather dies, he'll be left with everything. Just imagine how much money that man will have!"

"Yes, Mother, I am aware." My voice is muffled under my arm, but I'm sure she can hear the annoyance in my voice.

"And this sad, sad story about his mother. She died in a tragic car accident with him in the car."

My head perks to attention. "What else does it say?"

"How his heroic grandfather took him in. The man is a saint. He was the only living family the boy had. I don't know how you are able to look at that man without your heart breaking every day."

I sit up and reach over toward my mother. "Can I see that article?"

Gwen hands over the magazine, and I read through it. In there, it talks of the empire. Wow. The Asher family does control as much as Gabriel said they did. I can see why gluttony and greed are synonymous with the Asher name.

My eyes glide through the article, trying to find the part about the mother, when the garage door opening disrupts me. Gabriel is home. I have to talk to him.

His dark, wavy hair has fallen haphazardly on his face. He must have been running his hands through it a lot today. He looks more beaten and battered than I do.

"Hi, baby. How was your day?" I stand to join him by the table.

I gently put my hands on his shoulders, but he brushes them away.

"I'm sorry. It's just been a long day. I want to go upstairs."

Gabriel kisses me on the forehead and makes his way up to the bedroom. I stand here, listening as his footsteps climb the staircase and the door to the bedroom closes behind him.

This isn't the way tonight was supposed to go. My heart actually aches inside my chest. I grab Gabriel's car keys off the kitchen counter and head to the garage.

"I'm going out," I shout over my shoulder to Gwen, who watches me, stunned.

Ω

Crack!

I love the sound of a metal bat as it hits a ball. I especially love it on days like these.

Crack!

This one is for Gabriel and his bipolar moods!

Crack!

This one is for Becca with her perky boobs and platinum-blonde hair!

Crack!

This one is for Erik and his goddamn deadlines!

Crack!

This one is for Heather and her bitch attitude!

Crack!

This one is for Malory and her perfect body and evil words!

Crack!

This one is for me being such a chickenshit all the time!

Crack!

"I thought I'd find you here."

I should have known she'd follow me.

Crack!

This one is for nosy mothers who can't stop meddling!

"You always did run to the batting cage whenever you got angry." Gwen is standing behind the fence as I take my next hit.

Crack!

"Leave me alone, Mom. I just need some time to think."

Crack!

"I remember the day of your father's funeral. You didn't think I knew where you were, but I followed you to the cages. You hit balls for hours. I was afraid you'd sprain your wrist."

Crack!

I step back from the batter's box. "I didn't know you'd followed me."

I remember that day. After the burial, everyone went to a local restaurant to toast my father's demise. At least, that's the way I saw it. I couldn't bear to hear happy stories of my dad's life. I was too sad. I wanted to go somewhere I could connect with him. Where I could connect a bat to a ball. It's how Gabriel feels about sailing; it connects him to his home.

This must be how Asher feels about music. Why he pours himself into it. It connects him to his mother.

"You are your father's daughter, Kathryn." Gwen steps around the side of the fence. "But you'll always be your mother's daughter. That means, you want it all."

I look away from her.

"That's not what this is about, Mom. You don't understand…"

"A husband's neglect? Honey, if you don't think a woman who was married to a man who was always on the road doesn't understand neglect, then you know nothing about me."

"At least Dad had an excuse."

She has no idea what I'm going through. Keeping my eyes forward, I take swing after swing. She's still standing there, watching.

"Are you going home tonight?" My words come off snarkier than I intended.

I hear her shuffle her feet from side to side as she decides what to do.

"Yes, Kathryn," she says with a pause. "I was just stopping by to let you know that I'm heading back tonight."

I take a few more swings and wait for the sound of her car driving out of the parking lot. I know she means well in her own way, but I just can't deal with her tonight.

chapter TWENTY-ONE

"A week!"

I'm pacing the hallway outside our bedroom. *Is he kidding me? Chicago? Now?* We were supposed to talk.

"I have no choice, Kat. I told you, if I'm going to get this guy a good deal, it will take a lot of work." Gabriel pulls his suitcase from under the bed and starts to pack.

"I don't give a shit about your work. What about my work? The concert and gala are in three weeks!" I throw my arms up in a dramatic gesture.

"Really? You think your job is more important than mine? Last I checked, I was the one paying the bills around here."

Gabriel knows I despise when he throws it in my face that he makes more money than me.

"You're an asshole, Gabriel Monroe."

"And you're being unreasonable," he says, placing his dress shoes in the bag. "I have no choice. My client is taking off for a few days, so I need to get into his office and go through every piece of paper he hasn't shredded yet. This case goes to trial in four weeks."

I storm around the bedroom, looking for something to throw. "How can you think it's acceptable to tell me at ten o'clock at night that you're hopping on a plane at six in the morning to head to Chicago? Do you comprehend how wrong this is? You have a wife and a baby. You can't just take off on a whim!" I stop to catch my breath. I didn't realize I had been screaming.

"Kat, please, you know I don't want to do this, but there really is no option." Gabriel places two suits in a garment bag. "Besides, you have Carmen."

He just doesn't get it. I have to work late this week. I can't leave Jackson with Carmen all day and all night. It's not right.

The phone rings. I can't deal with whoever is on the line so I motion for Gabriel to answer it. I immediately know it's bad news.

"Fuck!" He slams the phone down.

I shoot up from the bed. "What is it?"

"That was Carmen." He runs his hands across his forehead. "Her mother is sick, so she's taking the train to Philly to tend to her. She said she'll be in Philadelphia through next week."

Gabriel is now equally as pissed as I am.

Good. Welcome to my world.

I fall back on the bed. No husband, no nanny, and I can count down the days until my event.

"What about your mother?" He suggests.

"My mother *just* left! She is not driving from upstate to stay with Jackson for a week."

"Bring Jack up there then."

"No, Gabriel, I am not going a week without seeing my kid."

"Well, Kat, you can't have it all."

He can be such a jerk sometimes.

My feet find the ground faster than my mind can grasp words for a comeback. I storm out of the room and grab Jackson's bag to pack. Ten o'clock at night, and I'm driving upstate.

Ω

By the time I get back home, it's almost four in the morning. My mother insisted on talking about my argument with Gabriel. She, of course, took his side. The woman is in love with the man. If I hadn't married him, I'm sure she would have.

I turn off the ignition and undo my seat belt. Unplugging my iPhone, I open the center console and put the charger away. As I place the white cord inside, I feel something soft at the bottom of the compartment. I didn't notice it when I took the cable out earlier. My fingers pinch the material and lift it out.

In my hands is a black lace thong.

I own lace thongs, but the label inside, Agent Provocateur, confirms this lacy undergarment is not mine. Upon further inspection, I see the thing has a clasp at the bottom, where you'd attach a garter belt. This is the kinky stuff you give your friends at their bachelorette party.

I panic as I shove the thong back into the center console and close it.

Like flashes from a movie, the scene plays before my eyes. That little tramp, Becca, buying underwear at Bloomingdale's. She was on the phone, talking about some guy she'd met in the park.

My body begins to spasm as I punch the steering wheel in front of me with the palm of my hand.

I knew it. I absolutely knew something was up. But instead of saying something, I decided to let it go.

What I should have done was hired a private investigator. I should have had documentation of this little affair. I should have gotten a lawyer. I should be making him pay.

"Just breathe," I attempt to say the words out loud, just as I have almost my entire life.

Well, not anymore!

I storm into the house, looking for Gabriel. Taking the stairs two at a time, I call out his name, but he's not there. He must have left for the airport already.

What time was his flight again?

I can't think. I can't breathe. My chest heaves. I place my hand over my heart to calm my erratic pulse. I think I'm having a heart attack. *What is going on? Where is my husband? Why is there another woman's underwear in our car?*

Our bedroom is empty, the bed is made, and the light is turned off. I turn to his dresser and start rummaging through his things—pants, sweaters, shirts, everything—trying to find a clue, any clue. *Isn't this what they do in the movies, go through the husband's things after suspicions of an affair? But to look for what? What am I looking for? More underwear? I don't know.*

I virtually spray the room with Gabriel's clothes, pulling pants pockets inside out and finding nothing, before heading to his closet. In the movies, the wife always finds an incriminating receipt in her husband's suit jacket.

One by one, I inspect his suits—the chest pocket, the inside pocket, the pants—but I find nothing.

Putting my hand on my forehead, I try to get my bearings.

The dirty clothes.

Running into the bathroom, I dump the hamper upside down, digging through its contents. I even smell each shirt, looking for a sign of perfume, and inspect the collars for lipstick stains, anything.

My breath quickens. My heart is leaping out of my chest. I'm anxious and nervous for what I might find.

As I inspect the last shirt and find…nothing, my body gives way and collapses on the floor. The tears discharge and fall down my face. I cry big, heavy, ugly tears. My breath hitches, and my nose runs. I rub my face with my shirtsleeve and try to pace myself. The release is refreshing as I finally begin to catch my breath.

I stop and lift my head to peek into the bedroom to take a look at the warpath I left behind. Clothing on the bed, dresser, across lamps, and on the floor. It looks like a mental ward.

I'm going insane. That's it. I have officially lost my mind. Maybe I made up finding the thong in the car.

208

My head in my hands, I sob and expel weeks of frustration and disappointment. Hell, I'm releasing two years of frustration and disappointment.

What happened to us? What happened to the young couple who met on a stairwell and couldn't resist the passion they'd ignited in each other? What happened to the young couple who had promised forever and dreams to each other on a sailboat?

Well, one is crying on the bathroom floor, and the other is on a plane to Chicago.

I lie on the bathroom floor for what feels like forever. I lift my head and see the sun is threatening to make an appearance. After my sob fest, I feel weak and numb. Slowly, I get up from the floor. I mechanically pick up each piece of laundry from the bathroom floor and place it in the hamper. Next, I move into the bedroom and carefully place every article of clothing back in its respected drawer or hanger, exactly as I found it.

Looking in the mirror, I can see but a shadow of myself. Eyes puffy and splotchy. My hair is a mess. I'm exhausted, but I can't stay home. I can't stay in this room. There is only one place I can go.

After a quick shower, I throw on a new skirt suit and head out the door.

The morning's events have left me distracted. As much of a confirmation I have in the form of sexy underwear, I can't help but wonder how the hell this happened.

God, I'm so naive. Even Malory saw the writing on the wall, but I kept pushing it to the side. It was easy to.

Gabriel is the most dedicated husband and father I have ever met. His parents have been together for forty years, and he's always said he wanted to grow old together just like them. No, this is not my Gabriel. The man I've been with for ten years. The only man I've ever been with.

Could that be the problem? Am I boring in bed? Have I become unattractive since having the baby?

When Gabriel and I met, he loved my inexperience. He indulged in teaching me how to love my body and use it for pleasure. We spent the first years wrapped in each other, all arms and legs and wet kisses. No matter where we were, we found a place to escape to be alone.

But then what happened? Life happened. He spending more time at the office than he did at home. I found myself traveling for work and going out for dinners with colleagues when he wasn't around.

Jackson came, and romance went out the window. Quickies were the new norm. Both with conversation and in the bedroom. *Was it enough to drive him into the arms of another woman*? I was available. I would have responded.

Maybe he doesn't want to be with me anymore. Especially the last few weeks, I've been distracted with work and…Asher. No, that has nothing to do with it. No matter how attracted I might be to my boss, that is where it ends. I would never…ever do anything to jeopardize my marriage.

Would I feel the same way if Gabriel had a little crush? I know the answer. I would be furious. But it's different. Women have more control than men do. Don't we?

And now, Gabriel is in Chicago, doing God knows what. The thought leaves me feeling ill.

Only five years in, and infidelity has reared its ugly head. I feel like I'm sitting in a fog as I travel to the office and sit at my desk, staring at the blinking cursor on my computer screen.

"You look upset." Asher startles me, awakening me from my daze.

He's the last person I want to see right now. My head is clouded with my husband's lack of desire for me. The last thing I need is to talk to Mr. I Have Absolutely No Interest In You Asher. Just looking at him in his herringbone suit and pale green tie, I'm reminded once again that I am not one of his beautiful models.

"Gray, what's wrong?"

I can't tell him about Gabriel. It's so embarrassing. He'd probably sympathize with him, too. Men will be men, and no one knows that better than him.

"I'm fine. I have a lot on my plate."

Asher looks genuinely concerned. "If it's work, I can get you help."

Oh no, he can't think this is about work. He'll give my responsibilities to someone else, and then everyone will think I'm inadequate.

"It's a personal matter. I'm fine, Alex, really. I promise."

Asher looks at me curiously. "I don't know what you're going through, but please know you can talk to me."

I give him a nod in understanding.

He eyes me up for a few more seconds and rubs his full lips together, as if trying to decide if he should pry further. He must decide not to because his body relaxes, and he walks backward toward the door.

"I just swung by to tell you that I'm heading out of town, so I won't be able to go through the final rundown with you."

"You're leaving? Where are you going?"

"Miami for a few days. I'm going there to wine and dine some donors. Malory was supposed to go, but she's off to LA for the weekend, so that leaves me to seal the deal." He stops with his back to the open doorway and places his hand on the frame. "Actually, I was going to ask you if you could join me since we're soliciting money for your event, but I understand it probably isn't enough time to let your husband know."

Under normal circumstances, I would never dream of leaving town without Gabriel and Jackson. But one is upstate with my mother, and the other is in Chicago, doing…I don't even want to think about what he's doing.

I thought I had this job under control. Instead, I have a world of work ahead of me, and after talking to Erik, I know if this production isn't top-notch, I'll be out of a job.

"Thank you for the offer, but Erik requested final production notes by tomorrow."

His face lights up as he releases the doorframe and takes a step toward my desk. "That's perfect. We can do everything on the plane. I have a phone, fax, Wi-Fi, and...me." His smile broadens as he raises his hands and points his thumbs in his direction. "You can't hand in anything to Erik without me looking over it anyway."

I roll my eyes at his arrogant approach. He has a really good point. There is no use in doing all this work and then waiting days for him to get back to give me an answer. I could get a lot done with his undivided attention, and I'd be able to hand in a final packet with Asher's seal of approval.

This is also my event we're getting money for. I should be the one to go. This is my job. I am one hundred percent capable of wining and dining some business people, closing the deal. Plus, I could use a day or two away from home to get my head together.

"I'll go."

Asher's jaw drops. For the first time, I think I've completely shocked him. I like this feeling.

"Really? What about your husband?"

"He happens to be away on business as well. This couldn't have come at a better time."

"Excellent. I'll let Erik know you're traveling with me. However, my plane leaves in an hour. You won't have time to go to Long Island and back. We'll have to buy you some new clothes."

"No!"

Asher knows my strong position on no gifts.

"Yes." Asher is stern, his voice commanding. "You will buy new clothes and expense them. Don't think of them as being a gift from me. They are a necessary business expense. That's final."

chapter TWENTY-TWO

I have never been this impulsive in my life. Leaving home without a thing on me. This is crazy.

I run through the checklist in my head. The alarm is set, the iron unplugged, the lights and televisions off…all the things that would concern me if I were going away for a day or two.

I call Gabriel to tell him I'll be in Miami, but I get his voice mail. Part of me is relieved. I want to yell and scream at him, but I can't be too impulsive. If he is having an affair, he'll just lie, say they were someone else's lace panties. I have to be smart about this. I feel nauseous at the thought of Gabriel being with another woman.

Asher and I sit in silence on the way to the airport. We are in his massive SUV, the one that drenched me the first day we met. We have come so far since that day. I was furious with him, but now, I've grown to enjoy his company.

He was right. We could be friends.

I never would have thought it possible.

I turn my head away from the window to see he's staring at me with a puckered brow. I reply to his expression with a softhearted smile. I don't want him to worry.

Although I have known him only a few short weeks, I feel like I've known Asher forever. He said I could tell him anything, but this matter is just too personal, and I fear he'd tell me exactly what I know is true—that my husband is having an affair. I'm just not ready for him to know. I already feel like a failure.

We pull through a gate and into the departure entrance at Teterboro. The car stops at the bottom of a stairwell, leading to a private plane with *ASHER* emblazoned on it. A beautiful brunette is waiting at the bottom of the stairs. She opens our car door, surprised to see me exit. Perhaps she was hoping for some alone time with Mr. Asher at forty-thousand feet. She definitely looks like the president of the Mile-High Club.

Asher greets the stewardess with a knowing glance. Yes, these two have been acquainted before. *Gross.*

The plane is more than I ever could have dreamed of. There is ample seating for eight passengers with plush leather seats and a place for dining. The table and consoles are a shiny birch veneer, and a large plasma television screen hangs on a wall adjacent to a kitchen. Beyond the seating area is a bedroom of the same colors. The full-size bed looks inviting, and I imagine the Mile-High Club has their weekly meetings in here.

I take a seat in one of the deliciously comfortable leather chairs. Asher sits next to me, pulls the newspaper out of his briefcase, and grabs my hand. We haven't said a word to each other since he asked me to join him in Miami. It's amazing to be so comfortable with someone and sit in silence.

I rest my head back on the seat and drift into a quiet slumber, pushing thoughts of Gabriel and those lace panties out of my head.

$$\Omega$$

"Wake up, sleepyhead."

I don't know how long I was sleeping, but I wake to Asher gently rubbing my cheek. Somehow, my head found its way onto his shoulder, his arm tucked around my back, holding me tightly to his chest.

"We're starting our descent. You should sit up for this."

I blush at the thought of lying in such an intimate position with my boss for the last three hours. I didn't realize I was so tired. The stress of last night had given me a mental and physical workout. Not to mention the fact that I hadn't slept a wink.

So much for getting work done on the plane.

I look out the window and see crystal-blue water and miles of beaches. I still can't believe I left the city without a thing on me.

When we arrive at the airport, Devon greets us at the foot of the plane with a Mercedes SLS AMG Roadster with a black exterior and matching interior. Asher and Devon speak for a few minutes, and Devon hands Asher the keys. He nods for me to get in the car, and I follow.

We drive down State Road A1A with the top down and the sun beating on us. I wish we were enclosed with the air conditioner on. My hair, which was neatly done up in a bun earlier, is getting disheveled, stray hairs flying around my face.

Asher looks cool and comfortable behind the wheel despite the fact that he's wearing even more layers than I am. Not shaking my mood from earlier, I turn my head away from the sun, slide on my sunglasses, and let out a sigh.

Asher plays with the radio dial, skimming through static and talk radio. His broad white smile lights up when he hears a fun Latin song. His shoulders immediately move. My mother always told me never to trust a man who could dance.

Asher breaks out in fluent Spanish, singing every line of the song. The sounds from his mouth are smooth and sexy. His voice is gorgeous. I could listen to him sing in a foreign tongue all day. He looks vibrant and free. I like this Asher.

With his coat lying across the backseat, he undoes his tie and throws it back as well. I watch him unbutton his top two buttons, unveiling a sneak peek of his perfectly sculpted chest.

Asher reaches his arm out toward me. It takes me a moment to realize he wants me to remove his cuff link. I raise my hands and unclasp the diamond-and-onyx cuff link from the French cuff and roll his sleeve up above his elbow. When I'm done with his right arm, he crosses his left toward me, and I do the same to the other arm, having to reach over him a bit to do so.

Wearing black aviator sunglasses, the man has transformed in our short drive from polished CEO to fun, sexy, and cool. A thousand light-years from how I feel right now.

I glance down at my beige skirt and matching jacket. It's ninety-one degrees outside, and the wind from the ride is doing nothing to relieve the heat. Following his lead, I take off my blazer and throw it into the backseat. I unbutton one button from the top of my cap-sleeve blouse and let the wind skim up my arms and inside my top. I take the hair tie out of my bun and shake the strands down my shoulders.

Asher casts one of those gigantic white smiles my way and starts to sing louder to the music. I don't know the song, but it's rather catchy, and I slowly start to move my shoulders to the music. My head sways a little as the chorus picks up, and I let go a little.

I throw my arms up and start moving to the beat of the music. A smile creeps across my face, and Asher lets out a laugh. He grabs my hand and kisses my knuckles.

Yes, this is what I needed.

We pull up to the W Hotel in Miami. As we exit the car, Asher walks to the trunk and removes two shopping bags I didn't even know were in there. A bellboy quickly retrieves the bags and the overnight bag Asher brought with him from the office.

Asher has secured two rooms—a penthouse suite for himself and a room on the sixth floor for me. He insisted I stay in the suite with him since there was another bedroom, but I would never feel comfortable, sharing a room with a man who was not my husband. I have boundaries. Thick, cemented-floor boundaries. A single room for me is perfect. I don't need the bells and whistles.

Well, I might not need the bells and whistles, but my hotel room certainly comes with them. Modern and chic, the room is decorated with white and silver. The spacious room has a king-size bed and an ocean view. The luxurious linens rival anything I could ever imagine. The bathroom has a shower that could easily host a small party and a soaking tub made for two.

"You like?" He follows me into my room and places the shopping bags on the bed.

"I love. The view is amazing."

His eyes focus on me. "I couldn't agree more."

I blush, thinking that comment sounded like he was talking about me. I look over in the mirror and see I've regained some color in my face since the early morning hours. The nap on the plane and sunshine from the car ride agree with me. I'm relieved.

"I have a meeting I have to attend, but I'll catch up with you by the pool." His glowing skin also agrees with the little bit of sunshine from the car ride.

If he has a meeting, then I should go. That's why I came here.

"I'll freshen up and go with you," I offer.

"It's a private meeting." Asher glances at his Rolex. "Why don't you put on a bathing suit and meet me by the pool in two hours?"

"I have work to do," I say, walking over to the desk where I left my bag and all my files.

"You can do it by the pool. Put on a suit and enjoy yourself. When I get down there, we'll go over everything," he assures me.

I assess the situation. I don't have a bathing suit. I don't have anything for that matter. I still can't believe I traveled thousands of miles with literally just the shirt on my back.

Asher sees the hesitation on my face and points to the bag on the bed. "Devon went out this morning and bought you a few items."

"Bought me a few items," I repeat. "Devon? The driver?"

My jaw falls as I try to take in just how insane that sentence sounds. My boss sent his driver out to buy me a few things. If that bag contains more gratuitous offerings, then I cannot accept them. I have my own money and can easily head out to Deco Drive and buy myself something to wear. I give Asher a knowing look, but he's already read my mind.

"Stop thinking and just accept them. End of story. I'll see you by the pool."

When he leaves the room, I inspect the contents of the bag—a sleeveless pale blue dress and metallic-gold sandals; a black bikini with gold rings on the hips and bust with a matching black cover-up; a long, one-shouldered green dress; strappy gold stilettos; a nightie; and two bra and panty sets.

Before I can even get upset about my boss having his driver buy me underwear—or shall I more appropriately call it lingerie?—I find a card from a personal shopper named Avalyn at the bottom of the bag. I feel better, knowing a female third party selected these items. The card suggests I call if something doesn't fit.

To my surprise, everything fits perfectly. I organize the items in the closet and make outfits from them. It's a sparse selection, which means they were specifically chosen for meetings I'll be having this weekend. They're not necessarily my style for the workplace, but this is what the boss wants.

After a shower, I dive into the bag and put on the bikini, cover-up, and sandals. I can't help but notice I look pretty good. I should, considering the price tags. Thankfully, the full-service hotel sent up a razor, toothbrush, and all the toiletries I need to get bikini ready. I'm also thankful Avalyn threw in mascara and lip gloss. She was clearly informed I was traveling down here sans everything.

Ω

With my hair tied in a ponytail and my sunglasses in place, I make my way down to the pool area. The lounge chairs are soft and luxurious. As the sun hits my skin, I relax into the much-needed therapy.

I don't have a laptop, so all my work is in printouts on my lap. I go through each document and make markings of the changes that need to be made. Erik was right. I am behind on my work. I compile a list of what needs to be done. I've found myself making a lot of lists these last few weeks without actually accomplishing everything on them.

Glancing at my phone, I see it's already close to four in the afternoon. I can't believe I lost an entire day to traveling. I will feel a thousand times better when Asher and I get to work.

A Pitbull song plays through the pool area, and I absentmindedly sway my hips to the melody. I'm not a dancer—at all. I love music but have always been rhythmically challenged. Even still, I am a fantastic seat dancer. Kind of like how I was dancing this morning in Asher's car. I smile at the thought of Asher letting loose, too. It was a completely different side of him I'd never seen before.

"Enjoying yourself?"

My sashaying hips are halted by the sound of said fellow seat dancer. If I thought him dancing was a new experience, seeing him in shorts is another. He looks so casual.

Wearing a black bathing suit and white shirt, Asher saunters up to my chair with two drinks in hand. I grab mine from him and take in how his highlights glisten in the sunlight.

He must sense my embarrassment, as he quickly settles himself in.

"Glad one of us is having a good time. I just had the meeting from hell. The fucker won't give in to my offer." Asher takes the seat next to me, his skin glowing against the crisp white of the lounge cushion.

I sit up slightly. "Sorry the deal's not going to happen."

His enigmatic smile crosses over his face. "Oh, it's going to happen. I always get what I want. Some things just take a little more time."

He kicks off his shoes and leans forward, grabbing the back of his shirt and hoisting it over his head. The muscles in his back flex as he raises his body back up.

My jaw unlocks at the sight of perfectly formed abdominal muscles…six…no, eight of them. I'm thinking this is what the term *washboard abs* means.

His waist is narrow and widens on the way up, revealing a broad chest and broader shoulders supported by two beautifully sculpted biceps and forearms. Asher throws his shirt it on the end of the chaise. He's like Thor but without the hammer.

Thank God for sunglasses. I place my head back on my chair and wipe the drool from my mouth. I hear Asher laugh, and I hope it's not at me. I grab my cocktail and inhale it, looking for a distraction.

Seeing my glass empty, a waitress no older than twenty-two saunters up. Before I can ask for a refill, she stops in her tracks to admire Apollo, the god of sun, sitting to my left. I immediately hate her.

Asher places his hand on mine, and the waitress frowns.

That's right. He's mine!

Wait, what?

Looking down at our hands, I realize he's merely getting my attention.

"Let's have Sex on the Beach," Asher says haughtily.

My head leaps up. "What?"

His husky laugh penetrates my body. "To drink. Let's have two Sex on the Beach drinks. Though I like where your head's at."

I nod to the waitress, confirming that's what we'll have, and she scurries off.

"You're incorrigible!" I take my hand back.

"God, I love spending time with you." His smile eases me. "Don't get mad at me, but I'm going to say something, and I'll have no apologies for saying it."

I raise my eyebrows in curiosity.

"You look fucking hot in that bikini."

I am beyond taken aback that my boss thinks I'm hot. Especially since he's this beautiful, successful, giving man who teaches music to underprivileged kids yet has time to run a multimillion-dollar corporation.

"Thank you. You look pretty good yourself." I try not to give away too much. I want to lick the sweat off his chest, but that would be entirely inappropriate.

Jesus Christ, what is wrong with me?

"I'm glad you approve. I have to thank the woman who picked out that suit for you. Did you have any trouble with the sizes?"

"Her name is Avalyn, and I've already made a mental note to thank her. The sizes are perfect. How did you know?"

"Years of practice, I guess," he says as the waitress quickly returns with our drinks. "Come on. Let's get drunk!"

I lift my files from my lap and hold them in front of his face. "Work first," I reprimand.

He lets out a deep laugh. "Yes. I want to hear all the ideas you have in that pretty little head of yours."

Asher walks us over to a private cabana, where we can sit at a table and get some actual work done. It's beyond bizarre, conducting business in a bikini, but when in Rome…

Thankfully, Asher has put his shirt back on and grimaces at my paperwork, confused as to why I'm working without a computer, "like a Neanderthal." His words, not mine.

I'm pleasantly surprised he likes most of what I've completed. If he's disappointed that I don't have some things in the final stages, he doesn't let on. Not surprisingly, he has a few good suggestions of his own. I write them all down with pure anticipation.

When we're finished, Asher has our private concierge deliver a special meal from Mr. Chow. We spend the rest of the early evening eating sushi, drinking sake, and talking about how we made our respected careers. My career path is shorter and not as exciting, so my contribution to the conversation is short.

The sun starts to set as he tells me about interning at other companies at his grandfather's insistence and learning about buying companies and rebuilding them. I am shocked to learn his first business venture was more about impressing a girl than it was about making money.

"Candy."

"Candy? Was she a stripper?"

"No, she was not a stripper."

"Was she a candy striper?"

"No! She was not a candy striper." He laughs. "What is it with you trying to ruin the story of my first love?"

"Spill it, Asher. Was she a palm reader?"

Tossing a bite of sushi in his mouth, Asher holds up a finger, his mouth still chewing. "*Candace* was the daughter of an executive I worked for. He didn't think I was good enough for her because I worked as a broker, and he had bigger plans for his little princess. You see, even though my name is Asher, I was a troublemaker, and people assumed I'd only gotten the job because of my grandfather's connections. Well, actually, that was why I'd gotten the job. No one thought I'd amount to much. Truth is, I didn't care if I did or didn't. All I wanted to do was play music. I wanted to work for a record label, but my grandfather insisted I take a job as a broker."

I eye him inquisitively. "You don't seem to me like the kind of person who does what others tell him to do."

His brow furrows with a look bearing a hint of resignation.

"At the end of the day, I am an Asher, and with the family name comes great responsibility. My grandfather...he has rules and is very strict about how they should be obeyed."

From the little I know about Asher, I understand he's an orphan. A boy who lost his mother at ten years old and went to live with his grandfather, who seems like he was a tyrant at home. From my head to the tips of my toes, I am dying to ask him more about his family, but I know, with Asher, there is only so far you can go without him diverting the conversation.

"So, how did you prove to the girl you were good enough?" I ask instead.

Seemingly grateful for the question, he nods and answers, "By making my first million, buying a small textile company and reselling it, which I was only able to do because my grandfather had given me the capital. I don't like to lie about how I got started. After my first big venture, everything snowballed from there. It was easy to buy and sell, and if all goes well, I will be buying my own record label, so I can follow my passion—music."

"And philanthropy!" I interject.

"And philanthropy. Yes, it's a large part of my life."

"So, what happened? Where is Candy? Why aren't you married with kids and living in Greenwich or somewhere?"

He kicks back a shot of sake. "Well, she did want me but for all the wrong reasons. I knew then that I would never know who loved me for me and not for this," he says, waving his hand in the air at our surroundings. "I don't trust people for a reason."

I swallow a lump and try to keep my mouth from falling. "Oh. I'm sorry. I didn't realize—"

"Don't worry. I don't mind."

"But I do. I assumed you liked being a bachelor, that you liked having a different woman every night." I pause before making my declaration. "You wanted more in life."

Asher leans back and laughs, his hand winding behind his head as he rubs his neck, his eyes darting around the table. "I think you've misunderstood. I quite enjoy the women I have in my bed."

My head tilts to the side as I continue to look at him. As his hand returns to the front of his body, Asher lifts his head, and his eyes meet mine. His cavalier grin melts as his eyes take in mine. His forehead crinkles.

Asher is avoiding my observation, and he knows I know it.

He looks at me as if conflicted about responding. "My grandfather pushed the thoughts of settling down out of my head. Said it causes more heartache and distraction than it's worth. He should know. He lost a daughter and took in her kid." His gaze drops to the table. "Growing up without a family makes me want one even more." There is a pause before he adds, "I've never said that out loud before."

Tears well up in my eyes.

When Asher said he wanted to be friends, I thought his tale of not being able to trust anyone was some sort of ploy. Now, I see it's merely the truth.

Is it possible that the sinful Asher who feasts on twinkies is really a romantic deep down? Could I have been so utterly wrong about this man? Have I been wrong about…everything?

He slowly leans across the table and gently cups my face, wiping my cheek with his thumb, catching a stray tear. "No, please, don't cry. Not for me. I don't deserve tears."

My breath hitches at his touch. His hand is so warm and comforting. My head falls lightly into his palm.

His eyes are sincere, and I bite back the sting of my tears to show him I'm okay.

"You are a great man. You deserve so much more than you allow yourself." I mean it.

Getting to know him over the past few weeks has been a pleasure. He might be inappropriate at times and even bossy. God, he can be downright pompous. Yet he is, without a doubt, the most amazingly contradictory person I have ever known.

"I have done some bad things over the years. In life, in business, and to women. Especially to women. They're my toys. They use me, and I use them. I like my lifestyle. I don't have to answer to anyone, and at this stage, I've grown accustomed to doing whatever the hell I want."

He releases my face from his grasp as I wipe the dew from my eyes.

I can't make him out. He is damaged but not irreparable.

"You need a shot!" Asher motions for the waiter. "Tequila, *por favor*!"

"Oh no! I haven't had tequila since college!"

"How I would love to have known you at eighteen."

Letting out a slight laugh, I release a deep breath and shake my head. "I'm sure you would." There's the Asher I know so well.

The waiter brings back three shots of tequila...each. I explain to Asher that this is way too much alcohol, but he assures me this is top-grade liquor and I can handle it.

"Lick your hand," he directs me.

I scrunch up my nose at the thought but shrug my shoulders and figure I'll give it a shot—pun intended. Tentatively at first, I poke my tongue out and touch the back of my hand.

Asher raises his hand to his mouth and glides his smooth, slick tongue across the back, like he's licking up ice cream. My lips part with a breath. I lift my hand back to my lips and try again, this time sliding my tongue across my soft skin, and look up to see Asher's eyes following the motion.

Asher lifts the saltshaker and sprinkles our hands. "Lick, sip, and squeeze." He offers me a lime. "Ready?"

I nod. *Here goes.* I lick my hand, gulp the shot of tequila, and squeeze the lime into my mouth. *Wow, that burns!*

"Feels good," he says and pushes the next shot of tequila in front of me.

We repeat the process.

We share a few good laughs, talking about some of our worst drinking experiences. My head feels lighter, and I start to sing along to one of the songs playing over the loudspeaker. It's a popular dance tune that has been remixed to a low downbeat, more laid-back for our setting.

After the third shot, I'm brazen. "Dance with me." My voice sounds impish and naughty, which makes me laugh because I am neither of those things.

Asher grabs my hand, and we stand, still inside the secluded cabana. Our bodies close, he wraps his arms around my waist and pulls me in tighter. My breasts rest on his chest; our groins connect. Not being the best dancer, I let him to lead the way.

I've danced with him without music before. He was magnificent then and even better now. The freeing feeling I have from the little bit of alcohol I drank allows me to move along with him, and I'm comfortable, even confident, in my movements. Our hips, bound together, sway from left to right and around in tiny circles.

Asher traipses his hand until it's firm on my lower back, causing my upper body to arch. He dips me and places his other hand on my chest, letting it travel down my body, from clavicle to navel. As he returns me upright, my body inches up in one smooth movement until I'm resting back on his chest.

My eyes widen when I feel his arousal through his bathing suit. My pulse quickens. My ears burn with heat and energy. My body is awakened.

Placing his hands on my hips, Asher spins me until I'm facing away from him. His palms rest low on my belly, and heat stirs within me, down in my sex. With his arousal pressing hard into my backside, I lay my hands over his, feeling my own throbbing deep in my core.

I lay the back of my head against his chest. We continue to move with each other, our hips now dipping in deep, erotic sways. With his mouth at my ear, I can feel hot, moist, erratic breaths against my neck. His lips lower to my skin, this time taking my neck in his mouth with warm, wet kisses. Tingles travel down my skin. The hairs on the back of my neck stand, and my nipples become erect, pleading, wanting, and needing. My breath hitches, and I drink in every sensation his luscious mouth gives me as he devours my skin.

With my hands still over his, I lower them, guiding him down my body, pleading for him to touch me.

Asher twists his hands in mine and grabs them to turn me back around. He is breathing hard, and his face is flush. "I'm taking you to your room," he whispers.

The walk to the room is faster than I thought it would be. My head spins a little. I think I fumble a few times on our way back. I drop my bag as I try to gather my room key. Asher lifts it from the floor and removes the key to open the door.

Before I can move my feet, he bends down and lifts me off the ground. We enter the room, and he kicks the door closed behind him. The room is dark, but the moonlight illuminates the space. Asher places me on the ground beside the bed. He walks over to the closet and removes something.

"Lift your arms." His voice is sultry.

I comply as he discards my cover-up.

"Again," he commands.

When I lift my arms, he places the nightie over my head, and it falls down my body. Turning me around, Asher undoes the strings of my bikini top, and it drops to the floor. He undoes my hair tie, and my hair tumbles past my shoulders.

Asher leans over the bed and pulls back the blankets. He lifts me in his arms and lays me gently onto the bed. Tucking the blankets over me, he leans down and places a kiss on my forehead.

"Good night, Gray," he says.

With the room spinning, my head is a mess of confusion, and I don't have the energy to fight. When the door closes, I lean over and place the pillow over my head to block out the moonlight.

Maybe, if I'm lucky, I'll suffocate.

chapter TWENTY-THREE

I have no idea what time I went to bed. I wake up at an ungodly hour with an ungodly hangover and an ungodly temper.

Last night, I thought he was going to make love to me. I thought he wanted me. I felt his need for me. I felt his lips on my skin, his palms on my body…I felt *him*!

When we came to the room, I thought this was it. But, no, he made me look like a fool—again! I can picture him laughing at me.

They're my toys. They use me, and I use them.

He probably ropes them all in, like the puppet master he is, with stories of his dead mother and wanting one of his own. The big, brooding billionaire can't find anyone who loves him for him. I can't believe I let him get to me. And with tequila!

Tequila.

My stomach dances, and I can't make it to the bathroom fast enough. The contents of my stomach expel from my body. My limbs go limp. My head pounds. I wish I could die here on the bathroom floor. This is the second time in two days I've found myself lying on porcelain. I seriously have to stop having such intimate moments with bathroom floors.

And then I hear the door open.

"Are you okay?" Asher rushes to me and wipes the hair away from my face.

What is he doing here?

"Get off me. I'm fine. Get out of here!" I shout and feel the need to get sick again.

This time, Asher grabs my hair and holds it as I empty what's left in my belly into the latrine. If I wasn't so sick, I'd be embarrassed.

No, scratch that. This is definitely the most embarrassing moment of my life.

When I'm done throwing up, Asher hands me a towel, and I wipe my face. I look up at him, wishing it were all a bad dream.

"Come on. Back in bed." He leans down and carries me back to the bed.

"What are you doing here?"

My head throbs and pulsates. Remember that throbbing I felt last night in my groin? Yeah, it's relocated to my brain, and it hurts. Or is it my heart? Could my heart have relocated to my brain? It's quite possible.

"I brought you room service. I'd figured you'd be in bad shape, so I ordered the Alexander Asher hangover kit."

His smirk needs to be smacked off his face.

He thinks this is funny. The bastard.

Asher sits on the bed next to me while I lie in my shame.

"First order of business," he says, "is Tylenol. Extra-strength. Open up."

I open my mouth, and he places two white tablets on my tongue.

"Now, wash it down with this."

I shake my head. "A Bloody Mary? I think I've had enough to drink."

"Nothing cures a hangover better than more alcohol."

He puts a straw to my mouth, and I inhale. I feel so shitty. I'll try anything to feel better.

"How are you not hungover? You drank as much as I did," I say, taking a bite of the toast he holds to my mouth. I take the toast from his hand and watch as he uncovers a dish of varied greasy breakfast foods.

"I'm twice your size. I should be able to handle more liquor than you. Though, I must admit, I didn't expect you to get as out of control as you did."

I drop my toast and feel the need to get sick again. For a second, I forgot about what had almost happened.

"I want to apologize for getting…carried away. Last night, I—"

My eyes shut in mortification. "Save it, Asher. I was drunk and clearly had no idea what I was doing. There's no way I would have danced like that if it wasn't for the tequila…and the sake…and the Sex on the Beach…" My stomach rolls, causing my eyes to open and face the source of my unease.

His face is pulled in, the corners of his eyes pushed down. His shoulders fall, and he lets out a breath.

"That's good news then. Here I thought, I'd have to let you down easy or something. I will now make a vow never to drink with you again." He smiles and gives me his phony Scout's honor salute.

My throat feels sore, and my chest surges upward as I fight the urge to cry. I take a deep breath instead.

"Good. I'm glad we're on the same page. I promise it will never happen again." I feel tears forming behind my eyes. "Now, if you don't mind, I need to get ready. Please leave."

Slowly nodding in agreement, he places his hands on his thighs and rises from the bed. His hand on the knob, Asher opens the door and pauses for a second. His broad shoulders rise and fall a few times, his muscles expanding up and out, visible through the button-down shirt he's wearing. His head sweeps to the right, and he talks over his shoulder, "You are expected downstairs in the spa at two to get ready for the benefit tonight. They know not to let you pay for a thing. No arguing."

He closes the door behind him, and I sob into my pillow.

I sleep the morning away. When I wake, I call Gwen to check on Jackson and feel much better after hearing my little man squealing on the other end. I search my phone for any missed calls from Gabriel, but there are none. If it wasn't for Jackson, I'd swear off all men.

When I put the phone down, I notice Asher left an invitation on the nightstand. It's for a party. The Asher Foundation is hosting a soiree in the hotel event space. I glance over to the closet and spot the emerald-green dress peeking out. I guess that's my uniform for tonight's event.

$$\Omega$$

I make my way to the spa on time. When I check in, I'm surprised to see I have a full itinerary prepared

For the first hour, I have a steam shower and my body scrubbed…literally. A brute of a woman rubs my body down with sea salt and washes all the toxins of Asher and tequila off my body. I'm thankful for her.

Next, I have a full-body mask. Sitting in a pile of seaweed and mud, I let the good nutrients enter my body. I indulge in a full massage, a facial, a manicure, and a pedicure.

I can't believe how fast the last four hours have gone. I could get used to this.

Finally, I'm escorted to the salon, where my hair is washed and styled. Due to the heat, I ask for something simple and off my neck. The makeup girl is heavy on the eye makeup. She wants my green eyes to "illuminate." I let her have her way but ask her to go soft on everything else.

I make it to the room with just enough time to get dressed. I pull out the one-shouldered, crepe Lanvin dress that falls above the knee. It is exquisite without being too formal. The stilettos go perfectly with the dress, but I'm not surprised, as a personal shopper selected them. I wish I had a bangle or cuff to go with the outfit, but I'm happy that I wore gold earrings yesterday, so I can pair them with the dress this evening.

Asher never said whether we'd meet in the lobby or in the room. Hell, he never said if we were to meet at all. I decide to head downstairs on my own.

The ride in the elevator has my stomach in knots. I still feel so foolish for the way I acted last night and angry over his reaction to it all. If I didn't have to work with him, I'd vow never to see Alexander Asher again.

The elevator slows, and the doors open, revealing a beautiful figure standing in the center of the space. A white dinner jacket, crisp white shirt, black pants, and no tie. His blond highlights look lighter from the afternoon sun. Further confirmation that they're natural.

Placing my hands on my belly, I try to calm my nerves. Pushing my shoulders back and lifting my chin, I exit the elevator. His golden eyes light up as I approach him, and it forces me to stop and take a deep breath.

His lips part as his eyes travel the length of my body, taking in my appearance. He opens his mouth further to say something, swallows, and then speaks, "You. Look. Beautiful."

The words travel off his tongue like a song. My favorite song. I wish I could stay mad at him, but against better judgment, I smile back at him and feel my guard being quickly let down.

"Shall we?" Asher offers me his arm.

Hesitantly, I take it as he escorts me to an outdoor area at the hotel where the cocktail portion of tonight's event is being held. Retro antiques and lanterns adorn the space, making it overflow with sensuality. Twinkling lights line the palm trees, as waiters walk by with champagne and hors d'oeuvres. After last night's fiasco, I forgo the champagne. I need to keep my head on tonight.

Asher walks me around the room, introducing me to Miami's elite and many others from the southeast region, whom Asher invited here for a fiesta. Most people have at least a decade on us, yet they all show extreme respect for him. For someone so young, Asher radiates wisdom, and his presence displays authority. People respond well to it.

Our goal for the evening is to solicit large sums of money for the Asher Foundation. Since these people won't be traveling to New York for the gala, we're looking for donors to promise five- or six-figure checks to be presented during the broadcast. For Asher, it's their way of showing respect. From a producer's standpoint, it would make for better television if we could display on the screen an unbelievable amount of money being donated.

Asher makes a short speech, welcoming everyone, and explains why funding music programs is important. Knowing his crowd, he keeps things very professional and speaks in numbers. The number of schools whose music programs have lost funding and the rise in adolescent arrests and drug use, which he feels is because young people need a place to focus their energy after school and music is the answer.

He gets a huge laugh when he assures everyone their donation is tax deductible, and he seals the deal by discussing the public relations explosion it would be for everyone and their businesses.

When he's done, he gets a few promises on the spot for sums of money I can't even believe these people can give up so easily. When people have further questions about the production going on, Asher lets me explain the various elements we have planned and when and where they can see it once it's filmed.

We continue to circle the room, mingling with guests, but there's one I have my eye on. One of the out-of-towners. We make our way over to a short, balding man and his well-tanned, ever-youthful wife.

"Oswald Thompson, may I introduce you to Kathryn Grayson? Ms. Grayson is heading our private benefit concert at Lincoln Center. Gray, Mr. Thompson here is…"

"An avid sportsman, I understand. Pleasure to meet the man who recently purchased a Minor League team. Congratulations, sir," I say.

Asher gave me a few names of who would be at the event tonight, and I remember Malory telling me about one in particular. I wasn't about to let Asher take this away from me. I am here to prove myself.

"Thank you, Ms. Grayson. May I introduce you to my wife, Ellie? Ellie has been incredibly bored since we got here. Perhaps you two could enjoy the party together."

Ellie looks at me with disdain, the same look I get from Heather at the office. I eye Thompson, who has already started chatting with Asher.

Accepting his dismissal of me, I turn to Ellie and speak a little louder than usual, "Ellie, you must be quite impressed by your husband's accomplishments. Especially his early career markings in the Minor League." I direct my attention back to Thompson. "I understand you had a one-point-two-three earned run average. I heard you had a curveball that would have sent the Babe swinging."

Thompson's ears perk up, as do his brows. He turns his attention from Asher to me. "I do know how to throw a ball, but my damn shoulder ended my career."

"Better off. The way they build parks today, with the fences drawn so close, they're made for The Home Run Derby. Pitching isn't the art form it used to be. It's all about the hitting now." I've been privy to plenty of conversations with my uncles.

"Sports fan, huh? What's your team?" Thompson asks.

I know he's a White Sox fan from his Minor League purchase within the franchise, but I'm not taking the bait. If I've learned one thing from Asher, it's that men of their caliber are tired of being told what people think they want to hear.

"New York Mets," I say proudly.

"Mets? I thought all respectable New Yorkers were Yankees fans?" Thompson laughs. "At least you didn't lie to me and say you were a Chicago fan to get on my good side."

Asher puts his hand on my back. "If I can assure you of one thing, Oswald, this woman doesn't lie. That's why she's on my team."

The heat of his hand burns into my backside.

Despite my distraction, I try to speak calmly, "Actually, Mr. Thompson, my father was a ballplayer. Have you heard of Frank Grayson?"

"Holy God in heaven. Your father was Catch Grayson?" Thompson throws his hands in the air in surprise. "Fine ballplayer. Mighty fine ballplayer. I saw him in New York right before he died. What an arm. What an arm!"

"Thank you, sir. He was a good man. It warms my heart to hear you speak so well of him." I will never tire of hearing stories of my father.

"I think this conversation calls for some champagne." Thompson waves over a waiter, and we each take a flute.

Once she has a drink in her hand, Ellie looks pleased for the first time all night.

As Thompson and Ellie take a sip, Asher leans into me, his voice low. "Be careful with this one." He steps back and eyes Thompson.

I roll my eyes at him and sling back my glass of champagne. "I can handle it."

The four of us toast, and Asher steps away as Thompson and I spend the next thirty minutes or so sharing sports stories. He asks me what it was like, growing up as a kid on the road, and I ask him about his Minor League career and thereafter.

The evening is going beautifully until Asher returns, letting me know there is someone he'd like me to meet. His voice is commanding, as if he thinks I'm going to say something wrong to Thompson and he wants me away from him.

"I've been enjoying the company of your date, Asher. Where did you find such a woman?" Thompson says.

His lips in a tight smile, Asher replies, "Not my date. Mrs. Greyson here is already spoken for."

Thompson looks from Asher to me and then winks at Asher. Their exchange is halted when someone taps Asher on the back. Both Asher and Thompson can't take their eyes off the busty brunette who enters our circle, and my mouth falls to the floor when I see it's Simone, the woman I saw exiting Asher's office many weeks ago.

She's wearing a skintight fuchsia cocktail dress that leaves little to the imagination. Her hazel eyes look up at Asher, and from under her lashes, I can see her giving him *the look*. The one that says, *I'm not wearing anything underneath this dress.*

"Sorry to crash your party, but I was hoping for a dance," Simone says.

Asher looks over from Simone to me to Thompson, his eyes landing back on Simone in agreement. "When a beautiful woman calls..." He smiles and slowly backs away. "If you'll excuse me."

Thompson's eyes are fixated on Simone's backside. Ellie doesn't seem to care.

I watch as Simone leads Asher to the dance floor. There are very few people dancing, so it's hard not to watch. She leans up and wraps her arms around him. Her short fuchsia ensemble climbs higher up her thighs as she dances. Asher places his palms on her hips, as he did with me yesterday, and my stomach drops.

Their bodies are so familiar with one another. They're graceful, and they fit together perfectly. Her dark skin against his bronzed, statuesque figure, they look like a Rodin statue in a heated embrace at the gates of hell.

The gates of hell—the exact place my thoughts have gone time and time again with this man. The place my thoughts are right now.

"If you continue to stare like that, your eyes will fall out of your head," Ellie says with a mischievous laugh.

Thompson chuckles along.

Snapping out of my daze, I turn back to my company. My cheeks redden, and I fluster.

"It's okay, girl. It's hard not to be taken by Asher. He has so many…assets." Thompson sneers.

My mood turns quickly from feeling foolish to furious.

"I am a married woman, Mr. Thompson. The fact that you think I would be interested in Mr. Asher for his…assets is the most intolerable thing I have ever heard," I declare and then regret raising my tone to the man I came here to beg for money.

I'm relieved to see Thompson chuckling again. Okay, so he's not insulted by my outburst.

"Asher was wrong about you." The little man continues to smile, wickedly.

"Excuse me?"

Thompson rests on his heels, his finger pointing at me in an accusatory manner. "He said you didn't lie."

I'm so confused. I don't know what to do with myself. I excuse myself and stalk toward the exit, glancing at the dance floor but noticing Asher is gone. I stop and scan the room, looking for his white dinner jacket, but I don't see him…or Simone.

My heart races, and I quickly make my move toward the lobby.

I shouldn't be surprised he would leave my side the second a sexy brunette approached. He is a cad and a snake. He uses women like I use Kleenex.

I spot a waiter walking into the party with a tray of champagne glasses and a bottle in his hand. I take a glass of champagne and quickly pound it before grabbing another. I drink that one before cutting to the chase and grabbing the entire bottle of Veuve Clicquot from his hand.

Briefly considering entering the party again, I think of what a fool I've made of myself and turn in the opposite direction. Heading out a glass door, my bottle and I follow the path to the beach. My steps start by walking but get caught in the sand so I take them off. Faster, my feet move toward the shore until I'm running. Faster and faster. The champagne spills out of the bottle as I leap across the sand. In the dark of night, the only sounds I can hear are the waves crashing. There is nothing. Just me and the beach, where no one can hear me.

I scream.

I scream from the pit of my stomach, out of my chest, out of my feet, and out of my hair. I scream out of my lungs and let out my soul.

I scream so loud that it hurts.

The past forty-eight hours have been the most miserable of my life, but what I really can't take—the piece of me that hurts so much that I don't know what to do with it—is the fact that despite everything, despite the last forty-eight hours, the truth, the plain truth, is that I think I'm falling for Asher.

I can't breathe.

I try to fight it. I've been trying to fight it. As much as I want to deny it, I can't help but find myself so incredibly drawn to him. He is an awful person. I know it. He leads me on and then leaves me hanging. He plays me for a fool time and time again, and I fall for it time and time again.

He is a walking contradiction. He's arrogant, but he cares so much for those less fortunate. He is rude and dismissive, yet he gives me time to share my stories. He is insightful and funny. He always knows how to make me laugh, and he gets me.

I hate that I'm so attracted to him. He's so physically attractive that my body doesn't know how to be in a room with him without wanting to jump on him.

"There! Fine, I admit it. I want him!" I shout into the ocean. "You happy, Karma? You're a bitch, and I know it!"

I am so upset that I can't even cry. I physically don't have the energy to cry. I'm so hurt and sad and disappointed that I just want to scream. I can't believe I thought for a moment that Asher wanted me.

Why would he want me when my husband doesn't even want me?

Collapsing in the sand, I raise the bottle to my mouth and start to drink. The sand feels cool. It's refreshing against the warm night air. I feel the bubbles of the champagne down my throat as I continue to listen to the waves. I drink in the moment. I know, in years to come, I'll remember this as the beginning of the rest of my life.

From here on out, it's just me and Jackson.

I raise the mostly full bottle of champagne and stare at it.

This isn't who I am. I don't leave an important work event and get drunk on a beach. I don't fly off the handle and make irrational decisions.

I let myself go.

Breathe.

I gather my shoes and start walking back toward the hotel. My dress has gathered sand on the bottom of the hem. Such a shame. It was a beautiful dress. I can't go back to the party, looking the way I do. It's time I head up to my room and get the old Kathryn back.

I'll book myself on the first flight out of here. I need to see Jackson.

I divert from the party and enter the hotel through a separate entrance. I have champagne on my dress and sand on my feet. I've made enough of a fool of myself tonight.

I get on the elevator with a young couple in the throes of passion and an elderly woman who looks at me in concern. I slide into the corner of the car and hang my head low. After stopping on the third and fourth floors, I'm relieved to be alone. When it reaches my floor, the doors open, and I head down the hallway toward my room.

My feet stop in their place. Outside my door is a man in a white dinner jacket with his head bowed, one hand resting against the door and a cell phone in the other, up against his ear. He looks concerned. He lifts his head as I approach and turns off his phone.

chapter TWENTY-FOUR

"Gray." Asher looks at me in concern. His body turns toward me with his arms stretched out. "Where have you been? I've been calling you."

I shrug my shoulders. "Don't you have somewhere else to be, Asher? Shall I say, somewhere else with *someone* else?"

"What are you talk—" His brow furrows before rising, his head slowly nodding in understanding. "Simone? Are you upset about Simone?"

I move my arm to motion him out of my way as I move past him and to my door. "Enough. I'm tired, and I want to go home." I open the door to my room and am surprised when Asher catches it before it closes and pushes it back open with his right hand.

"You're going home?" His left arm wraps around his head, and he rubs the back of his neck, making the shirt wrinkle out of his jacket.

My voice rises in a harsh tone. "Please leave."

Asher releases the door, and in one stride, he makes his way toward me. With both hands, he takes my face. "Please. Talk to me."

My heart wants to melt, but I can't be roped back into the vicious cycle. I remove his hands from my cheeks.

"This has to stop," I cry.

"What has to stop?"

"This." I motion to the space between us. "All of this. The talks, the gifts, the touching, the dancing, the kisses…all of it."

His body is bowed toward me in a plea. His face is in anguish, and that deep voice of his loses its footing. "What happened? Please. Talk to me."

I can't do this anymore.

"Go back to Simone. Go fuck her for all I care. Just leave me alone." I take my clothes from the closet and make my way toward the door.

My heart nearly leaps out of my chest as Asher grabs my shoulders, holding me still. I can't move from his grasp.

"I don't want Simone. Why do you think I'm here?" His eyes search mine for the answer, for recognition that I understand what he's saying. "I walked her to the elevator. She wanted me to come up, but I didn't want to. I went back for you. I went back, and you were gone."

He went back for me?

I will not get my hopes up. I can't go into the darkness with him any longer. "No, Alex. I can't do this. I can't be your friend anymore."

I try not to look into his eyes, but he grabs my chin and forces me to look at him.

"Why can't you be my friend anymore? Tell me!" His voice is stern.

"Because of this!" I move backward out of his hold. My eyes brim with tears, but I will them away. "Because when you touch me, I melt. When you stand near me, my body lights on fire."

I can't believe these words are pouring out of my mouth. I don't care. He has to hear this. I have to put an end to this.

"You say you want to be friends, but I can't. You say I'm refreshing and you love spending time with me. You say you're relaxed around me. But I…I'm a ball of knots around you. I can't breathe half the time."

Asher screams out, "You think I'm relaxed around you?" His eyes are on fire.

The controlled man starts to pace in front of the door. The only door that marks my escape. He runs his hands through his golden hair and tugs at the ends in frustration.

Exasperated, I don't know what to do to make him move and let me the hell out. I try to reason with him. "You said…you always…you say you want to be friends, and then this happens…"

"I know what I said, but it's a lie. I said that shit about being friends, so you'd spend time with me, so you wouldn't run from me every time I entered the room." He stops pacing as his body tenses, raising his hands into tight fists, punching the air around him. "You think I'm relaxed? I've been a nervous wreck for weeks!"

He hits the dresser with his fist. My body flinches at his action.

"Damn it! I've wanted you from the first time I saw you in the rain. I swear I didn't know who you were, but you were the most beautiful creature I'd ever seen in my life. Then I found out you were married. It nearly killed me."

He swallows hard and walks toward me, determined.

"Don't say it," I plead, yet inside, I desperately want him to keep on going.

"I want you, Kathryn." When Asher says my name, my real name, it sounds like a prayer on his lips.

My face flashes hot, and tears begin to form behind my eyes. "No, you can't."

"I. Want. You. Kathryn. I want you. I want you. I want you!" He pauses for a second, and with no warning, his body comes crashing toward me like a bulldozer. "Fuck it…I need you."

His lips press hard on mine, and in animalistic passion, our arms lock around each other. Yearning, wanting, needing…our lips move fast and steady. Our tongues dance, and I find it hard to breathe. Not from nerves, but from the sheer pace of our actions. I steady my lips, trying to fight the urge, but he has ahold on them. He tastes so sweet and smells so exotic.

I try to fight it...

I try to resist it...

I try...

I try...

I fail.

With pure abandon, my lips answer his with equal earnest. My body follows suit, pressing my weight back into his. Not in my wildest dreams did his mouth taste as sinful as it does right now.

All inhibitions are lost. My soul is his for the taking.

"I've wanted you for so long," Asher murmurs through our kisses. "Let me make love to you tonight. Just one night. That's all I ask." He pulls back, and his eyes search mine for approval.

My body craves him, my mouth needing his taste again. I'm at the point of no return. I know this is wrong, but I am so tired. Tired of fighting whatever this is.

"Yes," I cry out.

And that's all he needs. Asher bears down on me, forcing my back against the wall. I drop the suit I was holding in my hand His lips move brutally across my mouth, his tongue performing dangerous acts against mine.

Taking my hands in his, Asher raises them above my head, pinning me to the cold, hard surface of the wall. His full weight presses against me, and I can feel his arousal against my belly. Every divot and sculpted muscle is hard against the front of my body. With his hands strong in mine as they hold me in place, I am at his mercy.

Asher's mouth travels along my jaw, taking tiny bites of my neck and along my collarbone until he is nipping at my ear and sucking on the lobe. The sensation traveling through my body sends a tingling down my spine and deep into my core.

My mind knows this is wrong, but my body can't resist. I want this man. Hell, I *need* this man. I've never craved anything more in my life.

Taking my head in his hands, Asher tugs my hair, forcing my mouth up. His kiss is explosive. I can feel his desire continue to build as his kisses quicken.

In one swift motion, Asher's hand slips along my neck and pulls at the string of my dress, sending the silky fabric down my body, pooling at my feet. His hand slides down my neck and rests on the clasp of my bra, and he unhooks it with the tips of his fingers. That, too, falls to the floor.

My breasts exposed, I feel helpless. Asher takes my nipple between his fingers and tugs at it. I cry out in pleasure. His other hand cups my bottom and pulls me tighter into his groin.

I can't take any more. I need to feel his skin. Hungry with the thought of feeling him, I lace my fingers between the openings of his shirt and rip it off his body. Buttons fly across the room, but I have no apologies.

Asher lets out a deep growl from within his chest and leans down. Taking my breast in his hot mouth, he sucks on it, licking circles along the rim.

My cries must do something to him because he rises back to his feet and takes my mouth in his again, and I can feel the rock-hard impression of his desire so heavy against me that I can't imagine what it will feel like without the clothes between us.

I press my body against his and nearly collapse at the feeling of his hard chest against my breasts. My hands caress his firm torso and move toward his strong back, pushing the shirt and jacket away from his body.

Releasing our mouths, I steal a glance to appraise the man. Asher stands in front of me, panting, wearing nothing but satin skin over hard muscle and a black pair of pants.

I can't believe this is really going to happen. This incredible, sexy man is mine. Even if it's only for one night, this ultimate Apollo, the great omega, is mine.

I drink him in.

My eyes rise, and I startle when I see his looking down on me, not at my body, but straight into my soul.

"You are so beautiful," he says, his chest rising and falling so fast and hard that I almost didn't hear him.

He took the words right out of my mouth.

Asher grabs my backside and hoists me up to him, forcing my legs to wrap around his waist. He carries me to the bed and lays me down on the soft duvet.

I sit up on my elbows and watch as he slowly removes his belt and pants, leaving him naked in front of me. I have to blink twice to make sure I'm seeing him properly.

He is as impressive as I dreamed he'd be.

Asher climbs onto the bed, his masculine, hard body hovering over mine. Sitting on his knees, he stops and stares down at me, his hands massaging the inside of my legs as they travel to my lace panties. Hooking his two forefingers inside, he skims them down my legs and throws them onto the nightstand beside the bed. He slowly licks his lips, and his pupils dilate as he lowers his head toward me. My legs widen to accommodate the width of his shoulders as he settles between my thighs. He dips his head and kisses my navel, plunging his tongue in and out.

My hips arch off the bed, pleading for him to move down. His mouth feels so good that I jump out of my skin. My body is wet, and heat pools deep down inside of me, begging for him to be nearer. His tongue glides down my inner thigh, kissing and nipping my skin and nearly sending me over the edge.

"Alex, please," I beg.

"No." His head lifts, and carnal eyes meet mine. "If I only get you once, I need to soak this in. Tonight, we play by my rules." His commanding tone drips with sex.

I grasp his hair in my hands and guide his mouth to the height of my desire. His tongue knows exactly where to go and starts by licking the sensitive folds already hot with lust.

"Do you know how long I've wanted to do this?" he says, lapping up my wetness with the smooth velvet of his tongue.

I let out a loud moan of pure pleasure. He rewards me with a lick to my swollen clit. I gasp for breath.

"Hold on, baby. Now that I've tasted you, I can't stop," he says just before lowering himself back down. He quickly starts circling my need, flicking, licking, and sucking at a pace I didn't know was humanly possible.

I tug his hair in approval, and he continues on, his tongue vibrating on my clit. There is no downtime, no need for him to go faster. My body is trying to back away because the gratification is too much and too fast, and too good.

Asher dips two fingers inside me, making a come-hither motion, and my need rises. When he quickens his fingertips to match his mouth, my body is close to bursting. Sweat pebbles on my chest, and my ears burn so hot that I might explode. My mind goes blank, and my voice is crying out in sounds that aren't human.

I need it, want it, feel it…fuck it!

My body collapses around his fingers, my desire pooling into his mouth. My torso, so far off the bed, crashes down onto the duvet. Instead of being spent, I'm ignited. I grab Asher's head and move his gorgeous, full lips closer to mine, tasting my arousal on his beautiful, pout.

"I need you inside me," I say, taking his tongue so deep in my mouth that I swallow him whole.

Asher pulls back and reaches over to his pants that were left on the edge of the bed. Producing a foil package, he rips it open and slides a condom down his very impressive manhood. His eyes spy mine eyeing up his erection.

"You have no idea what you do to me." Asher mounts his body on top of mine and positions himself so that his hard length is settled just outside my wet entrance.

Taking my hand in his, Asher holds it over my head and pushes it down into the bed, pinning me in place. His other hand wraps around my waist and braces me for what's about to happen.

Holding his head just above mine, he looks down at me, his golden eyes intense on mine. "I need to watch you," he says.

I nod, looking deep into those brown flecks you can only see when you're really looking at him. Without warning, Asher presses himself hard inside me. I gasp in desire

Asher stalls for a second, waiting for my body to adjust to his. He retrieves himself and slams back into mine once more, rubbing my body from the inside out with his. I feel myself begin to climax again.

He feels it, too, and quickly slams his body into mine, harder and faster with each thrust. My internal orgasm builds deep inside my belly. My eyes roll into the back of my head, the intensity of each movement forcing them to close. I have never in my life experienced this much pleasure.

"Kathryn!" Asher cries out.

The sound of my name pouring out of his beautiful mouth in ecstasy is all I need to push me back over the edge. My body explodes.

Fingers gripping the sheets, I try to stabilize myself. I'm having an out-of-body experience.

Asher collapses on top of me, burying his head into my neck. We lie there, all legs and arms wrapped around each other, as our heartbeats steady.

Asher runs his hand up and down my arm as I catch my breath.

Coming back to my senses, I shouldn't be surprised how natural it feels to be in his arms. I bathe in the warmth of his skin.

His hand moves up to my hair, and he softly brushes it away from my face. His lips kiss my head. I inhale his intoxicating scent, drinking in this incredible creature.

"I dreamed of this," he whispers in my ear.

I look at him, still not believing I'm really here, naked in bed with Alexander Asher.

Raising my right hand, I tenderly caress the side of his face. He closes his eyes as I run the tips of my fingers across his strong jaw and trace the line up to his temples and down the slope of his nose and the curve of his soft lips. He lets out a breath when my hand moves down to his neck and over his Adam's apple to rest on his chest, his heart. Under my palm, I can feel his chest rise and fall in a deep, rhythmic pattern. His heartbeat quickens.

"What are you thinking about?" I ask.

His eyes flutter for a second before he answers, "You." He leans down and kisses my lips, softly. "I'm waiting for you to leap from this bed and scream about how wildly inappropriate this is."

He's right. I should be running for the door. But I can't.

"You asked me for one night. The damage is done, and I don't regret it. At least, right now, I don't regret it. I'm here. I'm staying…at least for the night."

Tomorrow. I can deal with this tomorrow. For now, I am content in his arms.

chapter TWENTY-FIVE

The room is pitch-black when I wake. *What time is it?* I turn to the side, but I can't see the alarm clock. I try to lift my head, but Asher's arm is tightly wrapped around me. So is his leg for that matter. I take his hand and unravel it from my body. His leg is more difficult. I have to catch my breath after trying to remove his massive leg from around my hip.

I crawl out of the bed, placing the covers back on top of him.

Trying to navigate in the darkness, I tiptoe across the room and into the bathroom. The light is too bright, and I contemplate turning it back off.

I lean over the sink and wash off the heavy eye makeup. I pull the pins out of my hair and shake out the curls. Looking up in the mirror, I assess the damage. Surprisingly, I don't look that bad. My hair is long and wavy from being pulled up for the gala. My skin is red from sun and sex. Spending an exhilarating night with Alexander Asher seems to agree with me.

Exhilarating it was. His body is incredible, and his mouth can do extraordinary things. Even more extraordinary than the physical were his words. He needed me. He dreamed of me.

I look back at the woman in the mirror. Yes, she is a woman. A hot, attractive, feral woman.

Grabbing a soft waffle robe from behind the door, I wrap it around my body. The man has already devoured my body, but there is still a sense of modesty to be upheld.

I open the door and am startled to see Asher sitting up in bed with the sheet draped across his hip. I want to crawl on top of him. The light from the bathroom casts a heavenly glow. He looks godlike. The hard stare of his eyes boring into mine looks primal.

I walk across the room to open drapes that lead to the patio overlooking the ocean.

"Don't," he commands.

"Don't open the window?" I ask.

"No. I closed the curtains after you went to sleep."

I raise an eyebrow at him. With the bathroom as my only source of light, I scan the room and notice the alarm clock is unplugged. "Did you also unplug the clock?"

"Yes."

"Why in the world would you do that?"

"You said I could have you for one night, and I don't want this night to end."

"Alex, this isn't going to…"

Asher rises from the bed, standing tall in his naked glory. "Don't overthink this, Kathryn. We've already sinned, and I have no regrets. I just want you, and if I have to make time stand still, I'll lock myself in this room with you forever."

He takes my head in his hands, his thumbs grazing my cheeks, his lips firm and his eyes serious. "Tonight isn't over. It's just you and me."

Asher leans down. His kiss is soft and gentle, more passionate. I can feel his desire for me, and I reciprocate. I don't want the night to end either.

"Shower with me." I grab his hand and lead him into the bathroom.

With a boyish grin, he obliges, taking a foil packet on the way in. Asher is already naked, so he walks into the massive shower and turns the water on. I can tell it's hot from the steam that billows out against the glass door. He reaches out his hand, and hoists me into the shower with him, robe and all.

I laugh out loud as he wraps his arms around me, and we kiss under the warm water. The weight of my robe grows heavy, and I'm relieved as he unwraps me like a Christmas present, our bodies becoming one under the steady stream.

His lovemaking is slower than before, but the intensity is the same. I fall apart in his arms, and my legs are jelly once again. I feel as if we were made to pleasure each other.

When we both come to, we slowly explore each other's bodies with soap. I place soft kisses on a scar that rests below his shoulder blade. Asher spends too much time admiring a beauty mark on my inner calf.

We wash each other's hair and have a soap fight with the bubbles from our overuse of body wash. The water runs cold, and our fingers start to prune from too much time spent under the shower.

We dress ourselves in towels. I hang back and take a moment to dry my hair and freshen myself up. Exiting the bathroom, I'm shocked to see the room illuminated in the soft splendor of candles.

"Aren't you full of surprises? Where did you get candles?" I ask.

This man is always such a mystery.

"Maybe it's magic," he says from his place by the bed.

"I doubt it. Let me guess. You texted Devon to buy candles."

Asher lets out a laugh and hangs his head in mock shame. "You know me too well."

Even if this is only for one night, Asher is pulling out all the stops. I wonder if he's like this with all his women. I push the idea out of my head. I'm not ruining this moment. If it's only for one night, I'm going to enjoy every second of it.

"I've ordered in. Come, let's eat." He places a soft kiss on my neck and leads me to a table by the window.

His towel is too small for his frame, and I giggle at the sight of flesh peeking out from beneath.

"What I would give to know what goes on inside that little head of yours." His luminous smile glows brighter than I've ever seen it.

"Very dirty thoughts."

"Care to share?"

"You can use your imagination. Mostly revisiting the act of you ravaging me in the shower. You have given me plenty of moments to relive once this night is over."

A frown registers on his face.

Did I say something wrong?

His eyes look down at the table. "Let's not talk about tonight ending yet. The night, as they say, is still young."

I nod and take a seat. Asher ordered a smorgasbord of food—from pancakes to lamb chops, chocolate cake to a Caesar salad.

"Since we have no idea what time it is, I didn't know if you'd want breakfast or dinner." His full mouth is mesmerizing as he speaks, and I lean over to kiss it.

"This is perfect. I'm starving."

He laughs heartily. "What would you like?"

"Pancakes!"

"I ordered them especially for you. You told me that night we went out to the bar. You were standing under the streetlight, looking like heaven. I wanted to kiss you then, but I knew you'd just run."

I recall that night. Thank God he didn't kiss me. I would have quit my job.

"You were my knight in shining armor. You took care of me that night. There is something about you. I fall apart when I'm around you."

"That's good to know because I feel the same way about you."

The pancakes are warm and buttery, as sinful as the act they followed. I dive my fork and marvel at how easily they separate. They remind me of the first night I spent with Gabriel—or shall I say, the first morning?

$$\Omega$$

I awoke to the smell of butter on a frying pan. I knew something delicious was cooking in the kitchen. Yes, there was something very delicious—Gabe in nothing but sweatpants and a spatula, making me pancakes in the very modest kitchen of his college apartment. I must have startled him when I entered the room because he dropped a pancake on the floor at the sight of me.

His face was young and eager, his smile broad and excited to see I was still there.

Gabe ushered me to a chair and poured me a glass of orange juice. I couldn't deny my surprise that he had the ingredients to make breakfast. Not many boys kept a stocked refrigerator or anything other than beer and ramen noodles. Even still, he didn't strike me as the type of guy who made breakfast often.

I raised the fork to my mouth and took a bite. One bite, and, boy, was I right about this one.

How on earth did he make them so hard?

Maybe if I tried adding more butter or syrup, they'd taste better. No, no help.

I looked up to see Gabe staring at me, watching me eat. I put on a gracious smile. It was so cute that he'd cooked for me. I couldn't insult him.

When Gabe finally took a bite himself, he immediately spit it out. "Oh my God, that's awful!"

Call it nervous energy and completely inappropriate for the mood, but I broke out into complete laughter. I was so relieved that he felt the same way, and I just let out the biggest, gut-wrenching laugh. I nearly fell out of my seat. After a few beats, Gabe joined in, laughing, too, and that felt even better.

When our nerves and laughter settled, we sat for a few seconds and caught our breath until a frown formed across Gabriel's eyes. He stood and walked toward the kitchen. Pushing his hair off his forehead, he took a few paces in the kitchen before returning to the table and taking his seat.

"What's the matter?" I asked.

Leaning back on his chair, Gabe crossed his arms across his hunched chest. His chin lowered as he shook his head. "I wanted to impress you," he said.

Lifting myself from the chair, I walked toward him. Uncrossing his hands, I pulled them apart and took a seat on his lap, wrapping my arms around him. I landed a sweet kiss on his lips and looked into his navy-blues.

"You are the most impressive man I've ever met. I don't need pancakes. I just need you."

His grin melted my heart and widened into a gorgeous smile that reached his eyes. Tugging me closer, he kissed me with his whole body, and I reciprocated.

"Come back to me, Kathryn."

I smile at the memory of a simpler time. A time that wasn't that long ago yet feels so far away. It's amazing how much people can change in a day, a year, a decade. It's a hard lot to swallow when you're promising an eternity.

"Stop overthinking." Asher's eyes are on me. He stands up and makes his way around the table. He leans down to me, placing soft kisses on my shoulder. "Come. Back. To. Me."

Even though we've been more intimate than some married couples, I still feel nervous around him. I smile and try to ease his curiosity. He wants one day, and I want to give it to him. With Asher, I feel as sexy and alive as I did when I was a teenager. I want to live in this moment.

"I know you like living in our cocoon up here, but we should get some fresh air," I suggest, turning to my side and facing a kneeling Asher.

"I don't trust that you'll leave this room and not freak out." He leans back on his heels. "I meant what I said. I need you. What you've done to me in the last few weeks has been amazing. I've never woken up with a woman and wanted to spend more time with her. Usually, it's the complete opposite. But you, you make me thirsty for more. I'm not ready to give that up. If you walk out that door, it's over between us. I know it."

He's right. I haven't told him about Gabriel's affair, and when I do, this thing between us will be over. We both know Asher only wants me because he can't truly have me.

"I'm a grown woman. I know what I'm doing." I rise from the table and walk back toward the bathroom.

"Where are you going?" He sounds concerned.

"Swimming."

Ω

Asher calls for an attendant to set up a cabana with two lounge chairs on the beach, facing the water. Again, we're in our little cocoon, but I'm enjoying my time with him, so I can last for one more day. Besides, what am I rushing home to?

His skin glistens in the sun. It's an added bonus to be able to pay homage to him in the daylight instead of our love den upstairs. I pull my chair out of the cabana and into the light. I still haven't looked at a clock, but I assume it's close to one. Asher has also sworn off cell phones for the two of us, and so far, I've obliged.

The waves crash nearby, and I dance in the sound of them. There is no greater feeling. I lie back, close my eyes, and daydream about the amazing last few hours. Up against the wall, the bed. The shower…it was hot. Asher is more than I could have imagined. Who knew my body could respond like that?

I fantasize about his beautiful body and gorgeous face—him touching me, tasting me, doing incredible things to me. I relive every caress and recount every thrust. If the sun wasn't making me sweat, the thoughts of last night would.

Sinking deeper into my dream, I lick my lips in satisfaction. Yes, it was that good.

I am lost in my dream until…

I'm wet!

I let out a girlish scream.

I'm wet. Literally, not in a turned-on kinda way.

I look up to see a grinning, devilish Alexander Asher with an empty glass, which the remains of, I can only assume, are now on me. The ice-cold liquid against my heated body is painful, and I instinctively want to hurt him.

Asher laughs and backs away toward the beach. "You looked like you needed to cool off," he chides. "You should stop fantasizing about me and enjoy the real thing."

He grabs my waist and hoists me toward the water.

Like he always does, he makes me hate him and want him in the same breath. The ocean water is warm in comparison to the cold drink yet freezing compared to the heat of my body. I thrust myself up against Asher in search of body heat to protect me from the cold current. With one hand around my waist, the other locks around my ponytail and pulls my head back until my lips are facing his. He leans down and takes my mouth in his, and I immediately begin to warm up. With his body tight against me, I can feel all of him.

When he finally releases me from our kiss, he steps back and splashes me. I splash back, and like teenagers, we're wrestling and playing in the water, stealing kisses when we can.

Parasailers glide above us and shout obscene things, but I can't hear exactly what they're saying. We're too into each other.

I'm amazed how much fun Asher can be. We have handstand contests and show off our best skills. When the waves pick up, Asher challenges me to a body-surfing competition. I win by default when my bathing suit falls off. My prize is getting it back after much embarrassment.

Growing hungry, Asher races me back to our chairs, which I legitimately win, and we dry each other off with oversize beach towels. Asher orders oysters, mini sliders, and Coronas.

After enjoying my meal, I lean back into the soft cushion of my chair and take in the beautiful day.

To the right of us, a little girl is playing in the sand. She has black hair and black eyes with a bright white smile. She's wearing a one-piece suit with pink hibiscus flowers. I watch her diligently shovel sand into her pail and haphazardly dump it out. She is a sweet sight, reminding me of my angel. My sweet boy with his wavy hair and navy eyes. My boy who drools all over me and refuses to say my name. My cherub who loves to kick his feet in the bath water and is probably learning how to walk at this very moment. My baby who I'm not with right now.

"Jackson!"

I pop up from the lounge chair and look over at Asher, who is staring at me with a confused expression. I turn back at the hotel behind us, the beach in front of us, the cabanas around us, and the little girl to my right.

What am I doing here?

This is not me. The kind who runs off to another state with her boss and…oh my God…has an affair.

Who am I?

I am a mother.

How could I have forgotten that?

Despite Gabriel, despite Asher, there is a boy whom I love more than anyone in this world. He isn't home, and he is certainly not with me.

Not too long ago, I yearned for a day when I would get out of the house, go back to work, and become the successful woman I'd once set out to be. I wanted my son to be raised by a strong, independent woman. To show him that you could achieve anything in this world if you put your mind to it. I wanted to be his greatest role model.

This is not the life I'd want my son to be proud of.

"I have to go!" I practically jump out of my chair. I throw the cover-up over my head and grab my purse before storming off toward the hotel.

"Kathryn!"

I leave a stunned pair of golden eyes in the cabana as I race through the hotel grounds and inside, making it into the elevator just as the doors are about to close.

Seconds before they shut, I see Asher darting through the lobby.

"Kathryn!" he calls, but the doors shut tight and the car rises up to my floor.

I need to pack. *Pack what?* I need to change and get the hell out of here.

I get to my room door and go to open it. My key! I need a key. It's in my bag.

I'm searching for the key when I hear the elevator ping. I gather the key out of my bag as Asher darts down the hall.

I open the door and enter the room, marching straight to the closet. I need the clothes I came in.

Asher is right behind me. "Where are you going?"

"Home." I grab the suit off the floor where I dropped it last night.

"Shit!" he swears, placing his hand on the back of his neck, rubbing hard. He's wearing nothing but his trunks. "I knew we should have never left this room."

"I'm sorry, but I have to go home." I slip my skirt on over my bathing suit. I'll pay him for it when I get back.

"Don't go," he pleads.

Stretching the button-down over my arms, I make sure not to look at his eyes. They'll force me to stay; I know it.

"Asher, please…"

"Asher? What happened to…" He fumbles over his words. "Just stay the day. We'll leave together in the morning." He approaches me, trying to make contact.

"I have to see Jackson!"

He looks at me, aggravated, agitated, confused.

"*Who is Jackson?*" he nearly screams the question at me.

Holy. Fuck.

My hands stop buttoning my blouse, and I look up to see his gorgeous face pleading, desperate.

"Jackson is my son," I whisper. *How does he not know this?*

"You have a son?" He makes it sound like he just swallowed a bitter pill.

I take a step back.

How does this man not know I have a son? We've talked about this. Haven't we?

FUCK!

"I have a child. You know this." I continue buttoning my shirt.

"I had no fucking clue you had a kid." He turns from me and rubs the back of his neck with his hand, harder this time. "How old?"

"A little over a year." My voice is low, and my head is down.

What have I done? I throw my jacket on.

He shoots around, and I can see the hurt around his eyes. "You have a baby?"

I've never felt lower in my entire life.

I slide on my shoes and grab my purse. I don't belong here.

"I have a baby named Jackson. I need to get home to him. He is who I should be with. I shouldn't be here with you." I head toward the door, stopping just before leaving. "I thought you knew."

I pause for a second, staring at the floor, waiting for…I don't know what I'm waiting for. His silence is deafening, yet his body is screaming at me with tension. Turning the handle, I swing the door open and let it close behind me as I walk away.

Just like that, I exit the hallway. Exit the elevator. Exit the lobby and hop into a cab.

Asher doesn't follow me.

Ω

Why I thought I could easily hop a flight back to New York is beyond me. I sit in the airport for hours, waiting to board my plane. I try calling Gabriel from the terminal, but he's still not picking up. My battery is dying when it's time to board the plane. I turn it off to save a little bit of juice.

My seat is 33A, in coach, a far cry from the private jet I arrived in yet exactly what I deserve. The girl next to me is afraid to fly. I can tell because her guy next to her is holding on to her hand and comforting her sweetly.

Great.

I stare out the window, watching the world below me disappear. The last seventy-two hours have marked me in a way I'll never be able to undo. This whole time, I've been focusing on a lost marriage when I've been losing myself. Going back to work isn't the problem. My husband working late isn't the problem. I'm the problem. My priorities have been in the wrong place.

What's wrong with being a stay-at-home mom? What's wrong with cherishing my little boy? Was it so bad? Did I have it so rough that I couldn't just be happy?

And Gabriel. So what if he did run into the arms of another woman? Isn't that exactly what I just did?

I've made a mess of everything.

I need to make it right.

But can I?

Ω

I exit JFK International Airport and catch a cab. The New York sky is thick with clouds, a complete contrast to the beautiful blue sky of Miami.

I try Gabriel's cell phone again. No answer.

With my legs crossed, my dangling foot shakes a mile a minute, banging on the seat in front of me. I know it's bothering the driver, but I can't stop. Scrolling through my phone, I bite my thumbnail as I wait for Gabriel to call me back.

Why isn't he calling?

My phone chirps the familiar sound of a new email coming through. I open the email app and see a message from an unfamiliar address. I tap it open and download the attachment.

Before my eyes, an image pops up on the screen that makes my heart fall down to my stomach.

It's a photo of Asher and me from this afternoon, making out like teenagers in the water. I can feel the blood rushing from my face as the horror of the situation becomes reality. Someone knows what happened in Miami, and they have the pictures to prove it.

Who could have sent this to me?

I go back to the original message and look at the address. I don't know who it is. But the photos were forwarded to someone else. I stare at the other email address, hoping, praying it's just my imagination. I blink once, twice, but there's no use. It's still there. These photos were sent to someone else. It's an address I know all too well, and the sight of it makes me want to vomit.

Gabriel.

What have I done?

chapter TWENTY-SIX

I scream at the cab driver to drive faster down the Long Island Expressway. I have to get home. I need to find Gabriel. I try calling his phone again, but my phone dies.

The cab pulls up to the curb outside our house, and I throw money at the driver before he speeds off.

The house is pitch-black. I don't know if I should wait here for Gabriel to call or get myself on the first flight to Chicago. I need to see my husband. But first, I have to change. I have to shower and get Asher off of me.

I rush through the front foyer and up the stairs. I open the door to our bedroom and head toward the bathroom when a shadow frightens me.

A tall, dark figure is sitting in the chair in the corner. I switch on the lamp beside the bed.

It's Gabriel.

Red, puffy circles hide his navy eyes. Dew streams down his cheeks. Wavy brown hair stands up on all ends. Disheveled.

"Gabe."

I start toward him, but he holds up his hand, halting me in the middle of the room. A glass of dark brown liquid is in his other hand. A half-empty bottle beside it. He is still in his suit pants, his jacket thrown haphazardly on the floor. His sleeves are rolled up, one three-quarters and the other hanging lower. His tie is undone, and his shirt is unbuttoned halfway. He has water stains on his hands from either the liquor or the tears.

He's looking in my eyes, but instead of a gaze of love, there is only despair.

"I can explain."

I take a step toward him again, but his mouth opens to speak.

"Explain what?" His voice quivers. "This?" He holds up his phone to show me the same photo I saw in the cab.

I turn my head from the sight. Bile rises in my throat. *Where do I begin?*

"I left, Gabe. I couldn't do it. I left to come home." My bottom lip trembles.

"Did you fuck him?" The accusation comes out of his mouth like venom, filled with anger and resentment.

I stand there, stunned.

"Did. You. Fuck. Him?" His jaw is clenched, eyes burning with rage.

With my head lowered, I answer the only way I can, "Yes."

"AHHH!" Gabriel screams.

Rising from the chair, he throws his glass toward the wall. I jump and step back, afraid for what his next reaction might be. Not that I'd blame him.

Gabriel turns his body away from me. His hands are on his hips, his body grows rigid, his back muscles tighten, and I can see his rage building.

He turns suddenly and looks at me with fresh tears in his eyes. "You whore!" he screams.

Air leaves my body, and I struggle to breathe. I have never seen such hate in his eyes. He called me a whore. *Isn't that what I am?*

Wait a minute. Doesn't it take two to tango?

My fists ball up at my sides. *How dare he treat me like this when I at least had the decency to wait to talk to him about his own indiscretions!*

"You *hypocrite!*" I cry.

His eyes look at me in astonished confusion.

"Don't you pretend you had nothing to do with this." I violently point my finger at him. "Don't tell me there is nothing going on between you and that tart in the park. What's her name? Becca!"

Gabriel's jaw drops with amber liquid wet on his lips. "Are you fucking kidding me? What the hell does the girl in the park have to do with any of this?"

"I heard her, Gabe. I heard her talking about you!" Finally, I'm letting it out. "And I found her panties. You asshole! I found her underwear in the car!" My eyes well up with tears. Saying it out loud makes it so real.

"What are you talking about? Why would Becca's underwear be in our car?" He's trying to control his breath.

"Well, if they're not hers, then whose are they?" The thought frightens me. "Who are you fucking, Gabriel?"

He looks at me with clarity. His eyes widen in a stunned expression. "Is that why you did this? Did you throw away our marriage because you thought I was having an affair?" He covers his mouth with his hand. "Is that what this is about, Kat? An eye for an eye?" He lowers his hand. "Would you really throw away ten years because you thought I'd cheated." It's a statement more than a question.

Have I been wrong this entire time?

No. I'm not wrong. I know what I found.

"Don't make me feel crazy, Gabriel. Whose underwear did I find?" It's a simple question.

Staring at me, his eyes search mine for something. An answer? A reason? I don't know.

His lean, strong frame looks downtrodden. From his perfectly straight nose to the cheekbones that make him one of the most beautiful people I've ever seen, only sad features mask his melancholy face.

I stare back at him and wait for him to do something. His jaw remains clenched, and his eyes grow redder as they continue to glower back at me.

"Good-bye, Kathryn," Gabriel says, turning to the left and walking out our bedroom door.

He slams the door behind him, and he leaves down the hall, down the stairs, out the front door, and out of my life.

I sit on the bed and grab the house phone. Reluctantly, I make the call and have the conversation I've been dreading for days.

Gwen promises to have Jackson here first thing in the morning.

$$\Omega$$

I wake, not knowing what day or time it is. Hell, I don't really know where I am at first.

I'm home. It's Sunday. My husband's side of the bed is empty. Proof that my greatest nightmare has become a reality.

Throwing the comforter off my body, I get up and head into the bathroom and run the water. I slept in my suit last night, too intent on crying to change my clothes.

Unbuttoning my shirt, I see my bikini top. I rip it off in haste, desperate to wipe away my sins. I do the same with my skirt and bikini bottom. If I could, I'd burn them.

Stepping into the shower, I let the hot water wash away all traces of Asher from my body. The way he kissed me, caressed me, all the memories. Taking the loofah, I scrub my body raw.

It's no use. I can sanitize my skin, but I can't erase his touch or, more importantly, his words.

"I. Want. You. Kathryn. I want you. I want you. I want you!"

Get out of my head, Asher!

"Fuck it…I need you."

Please. Stop.

"What you've done to me in the last few weeks has been amazing."

"You make me thirsty for more. I'm not ready to give that up."

His words are still sweet in my head.

"If you walk out that door, it's over between us. I know it."

I walked out on Asher.

Gabriel walked out on me.

Ω

As promised, Gwen pulls up bright and early with my sweet angel in tow, and in a very un-Gwen-like fashion, she doesn't say a word. I'm grateful for the silence.

Jackson and I spend the morning playing with his shape sorter. I try to teach him the different colors and shapes and how each one fits in a very special tiny hole designed just for it. The point is lost on his little mind, and all he wants to do is eat the blue circle.

Jackson has had enough of the shapes and takes off for the couch. His chubby, little legs crawl across the room, and he uses the cushions to raise himself up in a standing position. He must be very proud of himself because he sends me a beaming smile. I clap my hands and applaud for him. He claps as well.

Just when I think he's done with his tricks for the day, he brazenly turns around and stands freely with his weight against the couch. I'm surprised by his ability. I clap once again, but this time, Jackson doesn't clap back.

With determined eyes, he heads toward me. His hands up in the air, he takes a small, wobbling step toward me and braces his weight midair. I put my hands out in an attempt to catch him if he falls. I'm close but far enough for him to walk to me.

"Come on, Jackson. Walk to Mama." My arms are spread out, and I encourage my angel to walk forward.

Jackson takes another wobbling step with his other foot and follows it with a quick step before crashing into my arms.

"You did it!" I beam, kissing him all over his face. "You walked to Mommy!"

For the first time in a while, I cry but not out of sadness or irritation. No, these are happy tears. I am exactly where I'm supposed to be.

After the morning's excitement, Jackson is ready for a nap. I lay him in his crib upstairs and grab the monitor before coming downstairs. He should get at least two hours of sleep.

Entering the kitchen, I see Gwen standing at the counter, pouring two cups of coffee. I knew her silence would only last so long. It's time for me to stop being such a chickenshit.

Gwen leaves one cup on the counter and picks up the other, carrying it into the living room. I would have sworn she would want a heart-to-heart at the kitchen table. I watch her take a seat on the loveseat and pick up a magazine, casually reading it while sipping her coffee.

I grab the other cup and contemplate taking it to my room before following her into the living room. I sit on the couch opposite her and take a sip.

Gwen is sitting with her legs crossed and the magazine loosely lying open on her leg. She looks disinterested in engaging in a conversation with me. The silence is making me uncomfortable.

"Fine, I'll bite." I know what she's doing, and it's working. "Where would you like to start?"

Gwen is still thumbing through the magazine, taking in the pictures. "Perhaps you can start with why I woke up at the crack of dawn to bring my grandson home to a half-empty household?" she says without looking up.

I shift uncomfortably. "Mom, Gabriel..." I don't even want to say I out loud. "Gabriel walked out on us last night."

"Uh-huh," she says, still looking down. "And why did he do that, honey?" Her tone is nonchalant yet slightly condescending.

"Why do you think he left? To get into some other woman's panties, I presume." The anger comes raging back through my bloodstream as thoughts of Becca, the underwear, and who knows what else start to replay in my head.

Gwen just nods her head. "That's interesting. You see, I thought it had something to do with this devastatingly handsome man right here."

I look up to see Gwen holding the magazine open to the photo of Asher standing in his office. *Why do mothers always know everything before you even tell them?*

My mouth is dry. This is exactly what I was avoiding. I should tell her the whole story. I should start from the beginning. I need to explain what the last few weeks have been like—the park, the department store, the car. I need to tell her everything, but I have a feeling she already knows.

Tears fall slowly down my cheeks. "I've made a mess of everything."

Gwen puts down the coffee cup and closes the magazine. The couch dips as she takes a seat next to me, curling one leg under the other, leaning into me. Her hand rubs my back the way she used to when I was a kid.

"There is no mess too big to clean up."

I look up at her understanding eyes. "No, Mom, we both have made a mess of this. He's done things, I've done things, and words were said. I'm afraid it's irreparable."

"Kathryn Elizabeth, look at me." She lifts my chin with her fist, sternly looking me in the eye. "I look in your eyes, and I see your father."

The thought makes me smile. "You do?"

She continues, "But your personality, that's all me. Sorry, kid, but you are Gwendolyn's daughter. I tried to tell you that before."

I shake off the notion. My mother is flighty, irrational, and a total drama queen.

Damn it.

As the realization hits me, I pose the question, "Mom, you would have never, ever done to Dad what I—"

She stops me midsentence. "Don't be so sure about that, sweetheart."

I gaze up at her, stunned.

"It was a long time ago. Your father was on the road, and the other wives were always talking about who was screwing who in what hotel in which city. It's a lot to play with your head, you know."

"Every time your father walked out that door, I wondered what he was doing out there." Gwen leans back into the couch and takes my hand in hers. Her head turned toward the window, her gaze wandering off. "Maybe he was. Maybe he wasn't. That, I will never know." She sighs. "His name was Don, and he was handsome, charming, and attentive." She looks back at me, giving my hand a squeeze. "It was short-lived, but it was incredible. He made me feel complete when I didn't know I needed it."

Part of me wants to hate her for being unfaithful to my father. The other part completely understands how she must have been feeling to be drawn to someone else.

"What happened? How did you end it?"

Her eyes soften. "Your father got sick, and I knew there was nowhere I'd rather be than at his side." With the back of her hand, she brushes away the soft tears falling down her face.

After what I've done to my family, I have no right to judge. But I can't help it.

My father did everything to give her the house, the clothes, the lifestyle, yet once he was out the door, making the money to afford that life, she dived into the arms of another man.

All my father had ever wanted was to make her happy, and apparently, he couldn't.

Is that what Gabriel thinks of me? The house on Long Island, the clothes, the car...is that why he spends so many late nights at a job I know he doesn't love? And what did I do? I ran right into the arms of another man.

Like mother, like daughter.

"What if Dad hadn't gotten sick? Would you have left my father for Don? Is Don the man you should have been with?"

"You're asking for the answer to a question you're too afraid to ask yourself." She brushes my hair off my face and wipes a single tear from my cheek. "This is a decision you have to make on your own." She gives my hand one more squeeze and exits the room.

For the next few hours, we live comfortably in silence. I stop by her room to see if she has enough towels in her bathroom. On the floor, I see a full suitcase. It looks like she's staying for a while, and I'm glad. I really need my mother.

chapter TWENTY-SEVEN

I didn't have the energy to get dressed up. Jeans, a T-shirt, and a pair of Converse were all I could manage. I look like the suburban me again.

Exiting the elevator to the twenty-fourth floor, I notice an immediate change. I can see the redhead.

The flowers? They're gone.

The thought brings me a surreal kind of sadness. One I wasn't expecting.

For the first time since I started working at Asher-Marks Communications, I do what I've never done. I finish my work. I lock my door and put my headphones in my ears and listen to music as I write every document; answer every email; create timelines, contact sheets, script pages; prepare itineraries; and print packets beyond packets of information for everyone involved. I only remove my earbuds to make calls to vendors.

Contracts are faxed and sent directly to legal for approval. Gretchen emailed me all the information I'd requested, so I'm able to get green-room and transportation requests in order. Harvey sent me the revised speeches, and I forward everything Erik requested.

Relief floods through my veins at the feeling of accomplishment. Sure, the event is still two weeks away, and everything will have to be updated, but to have completed so much so far, I feel confident in my decision.

I grab my files and walk down the hall to Erik's office. The door is open, but I knock anyway.

Erik is seated at his desk, looking over his computer screen. His hair tied in a ponytail, he's wearing his signature black. He looks up, surprised to see me standing there.

"Kat, come in. I was just looking over the files you sent me." He motions for me to take a seat.

"No, that's okay. I'll stand. I came to drop off my hard copies and give you my resignation." I wanted to get the words out before I lost my nerve.

He sits there, taken aback by my announcement. "Is this because of what I said to you last week?"

"Partly." I let out a breath. "I have a few personal matters to attend to, and I'm afraid I haven't been giving you my all. I'm used to giving a hundred and ten percent. I've failed to do that here."

His mouth bends, and he lets out a heavy sigh. "This will have to be your two-week notice then. The concert is in that much time. I'm afraid I can't let you go before then. You're under contract."

I bite my lower lip. I can't stay here. "If I stay, it will be a…conflict of interest." I wonder how much he knows.

Erik nods his head in confirmation. He knows. His fingers tap on the files I placed on his desk. "I was worried you wouldn't be able to complete the task at hand, but it looks like you have everything in order." He scoots back his chair. "I was getting some bad advice," he begins to explain.

I hold up my hand to stop him. I don't want to hear what kind of lies Heather has been spilling about me. I've had enough, and it's time to move on. "Please, Erik. I don't need to know what people say about me behind my back."

"No, I suppose you don't. Otherwise, you wouldn't have taken off with Alexander Asher for three days," he says, seeming uncomfortable with bringing it up.

If feeling degraded were an outfit, I'd say I was wearing it from head to toe. "That was for business, I swear." Even though I'm leaving, I don't want him to think wrong of me.

"I thought you were different, Kat." He can't look me in the eye. The one person in this building who has been nothing but kind and warm toward me, who believed in me from the beginning, is let down.

I nod in agreement, my head still hanging low. "I thought so, too."

I make my way back to my office and gather my few small possessions, all of which I brought with me this morning. The room is still as bare as it was the day I started. The only personal thing it bears is a screensaver on my computer of the two people who matter most to me in my life. Two months ago, this room brought me joy and excitement. Now, I see it for what it is. Just four white walls and a window.

I turn off my computer and put the chair back in position, clean and neat for the next person who occupies this space. I make my way to the doorframe to take one last look at the room when I see something poke out from under the desk. I bend down on the ground and slide out the beautiful black umbrella with its white pearl handle.

I buried it under there for a reason. Subconsciously afraid to acknowledge what it meant. Afraid of what was happening and knowing I had no control to stop it.

The umbrella has a weight to it I didn't notice before. I grab it and hold it, reliving that day we met in the rain. My life would have turned out differently if we hadn't met under those circumstances. If the train had arrived on time or if it hadn't been raining, I would have been at the office on time. Asher and I would have met like a typical boss and colleague. He never would have acted the way he did toward me, and our conversations moving forward wouldn't have been so heated.

If just one thing had gone otherwise that morning, my life would have turned out much differently.

The weight of the umbrella feels unbearable.

What I cannot understand—and I tried to figure it out all last night—is how on earth Asher didn't know I had a son. Malory knows about him. She's mentioned him quite a few times since I've worked here.

Were my conversations with Asher so aloof that I never spoke to him about Jackson?

Freud would have had a field day with this. Some people believe there are no accidents; each of our actions has a purpose. In this case, I don't remember a single moment I purposefully did not mention my son.

I also wonder, had I mentioned Jackson at any time, would the outcome have been any different? I honestly don't know.

Grabbing the pearl handle, I head down to reception where I can see my redhead.

"Hey, Kat." Trish is seated behind the desk, her usual boisterous self deflated. "Shame there are no flowers today."

She's a sweet thing. I'm going to miss her.

"It is a shame."

"Yeah." She smiles coyly. "Well, come to think of it, they were getting a bit out of hand. The smell was starting to give me a headache." She scrunches her nose and wiggles her head.

I smile. "Yes, they were out of hand. Perhaps, now, Mr. Asher will put his money to better use."

Trish nods in agreement. "Listen, Kat, I've been wanting to talk to you about something…" She pauses mid-thought to answer the phone.

I place my ID badge and office keys on the counter.

Her face shoots up, and her mouth fumbles as she talks to the caller on the other end, "No, sir, she hasn't. Yes, she's standing right in front of me. I'll send her right up." Trish hangs up the phone. "Mr. Asher needs to see you immediately." Her voice is stern.

I wasn't planning on facing Asher today—or ever again for that matter. "Call him back and tell him I already left."

"No way. I already told him you were here. He called down here personally. My ass is grass if you don't go up there, and you know it."

I let out a breath from deep inside my gut and surrender. She's right.

"Looks like I'm going up." I step away and take the elevator up to face him.

What do I say to him? What does he want to know? Surely, he hates me, and I can't blame him.

The elevator stops on the floor, and as the doors open, I can already hear his voice.

"Where is she? Is she on her way up?" He's standing at the reception desk, next to Cecelia.

I take a step toward them.

"Kathryn." His resolve quickly morphs from exasperated to steel.

He's wearing his favorite black suit, and he looks like the epitome of control, except for how his collar is bunched up at the back of his neck. He glances back at Cecelia and decides we don't need an audience.

He opens his office door and directs me, "In."

I comply and walk into his office but stop not far beyond the door. No sooner does he close the door behind us than I am immediately overwhelmed with emotion.

Keep it together, Kat.

I look around the room. There is the bar and the fancy TV screens. I see the small conference table, the seating area, and the wall where the crux gemmata is displayed beautifully. I take another look at the artwork. Its gemstones of emerald, citrine, and sapphire pierce my brain, and I'm reminded of the awful mess I've made. My beautiful, blue-eyed husband and this golden god and everything they've done to my life. My alpha and omega.

Focusing on the art, I use it as a distraction not to look over at him. My head is craned so far to the right as I feel him moving around me, circling like a hunter on its prey.

I let out a deep breath and turn slowly toward him. I open my mouth to speak, but there are no words.

Deep, dark circles line his eyes. "You're leaving?" he asks.

"I have to." I close my eyes. I didn't think seeing him would be painful. "I hurt you, Asher. I hurt a lot of people."

"You lied to me." His jaw is clenched, but his voice sounds pained. "I bared my soul to you. I told you things I'd never shared with anyone, yet you held back the most important piece of you."

"I'm sorry," I murmur. "I promise you will never have to see me again."

Asher flinches like my words hit him with an iron brick. He closes the gap between us, his head bent down, looking right into my eyes. "Did you mean what you wrote me in the note?"

I look at him, confused.

"You wrote, *You make my life make sense.* I've kept it in my pocket since you gave it to me." He looks down and pulls the note out of his pocket.

There it is in his hand, that Asher stationery I sent him with the bottle of intoxicating cologne. The words were a cute play on the gift. The sense was the smell of cologne. The words didn't mean anything at the time. Not to me at least. Not then.

My bottom lip trembles. "I don't know what makes sense anymore, Alex."

He smiles at my use of his first name. That's our way of knowing we're okay.

Looking down at my hand, Asher notices the umbrella.

I hand it over to him. "Part of the no-gift policy," I say with a shy smile.

He knows better than to argue with me over this. He takes the pearl handle and places the umbrella on the floor by the door. If I didn't know him so well, I would have missed the wounded expression creeping across his face.

He looks back at me. "Why didn't you tell me you had a son?"

I shrug my shoulders. It's the question I've been asking myself all weekend. As confused as I am about why he never knew, the truth is once he found out I had a son, he freaked out. That is the type of man he is. He wants no strings attached. Fooling around with a married woman was the perfect situation. But throw in a child, and you change the game. That is a major string.

Ashamed, I turn my body and start to head toward the door when a strong hand lands on my shoulder. My body swivels around and into him, landing on his hard chest, and I stare up into the unwavering eyes of Alexander Asher.

"I never thought I'd find someone like you," he says.

I draw my hand up to his lips to stop him from speaking, but he grabs my finger and pulls it away.

"No, Kat. I've been thinking about you a lot. I don't know what is going on with you, with us…" He pauses. "But I can't lose you."

His hand holds tight to my cheek, and I try to gently pull away.

"I was never yours to lose." The words are as painful for me, coming off my tongue, as they are for him to hear.

He closes his eyes tightly and shakes his head. "No. I need you. I told you that. I need you any way I can get you." He opens his eyes and stares through my soul. Full lips so close to mine.

I remind myself that I can't lose myself in him again. His words are surprising. I thought he'd be disgusted by me. I thought he'd need me gone. Instead, he's asking for me any way he can get me.

I step away from his hold and back up a few feet. "I can't. I'm sorry."

"You can't quit. I have you under contract."

Two more weeks of this? It would be difficult to look at him every day. It would be too much to look at Erik, Malory, and Heather. I couldn't bear the rumors.

He won't let me walk through the door, so I round him and make my way toward the bar. I grab a glass and the first bottle I see. As long as it's strong, I don't care what it is.

Asher watches as I hastily make my drink. His hands in his pockets, he is back to being the one in control. "I'll let you resign as of today—under one condition."

I stop mid-pour, and my head shoots up in curiosity.

"Come to the gala as my date. You've worked so hard on it, and a lot of our contacts are expecting to see your face. The organization needs you."

I take a large swig and let his words set in. He knows where my soft spot is. I should go to the gala. I forgot how my absence would affect the charity.

"Yes. I will be there." I can do that.

Asher's face lights up, and he looks relieved for the first time since we were on the beach in Miami. Maybe we can make this work.

"You'll definitely be there?"

"Yes," I reassure him. "Yes, I will be there." I already dug my grave. Might as well lie in it. "May I use your bathroom?"

He laughs at my simple request, relieved I'm no longer running for the door. "It's behind you, to the left," he directs.

I take a final swig from my glass and set it down on the bar. In the bathroom, I evaluate myself in the mirror. Yes, she's still there. Loose hair, T-shirt, jeans, and Converse. Adulteress and mother but still me.

I splash some water on my face and look for a towel to dry with. There isn't one on the counter. I open a drawer under the sink. Nothing. I try the next, and there is one.

Hang on a second.

I go back to the first drawer and open it again. *How did that get here?*

I put my hand into the drawer and pull out the exact pair of black women's underwear that has been causing me to lose sleep.

What the fuck?

Either this is a very popular brand of women's undergarments or there is something completely fucked up about this situation.

I exit the bathroom with the panties hanging from my index finger. Asher is still standing by the bar. He turns from looking at the television, and his smile disappears.

chapter TWENTY-EIGHT

"Whose are these?" My voice is stern.

Asher's face is in a state of shock. His body tightens, and his hands rise in defense. "Where did you get those?"

"Who do they belong to?" My voice is deeper, angrier.

"That was from long before this weekend. The relationship is over. I swear."

He takes a few steps toward me, and I take the same steps back.

It doesn't matter whether these were before, after, or during our time together. It doesn't matter if they are from his long-lost love or the girl next door. I just need to know *whom* they belong to.

My fear is, I know exactly whose they are. There is only one person other than me who knows both my husband and my boss. It's all starting to make sense.

"They're Malory's," I state clearly.

By his lack of response, I know I'm right.

I throw the vile undergarment in his face and storm toward the door.

"Kathryn, wait." He takes off after me. "What difference does it make?"

I walk out the office door and catch the waiting elevator. "It makes more of a difference than you'll ever know."

I descend to the twenty-fourth floor and stop at my redhead. "You had something you needed to talk to me about?"

By the look on my face, she knows I've already figured out a thing or two.

Trish doesn't say a word but hands me a stack of emails she printed out. She clearly didn't have access only to Erik's files.

There are emails between Malory and Asher. They start when she submitted my résumé, boasting about my proficiency and knowledge on site surveys and production planning. Then, they get creepy. Many are explicit, recounting some of their nights together. I try to figure out why Trish printed them until I see my name pop up. That one is dated the week after I arrived. She suggests the new girl is "definitely willing to work her way to the top." Malory had no idea about my true affliction with Asher and the tumultuous relationship we had.

There are others where she tells Asher about how my marriage is falling apart, and if he's interested, he should stake his claim. I don't understand why she was pushing me toward Asher. I thought she wanted him. From the words I'm reading, she had him—many times.

Trish also printed correspondence from Malory to Erik, stating I was unfit for the position and he should reconsider whether I was appropriate to produce the gala. This is dated last week—the day Gabriel came to see me in the office. She was so mad at Heather that day—or perhaps it was really me. To think, I thought Heather was the one who had undermined me to Erik.

It all begins to come together with the final set of emails between Malory and Gabriel. This one is dated the day before his office visit. I didn't even know she knew him well enough to email him. It seems innocent enough. She's telling him what a great job I'm doing and how Asher and I did a site survey and how he's really impressed with my work, even providing me with one-on-one mentoring. *How did she know I was with Asher that day? And why would she tell Gabriel?* That was the night he fell asleep, reading the magazine. He came to the office the next day, and I reveled in the fact that he was jealous.

She had an agenda, and now, so do I.

Emails in hand, I storm my way down to her office with my phone in my back pocket and slam the door behind me when I enter. She doesn't seem concerned that I would even be there. It's like she's been expecting me.

"I thought you resigned," she states blandly.

"And I thought you were my friend," I spit out.

Malory leans back in her chair and rests her hands on the arms, willing the confrontation.

I throw the incriminating emails on her desk and hide my phone as I hold it low at my hip. "You brought me here on purpose. You got me this job for a reason. Tell me, was it my career you set out to tarnish or just my marriage? I seem to be a little lost on the details."

"Don't flatter yourself, Kat. You always did think it was all about you."

"Is this about Asher? I never wanted him, yet you were trying to get me in his bed before I even met him."

"It was never about Asher. I've had him tenfold, or did you really think you were the special one around here. I knew you would be easy bait for him. I just never expected the poor bastard to fall in love."

Fall in love? Asher's not in love with me. Even if he thought he was, he lost it as soon as he found out about Jackson.

This all couldn't have been about my career. *Why would she hire me just to tear me down? No, she hired me to put me in Asher's arms. And all for what?*

"Gabriel." I knew it when I found the panties in Asher's bathroom. "You're having an affair with Gabriel. You did all of this to drive us apart."

Her black eyes turn to ice. "How these men fall for you is beyond me. It's like talking to a fucking wall. You don't deserve Gabriel. You...you just push him aside like some lame suit who works his ass off to provide you with everything. I did all this to prove to him that you're unworthy of him, and you know what? I was right. You're just as low as the rest of us. While you were gallivanting with Asher, your husband has been nothing but faithful to you. Trust me, honey, I've tried, and I will keep on trying. Because you see, I was right. Gabriel is one of the good guys. If you did half the digging I did, you'd see that little tramp, Becca, got nowhere close. The man's a damn saint."

I can't believe what I'm hearing. She is obsessed with Gabriel. It all makes sense now—in a really bizarre way. "You tried to be with Gabriel," I state. "How? When?" My comments are a whisper to myself, yet she hears them and sighs.

"We have history. I always assumed since he never told you that it meant something to him. Gabriel wants you in the dark and there's a reason for it. I'll never understand that man. It's like you have some sort of vice on him and he never saw how flawed you are."

I thought this was my solace, and it's turned out to be my hell. I have to know just how evil she really is.

"Last week, you asked if I drove in. You left your underwear in my car to find. You wanted me to—"

"You did that all on your own, Kat. You were begging for an excuse to fuck Asher."

I can't even respond to that comment. Instead, my mind continues to piece it all together. "Did you send those photos?" I breathe out the question with every ounce of disgust I have in my body.

She looks at me like I'm the biggest idiot she's ever met. Perhaps I am. "You remember meeting Oswald Thompson in Miami, don't you?" she asks. I nod. "Ozzie sent those. I told him to keep an eye out on you, as it would serve both our interests."

"Why in the world would Oswald Thompson care that I cheated on my husband?"

"He's my contact, Kat. Did you think you were going to go to Miami and take credit for an account I'd been working on?" she says with both palms placed flatly on the desk, her body leaning toward me. "Bet you also didn't realize he's Gabriel's big client."

Gabriel's client? I would know that, wouldn't I?

Malory lets out a wicked laugh. "Keep your friends close and your enemies closer."

This is definitely hell. I grab my purse and leave the building quickly. My feet are on the concrete pavement of New York in less than five minutes, and the dark sky is peaceful compared to the world I just left behind. I open my iPhone and close the digital recorder app. I send the file to Asher and hope he'll see Malory for what she's worth. And if he doesn't, then it looks like I'll lose another friend.

Seems like I'm losing a lot these days.

Ω

The last five days have been quiet torture. I can't call Gabriel. I know he'd just hang up. I can't email. I know he'd delete it.

Gwen has been on the phone with Gabriel many times over the last few days. I know this because she scurries into the other room, whispering into the receiver. It doesn't surprise me. Gabriel needs to know how Jackson is doing. It's probably killing him to have gone days without seeing the baby. That's why I've suggested to my mother that Gabriel come to the house after work while I make myself scarce. It's the least I can do.

I've spent my time holed up in the house, feeling sorry for myself. Gwen gives me my space while I process everything that's happened. On Monday night, she watched Jackson while I cried myself to sleep. Tuesday, she kept a safe distance while I camped out in the living room with Jackson and watched him build blocks up high before we knocked them straight down. On Wednesday night, she made us cups of coffee and listened while I told her the story from the very beginning. The last two days, she offered me time to reflect.

Today, I have to get out. Whipping out the baby jogger, I start the day with a brisk walk, and Jackson and I enjoy the fresh air. Then, we take a go to the grocery store in town and start to get a routine back in our lives. It is reminiscent of our life mere months ago. It seems like an eternity has passed.

As the clock strikes closer to Gabriel's arrival time, I borrow Gwen's car and start heading west. I don't know exactly where I plan to go, but traffic is moving, so I just keep with the flow. I stop the car in a deserted parking lot overlooking the Long Island Sound.

To my left is the marina. Everything from grand sixty-foot yachts to motorboats and small fishing vessels line the docks. I love looking at the boats, especially the ones drifting in the harbor, waiting to be taken to some exotic destination.

$$\Omega$$

"Where are we going?" I asked with blindfolded eyes.

Gabe was in the driver's seat of his Mustang. It was old and made a lot of noise, such a boy car.

"I'm taking you somewhere very important to me. A place I want to share with you." His warm hand grabbed mine and raised it to his lips before falling onto his lap.

In the six months we'd known each other, we'd become inseparable. He waited for me after each class and carried my books everywhere we went. Most of his classes were early in the morning, so he was done before I even began. He even resorted to sitting with me during lunch, twirling my hair in his hand as I told him stories about my childhood and growing up with my dad in the majors. He was a big Marlins fan and went to quite a few games with his dad.

I felt the car slow down. Gabe let go of my hand, so he could use both hands to pull into a spot. I heard him get out and close the door behind him. Shortly after, my door opened, and Gabe's hand was in mine again, escorting me out of the car.

"Now, will you tell me where we are?" I begged.

The air was finally warm after months of the autumn chill and winter winds.

"If there is one thing you must know about me, it's that I love surprises. Consider this the first of many."

"So, that's a no?" I teased.

"Patience, baby. We're almost there."

He gently guided me along the walkway. I didn't know where I was, but I could smell the saltwater and hear seagulls. We were by the water, but where?

We walked a few more feet and stopped. Gabe braced me with both arms. I thought he was going to take the blindfold off. Instead, I felt warm, wet lips on mine. Lips I'd become very familiar with.

When he pulled away, he also took the blindfold off. First, my eyes fixed on his beautiful navy-blues. But then they drifted to a different sea of blue. We were at Baltimore's Inner Harbor.

"Are we going fishing?" I frowned at the idea. I wasn't much of a sit still, be quiet, and wait for a fish to come *type of girl.*

"No, we're going sailing!" His Robert Redford grin turned into a glorious smile. This was definitely something he enjoyed.

"Sailing?" I was impressed.

"It's my first love." Gabe pulled my hand and walked me over to, what I later learned was, a 1983 Catalina 25 Swing Keel.

Gabe had sailing paraphernalia around his apartment. He'd mentioned he loved to sail, but this was taking it to a whole new level.

"I had to mow a lot of lawns to afford her." He stepped on board and held out a hand for me to join. *"I just repainted the hull, and the wood has been redone."* His eyes were reflected in the sapphire sail. He was beaming with pride.

"She's beautiful. What's her name?" I took a seat on the white leather cushion.

"Breaking Wind.*" He cringed a little at the name. "She came with the name, and it's bad luck to rename a boat."*

I laughed for a solid five minutes. He joined in after about two.

He produced a white plastic bag I hadn't noticed before. He must have carried it from the car. There was a brown bag inside, a yellow smiley face on the outside. Gabe noticed me eyeing up the bag and explained, "Chinese. You do like Chinese, don't you?"

Chinese takeout on a sailboat didn't sound right, but I nodded anyway. "And what would happen if I told you I didn't like Chinese?"

"Then, I'd say, I'd just found your one flaw."

I laughed and sat back, watching him as the wind blew through his hair. His white windbreaker danced in the breeze as we left the dock and started toward the open water.

"So, tell me, Gabriel Monroe, why does a boy from sunny Florida, who loves to sail, want to go to New York and become a lawyer?"

His eyebrows caved in as he took a moment to think about his answer. "I guess because I want more out of life than my parents were able to give me. They struggled—a lot. I don't want that for my future family."

Family. I'd never heard a guy talk about family. It was usually taboo.

"Why New York?"

"I got into NYU Law. Figured I go there for a few years and then head back home." He turned his gaze from the

ocean and back to me. "But I met this great girl from there, so if all goes well, I might stick around."

I loved that he was already thinking of a future with me. I crawled over to him and took a seat beside him. Gabe's arm swung around my back, and he pulled me in.

"I'd like that." I kissed him on the neck. "I'd like that a lot."

"Okay, Twenty Questions. Me first. Favorite food?" he asked with his fingers twirling in my hair.

"Pizza. My turn. Favorite candy?"

"You." He smiled and placed a tender kiss on my lips. "And Skittles. Favorite movie?"

"Field of Dreams." It was my dad's favorite.

"Me, too! That, and Braveheart. It's a guy thing. Worst trait?"

I had to think on that for a second. "Being complacent. When I get mad, I do this weird breathing thing. It works, but sometimes, I worry that I let things that bother me roll off my shoulders too easily. I wish I were more headstrong. Like you."

He laughed and shook his head. "That's not your tell."

I sat back and squinted my eyes at him. "What do you mean?"

"I can always tell when you're angry or embarrassed or confused or, better yet, turned on…"

I hit his side. "Okay, I get it. I have a tell. What is it?"

Gabe raised a hand and massaged my earlobe. "Your ears turn red. It's the cutest thing I've ever seen. Your ears turn various shades from this adorable pink to neon red. They give away every emotion you have."

"What color are they now?"

"Pink. But I bet you I can make them turn red." His Robert Redford grin crept across his face.

"You're gonna try and get me mad?"

"I hope not."

"Well then, go ahead."

Gabe brushed a piece of hair behind my ear and slowly stroked it with his thumb. His eyes looked straight into my soul. "I love you. From the second I saw you on the steps, I knew you were my forever."

His words were like poetry in my ears. The beautiful, blue-eyed boy with dark, wavy hair loved me.

"Your ears are very red, Kat." His eyes searched mine for a response. His brow furrowed, and he took a cautious stance, waiting for a reaction.

"They're also very hot," I replied.

"What does that mean?"

"It means, I love you, too."

And I told him so over and over again in the confines of a small bed in the cabin below.

Ω

Sailing in that little boat became a part of our romance. Gabriel even brought it to New York when he started law school. We took a few trips with it on the Long Island Sound, but as his career blossomed, *Breaking Wind* got neglected. He sold the boat shortly after we were married, and he hasn't been sailing since.

God, I wish my dad were still alive. I wish I could talk to him just this once and ask him for advice. I want to know if he was as good a man as I think he was. I want to know if he would have forgiven Gwen for her indiscretions. I want to know how I can right my wrongs.

The problem is, I didn't just wrong Gabriel. I hurt Asher. He trusted me to be his confidant while I held back from him. I let him bare his soul, yet I only gave him a facade of myself. I never let him into my world.

Unfortunately, I let other people into my world. I let Malory in, and look what she did. I don't know what to do next, but I can't stand still. I hate running, but for some reason, I feel compelled to move. My feet lift off the ground, and I run the perimeter of the harbor until my heels hurt more than my heart.

Then, I head home.

Gabriel's car is gone when I return. I'm half-relieved and half-disappointed. I open the door to Gwen holding her finger over her mouth.

"Gabriel put Jackson to sleep before he left." She places the baby monitor on the counter.

I look at the black-and-white screen to see Jackson sleeping with his butt in the air. It's the sweetest little position.

"Did you tell him he took his first steps? He's probably devastated he missed it."

"I did, but I didn't embellish. Jackson put on a little show for him. He took a few more steps with Gabriel than he has with us. I think he was holding out for his dad." Gwen stalls for a second to make sure her words didn't hurt me too much.

"He's a daddy's boy; that's for sure. I hope he stays that way." My words assure her. I walk to the fridge and sigh as I open the door.

"Tired, honey?" Gwen asks, still standing by the counter.

"No." I scan the refrigerator. It's freshly stocked, yet there's nothing I want. "The opposite actually. I feel restless. I don't know what to do with myself."

She walks beside me and closes the refrigerator door. "Why don't you go to the batting cage? Take a few swings," she suggests. "It will help get a little aggression out."

She's right. I felt good after my run, but I still have more energy in me to burn. I kiss Gwen on the cheek and head to the batting cage.

Imagine my shock when I see I'm not the only one who had that idea.

chapter TWENTY-NINE

I haven't seen him look this free in a long time. Black T-shirt, jeans, and an old pair of Jordans. He looks a lot like this guy I once kissed at McCloon's.

Crack!

I assume he's picturing that to be my head. I walk toward the fence and stop just behind him. I'm safer behind the fence for more than one reason.

His back is to me as he keeps his stance for the next ball to be launched. "I take it, Gwen had the same great idea for more than one of us," he says, bracing for his next swing.

Crack!

Oh, Gwen. My mother, the meddler. She hasn't lost her touch. Gabriel must have seen me pull up, as he's not surprised that I'm standing here behind him.

"I suppose so. I'll go. You were here first." I try to appease him when I'm really longing for him to turn around. *Please look at me.*

Crack!

"No, stay. I'm almost done here," he says, taking one last swing of the bat.

He steps out of the box and removes the helmet. He replaces it with a baseball hat. I haven't seen him wear one in so long. I smile at the memory.

"What are you laughing about?"

I only make things worse. "I'm not laughing. I'm just remembering."

I look up into his navy-blues. The fence between us does nothing to still my nerves. I just want to touch him. His eyebrows rise, tempting me to share my thought.

"I was remembering our first date." I have to speak quickly or else he'll walk away. "You brought me to a batting cage, just like this one. You were terrible."

Gabriel pulls his hat lower over his face, but I can see his lips curl up on the ends.

"You're right. I was trying to impress you. I didn't know any other way." He shakes his head. "Lots of good that did." He bends down to collect his bag. He opens the gate to the batting cage and heads to his car. "It's all yours."

"Gabe, wait." I charge after him.

He turns around, sternly. "What do you want, Kat? Haven't you done enough?" His face is hard and cold, not the sweet Gabriel I know.

"I'm sorry. I am so sorry for everything," I plead. "I let other people and other voices get in my head. I know now that there was nothing going on between you and Becca. I was so terribly wrong."

His fist is clenched around his bag. The other points in my face. His body radiates tension. "You threw away ten years of happiness, five years of marriage!"

"I know. I'm sorry." *What's the use? It's over. I might as well just bare it all.* "I felt so lost for a while. You were off every day, working this fancy job, and lately, you've been staying later and later."

"You think I like my job? I do it for you and Jack." He throws his arms up in the air. "I hate my fucking job! I hate every client, every deposition, every amendment and appeal. I hate it all." His eyes are on fire. "But I do it for you. I do it to give you the life you deserve." He spits on the ground. "Or at least, the life I thought you deserved."

"I don't need this life, Gabe! I never asked for it. I only thought I would like it because it's what you wanted. I hate it out here. I don't fit in. This isn't us. It never was." I don't even remember how we made our way out here. That's when we lost each other. "If you're not happy with your job, quit. I'd rather have a husband who's happy and lives in a shack then a miserable one with a beautiful house we can't afford."

He balks at my response. "I'm miserable? Is that why you went to bed with the first man who gave you the time of day?"

"How dare you!" Now, it is my turn to be angry. "At least he wanted to touch me. At least he wasn't too tired to return my advances."

"You're a whore. It's all sex with you."

"You know that's a lie. Take it back!"

He doesn't say a word.

Taking a deep breath, I hug my denim jacket to me and walk toward Gabriel's car. I lean my head against the door and concede. "You're right. You're right," I repeat.

His body stills. I think I see his shoulders relax a bit. We stand in silence. I want to say something, but I'm afraid if I breathe too loudly, he'll move.

After an eternity, he finally speaks, "How's this for a cherry on top? Oswald Thompson is blackmailing me. Can you believe it? That criminal is blackmailing me." He shakes his head in disbelief. "I've been trying to get out of the case, but he said if I do, he'll release those photos to the media."

"You don't owe me anything."

"I know I don't." His words are calm, yet they hit me like a slap in the face. "I owe it to Jack to not have his mother smeared across the tabloids."

I close my eyes and breathe in deeply. I have made a mess of everything, yet Gabriel is still trying to protect our family. It's no surprise Malory is obsessed with him. He had to have known.

"Why didn't you tell me about Malory?"

His mouth nearly drops at the mention of her name. "What did she tell you?"

"Basically, she's in love with you and that she fucked with my entire life to get her hands on you." I can't believe I was so blind.

"Kat, listen, there is something I have to tell you about that." He tosses his bat in the back seat and closes the door. "Damn, I was hoping I'd never have to tell you. I guess it doesn't matter now."

My interest is piqued. "What doesn't matter?"

"I went out with her on a date when I first moved to the city."

I blink back at his words. *My* Gabriel dated Malory? We were together when he moved to the city.

He sees my concerned look and continues, "You were still in school then, back at Towson, and I was young and dumb. One night, at a bar, I was missing you so badly, and there she was. I was so stupid."

My mouth goes dry. Despite what I have done, it hurts to think he betrayed me at a time when we were still drunk in love. "How stupid were you?"

Gabriel is quick to answer; his hand rests on my arm in reassurance, then pulls back as if remembering he doesn't want to touch me anymore. "Nothing happened. It was just dinner. She started harassing me after that. Always making comments and telling me she was available if you and I ever broke up. For some reason I can't figure out, you started working with her. What are the odds? She started cornering me at your office parties when you were distracted. Propositioning me. She'd call when you were away on business. I never took her up on her advances." He takes a breath, seeming relieved to be unloading this information.

"I was happy when you quit two years ago. I didn't think it mattered anymore. Then, you got this job, and I was hesitant at first, but you were so excited. I never had a problem with you returning to work. I was afraid of what would happen with you working with Malory again…" He trails off. He removes his hand from my arm and takes a step back. "She told me you'd stray at the first opportunity."

There is an awkward pause. I don't want to say anything. I'm lucky he's talking to me this much.

His head is bowed, looking at the ground. I assume he pictures me on the same level as the dirt. He's standing so close, yet he feels miles away.

The one person I was closer to than anyone in my entire life is now my most distant acquaintance.

It doesn't feel natural. This isn't the Gabe I know. Then again, I'm no longer his Kat.

Gabriel's eyes start to redden. "It doesn't feel like it really happened. Like the last few days were just a dream."

"I wish they were just a dream. If I could take it all back…"

"No, Kat. You cheated on me. Don't you get it? You broke our vows. Everyone waits for the husband to screw up. It's the woman you have to watch out for." He turns his back and pauses just before opening the door. "You know, if I hadn't seen it, I would never have believed it. I just never thought you would do that to me."

I never thought I would either. Just a few weeks ago, I was devastated when I heard my cousin's wife had had an affair. I was the wreck, and it was Gabriel who seemed so nonchalant about the whole thing.

"What about those couples you were telling me about? The ones who moved on? You said it yourself. Couples get back together. These things happen." I try to bring back some of his own words from that conversation not too long ago.

"Not to us, Kat!" He nearly spits the words at me. "Don't you dare try to throw my words back in my face. Shit happens to other couples but not to us. We're better than this." His jaw tightens as he calms himself down. "I thought we were better than this."

I take a step toward him as he lowers himself into the front seat and ask, "Where do we go from here?"

He takes a deep breath before answering my question, "I'm going to see my lawyer in the morning." He closes the door. He turns the ignition and lowers the window. "I'll be at The Inn until I find a place."

I watch the man I promised my forever to drive away, ending our love story for good.

chapter THIRTY

GABRIEL

It's always the husband.

I've watched enough television dramas and seen the films. When a marriage goes wrong, it's the husband who strays. Science has deemed it our internal instinct. Men don't cheat because they can. They cheat because they *must*. It's part of our inner struggle.

That is bullshit.

I was barely a man when I met my wife. I'd seen her around campus many times. It was hard not to. Brown hair on porcelain skin and emerald-green eyes that made me speechless. The movement of her body was as graceful as a dancer, and yet I knew back then that if I could get a beautiful woman like that to fall in love with me, I'd better hang on to her for the rest of my life.

Approaching her was the hard part. She was a wallflower around campus, who was only seen walking from the dorms to class and back. My friends didn't know her name, and I looked for her at every party, but she never appeared.

I wanted to talk to her so bad, yet I couldn't muster up the courage. With timeless beauty like hers and the reserved quality she possessed, I didn't know what to say. Every opening line just seemed cheesy. I needed to think of something witty. So, I waited for my moment.

It came. Man, I hadn't been prepared for her to trip that day, yet I thanked my lucky stars she had. She was a fumbling mess, grabbing those books off the staircase at Towson. When she spoke, I found her looks to be a mere spec of how incredible she was. She had me so curious, and I needed to learn more about her.

Kat and I had an epic love story. Our passion was immeasurable, and our connection was tethered at our hearts. My friends thought I was crazy for settling down so young. I didn't care. When a man met the woman of his dreams, he held on to her tight.

I never wanted anything more than Kathryn Grayson.

"Can I get you anything else?" The waiter at the restaurant I'm dining in asks.

It kills me not to be at home with my family right now, but there's just no other choice.

"Just the check."

Being a bachelor was never the plan. As the son of a couple who has been happily married for thirty-five years, divorce isn't a word we utter. You find the one, and you get married. For better or worse, through thick and thin, you see it through.

Fuck.

I'm breaking my own damn rules. This is the worst, and in the goddamn thick of it, I'm sitting here in a restaurant, by myself, reading paperwork given to me by my attorney. How a man forgives his wife after finding out she had an affair is beyond me. I'm about to lose my dinner, just thinking about it.

His hands on her body.

His mouth sucking her breasts.

His cock buried deep inside her.

I could kill him. My fists tighten, and my jaw is clenched with the carnal need to mutilate the son of a bitch. The napkin in my hand is crumpled into a ball so small that I can practically feel it disintegrating.

I won't be able to go to Manhattan again without thinking of the bastard. His name is on everything. I told Kat that his family was synonymous with greed and gluttony. I never dreamed my wife would create the greatest sin with a member of the Asher family.

I pay the bill and rise from the table, tossing my napkin on my empty dinner plate. *Who the fuck am I kidding?* I'm not a fighter. I've never raised my fist to another man, and I don't have any plans to.

I can be angry with Alexander Asher all I want. Nothing compares to the hurt I feel in my heart when it comes to Kathryn, but she betrayed me. No one else.

My phone rings as I walk to my car. It's a number I don't recognize.

"Hello?"

"Gabriel." Her voice is a sinister hum on the other end of the line.

"What do you want?" I ask Malory. Anger and disdain are evident in my voice, as she has been the bane of my existence for years.

"We have to talk."

There's something in her tone that has me thinking she's actually concerned, so I give her a chance.

I lean against my car, and take a deep breath. "Talk."

"Kathryn had an affair."

"You know I'm already aware. You sent me the damn video," I say. I hear her start to speak, but I cut her off, "I know it was you who set this up with Oswald. He already told me. You asked him to keep an eye on them in Miami and to let you know if anything happened. The jerk was happy to throw you under the bus while he was blackmailing me."

"Gabriel, honestly, why would I betray a friend like that? Kathryn is my girl. You know I would never—"

"Malory," I say her name like a threat, and she lets out a deep huff. "What kind of scheme are you running? The lying and planning you had to do to piece together my relationship with Oswald just so you could, what? Embarrass Kat? Show me she's not worthy of our marriage?"

"I did you a favor, and frankly, I'm surprised you're not thanking me! I have no idea why you're even sticking up for that woman. She cheated on you, and you are acting like I'm the one in the wrong."

I rub my forehead and look up at the bright neon sign of the diner where I just ate. I told myself I wouldn't blame anyone but Kathryn, and here I am, taking it out on Malory. She might have had some sort of hand in pushing Kat into the arms of another man, but it was my wife who made the ultimate choice.

"I'm really upset, Malory. Now is not the time."

"Perhaps it is. Meet me for a drink. You need someone to take your mind off of this awfulness."

"No," I state clearly. "It's not going to happen. It's been eight years since we went out. I told you it was a mistake then, and I have no desire to relive it."

"Did you tell her we'd kissed?"

"I told her we went out. I didn't elaborate. She doesn't deserve the truth. Regardless of what happened between us, it pales in comparison to what she did."

"That's right. Gabriel, you must be hurting. Please, tell me, where are you staying? I can be there in—"

"I said, no."

"Why not?"

"Because I love my wife!" The words come out before I realize it.

Because that's the truth. I love my wife.

My fucking adulterous wife.

I love her so damn much. It puts my anger in overdrive, and tears well up in my eyes. I shouldn't still crave someone who betrayed me, and yet I still do. I hate her so much for making me feel this way.

"Gabriel, you're losing sight of what happened. She slept with another man. Here I am, throwing myself at you, and you're refusing me because you think you still love her?"

I sigh, shaking my head and looking down. My feelings are so jumbled that I don't know what side is up. All I know is the woman on the other end of this call has only the worst intention in mind.

"Good-bye, Malory. Don't call me ever again."

I hang up the phone and block the number she called from. I could have ended this years ago. I should have told Kat about that date I went on with Malory as soon as it happened. It was that kiss with Malory that convinced me I never wanted to kiss another woman besides Kat for the rest of my life. She felt wrong in my hands, she tasted horrible on my tongue, and even the scent of her was revolting. I wanted to erase the night from my history.

Still, I should have told Kat.

I was just so scared of losing her. Before now, trust and monogamy were a big part of her ability to love. If I'd lost her trust, she would have lost her sense of self. Without your whole heart in it, you can't fully give yourself to someone else.

My sweet Kathryn has always been the strongest yet most insecure woman. What she shows on the outside is just a front for the anxiety she hides on the inside. I could blame Gwen and her need for Kathryn to always look perfect. I know a lot of it has to do with Catch dying when Kat was barely a teenager, when she needed her parents to guide her. Gwen relied on her too much when Kat was growing up. It affected her social life and her ability to breathe. She told me so when we fell in love, and I helped her live again.

What we had was good. It was a bubble, just us, but we were happy in our world.

At least, that's what I thought.

I drive back to The Inn and check in to my room. Everything in here is impersonal. Her perfume is missing from the dresser. Jackson's pacifier isn't on the nightstand. And the wall is bare of our wedding photo.

I put on the television and watch the baseball highlights while I undress. This was always our thing—watching a game and razzing each other about it. She loves this sport so much, and I got into it just for her. Sure, I'm a Marlins fan, but my love of the sport isn't for the game. I love the way Kat's eyes light up when her player gets on base. She scrunches her nose on a bad play, and paces the room when it's the end of a crucial inning.

Never have I desired that woman more than when it's the bottom of the ninth and she's sitting on her knees, whispering obscenities at the pitcher on the mound.

It's going to take a long time for me to get used to not loving Kat.

Maybe in the morning, I'll figure out how.

Ω

Work is going to be the death of me. Now that I'm stuck on the Thompson case until the end, I'm been putting in extra-long hours. I've considered changing my game plan and letting the man suffer in court while under my counsel, but that's not my style. If I have a job, I give a hundred and ten percent. If not for me, I have to do it for the firm.

After being in the office all day, I work from my hotel room and then call my son. Gwen does a decent job of holding the phone up while I talk to him through FaceTime. It sucks. I miss my kid. I can't stand talking to him through a device, and I need to hold him. Being apart isn't what I want, and my new overpriced divorce lawyer is going to fight tooth and nail to get me full custody. The divorce is going to get ugly. I don't want that either. It's just the way these things go.

My body is exhausted, yet my mind is racing. I need to let out steam before I'm up all night, thinking about all the ways my life is messed up. It's late but not yet dark, so I change to go for a run.

The park is my favorite place to work out, and frankly, I need a sense of normalcy tonight. The fresh air feels good after a day indoors, and the summer heat is cooling as the sun gets ready to set. I pace myself and jog the path I've been taking since we moved into our house. It's a great house. I bought it after a coworker told me about a home for sale in his neighborhood. Three bedrooms, an open floor plan, and a gourmet kitchen. It is the perfect home for a family.

I showed it to Kat after I put an offer in and it was accepted. We arrived at the house, and I'd had a red bow put on the mailbox. She skeptically looked at me, and then I explained what I had done.

Her smile didn't come immediately. I forgot about that until this moment.

My pace slows as I recall the realtor showing up right then with a beaming smile. Kathryn stoically looked at her. She handed Kat a bottle of champagne. I took her hand and showed her the house—where we'd set the television and the state-of-the-art appliances. Upstairs, I outlined where we'd put the claw-foot tub she always said she wanted, and then I brought her into the nursery.

She was already pregnant with Jackson, barely showing. She rubbed her stomach and walked around the room, slowly taking it all in. When she turned to me, she had tears in her eyes and whispered the words I had been dying to hear since she got out of the car, "It's perfect."

We kissed for a long time in that empty room.

While I remember that as a good day, I have a pang in my chest. The house is amazing, but is it what she wanted? We had talked about it often. But it's possible I jumped the gun on the move.

Not long after that, she was put on bed rest. She had given up her job and moved to a town where she knew no one. She was home alone for seven months while I worked. Gwen came down often, but that probably wasn't any better. Kat spent a lot of time watching movies and browsing Instagram while I soared at work and got my last great promotion.

When she wanted to get back to work, she fought me so hard. It was like she had something to prove by going back, as if she felt inadequate in her skin.

"Everyone needs a sense of purpose," she said.

I didn't understand why Jackson and I weren't her purpose.

Yes, I know that's a misogynistic thing to say, but there's nothing wrong with a man wanting to provide for his wife and child, so they can live a stress-free life. It was always with the best of intentions. She acted like I was chaining her to the dining room table when all I wanted was for her to be happy. She could have done anything she wanted. Write a book, take up painting, join community theater. I wasn't telling her to cook dinner for me every day. I was giving her time to watch our son grow, be available to him, and have the freedom to invest in herself.

"You just don't get it," she said.

Maybe that was the problem. I didn't. And I'm pretty sure I'm starting to understand way too late.

As I trudge up the hill, I see the familiar blonde head of the woman Kat thought I was having an affair with.

"Hey there, stranger!" Becca waves an arm as she jogs in place.

"Hi there."

"I was looking for you. You haven't been around too much!" She gives a pouty face that makes her look like a duck.

"Been busy."

"I can only imagine. Wife, kid, and work. So much going on. I've been pretty consumed myself, too. Met this new guy who is just the sweetest."

Feigning interest in her love life musters up more energy than I care to think about. "Good for you. Hope it works out. Listen, I'm just trying to get a good run in before it's too dark." I'm still moving as I talk, hoping to get out of this conversation quickly and politely.

She nods her head as she falls in step with me. "Great! We can keep pace. Run with the wolves, right?"

I try to hide my disappointment that I won't be running alone tonight. This girl seems nice, and we've enjoyed some runs before, but it doesn't feel right tonight. Still, I hate being a jerk. "Right."

We run down our usual trail, and I remember why I like running with her. She kicks my ass. Every time I want to fall back, I look over and see her keeping stride.

"How's Jack?" she asks.

I, however, talk like I'm gasping for air. "Good. He should be in bed now."

"Bath, bottle, and bed. I remember." She giggles as we start going downhill. "Your wife seemed so nice. And she's so pretty."

I grimace at her description of Kat, mostly because I don't know the right thing to say about her. "She is."

"I only met her that one time. She must have thought I was loony tunes, coming up to her and talking about Jack like we were buddies. Tell her I said hello."

"I, uh, will when I see her. We're…not together at the moment."

Becca stops jogging, and it takes me a little time to realize she's behind me. I have to push down on my instep to keep from tripping as I slow down and turn.

"You broke up?" Becca's brows are curved.

My hands are on my hips as I take deep, erratic breaths. "Yeah, we're getting divorced."

This is the first time I've said it out loud. It feels weird.

She closes the distance between us. "Are you okay? That must be awful."

"I'm getting used to it. I think."

Her mouth parts as she nods her head, looking at me like I'm a wounded puppy. She places a hand on my bicep and tenderly rubs it. "Well, if you need someone to talk to, I'm here for you. Anytime. Anyplace."

I raise my chin as I look down at her, noticing the way her eyes are now hooded in a sultry way. I don't assume all women are hitting on me, but this is too friendly.

"Thanks." I step back and give a kind smile.

Becca takes a breath and then smiles back. Her eyes widen as she just stares at me for a beat too long. "Okay, so here's the thing," she starts, seeming almost nervous. "I'm sure whatever you're going through is super fresh, and maybe you're not ready to move on…yet. But I know that the good ones go fast, and you're not going to be on the market for long, so if you're interested, I'd love to go out with you."

Now, my eyes are widening, pretty much bugging out of my head. This girl is hot; don't get me wrong. Most men would kill for a chance with her. I'm just not ready for that.

I must be taking too long to answer because she starts talking again, "This is going to sound so weird. Before I met your wife—well, soon, ex-wife—I thought you were a single dad. You were so charming, and maybe you didn't realize it, but you were hitting on me. A lot. Super flirty. Before I started dating the guy I'm with now, I was really into you. Then, I found out you were married, and I didn't want to mess with that. But you're not married now. Well, you won't be for long. So, what do you say? Dinner on Saturday?"

I'm still speechless. For a man who argues for a living, I don't know what to say. "I was flirting with you?"

"Yeah. Why else would you run with me? Or let me bond with your kid?"

Fuck me. I am such an ass.

I mess with my hair while I look at her. Toned body and perky tits. She's cute all right, and I'd be a fool not to let her help me get through the next few months while I fight with Kat in court. Becca could most definitely distract me in the bedroom.

She is every guy's wet dream.

"I can't," I say. "I'm not ready to move on. Whatever you have going on with this other guy, you should keep it going. He might be the one for you. I'm not."

There's a reddish tint to her face, and I know I've embarrassed her. I don't want to be a dick, and there's no good way out of this, so I try to give her an out. "Why don't we finish this run? I'll leave you at the edge of the park, so you don't have to walk in the dark."

"Yeah." She nods, almost unsure, and then she smiles. "That would be nice."

As we finish our run, I know this is the last time I'll ever run with this girl again. Kathryn was right. There was something to be suspicious of. I might have thought my relationship with Becca was harmless. Hell, I didn't know her name until Kat brought it up, yet this girl thought I liked her. That's on me.

I leave Becca and run longer than I planned. My mind is all over the place. Kathryn found lingerie in our car and thought it was Becca's. It all makes sense now. I don't know who put it there, but I have a good suspicion. How fucked up the situation is, is remarkable.

The damage is done though. I am reminded of that when I find myself standing outside my house. The lights are out, and yet I yearn to go inside. I want to put my briefcase on the table, kiss my wife, and hug my son. I want my life back.

I'll never get it. What I thought was bliss was crafted in false expectations and good intentions.

The love story of Gabriel and Kathryn is over.

And it wasn't the husband.

It was the wife.

chapter THIRTY-ONE

KATHRYN

I regret my decision of agreeing to go to this damn gala. Even though I knew I should stay away, I feel like I need the closure. I started this project, and I have to see it through.

I step out of the bathroom, and Gwen beams at me like I'm going to the prom. Her one-week stay has turned into two. Believe it or not, I still don't want her to leave.

"Kathryn, you look…" Words fail her. "Oh, honey, after everything you've gone through, you deserve to see this event in all its glory. You worked so hard. I am very proud of you."

I give her my best Grayson smile. "Thank you, Mom. For everything."

We embrace, and she holds me—really holds me—for the first time since I was a little girl.

The dress looks as goddess-like as the day I tried it on—and with zero markings from the department store floor. I have on the most beautiful pair of strappy silver stilettos that cost me a fortune, making it the last big purchase this single mom will make in a long time. Gwen did my makeup, and I did my own hair in long, soft curls. I look demure, yet I'm ready to kick some ass if I have to.

Asher arranged for a car to pick me up. I think it's his way of ensuring I actually make it to the gala. I haven't seen him since that day in the office, and tonight will be my last. I am all too happy to see Devon round the SUV and open my door. When we pull up to the gala, he opens my door and takes my hand to lead me onto the black carpet.

It's everything I hoped it would be and more. Topiaries of dahlias, peonies, and roses line the carpet in an archway, leading people to the venue. At the far end is the photographers' pit with a step-and-repeat for interviews. The fountain is illuminated in lights, and a handmade marquee announces Asher's benefit concert. Spotlights stand on both sides of the venue, letting the city know there is an event happening right now that people have to take notice of.

I bypass the main entrance and make my way toward the side. I'm thrilled to see Trish wearing a headset and holding a clipboard. Looks like Erik and Asher did the right thing and promoted her to my spot. I want to say hello, but a quick wave and a nod for good luck is all I can spare, as she looks like she's in full producer mode. I can hear her telling the cameraman to get a pan of the exterior.

I walk into David Geffen Hall, toward the theater entrance. Standing there is a man wearing a black tuxedo, bow tie included. His golden highlights glisten in the pin lighting of the room, and I don't have to wait for him to turn around to see his eyes.

As if he can feel my presence, Asher turns and faces me with a mixture of elation and relief.

Golden eyes look me up and down. I know he approves.

"I've told you this before, and I will tell you again. You are beautiful."

"Thank you, Alex. So are you."

"So, we're back to Alex. Looks like I'm not in trouble anymore."

"No, you're not in trouble. We're friends, right?"

"Yes. Friends." He takes my hand in his and leads me around the room, introducing me to New York elite.

One person I don't see is Malory.

"She was fired," Asher answers my unspoken question. "I want you to know I never paid any mind to those emails. Once I got to know you"—he lifts my hand and brushes his lips against my knuckles—"I knew what was true."

We chat with dignitaries and celebrities, socialites and scholars. The room is filled with old money and new, and for Asher, they are willing to empty their pockets. Asher praises me to each and every one of them. And when he thinks I'm not looking, I catch him staring at me. He looks proud, and he should be. He's put on a spectacular event. No, two spectacular events. I'm sure Heather is doing an incredible job at the other.

Before the curtains go up and the speeches begin, Asher leads me backstage. Trish is keeping everything timed close to the itinerary, and I pat myself on the back for doing such a great job of putting everything together.

Asher and I stand backstage together, waiting for his cue to make his speech. I wonder if this is the life I would lead, sticking by Asher. Fancy productions, big events every weekend. If I'd met him at another time, would we be together?

He takes the stage with charisma and magnitude. The women in the audience gasp at his good looks, and I hear a few backup dancers backstage talk about getting in his pants after the show. I'm sure a one of them will succeed.

Harvey did an excellent job with Asher's speech. The audience eats it up, and I can hear the wallets in the crowd opening up.

Asher is soon by my side, and he takes my hand. "Come, let's go for a walk."

I hear a few whiny voices in the background. *Calm down, ladies. He'll be back!*

I take his hand and follow him out into the courtyard. He looks beautiful in the evening light. I will never tire of looking at this exotic Adonis of a man. Even at night, his perfect mouth and square jaw are illuminated against his tanned skin.

"Are you going to the park? I'm sure Heather will need you at some point. You are the face of the organization." I look over toward the park. I can see the lights of the event from here.

Turning back toward Asher, I catch him staring at me, mesmerized.

"No, Kathryn. I am exactly where I want to be."

He's smoldering, and I don't know if my heart can take it.

"No. Please. I know that look," I beg him for a reprieve.

"Good. Then, you know exactly what I'm going to say." His eyes lock on to mine.

"There is nothing we can do. It's over. It was a one-time—"

Before I can get the words out of my mouth, his lips are on mine. Warm, soft, passionate lips. They feel just as good as they did that sinful weekend.

I part my lips just enough, allowing him entrance into my soul. Our tongues meet, and his passion pours into me. With one hand wrapped around my waist and the other around my neck, Asher pulls me into his body, and I fall helplessly.

My arms wrap around his neck, and my fingers lace into his hair. I lose myself so easily when I'm with him. I have to stop. This isn't what tonight is about.

I release my lips from his and try to step out of his embrace, but his hold is firm on me.

"Don't leave. Stay with me."

"Stay with you? And then what? I move in? We get married? We raise my son together?"

He's not letting me go. Tobacco and vanilla eradicate my senses while eyes show something I've never seen before on him.

"I love you."

What? Love?

Alexander Asher doesn't fall in love. Once, but that was a long time ago.

I stare into those forbidden eyes and get swept up in the emotion behind them. Deep, soulful wanting hides behind those shades of gold turning into warm caramel. My breath is momentarily taken away by the angst hiding inside his heart. Conviction he has, but what he needs and what he wants are two different things.

"Asher...you don't love me. You *think* you love me. You're panicking, and you think the only way you can keep me is by telling me you love me."

"Listen to me."

"I am listening. I'm listening to a man who is so scared of losing his friend, so he will do and say whatever it takes. You're ready to be loved and to love someone, but it's not me. You don't love me." I place my hands on his face and take in his beauty.

"Stop it!" He grabs my waist and pulls me into him, close and protective. "Can't you feel it? Even Malory knew. She said it on that damn recording.

"I love you, Kathryn. Ever since I saw you in the rain. I've loved you from the moment I laid eyes on you. I loved you when you told me off in the elevator. I loved you when you came up with this crazy idea for two concerts. I loved you when you danced with me on that stage and when you let me share myself with you at the tomb. I loved you when you were standing in the halo of the streetlights, and I loved you when you let me make love to you.

"And I don't care if you're married or if you have a kid or if I have to give up everything I have to make this right. You make *my* life make sense."

My heart falls and loses beats in the process. His words are everything a girl could dream of, yet they're not right.

I shake my head and try to pull away from him. He holds on tighter.

"Kathryn, what can I do to prove it to you?"

I don't know what's right anymore. *Do I love Asher?* I've never taken the time to even think about that being a possibility. I did fall for him, but how deep? In love? In lust? I certainly wanted him, but did we both fall so far for each other when fate wasn't looking?

Or maybe it was fate all along.

"I need time." It's the only thing I can think to ask.

"Time." He registers my request and appears to be satisfied. "I can give you time but not too much. I know you, Kathryn. You'll run. I knew I should have never taken you out of that hotel room." He smiles that gorgeous smile and brushes a loose strand of hair off my face, cupping my cheek in the process. "Tomorrow. Meet me at the W Hotel. I'll be waiting for you. Take the night, but that's it. I love you, Kathryn, and I'll take you any way I can get you."

Time. I've bought myself time.

I lean up on my toes and kiss this impossible man on the cheek, holding on to it for what feels like an eternity. This hypnotic, successful man, who is also a philanthropist and classically trained musician, who has the world at his fingertips, wants me. *Me.* A soon-to-be divorcée, mother of one, with no job and no friends.

There is something incredibly wrong with the universe.

chapter THIRTY-TWO

Asher leads me back to the SUV, where Devon is waiting. He sends me on my way, hoping I'll return to him with the answer he desires. As magical as it seems, this isn't how I envisioned the night playing out.

Devon has special permission to drive through the park, as it's closed for the evening's event. I'm glad to be able to see it in all its hectic glory. The lights, the people, the security. It looks incredible. The music soars through the air, and I revel in the amazing production that was put together in a few short weeks.

Tomorrow, it will all be gone. This concert is just like Jackson's building blocks. Build them up to knock them down. There'll be another production for Erik, another sparring partner for Heather, another twinkie for Asher.

Asher. Why did you have to turn my world upside down? You are amazing in so many ways, but you had to play the love card.

Is it possible for him to love? Yes. He can love and will love deeply, but is it for me? And do I love him? Did I fall in love with him in Miami?

I did fall in love once. At a beer pong table? No. That was lust. I fell in love with Gabriel the next day, at breakfast. I fell in love when he made those god-awful pancakes.

I laugh to myself at the thought. Gabriel is a terrible cook.

Our first date was to a batting cage. It was a place I went often and hoped we could share it together. Well, one look at his swing, and I knew I was dead wrong. Sure, he hit the ball with power, but it went in every other direction.

He was sweet about it though. He let me show him the correct stance and proper follow-through. Now, he hits the ball fast, far, and on target every time.

My thoughts are disrupted when Devon pulls up in front of my house. I kindly thank him for the ride and wave politely from my front lawn as I watch him pull away. I take one look at my front door and know I'm not ready to go inside yet. However, I do for a second, only to grab Gwen's keys. I hop in her car and drive away.

I could go to the batting cage, but I'm in a dress. I could keep driving, but for some reason, I find myself in front of the hotel Gabriel is staying at.

I've never been at The Inn before. It has a gorgeous, rustic feel. As soon as you walk in, you're greeted by a large foyer with a stone fireplace. Tonight, the fire is roaring even though it's warm outside. To the right is a reception area with a beautiful mahogany desk and a large, ornate, winding staircase leading up to the second level just beyond it. To the left is a bar area. It's still early, and although I am slightly overdressed, I think I'll have a drink while I gather my thoughts.

The bar is empty, except for a few guests in the corner, who are seated at a table, enjoying a nightcap. I decide to take my party of one to the bar. I hop on the stool at the corner and order a whiskey. I need the strong stuff to survive.

I take one swig, and my throat burns. I don't drink enough to know if it's because he gave me the good, expensive stuff or the cheap lower-shelf brand. I might as well keep on drinking. I deserve the burn.

"Since when did you start drinking hard liquor?"

I'm surprised to see him standing there. Not for the fact that he's standing there since I am drinking in the hotel he's staying in. I'm surprised because the sight of him still does things to me.

"I guess I just wanted to feel like a grown-up for the night." I watch his navy-blues for any sign he doesn't want me here.

Shifting from one foot to the other, Gabriel scans the bar area before taking a tentative step forward, and he slides into the seat next to me on the corner of the bar. He motions toward the bartender. "Make that two."

The bartender hands Gabriel his glass, and I watch as he takes a slow and steady sip. He looks good. He's in jeans and a plaid button-down shirt. No tie, no top button, sleeves rolled. His hair is long, much longer than he's worn it in a long time. He needs a haircut, but I like the mess of waves. He grabs his glass, and I hear the unmistakable clink of his wedding ring hitting it. My breath hitches.

"Guess I forgot to take this off." He motions toward his hand, flexing it out to feel the weight of the metal on his skin.

I look down on mine. "Me, too." I raise my glass. "Here's to our rings' last night out on the town until they get pawned and sold to some lowly sap."

He raises his glass to mine and adds, "And may their marriage last longer than ours."

We clink our glasses even though his words sting.

Gabriel stretches his strong arm across the counter, plucking an olive from a bowl, popping it in his mouth and swirls it around with his tongue.

I twirl my glass in my hand, watching the amber liquid dance in the glass. It's like a mini tornado. Glancing up, I look over and catch Gabriel staring at me through his long lashes.

"What?" I ask.

His eyes shift from side to side. His hand rises to rub his jaw and swipes over his mouth, coming to rest on his glass. "You know, when I came down the stairs just now, I saw this beautiful woman enter the hotel lobby. She was the most gorgeous thing I'd ever seen in my life. It made me stop and catch my breath. I actually followed her in here to buy her a drink, and when I got here, I found she was…you." Gabriel laughs at his idiocy and takes a swig of his whiskey.

I don't know if I should be flattered or disappointed by his words. At least he's still here, having a drink with me. "That reminds me of this guy I once met. You see, we were at this bar in Maryland. He had this charismatic smile, and soul-searching eyes. I waited for him every day after class to ask me for my name, and each day, I'd refuse, hoping he'd be back there the next day."

Gabriel lets out a shy smile at the memory. "I came back every day, hoping to learn your name. I fell in love with you on those walks." His eyes light up. "When I saw you that night in the bar, my life changed forever."

"I threw that game of beer pong just so you would take me on that date," I finally admit.

It's been an ongoing joke between us that Gabriel knew I'd wanted him as soon as I walked through the door. He was right. He's always right.

"I knew it!" His face shoots up in surprise.

I can feel the crinkle around my eyes from smiling. "Doesn't matter though because we didn't have to wait until that date." I look him right in the eyes. "We were so hot for each other that we walked right out of that bar and almost didn't make it out of the cab."

Gabriel takes a final swig of his whiskey and lets out a deep grunt. He stands up and takes his wallet out to pay for the drinks. "It was the best day of my life. Please don't ruin it."

"The next day, he made me these terrible pancakes because he wanted to impress me. As much as he wanted to do something nice for me, I knew I would spend the rest of my life doing everything I could to make him happy. But you see, I failed him."

Gabriel's body is tense. He looks like he's about to leave but stands there as I speak, his back half to me as he holds on to the barstool he just rose from.

"When he proposed, he promised to share my dreams, but I never did the same for him. He took a job he was brilliant at yet secretly hated, all so he could provide an amazing life for me and his son. I took it for granted. I thought I wanted more, yet I had everything I wanted. I forgot to give him what he needed."

"And what did he need?" he asks over his shoulder.

"Support," I say.

Gabriel runs his hand down his face and holds his mouth for a second, as if trying to think of the right thing to say. He turns back toward me, placing both hands on the barstool. "Kat, it's not all your fault. I know I'm not supposed to say this—my lawyer would kill me if he heard me say this—but I was a shitty husband. I didn't listen when you said you were unhappy, and I certainly wasn't as affectionate as I used to be. I just…I got so damn tired.

"I am so damn tired, Kat. This is not what I pictured our life to be. I swear to you, I planned it out differently. The truth is, we both screwed this up. I drove you into his arms."

I have to pull my mouth up from the floor. I wasn't prepared for him to take the blame. I don't know how I feel about that.

"And listen," he continues, "as much as I still hate you for doing it, with Malory torturing you and Becca—oh, that's another story. Let's just say, you were right about her. She definitely thought I was sending her signals that weren't there. Maybe I was. So, I can't say I entirely blame you."

"Gabriel, please. I hate myself so much right now I can't bear the thought of you thinking this has anything to do with you being at fault." I lower my head.

Running his hand through his hair, he says, "Listen, it's late. I'm going to head up. Do you mind if I take Jack for the day? I miss him so much."

I look up to see pain in his eyes. I shake my head in disagreement. He shifts back, but I clarify, "Why don't you go home and spend the night in your bed? You'll be there when Jackson wakes up. I'll stay here." I open my bag and take out my set of keys. I place them in his palm and close his fingers. "You should go and be with your son."

Gabriel's eyes relax, and I see a calming and almost-appreciative gaze. A hint of that Robert Redford grin I fell in love with makes an appearance. "Thank you," he murmurs, handing me his room key.

He tells me his room number and to help myself to anything from room service. I have no choice but to watch as he turns on his heel and heads out through the lobby.

All dressed up and nowhere to go, Cinderella retires to her tower for the night.

I make my way up to Gabriel's room and unlock the door. The room is spacious and elegantly decorated, yet it's nowhere for a man to call home even if it is only temporary. There is a large canopy bed in the middle, made of rich mahogany, with luscious cream-and-red paisley bedding. I stroll over to the mini bar and take out a bottle of water from the inventory.

The TV sits on a dresser in the corner, yet I have no desire to turn it on. I just let my beautiful husband walk out the door, and I didn't even put up a proper fight. In fact, I let him feel like shit about himself.

I should have said more.

I should have told him about the night Jackson was born. How frightened I was, yet he was right by my side, comforting me, encouraging me the entire time. And how, when we brought him home, I was so scared of being a new mom, but he assured me we would learn to do this together.

I never doubted how I'd be as a mom because Gabriel was by my side.

I should have told him about that time we backpacked through Europe and missed our train. We didn't know if we would have to sleep in a hostel or in a car or in a park. I didn't care because he was always ready with a plan and never faltered to protect us.

Or the night before our wedding, when the DJ called with the flu and canceled on us, he said it didn't matter if there was silence because we had our entire lives to dance. All he wanted to do was marry me.

I have a thousand stories I should have told him, but I didn't.

My pity party is disrupted by a knock at the door. I place the bottle of water on the dresser and make my way toward the door. My heart melts when I see him standing in the doorway.

Gabriel's right arm is stretched up against the doorframe. I can feel his weight swaying toward me. He stands there, looking down at me with sheer determination.

"Did you forget something?" I ask.

"I met this girl once. She had this long brown hair and gorgeous green eyes, and she had the most incredible smile I'd ever seen. I thought I'd died and gone to heaven." He takes a step toward me. So close that we're almost touching. "Tonight, I saw her again, and I'll be damned if I don't take her home just like I did then."

No sooner is he finished with his sentence than his body crashes into mine. Warm hands grab me by the sides of my face as his mouth lands on mine. My lips immediately part and welcome him in. His tongue is hot and burning with desire. We are all mouths and tongues and hands and body heat. His strong, lean body presses up against me.

I let out a moan as his mouth moves from my lips and finds the nape of my neck. His wet tongue French-kisses my skin. My body quivers. He briefly raises his head, and I get a good look at his face. Navy blue turns to midnight in carnal lust.

Gabriel spins me around, forcing my hands to brace myself against the mahogany post of the four-poster bed. He moves my hair off my back until it's cascading off my shoulder and down my front. Long, strong fingers slide the spaghetti straps of my dress, so they slip down my arms. His lips find my skin once more and kiss and lavish every nerve ending, sending shivers down my body, which instinctually falls back into Gabriel.

His fingers glide the zipper of my dress down, and gravity slowly pulls it to the floor. I'm left in nothing but white panties and a matching strapless bra.

He steps back, as I turn around. "I want to hate you," he murmurs under his breath.

I bite my lip at the sight of tears. Slowly, I approach him, gazing into his eyes. They are down and turned away. I catch their attention with my own and bring him back to the moment. Holding up my right hand, I gently place it on his cheek. His brow furrows, as if he's trying to fight it. Instead, he lays his head into my palm and closes his eyes, relishing my touch.

I lean up and lay my other hand on his other cheek. I place a soft kiss on his forehead and whisper, "I love you."

I do the same, kissing his eyes. "I love you."

His nose. "I love you."

His cheek. "I love you."

His temple. "I love you."

His lips. "I love you."

I lean back, and he opens his eyes. His heart caving in, Gabriel leans forward and wraps his hands around my waist, pulling me into him, kissing me passionately, his animalistic need replaced with love and desire.

No words are said. Everything that needs to be told is done so through touches, glances, tickles, and kisses. We have a conversation without words. Mine are words of love, and his are of acceptance.

We make love three times before the sun comes up. He makes my ears burn red hot more times in one evening than I can count.

The rosy hues of the sun are coming up over the horizon when I finally curl on my side with my back against Gabriel's chest. He drapes his arm around mine, playing with my hair before my eyes shut blissfully.

chapter THIRTY-THREE

The sun has risen and is cheerful. The heat of the sun shines through the window, yet I'm cold. I'm missing my very warm blanket. My Gabriel.

I roll over and place my hand on the mattress. He must have just gotten up. I sit up in the bed and look around the room.

His clothes are missing from the floor, his wallet and watch nowhere to be seen.

Did he leave? Would he leave after what transpired last night...and this morning?

Relief washes through me when the bathroom door opens, and Gabriel exits, pulling a crew neck shirt over his chest. I blush, thinking about the things I did to that chest last night. His chest, his thighs, his lips...

Gabriel sees me sitting in the middle of the bed and stops in his tracks. He looks hesitant, nervous even.

It feels like our first time all over again.

"Morning," he states politely, moving to the chair in the corner of the room. He sits down and puts on a fresh pair of socks. "I didn't want to wake you."

He looks handsome in a white waffle-weave shirt and blue jeans. He steps into brown loafers and adjusts his watch. "I'm going to the house to get Jack. Thought maybe we'd go to the park for a few hours." He glances out the window. "It looks like it's going to rain, so I want to get out before the downpour begins."

My heart nearly bounces out of my chest at the thought of Gabriel coming home. Wrapping the sheet around me, I start to make my way off the bed, surprised I have the need for modesty after ten years and last night's extracurricular activities. "Give me a few minutes. I'll just throw on—"

"No. You should stay," he states, grabbing his wallet and keys off the dresser.

For a man who just made love to me last night, he's not acting like he should.

My feet stop moving. I slowly turn around. Gabriel is on the other side of the room, yet his soul feels like he's miles away.

"Gabriel?" My voice is hesitant. I look down at the sheet, afraid to see the answer in his eyes.

"I don't want you to go home with me, Kat." His voice is steady and sure.

I bite my lower lip to keep it from trembling.

Breathe, Kat. Just breathe.

"You don't want me?"

He doesn't answer. I glance up to meet his face, but he's turned away. His brow is formed in a V, his lips mashed together.

"Answer me, Gabriel!" My voice is shaky yet commanding.

"No." His eyes dart toward the door. "I don't want you to go with me."

"But why?" I cry. "After everything we shared last night, I thought we were fixed."

His breathing is deep, his attention still focused on the door. He's trying to hold himself together. "I…I love you so much, Kat. More than you ever gave me credit for. Finding out what you did, that killed me. I lost a piece of my heart that I won't ever get back." He lifts a bag off the floor and walks to the door.

Everything happens in slow motion. It feels like it takes him hours to walk across the room and a decade to head out the door. I know I should say something. Begging comes to mind. I have no words. *Defeated* is the proper word. Before I know it, he's out the door—again.

With the sheet still wrapped around my shoulders, I fall to the ground. My forehead hits the bedpost.

There's nothing more I can do. I can't chase him anymore. What we had is dead. I saw it in his eyes. He doesn't want me anymore, and I destroyed the best thing I'd ever had.

Ω

In the most pathetic walk of shame I've ever known, I step through the lobby of The Inn in my thousand-dollar gown and head to Gwen's car to retrieve my gym bag. Gwen thought I should start going to the gym again to relieve stress. The bag has been sitting in her car for two weeks.

I ignore the stares and glares from the receptionist on my way out, but there is no avoiding them on my way in. Yes, I slept with a man last night in this hotel. If she only knew I was the adulteress, having an affair with her own husband.

The other man is at a hotel in the city, waiting for my answer.

Asher, you were such a vital part of my life, and now, I rue the day I met you.

There are so many aspects of him I am drawn to, but he's no good for me.

The man I love doesn't love me anymore, and the man I lust for says he loves me. Maybe Gabriel leaving me this morning a cosmic sign that I am meant to be at the W Hotel right now, starting my new life with Alexander Asher.

I strip out of the gown. I change into my black yoga pants and matching zip-up and lace up my sneakers. I have to get out of here.

I walk out of The Inn and to my car, heading toward the train station. I'm afraid if my nerves get the better of me, I'll crash the car.

There's no use in going home. I can't face Gabriel right now, and Gwen will have to wait for her daily update on the drama that is my life. I'm going to ask her to stay with Jackson and me permanently. Turns out, I need my mother after all.

She never did tell me what she would have done if my dad hadn't passed away. Perhaps she would have started a new life with the other man. If he was the man she was meant to be with, she would have betrayed her heart out of obligation to my father.

That is one reason why I want Gabriel. We took a vow. I am obligated to him, as barbaric as that may sound.

And, yet, people make new vows every day. Asher wants forever.

Mrs. Kathryn Asher. It has a really nice ring to it. We would be the Ashers. Our kids could have his bronzed skin with my green eyes. I'd even let them have his golden highlights. Jackson would love his new siblings. He's so young; he'd never know any other life.

How sad. He'd never know a life when Gabriel and I were together.

Tears pour down my cheeks, but I wipe them away.

No, Asher and I would have a great life. We'd spend the first two years naked and loving each other. The way we did in Miami.

Miami. Before that trip, I hadn't known how he felt about me. I had feelings for him, too. Otherwise, I would never have landed in his bed.

And, yesterday, he was so kind and considerate. He said he'd give me time. He knew I'd return.

The train comes to a stop at Penn Station, and I make my way to the restroom. I splash water on my face and apply mascara and a little lip gloss. Despite my morning sobfest, I feel surprisingly rested.

Probably because, for the first time in a long time, I know what I want.

I take the escalator up from the terminal and exit onto Eighth Avenue. The sky is dark and cloudy. The wind picks up. I relish the heaviness of the air. It matches how I feel.

I make my way down 42nd Street and walk across town. With each block, the heaviness of my heart sinks deeper hoping I'm making the right decision.

Lexington Avenue is quiet, as it usually is on Saturday. The cars move steadily up and down the street. I see the building in front of me. I should move my feet, but I can't. They feel like lead.

A drop of water falls from the sky.

We met on a day just like this. Gray sky and wind. Another drop falls, and I look up. Another falls and then another. Yes, we met on a day just like today. That was when my life changed forever.

On the other side of the street is a man who wants me, and I want him.

If I could take it all back, would I?

I'm standing on a corner in the rain. *How did I get here? How did I come to this point in the road?*

The rain starts to pour, the drops heavier. I don't have an umbrella. I didn't have an umbrella that day.

The corner is wet, and my clothes are soaked, but I can't move. I'm here to see him.

Asher gave me an umbrella. *So you don't get caught in the rain again.*

Yet here I am. In the rain. Again.

Him.

Asher.

There he is, walking out the front door of the hotel. Right where he's supposed to be.

He said he'd be here, and he is.

Through the parting umbrellas, I can see his face. Those golden eyes and chiseled chin are striking alongside his broad shoulders and strong thighs.

That could all be mine.

He's carrying an umbrella, shielding him from the rain.
The white pearl handle covered by his strong hands.
So in control. So dry.
He would take care of me.
He's wearing gray. That's the color. The color that defines my life.
He said it himself.
Nothing is black and white.
Just gray.
Gray.
I want to run, dash across the street, and grab him. Hold him in my arms, feel his tongue in my mouth.
I want to caress him, feel his hand under my skirt.
But my legs are lead. I cannot move.
He's waiting for me. This is my moment.
But do I turn to him or run away?
Far away.
What do I do?
What would you do?
Who would you choose?

EPILOGUE

Warm rays hit the deck of the boat as I raise my head to bask in the glorious day. Resting my head on the cushion, I lean back and let the heat hit my face. You can only get this sunshine in the South.

The boat is docked, and we're getting ready to depart. I don't know a thing about boats. My family was all about baseball. It took me a while to adjust to my new lifestyle, but I couldn't be happier.

"Enjoying the sun?" Gwen says, coming out of the cabin below, holding my son, Gray. "I think someone is hungry."

Gwen places my baby boy in my arms. I put my finger in his mouth, and he sucks immediately. Yes, someone is very hungry. Gwen laughs with her *grandmother always knows* attitude. I smile back as she returns to the cabin.

This sailboat isn't your average dinghy. Gwen says it's a yacht. When you step inside the boat, there is a sectional sofa with a seating area to the right and a television console to the left. Behind that living room is a dining area with a kitchen to the right. There are two bedrooms and two bathrooms, not to mention a small captain's quarters. The wood glistens under the pin lighting, and the cream color of the carpet and furniture upholstery make the space look luxurious.

I feed and burp the baby before taking him inside the cabin, settling him in his bassinet.

Grayson is the newest addition to our family. Jackson is so in love with his little brother. He gives him kisses daily. When he's not smothering him with hugs, that is.

"Where is Jackson?" I ask.

"Your men are on the dock, looking at the big boats."

I step outside and look down the dock for my husband and child. Two years ago, with all the trepidation and what-ifs playing in my head, I never thought I could be this happy. Now, I know I'm exactly where I belong.

I remember the day I had to make the most important decision of my life.

I was standing in the rain, watching Asher exit the W Hotel.

Ω

I was just about to step away when golden eyes caught me. I couldn't move. I was frozen.

Surprised to see me standing there, drenched in the rain, Asher leaped off the curb and ran across the street.

When I saw him darting toward me, my feet found their stride, and I started to move. I had to get away.

"Kathryn!" he called out, dropping the white pearl-handled umbrella to gain distance.

The rain picked up. I knew I shouldn't, but I turned around anyway, and just like the day we met, I was entrapped.

"Where are you going?" he asked, sounding confused.

And he had every right to be. I'd shown up, but I was walking away.

As I looked at him, that one last time, my heart clenched so tight. The man who had captured my soul and become my greatest friend, who had professed his love and life to me, was in front of me. The man who was so powerful and commanding was falling as he slowly understood what it was I was about to do. For a split second, I was afraid I was making the wrong choice.

"I came to say good-bye, but I couldn't do it." My hands rose to my face and wiped away hair that was sticking to me from the rain and wind.

"You know what that means, right? It means you love me. You can't say good-bye."

He took a step toward me, placing his hands in mine. I quickly pulled my hands away from his, afraid if I let him touch me, I wouldn't be able to pull away.

"No, Asher. You have it all wrong. I don't love you. I never have." I waited a second for my words to set in. "You have been an amazing friend to me. You've shown me there is more to my life, that I don't need to settle. You make my life make sense. For me, that means I needed to meet you to know exactly what I wanted."

"What do you want?" His face twisted in discomfort.

"I want my family. I love my husband. I love Gabriel."

His body stood straight, and he put on his affront. "But I told you, I love you." His words were pained.

"Yes, you love me as much as I love you." I placed my hand on his shoulder. "But it's not the love you deserve. You don't want to marry me. You don't want to have children with me. You are worthy of so much more, and you will get it. I think, for the first time in your life, you're ready for it. Now, you just need to meet the right person. Someday, you will meet her, and you'll let her know who the real Alexander Asher is. I only skimmed the surface. There is so much more you're willing to give. You just have to find the one to give it to."

Asher stood in front of me, soaked from head to toe. The commanding man who always got what he wanted was truly nothing more than just that—a man. "I told you, I always get what I want."

He does. He did. But…

"Not this time."

Asher shook his head and looked disheartened. He always marveled that I was the one who told it like it was. And with him, I could. I'd found my voice again with him. I'd discovered who I was, who the new Kathryn was.

He reached for my hand, and this time, I let him. I wasn't afraid anymore.

"I'll never forget you."

I smiled right back. "I will hold you in my heart forever."

Taking my hand back, I turned to head toward the subway, but Asher called out, "Take the car. Devon will take you where you have to go."

My body was soaked, and there was no way I'd hail a cab. Even still, I couldn't take his car. "No, this is something I have to do on my own."

And I left. Leaving the beautiful, exotic, successful, philanthropic man who had more to give than I would ever deserve on a street corner in the rain.

Ω

My heart leaps when I see them. My two men, holding hands, walking down the dock toward me with their navy eyes and wavy, dark hair. They are twins.

"Let's go get Mommy!" Gabriel says to Jackson, and the two run down the dock toward me.

My nerves catch up to me. I hate when he lets Jackson run on the dock. Especially since he's not wearing his life jacket.

Gabriel hands Jackson to me, and I raise him over the railing.

"Hi, Mommy!" My sweet angel beams. "Look what I have!" He holds out his small hand to show me a plastic bag of Goldfish crackers. "I was feeding the fish with fish!" His cherub cheeks lift into an angelic smile.

"That's awesome. Did you and Daddy have fun?"

"Uh-huh. Where's Grayson?" Jackson says as he shoves a handful of Goldfish in his mouth.

"He's inside with Grandma." I give Jackson a quick kiss before he runs inside to see his little brother.

Grayson Monroe, my second angel. My new beginning.

When I finally changed my name to Kathryn Monroe, it felt good. And when we were blessed with a second little boy, I knew there was no greater way to keep that piece of my family with me.

Gabriel lets out a laugh and kisses my hair. His fingers twist the soft curls in his hand. I let out a sigh. *This is bliss.*

"What are you thinking about?" he says with his lips pressed up against the top of my head.

"Just how happy I am." I smile and nuzzle closer.

"Good. Me, too," he says.

We are happy. It's amazing to think we almost weren't.

Gabriel starts the engine of the boat and drives it out toward the sea. The delicious scent and taste of the salt air bring on a sense of serenity. Once he guides the boat out of the harbor, the real fun begins.

With the boat as close to the eye of the wind as possible, Gabriel pulls the mainsail with the boom slightly over the transom. Seeing him pulling ropes, moving beams, and cranking away, I know he's in his glory. This is where he should have always been.

Since I'm a terrible seaman, Gabriel hired a deckhand to help him drive the boat. When the boat is cruising windward, Gabriel relinquishes complete control of the boat to the deckhand and takes a seat on the cushions of the deck sofa, holding his arms out to me. I slide into the crook of his arm and pull my feet up on the couch. I curl up as close as I can get to Gabriel without climbing on top of him.

"Now, this is the life," he says with his megawatt Robert Redford smile beaming into the sunset.

"Yes, this is where we should have been all along," I gush.

"So, you don't regret selling the house?" he asks.

"Not one bit."

"You don't regret moving to sunny Florida?"

"Never." I scrunch my nose at the thought of being anywhere else.

Gabriel lets out a laugh. I lean over and kiss him deeply and passionately.

It was never a choice of Asher or Gabriel. The choice was whether I would continue to fight for Gabriel.

I never loved Asher.

It has always been my Gabe.

Ω

After my corner encounter with Asher in the rain, I found my way back home. By that time, the rain had died down. I, on the other hand, was still wet, but it didn't matter.

Gabriel's car was still in the driveway. I'd made it in time.

"Gabriel!" I called out as soon as I entered the front door. I ran into the living room. "Gabriel!"

"What are you shouting about?" Gwen said as she entered the kitchen, holding Jackson.

"Where is Gabriel?" I asked.

"He left about ten minutes ago," she answered. "Is everything okay?"

I looked out the window. I could see his car. "His car is in the driveway."

"He must have gone for a walk." She looked out the window. "I don't know why. It was raining the entire time he was here. What's the matter?"

I ran out of the kitchen and out the door. I had to find him.

Exiting the house, I looked up and down the street. He was nowhere to be found. There was only one place he could have possibly gone.

I ran to the park. There was nowhere else close enough to walk to. I took the path I knew he usually strolled with Jackson and followed it up a hill. As soon as I rounded the bend, I saw him standing at the top of the hill, walking away from me.

"Gabe!"

Wearing a white shirt and jeans, he turned around at the sound of my voice, his face a mixture of surprise, confusion, and what I could only hope was elation.

I slowed my pace as I tried to catch my breath. My run turned into a power walk. Gabriel stood in place, waiting for me to get to the top of the hill.

"What are you doing here?" He was exasperated.

"I want my family back. I want you and me and Jackson. We are a family, and families don't give up. They fight. They fight every day for what's right. I know I betrayed our family, and I know I hurt you. The thing is...I love you. I mean it, Gabriel Monroe. I am in love with you. I will spend the rest of my life proving it to you, if you'll just give me a chance. I'm not asking you to forgive me. I'm asking you to try."

There, I'd said it. I'd laid my cards out on the table. And now, I waited.

We stood there, taking each other in for what felt like an eternity. I knew I couldn't say anything else. The ball was in his court. All I could do was wait.

And finally, after seconds, minutes, hours, I don't know...he spoke, "Every time I look at you, I'll be reminded of what you did."

His words stung, and as much as I knew I should turn around and leave this poor man alone, I just couldn't.

"Do you love me?" It was my Hail Mary. If I wanted my family back, it could only happen if he was still with me. I stood there, waiting for an answer. Praying for a miracle.

He lowered his head and nodded. "Yes." He swallowed hard before continuing, tears threatening to break through his navy-blue eyes, "Yes, Kat, I still love you. I don't like you, but you will always be the girl who dropped her books on the stairs and took my heart with her."

I couldn't contain the grin that appeared on my face. "Then, we should try. We love each other. We can do this. Let's get out of here. Sell the house. Quit your job. Start over!"

"You'd really let me quit my job?"

He let out a small laugh. I hadn't thought I'd hear that sound again.

"You hate your job. You hate it here just as much as I do."

"Where would we go?" he asked.

"Anywhere. As long as we're together, we can go anywhere."

Ω

And we did. We decided to live out the dream we'd had on our honeymoon. We sold our very expensive house in New York and moved to Florida. We have a beautiful home on the Intracoastal and a boat, *Breaking Wind II*. Hey, it was part of our history, and we couldn't resist.

Gabriel is still a lawyer but at a smaller firm, and I work for a local Miami entertainment show. We even catch a few Marlins games every year. We found a new favorite Chinese takeout place and enrolled Jackson in T-ball. You would think Gabriel would be the coach, but it's actually Gwendolyn. She's really good at it. Though I'm not crazy about the blue cheetah uniforms she designed for them.

It's the life we should have always had.

It wasn't easy. We've spent a small fortune on marriage counseling, and it's been worth the investment. I know there's a part of Gabe that will never forgive me. But that's what marriage is—working together.

We cried a lot in the beginning, but now, we laugh a whole lot more. I feel like I know Gabriel better now than I ever have. Because, now, I know the boy he was and the man he is now. And I love them both equally.

And Gabriel…he loves me. He tells me often. The fact that he's still here shows me he loves me more than I ever could have imagined.

"Are you going to tell me where we're going?"

We packed for a long weekend, but true to form, my darling husband hasn't told me our destination.

"It's a surprise." His face is illuminated in the bright Florida sunshine.

"And I love your surprises."

I fall deeper into the crook of his arm. He smells like sunshine and the sea.

"Twenty Questions. Me first. Favorite thing about Florida? And you can't say me or Jack or Gray."

That's easy. "The house. It's perfect." A modest-sized three-bedroom bungalow on the Intracoastal. I can walk to the beach with my boys.

Gabriel agrees, "Yes, the house is beautiful, like my wife. Although, I have to say, my favorite thing is the fact that we can take the boat out every day."

Yes, my husband, the sailor. This is the boy I fell in love with and the man he has become, wrapped in one delicious package.

"Me next." I love playing games with him. "Thing you miss most about New York?"

"The food," he says with a laugh. "You?" His navy-blues sparkle.

"The skyline."

"I promise I'll take you back." He leans down and kisses me passionately, his hand resting on my cheek, slowly pulling me in closer.

I can't believe I went so long without kissing this man. I mean, *really* kissing him, the way two lovers do. We were so caught up in life that we forgot to live for each other. I will never tire of kissing him again.

Gabriel smiles, breaking our embrace completely. I look up at him and see mischief.

349

"When do you want to start trying for a girl?" he asks, laughing a little since he knows it's ridiculous.

"I just had Grayson!" I hit him in the arm, my hair blowing in the wind.

He takes his hands and smooths the hair off my face, holding it in place on the side of my head. "I know, but I can't wait to have a little girl who looks just like you."

He kisses my nose, and I melt at the touch.

One corner of my mouth turns up. "Well…I am enjoying the practice. Maybe we can practice for a few more months and then try?"

Gabriel holds out his pinkie finger to me. "I promise to always try." His words have more meaning than ever before.

I smile, wrapping my pinkie around his. He looks down at our entwined fingers and kisses them, sealing our promise to each other.

"I love you, Mrs. Monroe."

The sun shines brightly on our backs as I kiss our fated hands. "I love you, too. Now, what do you say to getting some dockside delivery when we arrive at our surprise destination? I'm starving."

His eyebrows perk up. "Chinese?"

"You don't have to ask me twice."

BECAUSE YOU'RE DYING TO KNOW...

ASHER

I don't know why she always feels the need to shower at my place. It irritates the hell out of me, but at least I know she'll be gone as soon as she's done. Sex is the only reason I keep her around. She might be a vindictive bitch, but she's a great fuck, and she knows I'm not going to ask her to stay the night. I don't want her here all night. I don't want anyone here all night. I might hate to sleep alone, but that's my cross to bear. My penance for a wrong I did so long ago. I sleep alone, in the dark, and I like it that way.

I push the covers off my body and lean down to the floor, grabbing the dress pants she so carelessly threw on the floor in her rush to get me naked. I slide them on, going commando and shirtless. I know she's going to see me like this when she gets out of the shower and want another go, but I don't care. I want her gone when she comes out.

Walking down the hallway, I turn into the kitchen and grab the bottle of scotch I started before she arrived. I pour myself a fresh glass and savor the burn. Only alcohol that hurts is worth drinking.

I take my glass and move into the living room. It's a huge room in a huge apartment. Too big for one person. I know this, yet I don't know how to live any other way. My house is nestled on the top two floors of the Asher

Building. If you hit *Penthouse* on the elevator, you'll go to my office. A very public space that everyone and their mother goes through, trying to get a piece of me and the Asher dynasty. What most people don't know is, there is a private code for the elevator to bring you here.

It's three thousand square feet of *mine*. I only let a handful of people up here. It's one of the few things that keeps me sane. This, and music. When I'm up here, I can relax. No one is asking me for money, a deal, a favor. No one can pretend to need me, care for me, want me. There are no false pretenses up here, no bullshit.

I could have bought a place in another building. I could have bought one of those brownstones or mansions on Park Avenue. But this is my building, and I can control it. I know who goes in and what goes out. I can monitor my world from this building. For that reason and that reason alone, I created my sanctuary on top of the world that I control.

The living room is a two-story expanse of black walls and a black ceiling with floor-to-ceiling windows on the north and east walls. No curtains, no drapes. I can walk around, ass naked, and no one can see in.

I'm looking out the north window, seeing the lights of the city below and the red taillights in the distance. The suckers below are driving home on a Friday night, back to their mundane lives, wondering what kind of bullshit they'll open the door to when they get home. The holidays are approaching. You'd never know it, being up here. No tree, no lights, no cheer. Those fools below me, they're probably putting up their trees tonight. I can't remember the last time I had a Christmas tree. I'm searching my brain, trying to remember, when I hear the water turn off.

I take my glass and pad over to the table and pull out the white-and-blue documents my grandfather's attorney prepared. They're the final acquisition papers that make me the sole owner of everything Edward Asher built. It's the final piece of the dynasty I never had any intention of owning. His board knows this, too, which is why I've let them keep control of his businesses all this time. It's been long enough, and I have to take control of the lion's share, become an active member in the corporations. Not only will I have control of my own businesses, but I will also now have possession of the complete Asher dynasty.

The problem is, when I assume Edward Asher's role in the world, I'll have to disengage from my personal projects. There will be no time for my music lessons or charities. I'll have to sell my music and communications companies. Grandfather thought they were a waste of time. He'd be thrilled to know I was giving it all up. He should be. It's a stipulation in his will. When I take control, all of my personal companies and affiliations must be sold. The man never understood my love of music and the arts. They reminded him too much of my parents. They were two people we were never to speak of.

I *could* just rip up the papers. Say *fuck it* and live my life the way I built it. I have my own fortune. I can live my own life. But that's not who I was raised to be. I was born an Asher. This is my legacy. This is who I was groomed to be.

No time for Alex. You are an Asher.

My thoughts are invaded by the sound of high heels clicking loudly down the hallway. I drop the documents back on the table and lift my head to see her approaching with her head bowed as she buttons the last two buttons of her silk blouse.

She lifts her head, taking in my shirtless frame, and a wicked smile crosses her face. I know what she's thinking, and I'm already hitting the down button on the elevator to escort her out.

"I know you have a no-sleeping-over policy, but I could really make it worth your while," she says, putting her hand on my stomach and letting it graze its way south.

I'm seconds away from conceding when I'm saved by the chime of the elevator arriving. The doors open, and I place my hand inside, motioning for her to enter. That is, to exit my apartment.

"Mal…" I say with a condescending tone.

She knows the rules.

Malory removes her hand from my torso and grabs the glass of scotch from my hand. She lifts the glass to her mouth and takes a sip, savoring the burn, just as I was a few minutes ago.

"That's all right. You and I both know I'll be back." She hands me the glass and takes a step into the elevator.

I remove my hand from holding the elevator doors open and let them slowly close, her black eyes trained on me. They're the last thing I see before the doors close.

She's right. She will be back. Malory and I have had a thing going on for years. I give her what she needs, and I take from her what I want. She used to work for me in my production company, but she surpassed her disloyalty tenfold, so I had to let her go. These days, she works for some other company, where I'm sure she's screwed her way to the top, too. I would never have her work for me again. She's too much of a liability. But when it comes to a good fuck, she's an exceptional employee. I don't have to explain the rules, and she always follows them.

I start to walk back to the bedroom when I glance at the front table in the foyer and see a square white envelope. It's addressed to me at my office downstairs. Cecelia must have brought it up.

I turn it over. There's no return address. I put down the glass of scotch and open the seal. I pull it out and see a picture of a family of four, all wearing white sweaters and sitting on the bow of a boat. The father has dark brown hair and light eyes that match the little boy's in his arm. His other arm is draped around a beautiful woman with soft brown hair and gorgeous green eyes.

Kathryn.

In her arms is a small child, a new addition, who also looks just like his father. The inscription on the card reads:

FROM OUR GROWING FAMILY TO YOURS.

HAPPY HOLIDAYS!

THE MONROES

GABRIEL, KATHRYN, JACKSON, AND GRAYSON

She sent me a fucking Christmas card. The one woman who I'd let my guard down for, who I'd almost told my deepest secrets to, who I'd actually fallen in love with. The one fucking person I want but doesn't want me back went and sent me a fucking Christmas card with her asshole of a husband and fucking kids! Kids who, by the way, she hadn't told me about. That's right. I fell in love with a girl even though I knew she was married, but I didn't give a fuck. I didn't. I don't care what kind of man that makes me. I wanted her, and I got her.

I had her for a minute—until he took her away from me.

How callous is she to send me a goddamn picture of their perfect little family?

I turn the card over and see she handwrote a note. A short sentiment she had no business writing.

THINKING ABOUT YOU ALWAYS.

HOPE ALL IS WELL.

—KAT

The card crumples in my fist, and I throw it against the wall, followed by the glass of scotch I lifted from the table.

Storming into the kitchen, I grab the scotch and drink straight from the bottle. My sanctuary has been invaded. The one person who has no business even being thought about in here just penetrated these black walls. I think it's time I leave.

It's time I get out of here and go away…far away.

ALEXANDER ASHER'S STORY CONTINUES IN
RECKLESS ABANDON.

PROLOGUE

I open the car door, begging entrance into a world of speed and carelessness. I've always done things by the book. Tonight, I want to be reckless.

It could be the liquor talking, but I don't care.

"Where are we going next?" Luke turns up the stereo. All the way up to the point your eardrums try to close in protection of the onslaught of erratic beats and heavy metal.

"Anywhere you want, baby bro! Tonight, I feel like flying!" I bang my head on the doorframe as my butt falls hard onto the passenger seat of his Mustang. I raise my hand to the spot that should hurt but surprisingly doesn't.

Luke shakes his head and laughs. "You're gonna feel that in the morning. You're numb drunk."

I twist my face and think about how drunk I possibly am.

Do I know where I am? Yes. I am in Luke's car.

Where did we just come from? The bar? Yes. The bar.

I'm not too sure how many drinks I had. My guess is three, four, seven…wait.

My mouth pulls in, and my throat clenches as I release a warm-aired belch—the quiet kind that leaves a liquor aftertaste in your mouth.

Positive assessment: I am drunk. That is why my baby brother is bringing my ass home.

"Drive." I order.

"Yes, ma'am!" Luke salutes me and puts the car in gear.

When you live in a rural town, driving at night can be dangerous. With dark winding back roads and the only light coming from your own vehicle, you have to proceed with caution.

Not tonight.

"Let's run the night!"

Luke changes gears and we zip down the roads he knows like the back of his hand.

"I like drunk Emma!" he shouts over the music, and I just close my eyes and smile.

I like drunk Emma, too.

Sober Emma does everything right. Practices every day. Follows the rules. Dates the right boys.

Boys. Fucking boys.

I almost forgot about the douche who broke my goddamn heart. I spent the entire day torn up over him. I wasted years of my life being there for him.

And then he left me.

Just. Like. That.

"Faster!" I hear the words pour out of my mouth but don't actually feel my lips move.

"Really?" Luke asks.

I open my eyes and look over at him. My eyebrows scrunch close together and give my best stare down. "Faster!"

With a lead foot, Luke drives. Rapid, thoughtless, and uninhibited.

The heavy bass shouting through the sound system makes the car vibrate and my pulse race. I hear Luke sing along. My mind is a rush of adrenaline and my fingertips rise above my head and then out the open window. The passing wind makes me feel alive and wild.

Luke takes a hard turn. The tires of the car screech on the asphalt and my body slightly rises from the seat. I have to grab the door to get my bearings. He straightens out with precision and my heart pounds.

That felt so fucking good.

With his hand on the gear, he shifts with each sharp turn, losing ground over hills. The wooded confines become a blur in the black night. The fast-passing gravel ahead is all I see.

The world around me starts to move. Fixing my eyes on the dash, I try to ground myself, but it's not working. The wild movements make my head feel dizzy. My stomach rolls up and away from itself. I think I'm going to puke. We should stop.

We should…

The tires squeal. A loud bang comes from Luke's side of the car, and the force of the impact slams me into my door.

Spinning.

We're spinning.

Luke's hands are grabbing violently at the steering wheel. He's out of control.

It's happening too fast.

My head smacks against the door and then toward the windshield. Like a rag doll, my body is shifted. I have to grab hold of something but I can't reach anything.

The glass implodes. I raise my hands to cover my face from the shattering shards. My arms are shielding my eyes. I can't see anything, but I feel the weightlessness of antigravity.

I start to pray but the words can't get out of my mouth fast enough.

The car crashes hard onto the ground with a force so powerful…so fierce…so…

Silent.

PART I
CAPRI, ITALY

chapter ONE

"How much further to the top?" Leah whines, clenching her roller suitcase. The casters make a thumping sound, banging against each step as she pulls it up the mountain of stairs.

"We could have taken the bus." My voice is an I-told-you-so singsong, slightly wincing, as I try to tame the ache shooting up my left arm. It's my less-dominant one and not made for lifting a suitcase vertically up a hill.

We're both a little snippy from our long day of travel. It has been an episode of planes, trains, and automobiles to get us here. Yesterday morning, we woke up in Columbus and boarded a plane to New York, only to transfer to another flight to Dublin. After a serious layover and a few pints of Guinness, we boarded our third and final flight to Naples, Italy. With seventeen hours of travel behind us, we were elated to board a hydrofoil to take us to the island of Capri.

We are tired, we want showers, and a glass of Prosecco wouldn't hurt either.

I raise my gaze to the incredible surroundings. When the boat pulled up to the Grande Marina of Capri, I had to blink to make sure I wasn't dreaming. The sight so surreal, Schubert's Ninth Symphony played in my head as a virtual theme song.

Capri is a massive rock, shooting out onto the Tyrrhenian Sea. Rocky caves around the island can be made out as the water crashes at the base. Up top, a cloud hides the peak of the mountain, making it seem as if heaven is just beyond the fog. Cascading down the slope is fresh green, hugging the landscape like a blanket.

As you get closer to the island, the definition and vibrant colors of homes and hotels peering up from the greenery becomes clearer. Shades of gold, red, and orange reflect off the rooftops. At the foreground, vendors and shops are bustling with activity. Tourists are buying souvenirs or trying to get a glimpse of Mt. Vesuvius, while others are walking to the various restaurants that line the marina.

Stepping off the boat, Leah and I had rolled our suitcases along the stone path of the dock and over to where my map said we could hail a taxi or take a bus to our hotel. Leah being Leah, hell-bent on living life to the fullest, decided we should walk to our hotel, taking the narrow stairway paths that cut through the island. She said it would be "exciting" and would help us "stretch our legs." She had no idea how many hundreds of stairs we would have to climb.

"Buses are for tourists. We are here to enjoy this magnificent island, and the only way to do it is on foot!" Leah gives a loud huff at the end of her sentence, as she wraps two hands around the lever of her large suitcase and hoists it up.

"Switch bags with me," I say. My bag is much smaller and easier to maneuver. I pack light. We're spending a week in the exotic Mediterranean. How many pieces of clothing could you need?

Apparently for Leah, it's a lot.

I extend my arm, then quickly pull it back, realizing the one I was offering wouldn't be of any use.

"No, Emma, your hand." She stops her progression and looks down at me. "You must be having enough trouble lifting your own. I wasn't thinking. I shouldn't—"

"It's fine." I cut her off, stretching out my right hand, a constant reminder of the worst year of my life and all the dreams that faded in one awful weekend.

A heart-wrenching breakup with the man I thought I was going to marry?

Check.

The devastating loss of a family member that left my soul aching so hard I found it hard to breathe?

Check. Check.

An accident that crushed my desires and everything I'd worked my entire life for, leaving me virtually numb?

Triple check.

Yes, it has been the worst year of my life and we're only halfway through it. I've been so anesthetized and empty, that my family pushed their own grieving aside to make sure I'm okay. All they want to do is talk, when it's the last thing I need. That, and have them worry about me. They worry too much.

I shake off the thought and brush away Leah's concerns. "It's fine. I'm using my left hand. Keep going. This should be the last set of stairs."

With a nod, Leah continues up, me following, until we reach a road. Sure enough, our hotel is just to the left. I have never been more excited to see a hotel in my life.

I love vacations, don't get me wrong. But for the amount of travel and manual labor it just took to get us here, this better be the best vacation of my life. At least I hope it is. Leah gave up a lot for us to experience this together.

We enter the sliding glass doors of the Villa Marina Capri, and a lovely receptionist who speaks perfect English greets us. She takes our passports to make copies, as per Italian custom, and when she returns them, she escorts us to an outdoor waiting area while our room is readied.

I'm a bit unsure about leaving my bag. Ever since my luggage was stolen on a college trip to Cancún, I refuse to let other people handle my belongings. After Leah assures me this five-star resort is a far cry from that rum-soaked

Mexican hotel, I concede, but only after making sure my purse, along with my money and valuables, is with me.

Leah just laughs at my one OCD trait and heads outside with me.

"Oh my God." The words escape my mouth.

"Oh my God is right." Leah repeats, sliding her sunglasses up her perfect button nose.

The two of us stand in awe, gawking over the sight before us. If I thought the view coming into port was phenomenal, I was mistaken. This is the most incredible view I have ever seen in my life.

Standing about a third up the mountain, the island below us, and the sea beyond it, is the true answer of why God created the earth. So we can marvel at its beauty.

The afternoon sun is shining bright. The sky is a perfect shade of blue with a few stray clouds. The whiteness of them only illuminates the color of the sky. The rooftops below are a gorgeous copper hue and the sea is all but breathtaking.

With a slight breeze in the air, Leah's hair blows away from her cheek. Looking over at her, I see a look of melancholy on her face. A look so un-Leah, it makes my stomach drop.

"I knew this was a bad idea. I shouldn't be here. Adam..." The words choke in my throat.

"Adam is the most amazing man in the world." She finishes my sentence. It's not what I was going to say, but she's right. Leah's fiancé, Adam Reingold, is by far the most caring, understanding, and perfect man in the world. He is the kind of guy you want your sister to marry. It's *exactly* why I feel awful being the one standing here with her and not him.

Leah gives me this knowing look that she's been giving me a lot lately, followed by a hug.

"Stop it. We're here and this is happening. This week is about you and me. We are going to have the most spectacular vacation of our lives, and I don't want you feeling bad for one second. You hear me?" She holds me tighter and I return her embrace.

Sometimes, it's hard to accept she's the little sister. Not that she's younger by a lot. Hell, we were born in the same year—with her arriving the day before New Year's Eve. Irish twins. Most days, she's the wacky, wild sister who dances on bars and runs into oncoming traffic to get across the street. She never returns things she borrows and loves to sing karaoke, even when the establishment doesn't have karaoke. It can get quite embarrassing.

Back in Cedar Ridge, Leah owns a bar called McConaughey's. Yes, it's named after the famed actor and has Matthew McConaughey paraphernalia all around. There's no good explanation for why the bar exists, other than the fact she is a die-hard fan, and the cliental love to get drunk and chant, "Alright, alright, alright."

Leah is usually the crazy one getting the crowd riled up.

Yet there are times like this—like this entire year—when she shows more maturity and composure than you would expect from the wild child with the platinum-blonde bob and sheared jeans. This year had to be hard on her as well, yet she gave up so much for me, for our family.

Pulling back from her, I let out a large sigh and am relieved to see a waiter approach us with a platter of prosciutto and a bottle of Prosecco, compliments of the hotel. We clink glasses and salute the start of our sisters sabbatical.

"Do you know how much sex can be had in a tub like this?"

Leah is sitting, fully clothed in the empty bathtub in our hotel suite. The large porcelain tub is yet another reminder of the honeymoon this was supposed to be.

"Too bad it will be sexless for the next week." I say, putting my clothes away in the large wardrobe that sits opposite the massive king-size bed.

"Just because I won't be getting foamed up in here doesn't mean you can't." She wiggles her eyebrows.

"No." I shoot her an evil glare.

"What happens in Italy, stays in Italy." Leah sings, resting her head on the back of the tub and kicking up her feet.

I let out a laugh knowing that is not true. My sister has the biggest mouth in Cedar Ridge. The fact she is marrying a cop means Leah not only knows everyone's business from the bar, but she also gets the lowdown on every speeding ticket and arrest in town. If I hook up with a random Italian on vacation, every soul within a ten-mile radius will know, and I don't need my dad hearing about my rendezvous. My poor dad. He still has a hard time believing I'm twenty-five-years-old.

"I didn't travel five thousand miles for a random hookup." Placing my sundresses delicately on each hanger, I look over at Leah's suitcase, open on the sofa, in the seating area by the door. I'm sure that's exactly where it will stay.

"I didn't give up my honeymoon so you could wallow the entire trip." Her head peeks up from the tub's headrest, one eyebrow slanted up, her mouth in a lopsided smirk.

She's a conniving one. In one breath she tells me not to worry about hijacking her honeymoon and in the next she's guilting me over it. Nice to see she hasn't lost her sense of humor.

I shake my head and grin. Leah catches my laugh and points it out. "You're getting some action this week, lady. It's your debt to me. If you don't pick him, I will."

I turn around from my stance at the closet, placing my hands on my hips. "Why are you so hell-bent on getting me laid?"

"Because it pisses me off the last guy in your pants was that jerk Parker. He's an asshole, he fucked with your head, and it's been six months since you've been with anyone else."

I can't argue with her there. Six months ago, I thought I was in love with Parker Ryles. We met at Carnegie Mellon, where he was studying the flute, and I was on the violin. He was smart and sweet and made that instrument look super sexy.

After four years of dating, I was practically picking out bridesmaid dresses. That is, until he dumped me because he wasn't ready to settle down. That would have been fine and dandy if we hadn't started having "the talk." You know, the one where you discuss how many children you want and where you'll live. We were on the same page, or at least I thought we were. Now I know there is no way I could have married someone so selfish. My life has been destroyed, and I blame him every day for what happened.

At least it's easier to blame him than myself.

And right now, I'd really like to tell him what he could do with that flute.

For some reason Leah feels it's imperative that I meet someone new. As if going out on a date is going to make the pain go away. Well, it's not. I'm broken and loving someone or something is just not worth it because when you lose it…when you lose them…the pain is too much to bear.

Leah rises from the tub and stalks over to her suitcase. "Let's put on our sexiest outfits and hit this town."

I let out a stretch, arching my fingertips toward the ceiling. "Can we sleep first? I am jet-lagged and still on Ohio time."

Unzipping her bag, Leah moves some clothes around and talks over her shoulder. "No prob. I heard Italians like to eat really late anyway. You doze for a few. I'm too wired to sleep."

Leah pulls the largest pair of binoculars I've ever seen out of her suitcase and holds them up to her face.

"What the hell are those?" They look like they belong to the CIA.

"They're Adam's. He uses them for surveillance. I borrowed them for our trip." She walks over to the glass that serves as the main entrance into our suite. Opening the door, Leah steps out onto the veranda facing the marina and the view we were admiring earlier.

"Those things are huge. There's no way you're carrying them around. If you lose them, I don't care how much Adam loves you. He'll flip."

I walk over to the bed and fall into it. My body sinks into the duvet, and I actually sigh, it feels so good. My eyes are just about to set into sleepyland when Leah lets out a loud gasp.

I prop open an eye.

"Ems, Ems—come here, you have to see this." She's still on the veranda, her hand flapping at a million miles a second. Her eyes glued to the binoculars.

I let out a grunt and fall further into the pillow.

"Emma!" She shrieks. It's a hurry-up shriek, not an I'm-being-kidnapped shriek.

Unwillingly and very tiredly, I roll off the bed and pad over to where she's standing. When I reach her side, she hands the binoculars over to me and positions my body and the binoculars in the direction she was gawking. I lift the binoculars to my face and look out on the marina.

"What am I looking at?" I ask.

"The boat. Do you see the boat?"

"I see, like, a million boats." I reply.

"The ginormous boat, Ems. It's huge. You can't miss."

I pan the area where she's positioned me to look. Sailboat, sailboat, sailboat, smaller vessel, smaller vessel, motorboat, hydrofoil. Ahh, I see it. Ginormous isn't even the word. It's twice the size of the ferry we took from Naples this morning. It's impressive, I'll give her that, but so not worth getting out of bed for.

I hand the binoculars back to Leah. "It's very nice. Now, if you'll excuse me, I have some sleep to catch up on."

Leah pushes the binoculars back to my chest.

"Look at the upper deck, spaz."

With an eye roll, I take the binoculars back. There's the boat again. I see windows. I see a double staircase off the back of the boat. I see a seating area. I see…oh. *Oh, have mercy.*

I see a man. Not just any man. I see a naked man. Naked in all his glory.

Yup, I'm awake now.

These binoculars are really powerful—from the incredible distance we are from the yacht, I can see the clear definition of his ass.

It's a good ass.

It's a gladiator ass.

And that's not all. His back is rumbling with muscle, cascading with each movement of his incredible body.

Sweet Jesus, hallelujah.

I can't see his face because his back is to us as he is pounding into a woman. Maybe pounding isn't the word. Grinding, thrusting, plunging—take your pick. I can't see her at all because his masculine frame is blocking my view. All I can see of her is two legs wrapped around his lean torso. With each thrust, his gluts flex in and the lats muscles on his back pump out.

These two are having sex. And it's the really dirty kind.

A pool of heat settles between my legs. The nerve endings in my chest spark alive and my cheeks flush with heat.

It's like the first time I watched soft porn. My friends wanted to see what it was about so they turned on Cinemax, and we sat there in silence pretending we weren't being affected. The truth was, I was sitting there with a throbbing between my legs and the very strong desire to do something about it.

I have that exact feeling right now.

"My turn." Leah says, grabbing the binoculars from my face.

I breathe out through my puckered lips. That was hot. Really hot.

And really sick of us to watch.

"Leah, there has to be some law against you watching them have sex. Aren't there, like, stalker laws?" I ask.

"They're having sex in the open. If we were home, they'd be the ones getting arrested." She licks her lips and bites down on her lower lip. "I love Italy already."

Shaking my head, I walk back over to the bed and try to fall asleep.

My mind racing with visions of naked men, it's not as easy for me to fall into sleepy land as it was before.

chapter TWO

The first night of our sister sabbatical was more than I was ready for. After sleeping for five hours, Leah threw me out of bed and made me put on a very sparkly halter top and black capri pants for dinner. She insisted we wear capris in Capri. I couldn't argue with her logic.

After dinner, we went to the Piazetta Umberto I, the town square, got tipsy on limoncello and then followed a group of other twentysomethings to a club in town. Leah's idea, not mine. There we drank more limoncello, and by the end of the night Leah had the entire club singing a Katy Perry song.

Because that's what Leah does.

And apparently, even non-English–speaking Italians know the words to Katy Perry songs.

While they sang and danced, I sat at a table and sucked down my drinks, plastering a fake smile on my face, trying not to ruin Leah's "honeymoon" or elicit one of those looks from her.

I caught her inspecting me a few times, making sure I wasn't falling into a mood or withdrawing myself. She thought she was being sly, asking me if I wanted another drink when it was still full and hers was drained, encouraging me to drink up or telling me a joke and making sure I laughed at it, because, if I didn't, then something must be wrong. Each time her eyes drifted over to mine, I'd bob my head to the music pretending I was into whatever song the DJ was playing when I'd rather have been back in the room.

This morning, my brain does not like the Teenage Dream lived last night and feels like I have fireworks going off in my head.

Thank you, Leah, and thank you, Katy Perry.

And thank you, limoncello.

"Rise and shine." My chipper roommate bounces on the bed. Since I don't drink as much as she does on a daily basis, my body doesn't process liquor as fast. I think I'm still a little drunk.

"Go away." My voice is deep and hoarse.

"'Morning, Emma." A male voice echoes from Leah's speakerphone.

I glance up at the clock beside the bed. "'Morning Adam. Holy God, what time is it over there?"

Adam's chuckle pours out of the phone. "Four in the morning. Just getting off the nightshift. You sound like you had fun last night."

I grumble at his reference to my morning man-voice.

"You keeping my girl from getting into trouble?" he asks, knowing his fiancé oh-so-well.

"Her talents for entertainment have risen to international capabilities."

Adam laughs again. "That's my girl."

Leah talks back into the phone. "Okay, baby, let me go. I have to get this lazy ass out of bed or else she'll sleep the day away."

Leah lets out a loud air kiss and Adam does the same before they hang up. With her knees still on the bed, she rocks back and forth making the bed move beneath me. "Let's drink espresso and eat croissants. You'll feel like new in no time."

I look up from the sheets I pulled over my head. She is dressed in a denim miniskirt and a white peasant shirt. Her hair is blown out with the front pulled up in a mini poof, and secured to her head with a red barrette. Her pale eyes are light and bright; a far cry from what she should be looking like this morning after drinking her weight in lemon oil and sugar.

"Ten more minutes," I plead.

"Nope." She lifts the sheets off my body. "We have an island to explore."

"We're gonna be here for seven more days." My voice is starting to get back its natural characteristics. More feminine, less mannish.

"And I don't want to waste a second. Now, get out of bed and spend my honeymoon with me!"

I peer up from her with vulture eyes. She really knows how to guilt trip me.

I bang my fists on the bed and get up, not before getting my bearings and making sure the room isn't spinning. When I'm sure the ground is even, I straighten my back and walk to the bathroom.

There's a shower, a stall, and a sink for two in here. Since the bathtub is near the bed, there is plenty room for a large shower made for—you got it—two. I head straight in and let the hot water hit my head and my back until I feel normal again.

Out of the shower, I wrap my body in a towel and dry my hair over the double vanity made of rock. Like, literal rock that is jutting out of the mountain. It's crazy cool.

Looking at my reflection I see a girl who looks like Leah but so very different. Our features are fairly similar. Almond-shaped eyes, nice noses, and a heart-shaped face. But that's where the similarities end. Where her eyes are blue, mine are a light brown. She has Dad's eyes; I have Mom's. Leah also has this adorable cupid mouth that bows at the top. Yeah, mine doesn't do that at all.

And while Leah's hair is almost white, my hair is an ashy color. It's the kind of hair that's too dark to be called blonde but absolutely not brown. It's just ashy.

Some people say I should get highlights, but my schedule was always too busy to spend hours at a salon.

When you've been playing the violin since you were ten, there isn't much your life offers in the form of time. If I wasn't at school, doing homework, or grooming my career, I was practicing.

Well, now that that dream has died, I guess I have time to change my hair.

I look down at my right hand and flip it over repeatedly, flexing the nerve. Biting my lip, I look back up at myself in the mirror and continue to get ready. I don't want to think about that right now.

"She's doing fine." Leah is in our room talking to someone. I turn the sink water on low and prop my ear to the door to listen in on her conversation. "Yes, Mom, she's out of bed and in the shower...yes...yes...I'm making sure she's eating."

Being thousands of miles away from my family doesn't seem to change anything.

"She thought I didn't notice, but she didn't want to be out last night. She was a trooper. She's trying." Leah's voice is so hushed; I have to strain against the door to hear her muffled words. "I have her meds just in case."

My stomach rolls at the thought of those damn pills, which I spent three months on. I didn't know I was depressed. I just thought I was sad.

And tired. So very, very tired.

I didn't know it had been three weeks since I had gotten out of bed. I didn't know I wasn't eating. Who needs a shower when you have nowhere to go?

My behavior led to a meeting with a Dr. Schueler, who had a lovely parting gift in the form of antidepressants. I fought against taking them. I'm strong. I'm an accomplished musician with a world-renowned orchestra. I have a boyfriend, a happy family, and the world at my fingertips.

At least, I did.

Not anymore.

So, I took the damn pills and spent the next three months numb—so numb I was void of myself. I hated every minute. I only did it so I didn't have to see the look in my family's eyes. The one that said they couldn't move on until I did.

Two months ago, I told Dr. Schueler I wanted to do this on my own. She didn't think it was a good idea. I stopped them anyway. I've been doing really well for the last eight weeks. It drives me insane that Leah felt the need to bring them with her.

She probably did it for Mom.

When I hear Leah hang up, I grab the sun block and walk it into the bedroom, motioning for Leah to apply some. She doesn't even mention she was on the phone with our mom, and I don't bring it up.

Turning to the wardrobe, I pick out a pair of white shorts and a green tank top, opting for comfort over style. I slide on my Sperry Top-Siders and head out the door.

"You are not wearing a fanny pack!" Leah chides as soon as I step outside.

"Don't knock it. I have our passports, cash, and travelers checks in here. No one is getting away with our stuff." I pat down the bag holstered around my waist to make sure everything is secure.

"There are so many things wrong with that statement, I don't know where to start." Leah's arms flail about her body in mock exaggeration. Or maybe she's being serious.

"What's wrong with my bag?"

"Uh, everything?" She holds up a finger. "*Numero uno*, you are wearing a fanny pack." She stretches out the words *fanny* and *pack* as if I don't understand English and need to hear her diction perfectly. "Those are for tourists at Disney World and marathon runners. Are you riding the teacups or running twenty-six miles today? No. So take it off."

"It's practical and keeps all our stuff secure." It also happens to be super cute. It's gray with white chevron stripes. It's the most adorable fanny pack ever. If it were Gucci Leah probably wouldn't mind. Maybe if I got a Gucci one—

"*Numero dos*, that's what a safe is for. Why are you taking all of our valuables with us?" Her hands are still in front of her body making dramatic gestures. I think talking to the Italians last night rubbed off on her.

"It's *due*, not *dos*," I say.

Leah just taps her foot and waits for an answer.

"I am not leaving our money in some chintzy safe where anyone can walk out with it. Been there done that." Fool me once, shame on you. Fool me twice…you know how it goes. "If you want to get stranded in a foreign country with no way to get home, be my guest."

She throws her hands up in the air. "Fine. Whatever. Take the stuff. Just leave that horrible pack in the room."

Not wanting to cause a fight, I back up into the room and grab my shoulder bag, removing all the items from the fanny pack and inserting them into the new purse. It won't be as comfortable but it will be more stylish. I shouldn't worry. By midweek, Leah won't care what I'm carrying her stuff in. She doesn't carry a pocketbook at all.

Like Leah promised, after some espresso and a croissant, paired with some blood orange juice, my hangover is a dismal headache.

Leah made arrangements for us to take a boat tour of the island, starting with the Blue Grotto and then winding around the island to see the sea caves of Capri. Since the tides don't always cooperate enough for people to view the Grotto, Leah wanted to do this on our first day, just in case we aren't able to during the others.

We walk down to the Grande Marina and pass the vendors and shops we saw yesterday. Past the hydrofoil dock, there is a small area with several boats, anchored idly in the water.

I follow Leah down a concrete path to a boat about fifteen feet long with an Italian flag waving from a pole in the center. There is a day bed taking up half of the space with a small seating area in the back and motor for the captain to drive. It's a leisure boat made for tours of the island.

I take the gentleman's hand who will be driving us on our tour and take my spot on the day bed, sitting up straight and holding on to my bag. Leah stretches out next to me and leans back on her hands, looking up at the sun.

The gentleman escorting us on our tour speaks a little English, but it is very hard to understand with his thick accent. I know a tiny bit of Italian from taking it in high school, which doesn't amount to much. We nod and pretend we know what he's saying. All we can make out is his name is Raphael.

Starting the engine, Raphael drives away from the dock, and the rocking in the water forces me to brace myself. I place my hand on the bed behind me and lean back on my side, my back facing the water, my front to Leah.

We turn left and drive past the Grande Marina. Leah points out our hotel and takes a picture of it with her phone. Then, she snaps a few shots of me and asks me to take a few of her in return.

She slides the phone back in her pocket and goes back to taking in the sun.

Before long, Raphael slows us down and Leah and I peer up to see why we've changed speed.

Ahead of us is a sea of boats similar to ours and smaller wooden dinghies. They look like gridlock traffic, all idling in the water, dangerously close to the rock that is the island of Capri.

"Grotto Azzurra," Raphael says as he idles the engine.

Amongst the boats before us, there is a larger one with a sign over it. It looks like a concession stand of sorts.

Squinting my eyes, I try to make out what the sign says. It's where people pay their admission to see the Blue Grotto.

I notice there is a man to each dinghy and ushering tourists from boats like ours onto the wooden crafts, and then paddling over to the concession to pay an admission.

Leah asks Raphael why we can't take this boat to see the Blue Grotto. He points to a very small opening in the rock. We watch as one at a time, the dinghies approach the opening that looks entirely too small for them to fit through. The man on the boat instructs the passengers to lie down on their backs as he pulls himself, and the vessel through the opening by a metal chain that is mounted to the rock until they disappear inside the sea cave.

It looks slightly frightening.

I glance at Leah with an unsure feeling. She shrugs me off and tells me to relax.

We are waiting in a line of sorts. Tourist boats like ours are all gathered in a mosh pit, there's no telling who was here first. When it's our turn, Leah and I will board a dinghy and be swallowed up by the sea cave. My stomach drops at the thought.

We slowly inch up, getting closer to the mass of wooden boats. There have to be twenty in line before us.

Craning my neck, I look around at the sea around us. My eyes widen at the sight of a very familiar vessel.

I nudge Leah. "Look."

She turns her head and gawks over at the yacht we were spying on yesterday. It's about a two hundred yards from us, but it's so massive, it feels like it's on top of us.

"Looks like Mr. Sex-a-thon took a break for some culture this morning."

"How long did you watch them yesterday?" I ask.

"Over an hour. It was enough that I had to FaceTime Adam for some afternoon delight."

"Ugh! You did not do that while I was sleeping!"

"Actually, it was more like morning delight for Adam." She grins. "Calm down, I went into the bathroom. You didn't even know, so what do you care?"

I sock Leah in the arm and she laughs.

"Did they seriously go at it that long?" I am so curious. Parker and I never went longer than twenty minutes. And that was on a special occasion.

I once heard Seth Myers tell a joke. "A new study came out that women prefer sleep over sex. Who would want to sleep for two and a half minutes?" When I heard it, I thought of Parker and me.

"Ems, he had her in every position. And I mean *every* position. We're talkin' crazy Kama Sutra stuff."

I lift my fingers to my face, feeling the heat from my blush. I am not a blusher. Let's make that clear. But just thinking about what I saw through those binoculars yesterday made me hot all over.

"You are so getting laid this week." Leah winks and I glare at her. Getting in bed with someone is so far down on the list of things I want to do.

Thirty minutes later, Leah and I are still drifting in the boat, waiting our turn, when one of the dinghies makes its way over to us.

Leah lets out a huff. "It's about time."

She gets up and waits for me to stand as well. The small boat pulls up next to ours and Raphael holds on to it, trying to keep it positioned as close to ours as possible. The man in the dinghy holds out his hand and motions for me to grab it and come on board.

I rise and steady my feet to step over the wall and down onto the small boat. Holding my bag with my left hand, I grab the man's outstretched hand with my right.

"*Nessuna borsa.*" He says, motioning to the purse I have clenched tightly to my body.

I blink back at him. There is no way I am leaving my bag and all of its belongings here with a stranger, no matter how nice Raphael may seem.

"Emma, leave your purse. You can't take it with you." Leah translates in case I didn't get the message.

Still holding the man's hand, I turn to face her. I try to give her an eye that reads *over my dead body*.

"Give me the bag!" Leah orders and starts to snatch it from my hand.

"Stop that," I pull it back toward me.

Raphael releases the dinghy and stands to say something to the effect of why I can't take the bag. The man in the dinghy is now only connected to our boat by the strength of our hands clasped to one another.

"Seriously, you can't take it with you. Give it to me." Leah yanks the bag hard.

I release the man's hand and swing my right arm over to seize the bag back out of Leah's grasp. In doing so, I lose my ground and, more importantly, my footing and barrel ass up, backward toward the water.

I try to clutch Leah's hand on the way down but when I clasp my hand on hers, the nerve in my palm bites back and the pain shoots up my arm, forcing me to let go.

My arms flail and I hit the water with a splash, as the searing pain travels from my hand up into to my head.

Black.

All I see is black.

My lungs feel heavy and my body is lifeless. Ashy blonde hair floats around my face. I adjust my eyes and see water…everywhere. In front of me, next to me, above and below. The light in front of my eyes goes dark again and then comes back into focus. I reach up to grab onto something, anything, but all I feel is water.

It's dark.

My heart goes into panic mode as I spin around. I move my arms erratically and try to swim up, but I don't seem to be moving. A burning sensation settles in my throat, and my chest grows heavier as the air locked in my lungs begs to get out.

My body is trembling when two arms wrap around my chest and pull me back. My body arches forward, my head and feet curving in as I am dragged in retrograde like a rag doll backward and upward.

As soon as my head is above water, I gasp for air and start coughing from deep within. I sound like a barking seal.

Hair is stuck to the front of my face, and I can't see anything as my body continues to be manhandled. One very strong, thick arm wraps around my torso as the other releases its hold on me.

"Can you hang on?" A raspy, deep voice says from behind me. The accent is American.

Trying to process what is happening, I swallow back and attempt to understand what he's saying.

"I need you to hold onto the side of the boat. Can you do that?" The male voice asks again. Taking my right hand, I brush the hair away from my face and reach up, securing my body to the boat in question.

When I am in place, the American lets me go and hoists himself over the side in a rather rough manner. My body bobs in the water as the boat sways from his weight. No sooner is he on the deck does he reach down and lifts me from under my armpits and out of the water. His thumbs leave a prodding feeling in my skin.

He sets me down on a seat and my stomach curls in, hugging my chest to my knees. My clothes are soaked and I've lost a shoe. I'm shaking, frightened from what I can now acknowledge was a near drowning.

Looking around, I notice this is not my boat. It's slightly larger in size to the one I was on and far more luxurious. My eyes widen with panic until I hear Leah's voice yelling over the commotion.

"Emma! Oh my God! Are you okay?" Her voice is close but not coming from the boat I am on. I look around and find her, about thirty feet from where I am. She is standing up and visibly shaken from her place on Raphael's boat. Her clothes are also soaked. I must have pulled her into the water at the same time.

"I'm okay. You?" I assure her.

"Still intact." She calls out. "Where's your bag?"

My bag? I pat my body and then do a quick search at the space around me.

Oh, my God.

"My bag!" I exclaim, standing quickly, I nearly fall overboard again as I launch my body toward the side of the boat to look in the water.

A giant hand pulls me back. "It's long gone. No use looking for it."

I turn my head, and finally have a chance to look at the man who rescued me from the water. He, too, is dripping wet and wringing water from his green linen button-down shirt. Quite possible one of the biggest men I've seen in person, he looks like he could be a UFC fighter. His hair is buzzed close to his head and his brown eyes are large. His massive head is in proportion to his wide neck.

He's not fat in any way. To the contrary, he is rock solid with large forearms and a broad chest. His calves look like they're the size of my thighs.

Okay, maybe that's an exaggeration. But he's sturdy. This man is built to protect people.

My bottom lip trembles. The back of my eyes burn as hot water pools along the ridges. "You don't understand. I need that bag. Everything, and I mean *everything* I own is in that bag."

"Sorry to break it to you," he says, pulling his wet shirt away from his chest. "There is no way you're getting your bag back in this water."

My body starts to shiver as this terrible, awful feeling of helplessness pours over me. A dark, thick, sinister cloud of despair settles over my heart and my head fills with thoughts of desolation. It's a familiar feeling. The one Dr. Schueler told me was from post-traumatic stress. The one I have fought off yet sneaks back to pay a visit every once in a while.

What have I done? Everything is gone.

I start to cry uncontrollably, my sobs growing bigger and deeper. My lungs feel as if they are being crushed down by a lead weight. I try to breathe, but I can only gasp.

The stranger in front of me shifts his body to the side, leaning forward a bit and then pulling back. He has no idea how to comfort a woman. And it's a good thing. If he touches me, I just might flip out on him. If I can catch my breath, that is.

My daze is slightly lifted by the sound of Leah's voice. She is having Raphael drive her closer to me. When her boat reaches mine, she launches herself over the rails and swings her arms around my convulsing form.

"I was so scared. You didn't come up for air and I thought you were..." Her grip gets so tight on me I know exactly how she was going to end that sentence.

She lifts her head and I see her eyes bloodshot. She turns her head to the American sitting across from me, "You saved my sister." Leah launches herself onto the giant man and gives him an impressive hug.

How long was I under that water?

Another shiver runs up my spine as I shake off any thought of what could have been.

"It was no problem." His smile is polite. He acts as if anyone would have done the same.

"I dropped my bag on my way down."

Leah releases her hold on the giant and looks at me. Wiping a tear from her face, she asks, "I know you wanted to bring our things, but what exactly was in it?"

I glance up toward the sky and wish the bag would magically float to the surface of the sea. It doesn't, so I list the items that were in it.

"My passport, your passport, our euros that we exchanged at the airport, our credit cards and my phone."

With the mention of my phone, Leah pats down her skirt and feels for something. She reaches into her pocket and pulls her phone out. It doesn't turn on. "Shit. Mine might as well be on the ocean floor as well."

My shoulders lower and the darkness swells in the frontal lobe of my brain.

Leah nods her head and looks at me. "Okay, let's think about this. There has to be a way to get new passports. I'm sure people lose them on vacation all the time." She's trying to be positive and I'm trying to appreciate it. "How much money did we have in euros?"

I roll my neck and let out a large breath. "A thousand dollars' worth."

Leah swallows; obviously surprised I had that much cash on me. That much unrecoverable cash, that is.

"That sucks. As does your credit card. The good news is my credit card is still in the safe, so we can use that for expenses until we get home." She pats her knees and offers a cheery smile.

I lift my head and offer her the grimmest expression anyone can make.

Leah reads it right.

"Oh no. Oh no, no, no, no, no!" she exclaims.

I offer her a shrug.

Her blonde bob, now slicked back on her head, frays out when she stands up. "Are you kidding? Do you mean to tell me we have no passports, and no money whatsoever? Not even a friggin' credit card to our names?"

All I can do is nod. Slowly.

"Oh, my God, Emma! Because some lowlife in Mexico stole your suitcase eight years ago, you lost every penny we have. We're in a foreign country! We have no phones, no money, no way to get home!"

"I am so sorry." My voice is low and, most certainly, apologetic.

Leah sits down and rocks herself back and forth. I want to do the same.

Raphael says something in Italian that I have a hard time understanding until the giant American pulls a wallet from the cargo pocket of his gray shorts and hands over a soggy hundred-euro note. The American says something back to Raphael in Italian and then thanks him in English.

When Raphael turns the motor on to his boat, Leah and I both come to attention and get our minds back on the problem at hand.

"Did you just send him away?"

"Did you just pay him?"

We say both sentences in unison.

The American nods. "From the sound of it, you two weren't going to be able to pay him."

Neither of us can argue with that logic.

"We have to get back to our rooms. He was our way back," I say.

"He may not have spoken English well but he understood it and there was no way he was going to take you back without payment. I only gave him a tip for his services."

"So, he just left us here?" Leah rubs the sides of her arms with her hands.

"I told him to." He looks back from Leah sitting next to him, to me sitting across from him. "I can help you ladies."

"Thank you but you've already done so much," I say, but am cut off.

"I have a friend at the US consulate in Rome. He can rush you a pair of passports to Naples. While I make that call, you can use my satellite phone to call your credit card companies and see if they can get you a replacement card.

Maybe someone back home can wire you some money as well."

His logic is on point. Having a contact at the consulate would be incredible. I don't even know where the nearest one is. That said, this guy is a complete stranger and could hold both Leah and myself down with his pinky if he needed to. The offer is nice but we can handle the situation on our own.

"That would be great," Leah says before I can decline.

"I'm going to take you to my boat. You can dry off there while we make the arrangements." He stands up and starts the engine.

I raise my hand to tell him to take us back to shore but Leah stops me. "No, Emma. You lost our money and you lost our way home. I am not spending the next seven days standing in an embassy, God knows where, getting a new passport issued." Her tone is deep, bossy, and in full lecture mode. "The man saved your life. If he wanted you dead, he would have watched you drown. We are following him back to his boat and that is final."

Her brows are closed in and her button nose is pointed down.

"We don't even know where he's taking us," I whisper entirely too loudly. Obviously, he can hear our conversation, but if he is a madman, I don't need him knowing I think he's a madman.

"My boat is right there. I'll take you on board, we'll make a few calls, and then I'll take you back to shore." He points his finger at the boat he is talking about.

Leah looks over and I know her mouth is open just as wide as mine is.

He is taking us to the yacht.

Yes, the yacht.

The sex yacht.

Holy cannoli.

"Ems, we are so going with him."

WANT TO READ MORE?

RECKLESS ABANDON IS AVAILABLE NOW.

MORE BOOKS BY JEANNINE COLETTE

THE ABANDON COLLECTION

Pure Abandon
Reckless Abandon
Wild Abandon
Wild Abandon Christmas
Sinful Abandon
True Abandon

STAND-ALONES

Wrecked
A Really Bad Idea
Just Ten Seconds

THE SEXTON BROTHERS NOVELS (CO-WRITTEN WITH LAUREN RUNOW)

Austin
Bryce
Tanner

COCKY HERO CLUB (CO-WRITTEN WITH LAUREN RUNOW)

Layover Lover

KEEP IN TOUCH

www.jeanninecolette.com

www.facebook.com/groups/1671316156434656/

www.facebook.com/JeannineColetteBooks

www.instagram.com/jeanninecolette/

https://twitter.com/jeanninecolett

https://www.bookbub.com/profile/jeannine-colette

https://www.goodreads.com/author/show/13931286.
Jeannine_Colette

https://bookandmainbites.com/JeannineColette

ACKNOWLEDGMENTS

They say, "It takes a village…"

I'd like to thank my village for helping to make *Pure Abandon* a reality.

To my sister, Nicole, who this book was originally written for. She was the first person to read a line and brave my love of the run-on sentence. Without her, there would be no story.

To my editor extraordinaire, Jamie Chavez, for her incredible eye for detail and her help in forming *Pure Abandon* into a story worth publishing. I hired her as a developmental editor, but she did more for this book than I'd ever dreamed.

To Autumn Hull of The Autumn Review and Wordsmith Publicity for her unique ability to catch the unraveling threads of the story and sew them back together. Without Wordsmith Publicity, this first-time self-publisher would have had no idea how to get this book into the hands of readers and reviewers.

To Sarah Hansen of Okay Creations for the world's most beautiful book covers for this book.

To Cassie McCown of Gathering Leaves Editing for copyediting and dealing with my love of the word *that*.

To Jovana Shirley of Unforeseen Editing for making my words look beautiful on the page with magnificent formatting, and doing the 2020 re-edit that perfected this novel.

To Jennifer Windstein, my friend, roommate, and travel partner, who sat through two reads and gave equal love and insight each time. To Nanci Weaver for her constant support and guidance and for never making me feel like a fool in the process. To Nicole Lancellotti for her unwavering friendship, support, and creative input. To my beta readers, Tara McCormick and Nicole Parsons: I miss your face. And to my very own dark-haired mentor, Jill Meister for being this book's final line of defense.

To my friends and family for whispering words of encouragement, especially my mom for telling me to "go to work" and being where I couldn't while I pursued my dreams. I couldn't have done this without you.

To Starbucks for being my office.

To Snow Patrol, Sia, Adele, and Taylor Swift for being my inner soundtrack.

To my husband, Bryan, for always having my back and pushing me forward. He surprised me with his insights and ability to find holes within the story. I continue to be in awe that I married someone so brilliant…and funny…and witty…and handsome. *You're everything*.

And of course, to the two tiny people who rule my world: I love you.

Writing a book is fun.

Letting people read said book is the most frightening thing I've ever done.

Thank YOU for reading *Pure Abandon*.

I hope you were entertained.

ABOUT THE AUTHOR

Jeannine Colette combines humor and angst in her sexy, stand-alone romance novels. Her stories feature dynamic heroines and swoonworthy heroes, who have to *abandon their reality* in order to discover themselves…and love along the way.

A graduate of Wagner College and the New York Film Academy, Jeannine went on to become a Segment Producer at CBS News and NBC. She left the television industry to focus on her children and pursue a full-time writing career. She lives in New York with her husband, the three tiny people she adores more than life itself, and a rescue pup named Wrigley.